OATH OF EMBERS

FIRECALLER CHRONICLES
BOOK TWO

TRUDI JAYE

Hi! My name is Trudi Jaye, and I have a secret...

A secret society, that is.

Especially designed for people like you who love reading my books, the Trudi Jaye Secret Society is a place filled with magic, laughter, and most of all... free stories.

Everyone accepted into the society is given access to an ancient tome full of the stories, novellas, bonus epilogues, and deleted scenes from all the different Trudi Jaye series.

Called **The Shadow Archives,** you can access it by clicking the link below, and applying to join the secret society...

You'll also receive the weekly Secret Society Bulletin, with updates, ongoing stories and series, and early notification about sales and new releases.

Join my Secret Society today... if you dare!

www.trudijayewrites.com/shadow-archives

Oath of Embers (Firecaller Series, Book 2) is published by Star Media Ltd

Published 29 October 2025 by Star Media Ltd

Copyright © Star Media Ltd, 2025

Cover design: PCTC Design

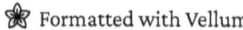 Formatted with Vellum

CHAPTER 1
JENA

Lightning flashed in the night sky.

Jena jerked back from where she was standing near the cave entrance, heart pounding. Her shirt and trousers were damp and her hair wet from their sprint through the rain. Her Hashishin knife sat in a leather case at her hip, and the fire ruby set in its hilt glowed softly. Thornal's ashes lay heavy against her chest, their small leather pouch attached to a leather cord around her neck. Goosebumps ran up her arms and she shivered. If she were wise, she wouldn't stand where the worst of the wind buffeted her body, leaving her chilled to the bone.

But she was too edgy to sit down.

The cave seemed too small, the darkness too great. It was the same kind of storm that had raged the night Thornal was murdered, and it was like she was experiencing it all over again. Wild rain, booming thunder and flashes of lightning threatened death and destruction. Rain pounding so fiercely into the hard earth it bounced back up into the air. Darkness so thick and heavy it felt like a heavy wool blanket thrown over them.

1

Even the volcanoes rumbling in the background sounded the same.

She shivered again and, for a fleeting moment, wished she'd never left the cottage. She could have ignored Thornal's instructions, lived a quiet and happy life hidden in the valley between the volcanoes. Tended the garden, dispensed the herbs. She could have pretended that Thornal was out whenever someone came to call.

She could have done that happily for years. She could have lived a careful, safe life.

Instead, she was here. Stuck in a cold and damp cave with her traveling companions of the last few weeks—the reluctant Firecaller mage Nate, the mercenary warrior Argus, and her newfound sister Bree. They were all watching the storm, just as she was, but from their seated positions at the back of the cave. Her sister's hair was tied back in a rough knot, there were dark circles under her eyes, and she was more disheveled than Jena had ever seen her.

But Bree looked happy. She sat close to Argus, under the same blanket and sharing his warmth, flicking the occasional glance up to his face, as if to make sure he was still there.

Nate sat a few feet away, arms wrapped around his bent knees, his black mage tattoo standing out starkly on his face. He looked lonely in comparison.

"We'll miss our deadline if we stay here too long," said Nate. His eyes were full of fire and Jena could see the agitation swirling under the surface. "Maybe we should—"

Lightning crashed close by, a burst of energy that made them all jump. Thunder rolled by only a moment later right over their heads, making the whole mountain shudder. Dust and rock fell from the roof of the cave, adding another layer to their dirt-covered clothes.

"We can't go back out there," said Jena. "There's something... *wrong* about that storm." The lightning strikes felt like they had a purpose. Almost like they were hunting for something. Or someone. She edged a little further back into the cave. The storm could be yet another attempt by Crown Prince Lothar to kill—or at least delay—them.

Her hands tightened into fists.

The prince had been chasing Nate for weeks now, trying to kill the one person standing between him and the throne of Ignisia. He'd almost succeeded with the fire hawks. She still wasn't entirely sure how Nate had saved them from being dropped into the center of the bubbling volcano, but he had.

She absently touched the almost-healed wound at her side and winced as pain shot up one side of her body. Bree had done her best, but Jena still ached across her middle from being carried by the giant hawk. Occasionally her breath would hitch in her chest as she remembered the feeling of being clutched in those enormous talons, dangling high in the air, completely out of control, with no way to escape.

And now they were stuck in this storm. Energy crackled in the sky outside as another bolt of lightning flashed. Was it truly possible for Lothar to control the elements like this?

"We should make a fire," said Bree softly, misinterpreting Jena's reaction. "We'll all feel better if we're warm."

"There's nothing we can burn in here," said Argus, his gaze searching around the tiny cave.

"And we can't go back outside," said Jena.

"Then we wait here until it eases," said Argus with a shrug. "It's not going to hurt us to be cold for a while." His gaze landed back on Bree again, like it was drawn by an unstoppable force. The mercenary had been like this ever since Bree broke the curse put on him by his old master, Remus, the shrinking mage.

"We can't just *wait here*. We have to keep moving," said Nate, gesturing toward the entrance to the cave. "We're so close. There's too much at stake."

She understood why Nate was objecting. It was his life that was being torn apart by Lothar. But they were all cold, tired and hungry. "We'd never make it to Remus tonight, not in this storm," she said gently. "Better to wait it out, get there tomorrow."

"What if it's our last chance to beat Lothar?" said Nate, his voice raw. He looked at the others, his expression haunted. "Remus told Argus we had to be back to him by now."

"Remus doesn't know everything," said Jena.

"Just enough to convince us to continue on, even though we don't have to," said Argus, his voice grim.

"Maybe we should reconsider," said Jena, for the first time voicing the thought that had been swirling inside her head since they arrived in the cave. "Maybe you were right, Argus. You and Bree could wait here, and Nate and I go alone to Remus. Or maybe we don't go at all and just go straight to the Utugani. Lothar knows exactly where we're going. It's too dangerous."

Silence greeted her suggestion. Outside, the rain pounded, and the wind howled, but inside the cave, they all just stared at each other.

"We have other options now," said Argus. "On that I agree." He looked like he wanted to say more, but he glanced at Bree and said nothing.

Jena stayed silent, waiting for more.

"Let's just rest a while," said Bree. "No need to decide right now."

Jena looked back out into the storm, unsettled and jittery. The rain was hammering so hard into the rocks outside the cave, it seemed like it might wash the mountain away. As she watched, a jagged branch of lightning launched out of sky and hit a nearby tree. The tree exploded into a thousand pieces, visible only for a moment before the darkness claimed it again. Thunder boomed, rocking the earth under their feet.

The raven fluttered its wings on her stomach, and she had a vision of it flying free, picking up tinder for a fire. She glanced behind her, but Nate was staring into the storm like he was waiting for it to clear up at any moment, and Argus and Bree were fussing over their shared blanket.

She lifted her shirt up from her stomach, and the tattoo immediately burst from her skin, making her wince again and wish she hadn't been so quick to let it free. As it emerged from her body, the tattoo transformed into a fully formed raven and dashed off into the rain. Lightning flashed, and she glimpsed the raven ducking and diving through the air, almost as if it were trying to avoid the raindrops. She hoped it came back unharmed.

She crossed her arms over her chest, trying to warm herself up a little. She didn't know what they should do, and it was making her crazy. It didn't help that she kept going over what she'd said to Lothar. Like an idiot, she'd told him she had the Book of Spells inside her. She was honest enough to admit that she'd been annoyed at how dismissive Lothar had been of her, despite already knowing who her parents were, and that she could do mage spells. He'd even known she'd killed his Hashishin with her silver flame, and he still didn't think she was worth anything.

At least she'd made him sit up and take notice. She'd surprised him.

It was also dangerous. He'd—

In a flurry of feathers and raindrops, the raven burst back into the cave, carrying three twigs precariously in its beak. It dumped them on the ground next to Jena, then took off. She looked down at the wet branches. It would take all her skill to get that drenched pile of tinder to light.

"Maybe we could use the shelter canvas to give us more protection from the storm?" she said.

There was movement behind her, and Argus stood—as much as he could in the low cave—and walked over. He glanced down at the soaked kindling at the entrance to the cave but didn't say anything. He'd probably seen much stranger things working for Remus.

Peering out into the storm, he nodded. "There's a rock we could tie a rope around. Might give us enough room for a fire." He went to get the canvas and ropes from his bag.

Another bundle of twigs landed at her feet, before the raven whooshed off again.

She crouched down to make the tinder into a stack. They'd need bigger pieces of wood as well if they were going to have a fire that would actually provide heat. Her palm tingled, and her silver flame burst into life in her hand. It didn't give off any heat, or she'd be using it to keep them all warm, but it could light the fire once they had enough tinder.

"That's an unusual flame," said a quiet voice behind her.

She flinched and closed her hand, before glancing over her shoulder.

Nate stood with his hands in his pockets, watching her closely with his dark eyes.

She wasn't used to others knowing about her magic. It still made her nervous. "It used to be normal flame colors.

After Thornal's death, it changed." Jena stood up again, wiping her hands on her trousers.

"Something to do with the Book of Spells?"

"Maybe." Lightning split the night and Jena shivered.

"It's definitely not a natural storm," said Nate, moving to stand beside her at the entrance.

She could feel his body heat radiating off him. She wished she had the courage to move closer to absorb some of his warmth. "No. It's not." There was nothing else to say. It felt like Lothar was watching and laughing maniacally to himself. He always seemed to be one step ahead of them.

A soggy clump of black feathers landed next to Jena's feet, dropping another few twigs. The raven shook itself, flicking water over their legs, then took off again.

"It's gathering wood for us?" asked Nate in surprise.

Jena shrugged. "It's getting a nice pile of soaking wet twigs that will probably never light."

Nate crouched down next to the wood and held out his hands. A warm glow lit his fingers, and his face reflected the color of fire. Steam rose from the twigs as his magic dried them out.

"You can control it," said Jena, her excitement making her forget everything else. It was one of their biggest issues; Nate's inability to use his magic properly. He'd never defeat Lothar if he couldn't figure it out.

"Not really," said Nate, making a frustrated face. "It barely takes any magic to do something like that. I still can't control my magic when I let it out fully."

"Oh," said Jena, disappointed. She'd vowed to help him with his quest to destroy Lothar, but if he couldn't even control his flames, she was afraid that they were doomed to fail before they even began. Which was why she'd been so ready to go to Remus, despite the risks.

Argus returned to the cave entrance, the canvas in his arms. He nodded to Nate. "Help me put this up."

Nate followed Argus outside the cave and rain immediately soaked both of them. Wind gusted at the canvas, making it flap restlessly. They worked quickly and soon had it attached to rocks and scrubby trees near the entrance. It flapped about in the wind, but it added protection from the storm. The three of them stood at the entrance, watching.

"Will it hold?" asked Jena.

"No guarantees," said Argus with a shrug. His hair was plastered to his head and his shirt was dripping. He looked like a drowned rat. They both did.

"Does Remus really know how to defeat Lothar?" asked Nate.

Argus hesitated. "That's what he told me."

Nate nodded sharply. "You think he would lie?"

"Yes," said Argus. "He's unscrupulous and cunning. But there's also a chance he knows something."

"We need him," said Bree from the back of the cave. Everyone looked at her. She had the flimsiest reason to be here, and somehow it made her voice weigh the heaviest. "We have nowhere else to go to find out more about Lothar. Remus might be untrustworthy, but what other mage is going to talk to us without trying to kill us?"

Jena nodded. Bree was right. Any other mage would try to execute Jena and Bree on the spot. And he'd be congratulated for doing it. "But what's stopping him from just lying to us?" asked Jena, frustrated.

"He needs something from Nate," said Argus almost reluctantly, his voice carrying across the small space. "That's how we make sure. We take advantage of his need."

Lightning flashed outside, showing the jagged barren terrain for a brief moment, then thunder boomed into the darkness. The raven appeared out of the rain with another bundle of twigs in its mouth. It dropped them at her feet, and stood, beak open and gasping for breath. She got an image of several large lightning strikes that only just missed.

"Aiming for you, huh?" said Jena.

The raven let out a single caw and an enormous bolt of lightning flashed overhead. Jena ducked her head, as if that would help if the lightning hit them.

"How are we going to do this?" whispered Jena, as thunder made the cave shudder.

"Light the fire?" said Nate, with a half-hearted smile.

Jena gave him a look. "Get to Remus without being killed by Lothar."

"We'll make it if we're careful. I've lived on this mountain a long time," said Argus, his voice stern.

Jena reached out with one hand and flicked her fingers. Her silver flame burst into life in her hands. She touched it to the now-dry tinder, and the wood started to burn.

"So we're all going?" asked Nate.

"When we get to Remus, we'll be safe from Lothar," said Argus, instead of answering directly. "But we won't be safe from Remus. We need to be on guard. He's not our friend. He might have valuable information, but he will take everything he can from us in return."

CHAPTER 2

NATE

The morning after the storm felt full of promise.

They were walking along a rough track that looked like mage fire had carved it out of the side of the mountain. There was a deep cliff on the left-hand side that made Nate feel queasy every time he looked over the edge. Overhead, the sky was gray and dull, interrupted only by the occasional red burst of light, the reflected glow of lava erupting out of the volcanoes behind them. Everything else seemed bright and sparkly, a little fresher than it had the day before. Even the low-lying shrubs seemed to glisten, and the occasional lizard scuttling past had a spring in its step.

The storm had blown itself out in the early hours of the morning, and they'd crawled stiffly out of the cave into the post-storm world. Nate had found it difficult to be patient while the others slowly ate their breakfast and prepared for the day. It felt like he'd been waiting for this moment for a very long time. He just wanted to get to Remus. He just wanted this nightmare to be over.

They were walking single file—Argus and Bree in front,

Jena in the middle. He took slow, even steps and kept his eyes on the path ahead. No one talked. They were all focused on not falling over the edge.

It suited Nate. He was still fizzing from the demons he'd called inside the Edges, even now. He could feel their combined magic, as if they still surrounded him, watching over his shoulder.

It was possible that was exactly what the demons were doing.

The Edges were a shadow world, adjacent to this one, where the demons lived, and the barrier between the two worlds was very thin in places—especially, it turned out, around Nate. He couldn't tell if the demons really *were* watching, not unless he used his powers, which he definitely would not be doing.

But it seemed possible.

Just ahead on the narrow trail, Jena glanced back over her shoulder at Nate and smiled her small half-smile. She looked tired, the dark circles under her eyes making the scars on her face stand out more than usual.

When they'd first met, she'd seemed so stern and angry. But that wasn't who she really was. It had taken him a while, but he now realized that the scars down one side of her face helped Jena protect her inner emotions from the world. They also protected her physically. She flinched any time someone tried to touch her, or came too close. But under that tough outer shell, she was kind-hearted and determined to protect everyone who needed it.

She'd been watching him closely since yesterday; grateful for how he'd saved her, but also curious over how he'd gotten free. He'd shut her down when she'd asked questions, but he knew he couldn't do that forever. He nodded at her but couldn't bring himself to smile. Not yet.

Just as she turned back to the trail, Jena's foot slid on a loose bit of shale, and she let out a squeal of surprise as she lost her balance and fell toward the cliff edge. Heart lurching, Nate thrust himself forward and stretched out his arm to save her. But he was too far back, and his hands grasped at nothing. Instead, as desperate fear surged through him, his feet became tangled, and he tipped toward the edge himself. Time slowed. The dark abyss below was a cavernous mouth ready to swallow him whole.

His heart constricted. He didn't want this to be the end. He couldn't die like this; not when there was still so much fight left in him.

He tried to stop the inevitable, hands reaching out, grasping at anything that might save him. Arms flailing, feet tangled, he knew that this was it... only to be pushed back up onto the trail by a powerful gust of wind.

He landed on his butt, safe but humbled.

Up ahead, Jena had regained her balance and stood bent over with her hands on her knees. He knew she'd sent the wind. It had been too powerful to be anything other than a mage spell. She glanced down at the gaping cliff beside them, then back at him, eyes fierce. He stared at her, recognizing her fear. He felt it pounding through his veins, too.

She blinked and took a breath.

"Come on, keep moving," said Argus from further up the trail. "There's a stop up ahead where we can rest." He said the words as though they'd just stopped to get an early break.

Nate wanted to yell at Argus, yell at the world, tell them all to go to the ashes. He didn't want this, he didn't want any of this.

But Argus and Bree had already turned and continued

walking. Jena was putting one foot in front of the other, although slower than before. They were only here because of Nate, and if they could keep going, then so could he. He moved closer to Jena; maybe he could do more if she slipped again. Maybe he could save her, instead of being saved.

Sometime in the night, he'd realized that even though he'd agreed to go to Remus, and even though he knew there was a strange and powerful flame magic inside his body, until yesterday, he hadn't really thought he'd have to battle Lothar. He hadn't really accepted he was part of the prophecy.

But meeting Lothar in the flames—hearing him discuss Nate's death like he was breaking a couple of eggs—then talking to the demon who'd saved him and calling all the other demons... that had made it all real.

Very real.

Horribly real.

Monstrously real.

So fucking real, he thought he might throw up.

Which was why he preferred not to talk to anyone right now.

And also preferred it if Jena didn't die.

According to the demon, he needed nothing more than his Firecaller abilities to beat Lothar. But he didn't know how to use his powers, and he didn't know if he could trust the demon.

Demons couldn't lie, but he'd seen them twist the truth many times. They'd resented it every time he'd called one of them, and he'd made it worse by only using them for menial tasks. In the Edges, he'd seen the demon's myriad expressions, the fall of muscles and flame over its body. There was more to it than pure energy. It had emotions and thoughts. The demon had been... proud. Almost... regal.

He winced. He shouldn't have been making them carry rocks.

But it still didn't answer the question of whether he could trust the demon.

Lothar had been planning this coup for years. He'd been honing his magic, creating alliances, plotting and planning. He'd also been raised amongst kings and queens. He knew what to say, when to say it. Nate was the grandson of a powerful mage, but he'd been raised in the recesses and corners of his castle. He'd lived in the shadows, hiding from a contemptuous grandfather who only seemed to know how to throw out barbs. Nate wasn't bred to be a king, even if royal blood flowed in his veins. All of which meant that Lothar had the advantage over Nate in every possible way.

If there was any other way to defeat Lothar, and to save Ignisia from his plans, Nate would have taken it. He didn't want to be King of Ignisia, and he certainly didn't want to put himself in a position where they'd ridicule him for his lack of social graces and knowledge of how to run a kingdom.

But he knew he'd be better than Lothar.

He knew he had the best interests of the people of Ignisia in his heart.

He knew now that this was his path, whether he wanted it or not.

CHAPTER 3
NATE

"Let's take a break here," called Argus from up ahead.

Nate looked up in surprise. They had walked only a little further up the trail. But Argus was standing in an area that had widened out into a small plateau that was perfect for a rest stop.

He eased his backpack from his shoulders, wincing at the stiffness in his muscles, and set it down next to a boulder.

"Want some?" said Jena, holding out a piece of jerky.

"Thanks." He settled himself on the boulder. He wasn't hungry but knew better than to let his energy get depleted.

Jena sat down nearby. He closed his eyes and tried to relax. He felt tired and confused. Maybe, if he was very honest about it, he also felt scared. Everything seemed too much. Who was he to—

In the distance, a volcano rumbled, and his fiery magic stirred in response.

"No, no, put your foot there," said Argus.

Nate opened his eyes, startled.

But the words weren't aimed at him. Argus and Bree

were standing in the middle of the plateau. Bree had her hands out in front, one foot in front of the other, in a fighting stance. Argus was walking around her, moving her feet into the right position. Nate watched, fascinated.

"Feet like this, so it's easier to spring to the side, or back. Always watch your opponent. Never get distracted and look away."

Bree nodded, her expression serious. "So how do I beat them?"

"You fight dirty."

"I don't want—"

"In a life-or-death situation, you fight using whatever it takes to survive, you understand me?" Argus ground the words out. "There's no honor in dying."

Bree nodded jerkily, her eyes wide.

"You aim for their vulnerable parts. Eyes, mouth, neck, groin. You punch and kick and scratch. Show me a punch."

Bree awkwardly hit the palm that Argus was holding up in front of her. Nate and Jena exchanged a glance. That punch wouldn't have hurt a fly.

Argus didn't seem to notice. "Basics of a punch: always hit with this part of the fist, and this way up. Keep your thumb outside your fingers, or you'll break it. Don't move your shoulder. The power comes from leveraging the movement of your arm."

"What if my arms aren't strong enough?"

"Do it like this," said Argus, and showed Bree a punch where he flicked his wrist at the last minute. His massive muscles bunched as he did it, and the air practically quivered where his fist stopped.

Bree watched Argus with a frown and then attempted to copy his movements. Her second attempt was better. Her next even better.

"She's a fast learner," said Jena, her voice low, just for Nate.

"That's good. She's the most vulnerable of us all."

"She has magic," said Jena defensively.

"It's all healing magic," said Nate bluntly. "That won't help her in a fight."

Jena flicked him a startled glance, like she hadn't expected him to notice what magic Bree possessed. He rolled his eyes. He wasn't blind. He'd even seen Bree use small mage spells, the kind that could get her killed, just as easily as Jena's more powerful mage abilities.

"She's determined to be here," said Jena. "When Miara suggested we travel with Argus to find you, she fought for it."

"Why would she do that?" Nate didn't want to be here; he couldn't understand why anyone else would.

Jena glared at Nate. "She knows it's important. That *you're* important. That something has been building around us all these years, and now it's overflowing. If we don't meet this challenge head on, no one will."

Nate considered Jena for a moment. She believed what she was saying, that much he knew. But he honestly didn't think Bree or Argus would follow them to Flame City. There might be trouble brewing, but they wouldn't be part of it. Argus would take Bree to his family, and he'd keep her well away from any confrontation with the deranged Crown Prince.

Nate agreed with Argus. He knew Jena could hold her own; she was smart and savvy. Strong. But Bree was...soft. Gentle. She didn't have any protection against Lothar and his allies, and a few lessons on how to punch wouldn't change that.

"You're not holding your arm high enough."

17

"I'm doing my best," snapped Bree.

Argus rubbed one hand over his eyes. "Sorry. I forget you're not one of my soldiers. You're doing great."

"For a healer," said Jena, with a grin. "Who's never had to fight."

"I suppose you'd be better at this?" said Bree, her voice sharp. Her eyes flashed at Jena, frustration in every tensed muscle.

Jena shrugged, shadows appearing in her eyes. "Probably."

"Come here then, if you're so tough. Show me your moves." Bree practically growled the words. Nate watched her closely, trying to understand where this was all coming from.

Jena hesitated, looking from Bree to Argus. "I'm not a proper fighter. Argus could knock me to the ground in seconds. Better to learn from him."

"But you think you'd beat me?"

"Yes." Jena's voice was soft, but sure.

Nate agreed with Jena. Bree might have discovered a desire to fight, but she didn't have the experience. He wasn't sure she had it in her to be a real fighter, someone who would kick and punch and harm her opponent.

Bree looked like she wanted to keep arguing, but Argus put one hand on her arm. "Bree, have some jerky. Rest a moment. We'll be walking again soon."

She glared at him, then stomped to a nearby boulder and sat down. Argus handed her a piece of jerky and sat next to her, a large calming presence.

Nate chewed on his own piece of jerky. It was the most upset he'd ever seen the usually serene healer. It was reassuring to see she was human after all.

"How far are we from Remus?" asked Jena.

Argus glanced up the mountain. "An hour, maybe. Depends how fast we walk."

"What happens when we get there? Do we just ask Remus for help?"

Argus shook his head. "We must be very careful. Remus is unscrupulous. We have to convince him that he needs us more than we need him."

"And how do we do that?"

"Just let me do the talking. Keep as quiet as possible. Don't give him any information." He glanced at the Hashishin knife that Jena had taken to wearing at her hip. "Hide anything you don't want him to know about."

Nate raised his eyebrows. "Is he as bad as all that? Surely—"

"He's worse," interrupted Argus. "He's everything you imagine, and worse." He glanced down at Bree and took a breath, like he was gathering himself to say something he didn't want to say. "Which is why we can't tell him that my curse has been broken. He *must not know* what Bree means to me. He'll use it against us."

Bree stood and turned to Argus, her white-blonde hair flowing behind her, small hands curled into fists. "I will not pretend you're nothing to me. I'm not going to—"

Argus placed one of his large hands on Bree's pale arm. "Remus is not like other people. He has no moral compass, no care for anyone other than himself. He will stop at nothing to get what he wants. If he thinks he can use you to get to me, he will."

"Won't he know?" asked Jena. "Surely if he cast the curse, he'll know it's gone."

"I don't think so. He used to test me sometimes," said Argus, his voice filled with a remembered pain. "Made me do things he knew I'd never do on my own, to make sure it still held. I learned to stay quiet and do everything he asked without question, lest he decide another test was needed. You need to prepare yourselves to deal with someone like that."

Nate stared at Argus, wondering what Remus had made Argus do. Based on the look on his face, it wasn't good. Bree must have decided the same thing, because she leaned in and wrapped Argus in a hug, his face against her chest, her arms wrapped tightly around his head and shoulders.

"Maybe you shouldn't go with us," said Jena tentatively. "He has no hold over you anymore. Surely we can—"

"You wouldn't survive without me," said Argus abruptly, pulling away from Bree to glare at Jena. "Having me there is the only way you'll make it out."

"But how? What will you do that's so special?" asked Nate.

"I spent years with that man. I learned every nuance to his expression, every emotion he hides behind his disgusting shrunken face. I know how to deal with him."

Nate shivered, foreboding filling his senses.

Suddenly he wasn't as keen to get to Remus.

CHAPTER 4

JENA

Jena rounded a corner on the track and almost bumped into Argus. Bree stood by his side. They were no longer holding hands.

In the distance was a small house made of lava rock that seemed to grow up out of the ground, like a strange, crooked, half-dead plant. Smoke puffed out the lopsided stone chimney; rocks had fallen down one side. There were vines growing through much of the outside. The small, crooked cottage felt precarious at best.

Argus stood as if he was stunned, his body stiff.

"This is it?" Nate came to a halt behind them.

"This is it," Argus replied, his tone grim.

"It's smaller than I imagined," said Jena.

"Remember, we keep my freedom from his curse a secret. He cannot know what Bree means to me," Argus whispered, his tone urgent.

Everyone murmured their agreement. They'd already agreed to his plan.

Several times.

Jena saw his fear and wondered—not for the first time

—if they'd actually be able to carry this off. Argus was wound up tighter than a coiled snake. Bree wasn't much better, her eyes wide as she looked at the crooked house.

"You're sure Lothar can't get to us here?" asked Nate.

"Remus has a powerful spell blocking his home. Only those he chooses can find him."

"Another reason why we needed you," said Bree softly.

As they watched, the door opened and a tiny man emerged. Feathers fluttered on her stomach, and Jena saw pictures of the same man at full height, standing straight and proud. He'd been handsome and confident.

The man in front of them had the same arrogant pride holding him erect, but he was half the size. It looked like he still had the same amount of skin on his body; he was wrinkled and bulbous in all the wrong places.

His mage robes had been shortened to fit his body, and he tottered on feet that seemed too close to their original size. His ankles—the only part of his legs visible under the mage robes—were bent and crooked. The mage's face was strangely lopsided, like the house, as if his head was too heavy for the rest of his body. One eye was lower than the other, and he was ever-so-slightly cross-eyed. If Jena had met him in any other circumstances, she'd have assumed he'd lost his mind.

Instead, she had to focus on holding her hand still to avoid casting a warding spell and giving herself away.

Argus straightened his shoulders and strode toward Remus, his long legs eating up the ground.

Bree and Jena hesitated, then followed at a slower pace. Nothing about this situation felt safe. The raven gave Jena more images of Remus when he was younger—a handsome mage in his flowing robes. Attractive. Powerful. She'd known he had a shrinking spell cast on him many years before, but she hadn't been prepared for this horrific deterioration. A chill walked down her spine. What kind of terrible deeds might a man such as this perform to regain his former glory?

There was an image of Thornal with Remus, both men tall and imposing. Even in the image, she could sense Thornal's displeasure with Remus. She was suddenly very sure he hadn't liked the shrinking mage either.

Remus moved awkwardly down the three steps from the veranda and came toward them, swaying and shuffling as he went. Argus bowed his head slightly, more subservient than Jena had ever seen him. "Master."

They caught up to Argus and stood just behind him, Nate taking his place on the other side of Bree.

Jena had to concentrate on not reacting to the excess skin that rolled over Remus's neck and arms. He smelled unexpectedly of basil and lemon.

"You survived," said Remus, his watery eyes moving restlessly within his face. His voice was reedy, created by the combination of a strong will and a deteriorating body. He sounded almost surprised.

"I did," growled Argus.

"You succeeded, then?" Beady eyes peered past Argus to Nate. "This is the mage Nathaniel?"

"Yes, this is Nate." Argus's voice had a sharp edge to it.

Remus's gaze fixed back on Argus. "You're late. I said the second moon."

"There was a storm. You probably had it here too," said Argus, looking around as if to find evidence. "It delayed us."

"Don't give me your excuses, Argus. I gave you one task. Be back before the second full moon. You couldn't even follow that one instruction."

"It was a long way. It's a miracle we're here." Argus

glared down at Remus, looking like he wanted to throttle the strange-looking mage. "We're less than a day late."

"I told you, that one day was the difference between life and death. You could have killed us all."

"And yet we're not dead," said Argus stubbornly. "Your deadline was impossible." Argus spoke through gritted teeth.

"You're lucky I didn't trust you. It would have been a disaster," said Remus smugly, one of his eyes tilting strangely to the side.

"What does that mean?" Argus took a threatening step toward the shrinking mage, as if he meant to strike him. He was doing a terrible job of staying on Remus's good side. But Remus didn't seem to notice. Jena had a feeling that Argus had always been like this toward the shrinking mage.

Remus waved airily in the direction of the sky. "You had until seven days *after* the full moon. But I knew if I told you the real time frame, you would have taken even longer."

"There was no need to trick me. You just enjoy playing the puppeteer."

"You barely made it," sneered Remus. "If I hadn't given you a false deadline, you'd have still been out there, struggling to return to me." He looked Argus up and down. "Actually, you'd probably have been dead."

Argus stiffened. He clenched his hands at his sides. "I said I'd be back, and I am." He looked like he was about to say something they'd all regret.

Jena glanced at Bree who looked equally worried. But Argus had been clear—they should allow him to deal with Remus. The shrinking mage was cunning and devious. He'd sniff out their secrets if they didn't keep their distance.

Except Nate obviously wasn't as worried about following Argus's rules as they were. He moved forward until he was standing next to Argus. "We're here because Argus said you knew something that would help me defeat Lothar," he said, before Argus could say anything unwise. "We traveled as fast as we could."

"I know many things that would help you defeat the usurper king," said Remus, looking Nate up and down like he was a cow he was considering purchasing at the market. "It is my burden to see the future in my crystal ball."

"A powerful talent," said Nate, with a slight bow of his head. "I hope you will consider using it for my benefit."

"You are truly the mage Nathaniel?"

"I am."

Remus sniffed the surrounding air, like he smelled something bad. "I don't sense your power." He turned back to Argus. "You've brought me the wrong mage, you imbecile. This idiot doesn't have more than a whiff of mage power about him." For the first time, Remus looked more than a wrinkled old man. He looked... vicious. Murderous. Cruel.

Jena's heart thumped heavily in her chest. They'd been here only a few moments and already Remus was sniffing out their secrets. Nate couldn't tell this man he was a Firecaller. It was too dangerous. She cleared her throat, trying to think of something to say that would ease the situation.

Except she needn't have worried.

Argus shifted forward and leaned down into Remus's space. "He's the correct mage. I have seen it proven many times. Lothar has been chasing us the whole way." He glared at Remus, daring the older man to disagree.

Remus hesitated, looking into Argus's face. "I will have to do a scrying to confirm. But I can see you are telling the truth. Your version of it, at least."

He transferred his gaze to Jena and Bree. A frown

appeared, creating a strange lumpy furrow between his eyes.

"And who is this? You know how I feel about strangers." Remus turned back to Argus, his uneven eyes glinting dangerously.

Argus paused, glancing at Bree, then away. "The High Witch Miara sent them to help me bring Nate safely to you. I would not have made it if they hadn't accompanied me."

Remus snorted. "The High Witch Miara is a meddling old fool. How was she? Still crying all the time?"

"She is well." Argus hesitated. "No crying."

"Couldn't get her to shut up at court. Husband died, and you'd have thought it was the only bad thing to ever happen to a person." He huffed in annoyance. "You're here now; you may as well come inside." He waved his arm, directing them into his home.

Jena exchanged yet another look with her sister. Bree's eyes were wide, her expression dubious. She seemed to agree with Jena's immediate assessment—this tiny, lopsided man wasn't completely sane—and he definitely couldn't be trusted.

They should probably run in the other direction. Find another way to get help with confronting Lothar. And if she'd been able to think of a single place to go that might give them what they wanted, Jena might have done just that. Grabbed Bree's hand and run the other direction. Instead, she followed Nate and Argus up the steps and into the house.

She couldn't help comparing it to the warm and inviting cottage she'd lived in with Thornal. Inside Remus's house it was dim and slightly damp. The curtains were all closed, and very little light from outside made it into the house. There were low lights glowing around the edges of the room and the light of a big fire burning in the hearth, but the shadows were large and jagged and almost seemed alive.

There were strange masks and stuffed animals on the walls—from tiny lava mice to larger wild cats and even a two-headed fire deer—all of them looking like they were in pain or angry or suffering some other disturbing emotion as they'd died. Their glassy eyes stared out at her, telling her to leave this place. A series of books lined a bookshelf, and even from across the room, Jena could feel their dark, terrible power. There was dark magic leaking out of the pages, crawling into the air around them, infecting them with their treachery. Jena took a step further away from the books. Thornal's magic had never felt like that.

On the shelves that didn't have books, there were bottles and vials and baskets and jugs, all filled with disturbing objects. Jena recognized herbs and other innocuous plants, but also a glass bottle filled with eyeballs in fluid, and another with hundreds of teeth that looked disturbingly human. One vial with a finger floating in murky water, yet another contained lumps that might have been internal organs. She shuddered. It felt like Remus was threatening them, without even saying a word. He had his trophies out on display, warning them of what was going on inside his head. Her every sense was yelling at her to run.

The raven shuffled on her stomach, and she saw flashes of Thornal in his potions room, jars of plants lined up on the shelves, paper thrown carelessly on the wooden tables, sunlight streaming in from the windows. He'd liked the mess, said it helped him think and work on some of his more powerful mage creations. Thornal had been a powerful mage, had delved into things that had sometimes felt like they were on the borderline of right and wrong, but it had never felt like this room.

Bree moved closer to Jena and put one hand in her sister's. Jena glanced over and saw the same apprehension on Bree's face. This crooked little mage was more dangerous than they'd given him credit for, even given Argus's warnings. She was glad she'd put her Hashishin knife and Thornal's ashes in her bag before they got here.

She smiled at Bree reassuringly. They could survive this place. She'd survived worse.

They didn't have to stay long. They just had to find out what Remus knew, then leave.

Fast.

CHAPTER 5
NATE

N ate shivered.

Despite the warmth of the fire burning in the grate, he felt cold. Perhaps it was because the last of his hope had died? They were sitting around the hearth in Remus's cottage, drinking the tea Argus had just made for them all. Shadows danced, and the disturbing masks and stuffed animals decorating the walls and shelves flickered ominously. Books and vials filled the rest of the space, plus bottles filled with unmarked floating organic matter. It was like a distorted, unhappy version of his grandfather's spell room.

And his grandfather's room hadn't been a barrel of laughs.

Nate clenched his hands around the mug he held, struggling to contain the emotions that surged inside him. After all their travels, after almost dying multiple times and the hope he'd been nursing about Remus being able to save him, it was a terrible disappointment to meet him. To know it was all a lie.

The warning he'd been given by the ghost when he first

met Argus was spinning around in his head: *Don't trust the mercenary's master. He means you harm.* He'd been hoping the ghost had been wrong or perhaps telling half-truths.

But as soon as he'd seen Remus, he'd known.

It wasn't just about his painfully shrunken body. Although that was disturbing and hideous. It took every ounce of Nate's concentration not to react to the wrinkles and rolls of flapping skin that were everywhere he looked.

No. It was Remus's beady little eyes.

Remus's loose facial skin was only just holding his features together, but it didn't stop his creepy eyes from peering out at them, calculation sparkling in their depths. There was something cold and devious about this man; it emanated from him, like a greasy mist, and Nate felt dirty whenever Remus came near.

"Argus, I'm pleased you succeeded," said Remus into the silence, lifting his cup of tea in a toast. "I didn't think you would." The shrinking mage smiled. It seemed an unnatural act, his lips stretching uncomfortably across yellowed teeth.

Next to Nate, Argus looked up from contemplating the mug he was holding in one enormous hand, his expression hard. "You said you could help Nate."

"Yes, I suppose I did." Remus's eyes bulged in the dim light. He was sitting on top of three ancient spell books, his need to be taller than everyone else while they sat in front of the fire outweighing the centuries of magic and knowledge they contained. How could Remus stand to be so close to the dark slithering power that emanated from the old texts?

How old was Remus? His age was obscured by the grotesqueness of his current state, his body wizened and wrinkled unnaturally, his lopsided face perched precariously on his birdlike neck. Nate watched Remus with narrowed eyes, trying to see through the surface to the man beyond. His imagination failed him. "And can you help me? Or is this some deception you've created?" His voice was harsh, and he was expecting an answer he didn't want to hear.

Across from him, Argus cleared his throat, clearly unhappy that Nate had spoken. But Nate didn't know how to keep silent when it was his whole life at stake. He ignored Argus's frown.

"I can help you, and you can help me. It will be a fair trade." Remus smiled again.

Nate ground his teeth. "How can I help you?" he said. "I don't have any useful powers. You've already established that." He didn't trust this shrinking schemer with the secret of the Firecaller abilities that burned inside him, itching to be released.

"I have searched far and wide for a way to reverse the shrinking spell that was cast on me. I have searched the future and have foreseen that you will be the answer to my problems."

Nate's heart pumped faster. What did the old mage know? What had he seen? "What do you want from me?"

"You will use a spell from the Book of Spells to save me." Remus leaned forward, his unsettling eyes focused on Nate. "I know you possess the book. It's part of the prophecy."

Nate's body relaxed slightly. Remus didn't know he was a Firecaller. But across from where he sat, Jena tensed and Bree put a calming hand on her sister's arm. Nate said nothing for a moment, gathering his thoughts. He was determined not to give Jena's secrets away, either. "What makes you so sure I have the Book of Spells?"

"It is written in the prophecies. Do not lie to me."

Remus made a wide gesture with one long, saggy arm, the huge spell books rustling as he moved. "I have studied for years to find a way out of this curse. It's in the Book of Spells. I know it is." His unsteady eyes flickered in the fire-light, and Nate's intuition kicked into full force. This man would never help them. He'd use them for his own ends and then spit them out.

The full force of their wasted journey hit Nate in the chest, and he struggled to take a breath. They'd made Argus come back here when he didn't want to. They'd put themselves in danger when they shouldn't have. It was all a waste of time.

Across from him, Jena stirred. "How did you come by this shrinking curse, Remus? It seems too simple a spell to confound a powerful mage such as yourself." She smiled, but it didn't reach her eyes.

Remus's face twisted for a split second, pulling his features into an even more terrible disfigurement. It seemed he might not answer Jena's question for a moment. Then he gave his chilling smile. "I was caught by a woman. Two women, actually. They were jealous of my powers and connived together to cast this spell over me."

Nate looked up, surprised. "The women cast mage spells?" He forced himself not to glance at Jena.

Remus shook his head impatiently, as if Nate were missing the point. "This was a long time ago, and both women were witches, so they had some power of their own. I taught them a few simple spells."

Nate blinked. "*You* taught them the spells they used to trap you?" The irony was almost laughable.

Remus saw his expression and waved away his breach of the centuries-old mage law with one arrogant flick of his wrist. "It seemed innocent enough, but on that day, I realized the Council was right to ban women from becoming mages. It leads to no good." Remus glared at Jena and Bree like they were cooking up trouble right at this moment.

"And how is it you can't remove a simple shrinking spell?" Nate felt his anger rising.

"Because one placed a shrinking spell on me, just as the other placed an eternal spell. Combined, they were powerful enough to entrap me."

"What happened to them? Why didn't they relent?" asked Bree, her eyes wide and her voice soft. She probably couldn't imagine a world where people weren't kind to each other.

But Nate thought he knew why they didn't relent. He wouldn't give in to this little monster either.

"Bah," said Remus, his expression like he'd just eaten a lemon. "I had cast a spell on them first, and it took effect before I could get them to reverse their spells."

Nate nodded to himself. It made perfect sense. The reason this horrible little mage was stuck in this position was because of his own actions. "And you couldn't take back the spell you cast on them?"

"What use would that have been? There was no guarantee they would have reversed their spells. If I had to be stuck shrinking through the years, they could be stuck in their assigned roles as well. It was a fit punishment."

"Even at the expense of your own health?" Nate couldn't believe it. Remus's pride was phenomenal.

"I was confident back then that I would find a way out of the spell. It has since come to my attention that although the eternal spell is small, it is surprisingly powerful. It does not detach itself easily."

"What's in the Book of Spells that will reverse the

shrinking spell?" asked Nate, trying to hide his distaste for Remus.

Remus made an irritated sound. "I don't know what it is. I just know it's there. Something in the Book of Spells can turn back an eternity spell." He leaned forward again, his strange, crooked eyes focused on Nate's face. "You have it, and in return for saving you from certain death at Lothar's hands, I want to look through the book."

A whisper of unease rolled up Nate's spine. What would Remus do when he realized Nate didn't have the Book? Would he stand back and let them all die at Lothar's hands?

Of course he would.

Nate glanced at Jena, wondering what she wanted him to do. She just shrugged, as if it were no concern of hers.

"And if I don't have it?" Nate asked softly.

"The Guardian might be dead, but the Book of Spells still exists. I know you have it." Remus's eyes gleamed in the firelight. Magic leaked from the books under him, swirling around his body like a lover. Even lopsided, his power was disquieting. He wouldn't let them leave without seeing the Book of Spells. It would just be whether they had the combined power to overcome him—or perhaps the wit to outsmart him.

Nate tightened his grip on the mug in his hands. "What makes you so sure?" He leaned forward in his chair, staring intently at Remus.

"Thornal couldn't destroy it. It's just not possible. What good is a Guardian without the Book of Spells to protect?" Remus shrugged, his head drooping to one side. "Impossible as it may seem, you are the one from the prophecy, and you are intimately connected to the Book of Spells in all the old sources. It is the only answer that makes sense."

Nate's stomach twisted at what Remus didn't realize he was saying. "But why?"

Remus huffed, sweeping his arm in an impatient arc. "I have studied for the last sixty years, trying to find a way out of this ash-begotten spell. I know the Rose King—Lothar—is finally moving, and the prophecy is underway. That means you have the Book."

"You seem to know a lot for a man who lives so far from anyone else," said Nate.

Remus nodded his head toward the hearth. "I have a Flame Echo. I hear the news; sometimes more than I should."

Nate jerked his gaze to the fire, its rosy flames taking on a sinister glow. Was Lothar about to appear? Had he been listening in already? Did he already know where they were? He glanced back at Remus. It took a complicated spell to create an Echo bond. Most of the Flame Echoes that existed were created by the Great Mage, centuries ago. It was a timely reminder that Remus was a powerful mage. He needed to be careful. "Can you control who comes into your flames?"

Remus smirked. "You're worried about Lothar?"

"Of course I am! He's trying to kill me."

"Lothar cannot access this Flame Echo, not unless I allow it. I prefer to keep him blocked."

Nate nodded, slightly relieved. "And if I help you undo this spell, what will you do for me?"

"I will help you defeat Lothar. I can show you his weaknesses."

Nate leaned forward. "His weaknesses?"

Remus patted the side of his nose. "I keep my secrets until you've given me what I need. Give me the Book, and I will tell you how to defeat Lothar."

Nate paused. "I need some time," he said. "I'll go through it to see what might be of use to you. It's not always a matter of simply reading the Book of Spells."

Annoyance flitted across Remus's face before he could hide it. "I'm a powerful mage. I can interpret it more easily than you ever could. Just give me the Book of Spells to study."

Nate frowned. "I gave an oath. It stays with me."

Remus smiled, a fake expression that was more chilling than conciliatory. "Then before you study the book, perhaps you could help me with a few tasks?"

"What kind of tasks?"

"I'm old and infirm, and I've missed having Argus around to help me." Remus widened his eyes, obviously trying to look infirm. Instead, he looked like his eyes were about to fall out of their sockets.

Nate glanced at Argus, trying not to react to the unpleasant sight. He didn't know what to say, but he felt churlish at this sudden change of direction. Argus gave a small shrug, like he didn't know either.

"Sure," said Nate, reluctantly. What could it hurt? It would give them more time to figure out how they were going to deal with Remus demanding the Book of Spells, which they clearly couldn't give him.

And they certainly weren't going to trust him with the truth.

CHAPTER 6
JENA

Jena stretched, trying to ease her sore muscles.

The raven fluttered on her stomach, stretching its wings around to her back, mimicking her movement.

She was sitting with Bree on the veranda, looking out over the barren landscape, trying not to be too impatient. Nate and Argus had agreed to go collect rocks to shore up the crooked little mage's crooked little house and had insisted she and Bree stay here and rest. She'd assumed Nate had wanted someone to stay and keep an eye on Remus.

Argus still hadn't told Remus that his curse had been broken, and the mage didn't seem to have noticed. He was ordering Argus around like a slave, and Argus quietly did everything that was asked of him. When Remus had asked them to collect rocks, Argus and Nate had packed up a bag and headed to the quarry.

So now they waited. It was early afternoon; steam rose from several rocky vents in the distance, and small animals occasionally popped their heads out from behind the sporadic underbrush.

"You'd think they'd know to stay well hidden," said Jena.

"What?" said Bree absently. She'd been staring in the direction Nate and Argus had gone.

"The animals. Otherwise, they'll end up on Remus's walls."

Bree shivered delicately. "How does he get their eyes to look so real?"

Jena shrugged. "Magic."

Bree returned her gaze to the narrow track.

"They'll be back soon. He's only sent them to get some rocks from the quarry. Argus said it wasn't far."

"I'm just nervous. Around...you know."

Jena nodded. She knew exactly what Bree was talking about. Remus kept watching them out of the corner of his eye, a faint sneer on his lips.

Even worse, Remus was desperate. She could feel it in every twitch of his eye, every wrinkle of his skin. He hadn't pestered Nate about the Book of Spells when Nate had stalled him, but he'd wanted to. He'd clenched his tiny little hand tightly and had just smiled and asked them to collect rocks instead. Like he was plotting something devious but knew how to play the long game.

If anyone knew how to play the long game, it was Remus.

He was also smart. He'd figure out her secrets if they stayed too long.

When Remus had questioned him, Nate hadn't looked at her and had answered calmly, but Jena's heart had been pounding loud enough to be heard across the kingdom. She felt like she'd given herself away.

"They're both big enough to look after themselves. They'll be fine," she said, although she wasn't convinced.

Jena crossed her fingers and stared nervously in the same direction as Bree.

"But why—"

Bree broke off as Remus came shuffling around the corner of the house. His beady eyes latched onto them, and he grimaced.

"Having a rest, ladies?" he said.

In the time they'd spent with him, it had become clear that Remus didn't like women. It made her wonder about the women who'd fallen in love with him all those years ago. Had he been so very different? Was it because of those two women that he was so distrustful of Jena and Bree? Or had all the years of shrinking simply affected his mind as well as his body?

"We've traveled a long way," Bree reminded him softly.

Jena glanced over at her sister, the edges of her mouth curving in a moment of genuine amusement. She honestly couldn't tell if Bree really thought Remus didn't remember, or if she was just playing games with him.

"Ah yes, I suppose you have." Remus came to a halt in front of them. He was clothed in a traditional mage gown that had been altered to fit his shrunken body, and his strange, wrinkled hands hung from the sleeves like they weren't even joined to the rest of him. He cast a considering look over their faces. "How much do you wish to help Nate?" he asked. "Do you wish him to succeed against Lothar?"

Jena tensed. Remus's expression was just bland enough to be suspicious, his eyes glittering with an excitement she couldn't easily explain.

"Of course we do," said Bree, frowning. Her hands tightened on the arms of the wooden chair she was sitting in.

"I hesitate to tell you this. I'm not sure you're strong

enough. Perhaps it will only upset you to know what you cannot do." He paused again, looking apologetic.

Jena raised her eyebrows but refused to bite. The more she knew of Remus, the more manipulative and devious he seemed. She wouldn't trust him to tell them the correct time of day.

When neither of the sisters asked him the question he was waiting for, Remus continued. "You can help Nate defeat Lothar. In fact, it is the only way to guarantee his success. But it will mean braving something rather frightening."

"What are you talking about?" said Bree, a small frown on her beautiful face.

"I could not tell you while the men were here; they would not have let you go."

Jena stood up. She'd had enough. "This is some kind of trick."

Bree pushed herself up from her chair and came to stand beside Jena in a show of solidarity that made Jena's chest tighten.

"My dear, this is no trick. It is within your power to bring Nate a lavaen stone from the core of the volcano. With such a powerful magical object on your side, Nate is certain to be victorious."

Jena's stomach dropped. "A lavaen stone?" Her one experience with a lavaen had been terrifying. She had no desire to repeat it.

"It is a powerful stone that comes from the very core of the beast. It forms like a pearl in an oyster. When it grows too large, they heave it up, vomiting a stone of such power and beauty, it is legendary among mages. The stone would give Nate the advantage he needs over Lothar. The lavaen on my mountain has recently created her very first lavaen stone."

Jena swayed where she stood as a page of the Book of Spells appeared in her head. It showed a picture of a gleaming red stone in the hands of a mage. Remus was telling the truth about that aspect of it at least. Except the page talked of lavaen stones as if they were a myth. Jena clenched her hands. "And how are we supposed to get it off the lavaen?"

"You must enter the lair of the lavaen and ask her for it."

Jena shuddered, images of fire and death flashing through her head. "We can't just ask a lavaen for a stone. It'd kill us."

"A normal lavaen, perhaps. But this is a special creature. She used to be human. If you appeal to her better nature, explain the quest you are on, she may give it to you. It is your only hope."

"Okay, well when Nate and Argus get back, we can talk to them, and—"

"No," said Remus sharply. "She responds only to women. Tears men to pieces. If I allowed you to take the men, they would only be a hindrance. You would fail. This is something you must do on your own."

Jena narrowed her eyes suspiciously. "Did you do something to her? Is that why she hates men?"

Remus waved a hand. "It hardly matters how it came to be. But the stone is there for you, if you are brave enough to take it."

"How exactly will the stone help Nate?" Jena knew there was a trick involved in Remus's suggestion, but she wasn't sure what it was. He was probably expecting them to fail. He assumed he was sending two helpless women into the lavaen's lair.

Horrible little ash-dweller.

How had Argus borne living alongside him all those years under his spell?

Although perhaps it explained the mercenary's surly demeanor.

"It is a power source. Lothar is gaining strength every day. Nate... is not a powerful mage. Fate seems to have chosen him, but if Nate is to have a chance of winning this battle, he needs help."

Nate was far more powerful than Remus seemed to suspect, but Jena wasn't about to contradict him. She thought of the murghah, and the small glowing ruby filled with souls the creature had carried. Lothar was using the souls of his own people to succeed in his terrible quest. It would certainly help if they had something similar. "Say we believe you. What do we have to do?" Jena asked. She ignored the flash of triumph on Remus's face. He knew nothing about them. He was underestimating their abilities.

"You must enter the cave and ask for the pleasure of speech with her," said Remus. "Always be polite and never turn your back on her. Explain your need and ask for the lavaen stone. Simple."

Jena turned to Bree and spoke in a low voice. "He's telling the truth about the lavaen stone. If it can be of help to Nate, I need to go. But you should stay here and wait for Nate and Argus, tell them what I'm doing."

"No," said Bree firmly, her eyes flashing. "If you go, I go. You might need help." Bree glanced over at Remus. "And I'm not staying here alone with him," she added under her breath.

Jena turned back to the shrinking mage. "How long will it take us to get to the lavaen's lair?"

"Just over an hour. It's very close." Remus waved one hand toward the summit.

She gazed up the mountain. In the distance, shots of red lava spurted out from the uppermost volcanoes. "She lives near the top of the volcano?"

"She lives *inside* the volcano." Remus's eyes glinted, and Jena saw amusement flit across his face. She let out an angry breath. He was a smoky, devious mage and this was a trick to get rid of them. He thought they wouldn't survive the meeting with the lavaen.

But he didn't realize who their parents were, or that her grandfather had taught her to be a mage. He didn't know she had the Book of Spells inside her head, ready to use at all times. He didn't know she had Thornal's raven attached to her body.

And the Book of Spells had confirmed that lavaen stones were real. That they held power comparable to the fire rubies that Lothar was already using. Maybe more powerful.

They—Nate—needed all the help he could get.

"Tell us how to get there."

CHAPTER 7
NATE

Nate's back was soaked with sweat, and his shirt was sticking uncomfortably to his skin.

He grasped another heavy lava rock with two hands and hefted it into his bag. Despite being small, they were compact—heavy with the minerals formed in the center of the lava. The sun was baking his skin, heating it until he felt like he was being burned alive inside a forge. This was much harder work than mining the volcanoes for salt; it was the kind of work he'd always called a demon to do, except he'd vowed not to do that anymore.

He paused and looked over at Argus. "How many more do we need?" he said, trying not to sound like he was whining.

"Not many," replied Argus from a few feet away where he was lifting a lava rock twice the size of Nate's.

"Did he make you do this very often? When you were under his spell?" Nate asked. He picked up another rock, and threw it into the bag, his arm muscles already aching.

"He enjoyed putting me in my place."

Nate winced. "And the reason we're breaking our backs lifting rocks for him now is...?"

"We needed more time to figure out what we're going to do. This gives it to us."

"And what *are* we going to do?" Nate was struggling to figure that out, even here, away from the dark swirling magic of Remus. He wiped sweat off his forehead with the back of his hand. "We can't show him the Book of Spells. And we can't trust him with any of our secrets. Which means he's not going to tell *us* anything useful."

Argus held one hand up to shade his eyes from the sun. "I know." He hesitated. "Is there any way Jena could tell him...?"

"No," said Nate sharply. "Remus can't know that she's a powerful mage. She's in enough danger already. She doesn't need someone like Remus having that power over her."

Argus shrugged. "Then we leave. Remus won't tell us anything if we have no leverage."

"What about telling him that I'm the Firecaller?"

Argus stared at him. "What would that achieve? Can you reverse his shrinking spell with your Firecaller abilities?" His large frame almost blocked out the afternoon sun.

"No. I don't think so." Nate squinted at Argus, wishing that he understood his magic and could get them out of this situation.

"Then he won't care. He only cares about reversing that spell. Nothing and no one else."

"Jena could search the Book of Spells for a spell that might work," said Nate. "But I'm sure she's already done that. And I don't think Remus would be satisfied."

"No. He believes he's the only one who can truly see the

potential in the spells he casts. He likes to pore over books, touch and feel them, read them over and over."

"He's not doing that to Jena," growled Nate. It felt like every hair on his body was bristling at the very idea.

"No. I thought not."

"What other options do we have?"

"We leave." Argus looked grim, like maybe it wasn't going to be that easy.

Disappointment swirled in Nate's stomach like acid. "But we spent all this time getting here. We were so sure he'd be able to help."

"He *could* help. But he won't unless we're useful to him."

"Is there anything else he might want to know?" Nate hesitated. "I have other abilities..."

Argus narrowed his eyes. "Like what?"

"I have a particular power; another part of being Fire-caller." Nate hesitated, old habits making him reluctant to spill his secrets. He took a breath, then blurted it out. "I can see and talk to ghosts. When you rescued me the first time, a ghost told me your master was lying and would only pretend to help me. It wanted to help me get out of there without you." Nate looked for shock or fear on Argus's face... and saw neither. The mercenary had lived with a mage for far too long.

Argus simply frowned. "How do you know the ghost didn't lie?"

"They can't lie. They can omit information, they can put it across in a certain way, but they can't outright lie. Kind of like demons."

"Then why come with me?"

"Aside from the fact that wolvans and a lavaen were attacking?" said Nate, raising his brows.

"Aside from that," agreed Argus.

Sweat dripped from his brow as Nate considered the rocky cliffs above them for a moment. Argus waited for his answer, patient as ever. "Ghosts... when they're living in the Edges between this world and the next... have to figure out why they're still here," he said slowly, trying to articulate it in a way that would make sense. "Sometimes they're just stubborn bastards who don't want to die, but mostly, if they find what it is they want to finish, they'll move on to the next world once they finish it. They get desperate as soon as they realize I have the power to help them do that."

"And that's bad?"

Nate shrugged. "They'll say and do anything to get me to help them, without considering the consequences for the living. They don't care about anything but getting what they want. It can be devastating. So, I went with you."

"And it landed you here, carrying rocks for a mean little bastard mage and trying to figure out what he's up to instead," said Argus dryly.

"Indeed." Nate paused and looked up. "But you *did* save my life several times. I don't know if I ever properly thanked you for that."

"You were too busy running away from me," said Argus, his tone amused.

Nate winced. "I didn't want to be King of Ignisia. Still don't." Except now he'd vowed to wrest it from Lothar's twisted hands. Nate tried to regret it and couldn't.

"Sometimes we don't have a choice in life. Things just happen a certain way." Argus's expression was haunted for a moment, before he hid his emotions again.

Nate hesitated. "Your brother's death wasn't your fault," he said cautiously. He didn't want to upset Argus, but his brother Eldrin had told them all the story of how their older brother had saved Argus at the cost of his own life. It was a burden Argus seemed reluctant to release.

Argus glanced sharply at Nate. "You don't know—" He stopped and took a deep breath. "I've carried that with me for a long time. It's hard to let it go."

"I know. But you've got a second chance now, with Bree. Don't mess it up by focusing on your past."

Argus paused in lifting rocks and stared up the mountain. "My past is filled with regret and difficulty," he murmured. "Remus used me as a mindless weapon for more years than I care to remember. But Bree has given me a reason to be more, she has given me a purpose and a life again. I would do anything to protect her."

The ferocity of Argus's answer surprised Nate. He swallowed over the lump in his throat. "That's a good reason to think about the future more than the past."

Argus raised his eyebrows at Nate. "Like you're doing?"

Nate ran one hand through his hair, frustrated. "My future isn't so simple. I have to battle a self-righteous mage more powerful than I, and if I succeed, I become king, a role I know nothing about and have no desire to hold."

Argus shook his head. "You're smart. You'll figure it out."

"Maybe." Blowing out a long breath, Nate sat down heavily on a nearby boulder. "So we really just leave here? Get nothing from Remus?"

"What makes you think I have the answers?" Argus lifted another rock and placed it into the closest burlap bag. He didn't even look like he'd broken a sweat.

"He was your master, you should know him."

Argus paused. Then he stretched his back and curved one corner of his mouth. It was the closest Nate had ever seen him come to being happy. "He's not my master anymore."

Nate grimaced. "Was it truly awful being his slave?"

"Worse than anything you can imagine," said Argus, his expression losing some of its satisfaction. "But I'm free now, and I don't intend to get myself caught up in another curse created by that man."

"So what do we do?" Nate tried to keep his voice calm, but some of his fear leaked into his words. He wasn't just asking about Remus. He didn't know what they were going to do once they left here.

"Your ghost was right. He's going to double-cross you if he can."

Nate nodded slowly. "I don't want to give him anything."

"Nor I. We need to leave here as soon as possible."

"Do you think Remus will just let us leave?"

Argus shook his head firmly. "No. We'll have to sneak out once he's asleep and we can't delay. We must leave tonight."

"You're really afraid of what he'll do to us, aren't you?" Nate had never seen Argus act like this around another person.

"He's not a good man. He will connive and lie and steal to get his way. We need to take these rocks back, do whatever he asks of us without question for the rest of the day, except give him the Book of Spells. And then in the middle of the night, we run from here. It's the only way."

"But where do we go? I was relying on Remus giving us some kind of direction." Nate tried to imagine where else they could go for help against Lothar, and failed.

"I think we should go to the Utugani winter camp

immediately. My father is a skilled leader and always has his ear to the ground. He will have some suggestions on where you can go next."

Nate clenched his hands into fists. Argus was talking as if he planned to let Nate continue without him. And he knew it made sense. Argus wanted to protect Bree, not go charging off on a suicide mission to fight a powerful prince. But he couldn't help the pang in his chest. "The idea of going home must be tantalizing," he forced himself to say. It wasn't Argus's fight. He couldn't force the mercenary to come with him to the Flame City.

Argus hesitated and his expression became almost wistful. "Yes, seeing Eldrin has made me long for home. I'm excited by the idea of hugging my grandmother and younger sister again, and I'm even looking forward to talking hunting with my father."

"What will you do once we get there?"

Argus took a deep breath. "I'm free to do what I want. I'm free to love Bree and settle down if she'll have me. I'm free to introduce my family to the woman I love."

Argus looked almost overwhelmed by the idea. It made Nate's heart swell and he felt churlish for wishing the big man would come with him to face Lothar. He went over to Argus and grabbed his shoulders. He grinned, then pulled Argus into a big hug—not caring whether the mercenary wanted it or not—slapping his back in congratulations. Argus stiffened, then relaxed and hugged Nate in return.

Nate stepped back, still grinning. "How long were you under his spell?"

"Too long. Since just after I left the Flame Guards."

"Eldrin said that was years ago…" Nate looked up at Argus. "I don't know how you're so calm about all this. Or why you're even here."

"I will do anything for Bree. She brought me back to life." Argus shrugged. "She wanted to come here, so I came here."

"Then let's get these rocks back to Remus and get the hell away from this place."

CHAPTER 8

JENA

T he hot sun beat down on Jena's body, making the scar tissue on one side itch uncomfortably, while the knots in her stomach tightened with each step. But she refused to give in to the urge to turn around again and see if Remus was still watching them from the veranda of his house.

An uneasy shiver crawled along her overheated body as she pictured him standing where they'd left him, a cold gleam in his eyes and a tiny smirk on the edges of his lips.

He knew something they didn't, and that felt dangerous. She continued to fight the urge to look back, to see if he was still there. Instead, she clenched her fists and forced herself to carry on.

It didn't matter. They were both strong, capable women with more power in their little fingers than Remus gave them credit for. He didn't know everything there was to know about their situation. They'd be fine. They'd faced so much already that it was difficult to imagine anything worse.

Except maybe Lothar watching them through the flames.

Firmly blocking the memories, Jena forced herself to focus on the uneven track ahead of her.

The mountainside was barren, and the path rocky and steep. The track was so rugged it was almost invisible in places. The only other movement came when they dislodged rocks and sent them tumbling down behind them.

Heat blanketed the landscape, getting worse as they climbed higher, closer to the molten lava at the crater. They both wore sturdy traveling shirts and long pants that kept the worst of the sun's heat off their skin, but it didn't stop them from sweating profusely.

She'd strapped her Hashishin knife to her calf, out of sight, and put Thornal's ashes in her pocket. But the knife was rubbing against her skin uncomfortably, and she was tempted to take it out and put it in her belt again. She squinted at the surrounding landscape, wondering about the risk of meeting someone who'd recognize the knife for what it was.

She didn't want anyone else to know she had a stolen artifact that was filled to the brim with Hashishin magic. She left the knife where it was.

"You good?" she asked Bree. Her sister was walking just behind her.

"Yes," said Bree, her gasping breath leaping over and around the word like a lizard in a lava bath. Jena winced.

Remus had promised them it wasn't far to the cave, but it was still a steep climb, and they were both already exhausted.

The wound from the fire hawk's talons burned on her side, and despite healing from Bree, it ached with every step. She was glad they'd left their bags with Remus, even if he thought he was tricking them. She knew he'd search them as soon as they were out of sight, but he'd find nothing of use.

She had everything important to her on her person. The wooden raven amulet that Thornal had given her was in one trouser pocket, the handful of ashes from Thornal in a leather pouch in the other. The knife from the Hashishin who'd killed Thornal was strapped to her calf. The Book of Spells Remus so desperately wanted was inside her head. For the first time, she could see exactly why Thornal had thought putting the spell book inside someone's head was a good idea. It was the perfect hiding place.

As long as Remus never found out.

Jena shuddered to think what he'd do to get the information out of her if he knew. He wouldn't be kind or considerate. She'd probably end up like one of those animals on his walls. She wondered what kind of expression he'd twist her face into. Fear? Horror? Abject terror?

She was glad to be out of his house. Remus was worse than anything she'd imagined, even after all of Argus's warnings.

She glanced around at the barren landscape, thoughts of Remus still bubbling inside her head. What if getting them out of the way so he could search their bags wasn't the worst of what Remus was trying to do? They *knew* Remus was trying to trick them, and they were still going. She was deliberately taking her sister Bree into a confrontation with a deadly beast.

Jena took a deep breath and tried to calm her nerves. She was confident in her mage skills. She had the Book of Spells inside her head and the raven on her side. It was all information Remus didn't have when he sent them up the mountain.

They would be fine.

This wasn't a terrible idea.

Jena slowed in her steady ascent, her legs unconsciously catching up to what her brain was thinking.

What were they doing? This *was* a terrible idea.

"Everything okay?" asked Bree from just behind her.

Jena glanced back at her sister. "Maybe we should have talked to Nate and Argus about this?"

"What would they have said?"

"That we shouldn't go. That it's too dangerous." Jena knew for certain that Argus would never have allowed Bree to come with her. "Argus wouldn't like you—"

"Argus doesn't get to speak for me, just because I've fallen in love with him," said Bree, her eyes flashing.

"I just mean—" Jena stopped. She didn't know what she meant.

"I love Argus," said Bree, more calmly this time. "He's a good man, and I want to spend my life with him. But he's not my master. I can make my own decisions."

Jena hesitated. "How do you know you're in love with him?" she blurted. Then winced and wished she hadn't said the words out loud. Nate's face flashed briefly into her thoughts, and she shook her head to clear it. She wasn't in love with anyone. She didn't know why she'd asked.

But Bree didn't laugh at her. She just looked thoughtful. "I just *knew*. I could see the real person under his mask. He was more than he pretended to be, and our connection is stronger than anything I've ever felt with another person." She glanced at Jena. "Except for you."

Jena blinked at Bree's words. Butterflies surged in her stomach, and she tried to understand why she was so scared by the idea of someone being close to her. Of loving her.

"What if he changes his mind?" The words slipped out

of her mouth before Jena could stop them. But they were at the heart of her most secret pain. She'd been abandoned or left for dead so many times in her life that it felt like it was all she could expect. *All she deserved.*

The idea of being in love with someone, of allowing herself to be that vulnerable to another person, made her squirm uncomfortably. She would run a mile in the opposite direction before allowing herself to be that vulnerable ever again. Even her newfound connection to Bree was pushing the limits of her hard-won boundaries.

"If he breaks my heart, I'll break his bones," said Bree with a small smile. "But he won't. I know him. He's strong and thoughtful, and he's just as committed to me as I am to him."

Jena found it hard to imagine ever feeling that sure about another person. "Then why risk everything to visit the lavaen?"

Bree frowned at Jena. "Do you think this lavaen stone will help Nate fight Lothar?"

The thought of Nate up against Lothar—a failed mage who didn't have a clue how to use his brand-new Firecaller magic against an experienced mage using dark magic— hardened her resolve. "Yes."

"And is Nate defeating Lothar the whole point of our quest?"

"Yes."

"Then stop questioning our decisions, turn around, and keep going." Bree's blue eyes flashed with fire, and Jena couldn't help grinning back at her sister. Bree was right. Whatever Jena could do to help Nate in his quest, she would do it.

She'd made a vow, and she intended to keep it.

CHAPTER 9

JENA

They traveled on in silence, both lost in their own thoughts. When Jena felt the impatient scratching on her stomach, she lifted her shirt, knowing right away what the raven was asking for. The bird leaped free with the usual painful twist. It flew straight up, high into the sky, then back down and landed on her arm, chattering at her in a way she hadn't heard before.

"What's the matter?" she asked it. "Have you seen something?"

It continued to chatter and caw, but when she lifted her shirt for it to go back on her stomach, the raven leaped back into the air, flying overhead in wide circles.

"It'll warn us if anything is coming," said Jena, almost to herself, as she watched it with one hand over her eyes.

"Why do you think Remus sent us up here?" asked Bree.

"I don't know. He might want us to succeed at this, so we owe him something. Or he might be trying to get rid of us."

"What does it say about lavaen in the Book of Spells?" asked Bree.

Jena scanned the pages until she found the notes on the fiery creatures. "They're born in the lava. It's possible they can read our minds, although that's just a rumor."

"Good skill to have. I wish we could use it against Remus."

"Yes. Although I'm not sure I'd want to know everything that's going on in his head."

"He's... off-balance," said Bree, thoughtfully. "It's the way he's shrinking. I don't know what he was like before, but he's crooked now. Askew. Not just in his body, but in his mind."

Jena nodded. She knew exactly what Bree meant. "He's also desperate," she said. "And arrogant. It's dangerous."

"Can Remus still overcome his shrinking spell? Perhaps it's already too late." Bree sounded hopeful.

Frowning, Jena scanned the pages of the Book of Spells in her head. "I'm still looking." She hesitated. "To be honest, I don't want to help him."

Bree nodded her understanding, and they climbed in silence, Jena still searching the Book. There were a number of spells that almost matched, and could possibly be altered to suit, but they could just as easily make his condition worse.

The eternity spell was difficult. It could backfire in so many ways.

"Enough about Remus. What about the lavaen? What else does it say about them?" Bree sounded nervous.

Jena read the collected mage wisdom on the lavaen. 'There's not much here. It says they'll sometimes work with humans when necessary." Jena glanced at Bree. "Let's just hope that turns out to be true."

"The one we saw was terrifying. It didn't seem like a creature we could negotiate with," said Bree, her expression pensive. Her horse had been killed by the last lavaen they'd met.

"This one is different. She used to be human. Perhaps she'll be more reasonable."

"I doubt it. Not if Remus thought he was tricking us by sending us up here."

"You're right," said Jena. "We have to be careful."

They trudged up the mountain, one slow step in front of the other. The heat that had been cloying and uncomfortable now became almost unbearable. Her scarred skin tightened painfully. Jena dealt with the discomfort by focusing inward, looking through the Book for something that might free Remus—if she decided to help him.

"There it is," said Bree, pointing ahead. "The rock shaped like a bird's head. That's the one he was talking about. We must be close." Bree crawled up and around the large rock, and then reappeared at the peak, waving at Jena. "It's just behind here."

"It's not very big," said Jena, peering around. The gap in the mountain wall would allow the women through, but the lavaen would never be able to use it. "Do you think she'll be happy about us coming in by an entrance she can't use?"

"This is the entrance Remus told us about." Bree shrugged. "We can only hope he was telling the truth about that, at least."

Jena turned to Bree, all her doubts pushing to the surface yet again. "Are you sure we should do this?"

"We can't back out now. We've just spent all this time climbing the mountain," said Bree, her voice gentle and persuasive. "Our reasons for being here haven't changed. We need to help Nate."

Jena took a fortifying breath and stepped closer to the

entrance, then hesitated again. She focused on the Book of Spells page about lavaen, just in case there was something she had missed. "They also hate not getting the respect they feel they deserve. So whatever you do, make sure you're polite."

"I won't say any of the terrible things I was planning to say," Bree said with the ghost of a smile. "The sooner we go in, the sooner we get out."

A cawing sound was all the notice that Jena had before the raven swooped down, demanding access to her skin. She lifted her shirt over her stomach, and the raven slammed into her side, making Jena wince.

"I never get tired of watching that happen," said Bree. "Can all mages do that?"

Jena shook her head. "One, I'm not a mage. I'm a woman, remember? And two, no. Thornal was special. More powerful than any other mage I've met. It's the only raven tattoo I've ever seen do it." The raven feathers ruffled on her stomach. "I don't know how he made it so that his tattoo would live on after his death, and I don't know how it is that his raven can fly free, or how I'm able to wear his tattoo." She wished Thornal had shared the secret of the raven with her before he'd died.

"Maybe because he was our grandfather?"

Jena flicked a surprised glance at Bree. "I hadn't thought of that. Maybe."

"It's very impressive. And I don't think just anyone could do it." Bree smiled warmly at Jena, her expressive eyes letting Jena know just what she thought.

"Maybe," said Jena, trying not to feel too pleased by Bree's compliment. She moved closer to the entrance, rubbing her side where the raven attached itself. "Come on, let's get this over with."

Together they walked into the gloom of the tunnel, hands running along the sides to keep their orientation. Bree grabbed one of Jena's hands and held it tightly as they walked into the murky darkness.

When the darkness didn't let up, Jena created her small silver flame in her other palm and held it up. The tunnel was narrow, the walls close. It was warm, the heat coming from the surrounding rocks. Unidentified creatures skittered back into the darkness ahead of them.

"How long is it?" whispered Bree. Her voice echoed into the darkness.

"It goes to the center of the mountain, directly to the lavaen's lair. It must be a fair distance."

They kept walking, stepping cautiously to avoid the rocks jutting out at irregular angles. Jena felt something slither over her foot and jerked to one side to avoid it, crashing into her sister.

Bree squeaked as they both fell against the wall. The light in Jena's hand went out, and they were plunged into darkness, clutching each other.

"What's the matter?" Bree whispered, her voice shaking. "What did you see...?"

"There was something—I felt it on my foot," said Jena, feeling stupid. She shook her head. "Sorry." She pulled herself away from Bree and drew forth the silver flame in her palm again. She held it high, letting the flickering light fall on the tunnel around them. It had a slight decline, and it was getting hotter and hotter as they got deeper into the mountain. The pungent odor of sulfur hung in the air, and Jena's nose twitched uncomfortably.

"Are we going to end up in a lava pool?" asked Bree.

Jena shrugged. "The lavaen swim in it."

"Of course they do."

They kept moving forward, Jena leading cautiously. As they moved closer, the tunnel became even hotter, and her doubts resurfaced. The memory of the lavaen as it swooped low over their heads was repeating in her mind. The only thing that had stopped the lavaen that time was Nate. Jena took a shaking breath, and her hand trembled, throwing strange shadows into the tunnel ahead of them. They should have waited for Nate and Argus. The four of them together could have taken on a creature like a lavaen. What had she been thinking?

"It's going to be fine," said Bree from behind her. "We'll charm the lavaen. Remus told us the creature doesn't like men. Nate and Argus would have been a hindrance."

"How did you—?" asked Jena, startled.

"I can...kind of...*feel* you thinking. It's just a vague feeling. I've also gotten to know you, and understand your tells. You're still regretting the impulse to come up here. But it's going to be fine."

Jena nodded, reassured. "Thanks. I needed that." She kept walking, this time with a steadier hand. The calming influence of Bree stayed with her. Jena smiled at the thought of having a sister to be there for her. It felt good.

The tunnel was narrowing around them, and the rotten smell of the hot lava was getting stronger. Under their feet, the stone was vibrating gently, and heat was rising up from the rocks. Up ahead, a glowing light became stronger and stronger, until it was brighter than the flame in her hand. Jena breathed a sigh of relief. The end of the tunnel.

They approached it cautiously, not sure what to expect. Jena peered over the edge into a massive cavern. The heat hit her like a wall. Lava bubbled in an enormous internal lake, flowing in from several tunnels, and swirling violently in red and orange patterns around large rocks and stalagmites. The lingering smell of sulfur was so strong, it was like another personality in the cavern.

In the center, an enormous lavaen lazed in the middle of a lava pool, eyes closed.

They'd found her.

CHAPTER 10
NATE

They were almost back at Remus's house, two enormous sacks filled with rocks hampering their every step, when a familiar rush of energy told Nate that a ghost was traveling alongside them.

He was so used to ignoring them that it was only when the ghost crossed his path that he realized it was the ghost mage. For the first time since he'd been visiting Nate, the ghost mage was agitated, floating back and forth and waving his hands, trying to catch Nate's attention.

Nate stopped, trying to figure out what was wrong. He hadn't seen the ghost mage since the fire hawks attacked and he'd taken over one of them. "What's the matter?"

The ghost mage grabbed at Nate's arm, trying to force him to keep moving. Except the ghost's hands just floated through Nate's body, giving him eerie chills. *"You must hurry. They're in danger."* The ghost mage's voice was louder than usual and it echoed uncomfortably across Nate's skin, making goosebumps appear down his arms.

An ominous feeling expanded in his chest. "Who's in danger?" He took a step toward the ghost, as if that would

64

help. Shale beneath his feet moved and he had to drop his bag of rocks, so he didn't topple over.

In front of him, Argus stopped. "Who are you talking to?" He turned back and dumped his bag of rocks on the ground as well.

"There's a ghost. He says someone's in danger." Nate tried to shake off the unease. They'd only just left Bree and Jena at the house. What kind of trouble could they possibly have gotten into? It must be someone else.

Except they'd left them there with Remus.

"Jena and Bree are walking into a trap," said the ghost mage urgently. *"Remus sent them somewhere. I can't tell where they've gone, but I know that if you don't hurry, they're both going to die."*

As if by magic, the words had Nate moving again. "Remus has done something to Jena and Bree," he said to Argus as he scrambled toward the bigger man. "We have to hurry." His heart was pounding uncomfortably in his chest and he struggled to banish the image of Remus pulling unseen strings, guiding them into a snare of his own making.

Argus's expression became thunderous. "If that shrinking monstrosity has harmed a hair on either of their heads, I'm going to kill him," he growled.

Nate just nodded as he lumbered past Argus, the rocks on his back feeling twice as heavy as they'd been a moment before.

The ghost scowled at Nate. *"Drop the damned sacks of rock and run,"* said the ghost, his agitation making his voice rise an octave. *"Only you can save them."*

The words were like a bucket of cold water being poured over Nate's head. He dumped his bag next to the path. "Leave your bag. We have to run."

Argus followed Nate without question, and soon they were thundering down the mountainside, their booted feet pounding over the landscape of boulders and sparse plant life. Nate couldn't think clearly—he just kept Remus's house in his sights and concentrated on not falling. What if something happened to Jena and Bree? He'd never forgive himself. They should never have left them alone with Remus.

His whole body felt twice as heavy as normal, and it felt like he was running through molasses. He couldn't seem to run fast enough.

We'll save them. It'll be fine. He kept repeating the words inside his head in time to the pounding of his feet on the rocky ground.

Nate rounded the corner of the crooked little house, going straight for the front entrance. He pulled open the door to find a cheery fire flickering in the grate and Remus waiting for them at a table filled with bread and butter and meat, like he hadn't a care in the world.

"Where are Jena and Bree?" Nate asked as he strode into the room. He didn't trust the innocent expression on the shrinking mage's face. Fear for Jena and Bree was buzzing through his chest—a swarm of bees ready to annihilate him.

"They went for a walk," said Remus, his expression quizzical.

"He's lying," said the ghost mage.

"A walk? Why would they go for a walk? They were both exhausted."

"They'll be back soon," Remus said in a calm voice. "Now, come, sit down. What would you like to eat after your busy morning?"

The ghost mage was pacing behind Remus. *"Make him tell you where they've gone. It's their only hope."*

"Where are they? Tell me now. Before I call some friends you won't like." A demon would torture Remus however he asked, with no second thoughts. Nate hadn't called a demon since he called *all* of them just outside the volcano —he'd been avoiding it, part of him scared of what it meant. But he'd do it every day of the week to save Jena and Bree.

Remus put his butter knife down and tipped his head to one side. "There's something different about you," he said thoughtfully. "You're...almost...glowing."

"Answer the fire-damned question." Nate ground out the words. A red haze came across his vision as he watched a smug look appear on Remus's face.

"Sit down and I'll tell you everything you need to know about Lothar while we wait for them," said Remus soothingly. He waved a hand at the grate. "Argus, tend the fire."

Argus didn't even pretend to move. "Where are they?" the big man growled.

Remus's eyes narrowed ever so slightly. He'd finally noticed Argus wasn't doing his bidding.

Nate loomed over the shrinking mage, using his height and letting off waves of power. "I have no time for your lies. Tell me where we can find Jena and Bree." The magic inside him was waking up, the smoldering flames getting ready to burst free. Nate clenched his fists, trying to control the fear and anger that were setting off his magic.

"Hold it in," said the mage ghost in his ear, making Nate jump. *"We need your powers to save the women."*

Remus blinked up at Nate. "Fascinating. I can feel the power growing inside you. Almost like it was hiding itself away." He glanced at Argus again, who was still standing ominously by the door.

"Stop avoiding my question," growled Nate.

"They just went for a walk. I don't know why you've decided otherwise." Despite his ingratiating tone, Remus was starting to look uncomfortable.

"I don't believe you. Try again," snapped Nate.

"You'll feel bad about this when they arrive back at the house." Remus tried to smile, but his thin lips parted awkwardly over his crooked, yellowing teeth, and it just made him look more grotesque. His eyes kept darting between Nate and Argus.

Nate almost snarled. "Tell me where the women are, and I might not kill you." He was on the edge of his temper. The fires were boiling over inside his chest, and he could feel the room heating up.

He was about to snap and kill Remus right here and now.

CHAPTER II
NATE

Remus stared intently at Nate, and then all of a sudden he leaned forward. "I can see now that you're the correct mage. You're even more powerful than I could have hoped for."

This time, Nate did snarl.

Everything turned red, and the fires inside him rose up, ready and blazing. "I don't care about you or your stupid spell. Tell me where you've sent Jena and Bree," he seethed. "Tell me, and I might not kill you."

Remus stilled, like a mouse caught in front of a cat. He'd finally realized that Nate was serious. "I told them not to go," he said. His tone was petulant. "Why don't we just sit here and—"

"Where. Are. They?" Nate's voice was as hard as steel. Panic was clawing its way up his throat. He grasped the front of Remus's mage robe and finally let the flames burn inside his eyes.

For the first time, fear emerged on Remus's face. His hands clenched in front of him on the table, and his left eye twitched. "Don't take it out on me, just because you can't control your women. I could have told you they'd disappoint you."

Nate growled, and lifted Remus up out of his chair. Legs dangling, Remus pulled frantically at Nate's hands. "Let me go," he screeched. "You'll regret this."

"You have five seconds. One." Nate pressed his face close to Remus, fires blazing in his eyes. His whole body was heating up, and his patience was completely gone. "Two."

"Don't be so hasty—" Remus was still wriggling in Nate's grasp.

"Three."

"Stop counting, I—"

"Four." Nate said the word through gritted teeth. His eyes were blazing and he only just had control over the fires inside him. He was almost glad that Remus wasn't going to tell them. He was going to enjoy watching a demon rip him apart.

But then Remus sagged. His hands dropped to his sides. "Okay, okay. Put me down. I'll tell you."

With a growl, Nate lowered Remus back to his seat but didn't let go of the front of his robe.

"They went up the mountain to the lavaen's lair," Remus said. "They wanted to collect a lavaen stone to help you with your upcoming battle." His voice rose to a squeak as Nate tightened his grip.

Argus's hand whipped to his sword as if he wanted to pull it out and run Remus through. "That beast is insane. You know she is. And you sent them to her *lair*?"

Remus gave Argus an irritated glare. "Since when do you care, Argus? This isn't the first time I've sent someone to the lavaen's lair."

Argus clenched his hands at his sides. "You no longer

own me. I get to have my own opinions now." He strode over to the other side of Remus and loomed threateningly over his ex-master.

Remus peered up into the mercenary's eyes. He pursed his lips like he'd just tasted something sour.

"They insisted on going. I tried to stop them," he said. "They're both stubborn women."

Nate couldn't help himself. He called a fire demon, and the glowing ball immediately appeared in the room.

"Master, how may I serve you?" The demon bowed to Nate, which confused him for a moment before he remembered how he'd called all the demons.

He suppressed his shudder and scowled at the demon. "I need you to watch this mage for me."

"Just watch?" said the demon, clearly disappointed.

"Maybe more, depending on what he decides to tell us."

The demon glowed a deeper red, pleased.

Remus held up his hands, palms out. "Now, now, don't be hasty."

"Tell us exactly how to find the lair and how long ago they left. And how you convinced them to leave this damned crooked hut, and I might consider it. But so help me, if you lie, you'll live to regret it," hissed Nate, the red demon glow adding unpleasant shadows to all their faces.

Remus cleared his throat, glancing from the demon to Nate. "I see now why you're in the prophecies. I must admit, it seemed a little far-fetched when I first met you." His eyes were glowing like he was a kid at a Flame Festival.

"Demon," growled Nate, unable to hold himself together enough to say more. He stepped back to allow the demon closer to Remus.

The demon moved next to Remus, hovering near his chest. "Where would you like me to burn him, master?"

"Anywhere, I don't—"

"I simply told them about the lavaen stones," interrupted Remus hastily. "They could help you destroy Lothar. I might also have mentioned that the best way to earn the favor of the lavaen was to go in through the entrance on the Bird Head side."

"You sent them into the lavaen's lair via the same entrance you always use to provoke her?" Argus lurched toward the little mage, grabbing Remus's robes at his neck, yanking him into the air and knocking over his chair with a clatter. He gave the mage a shake. "I will kill you with my bare hands."

The ghost mage moved in front of Nate again. *"You have to hurry. I've found them, but they've already entered the caves. You're going to have to run to catch up with them."*

"Stop it Argus." Nate pulled at his arm. "We don't have time. We have to find them. Do you know this entrance he's talking of?"

Argus nodded, giving Remus a shake before dropping him to the floor. The ungainly mage landed heavily and looked sulkily back up at them. "Before you go, just tell me the spell I need to release me. I know it's in the Book."

"I don't have the Book of Spells," said Nate, satisfaction flowing through his body as Remus frowned in confusion. "*Jena* has it. Your interpretation of the prophecy was wrong. You've just destroyed any hope you had that she'd help you." Nate cut himself off before he could say anything more, already regretting his angry words. Women weren't supposed to carry the Book of Spells. It was the kind of information that could get Jena killed.

"What? That can't be right." Shock ricocheted across Remus's expression.

"You better hope they're still in one piece, or you won't

have to wait until you shrink to death. We'll murder you ourselves."

"*She* has the Book of Spells?" He looked to the bags that Jena and Bree had neatly stacked to one side. "But I checked —" Remus's face went white. "Why didn't you tell me?"

"Because we didn't think you could be trusted," snarled Nate. "Which you've just proven by sending Jena and Bree off to be killed."

As Nate watched, Remus's face took on a sly expression. "A *woman* has the Book. Now that is an interesting situation. Any help you need, I'd be glad to give it."

Nate swore under his breath. The devious little mage was going to use this against them. The knowledge sat like a stone in Nate's belly, making him feel sick. He already regretted the petty urge that had made him blurt out Jena's secret. He looked over at the demon, tempted to let the creature do whatever it wanted to Remus. The demon beside him moved forward eagerly, as if it could read his thoughts.

"If you so much as blink out of line, we will kill you," said Nate grimly, his eyes flashing with fire as he turned back to Remus. "For your sake, you better hope we find them in time."

"It's not my fault they took off up the mountain," said Remus, his voice turning petulant.

Nate stared down at Remus a moment longer. "You did this to yourself," he said. "Just like you did it to yourself all those years ago. You haven't learned a single thing in all your years."

"I didn't need to learn a lesson," snapped Remus, his face twisting with long-ago anger. "I just want my life back."

"If you'd been a better person, you'd have had it back by

now." Nate paused, then looked at the demon that was hovering hopefully next to Remus. "He's coming with us up the mountain, and I need you to guard him. It's your job to make sure he doesn't try to escape."

Remus looked horrified. "Climbing the mountain? I can't do that. I'll just wait here for you."

His expression would have amused Nate if he hadn't been so worried about Jena and Bree. "You're coming with us, so we can throw you to the lavaen, should we need bait."

Remus sputtered and skittered away from Nate.

"Let's go," said Argus, grabbing Remus's arm and pulling him out the door.

CHAPTER 12
JENA

Fires burst forth from the cave entrances below where Jena and Bree stood, sending swirls of smoke and steam into the air. Across and down from where they peered out of the tunnel, other similar cave entrances darkened the rocky walls. Lava bubbled and curled below, pushing waves of hot air upward. The heat was so intense, it was hard to breathe.

The entire cavern glowed red, lighting up their faces eerily. Bree looked just as uneasy as Jena felt about being here.

But instead of moving away from the heat, Jena and Bree edged forward, as if compelled. The glow called to them; it felt warm and cozy and familiar. Jena wanted to get closer, to feel the warmth against her skin. She took another step forward, out onto the small ledge in front of the tunnel, and rocks skittered over the edge, tumbling into the lava pool below.

Jena's scars prickled uncomfortably. Something was wrong. The raven pecked her on the stomach, and she jerked at the sudden pain. She shook her head to clear it. The compulsion to leap off the edge into the lava receded.

Taking a quick step backward, Jena moved back into the tunnel, pulling Bree with her. Her sister fought her for a moment until she shook her head and looked around like she didn't know where she was.

"What just happened?" Bree asked in a small, scared voice.

They'd almost walked over the edge into the lava without even thinking about it.

"Some kind of mesmerizing spell to capture her prey," whispered Jena. "We have to be more careful." It wasn't normal behavior for a lavaen. They didn't set traps and think about how they would catch their prey. What kind of lavaen was she?

Jena peered over the edge again, and this time she saw the lavaen, her black scales reflecting the light from the fires. Jena's breath stuck in her throat, and she had to suppress the urge to cough over her dry mouth. The lavaen was easily three or four times larger than the one they'd faced before. Lava spilled over the rock where the immense creature perched, lapping at her enormous black, clawed feet. The gushing orange-red glow of the lava pool echoed the molten magma that simmered between the lavaen's own scales. Its wings were tucked against her sides, and her eyes were partially closed.

Suddenly, those molten eyes opened fully, and the lavaen lifted its head to stare directly up at Jena. The creature's cold eyes reminded her of Remus's, and she shivered, despite the terrifying heat of the cavern.

Who dares to interrupt my sleep? The lavaen's voice reverberated around in their heads, echoing uncomfortably several times. Jena held her hand to her forehead. Her instincts were screaming at her to run. The lavaen watched them coyly, and Jena was reminded of a snake waiting to strike.

Bree took a few steps forward, her hands reaching out to calm the creature. "A friend of yours told us you might help us. The safety of the Kingdom is at stake." She stood on the ledge, staring down at the lavaen like she was asking to borrow a cup of sugar.

The lavaen's eyes glittered. *Who might this friend of mine be?*

"Remus." The name was out of Bree's mouth before Jena could stop her. She didn't think Remus was a friend of anyone's, let alone this lavaen's. In fact, she was pretty sure he was counting on that fact to ensure they didn't survive this encounter.

Ah, Remus. The lavaen spat out his name, her eyes swirling with anger. *He is a friend of yours?*

"No. He's nothing but a dirty little sneak," Jena quickly interjected, trying to prevent whatever was about to happen. She took a step forward, meaning to stand next to Bree.

But she was too late.

So fast it almost seemed like she might have imagined it, the lavaen's body rose from its lava-encrusted perch, its enormous black wings pushing outwards for balance, making a heated wind blow over them and throwing up stones and dust. Jena scrunched her eyes shut for a moment, trying to protect herself from the debris. When she opened her eyes again, the lavaen's arm was already snaking out...

"No!" Jena leaped forward, arms outstretched.

But it was too late.

The lavaen grabbed Bree in her scaled hands and

returned down into its crouching position. She held Bree's struggling body up to the light of a nearby fire like she was a toy.

A pretty young female. Did you think some of my jewels would make you even prettier? Or is it my gold that you're after? Is that why that disgusting rodent Remus sent you here?

The words were heavy inside Jena's head, this time laced with a pungent bitterness that she hadn't noticed the first time.

Bree screamed, her legs thrashing uselessly as they dangled below the lavaen's scaled hand.

"Leave her alone!" yelled Jena. Fear made her vision blur for a second, but she didn't have time to fall apart. She had to save Bree.

Her heart pounding, Jena leaped through the air and landed on the back of the giant creature. Steadying herself on the lavaen's back, she dug her fingers into the gaps between the scales. The heat from the lava behind the scales seared her fingers, and she screamed with the pain on her scarred side. But she didn't hesitate. She climbed up the back of the lavaen, ignoring everything but the need to rescue her sister.

The lavaen roared louder this time. *You think I would give you one of my precious gems?* She reared up on her hind legs, trying to shake Jena free.

Bree screamed as the creature tightened its hold on her.

"Stop that! Stop hurting her," Jena shouted, her voice almost a scream.

The raven twitched on her skin, and she felt an insistent peck before it pulled itself away from her body, escaping out from under her shirt in a flurry of feathers. The raven gave a loud and insistent caw, and then she felt the brush of its wings as it flew past her face. Her sense of relief was out of proportion to what the raven could actually do. But it was good to have help.

The raven flew up past Bree, cawing madly at the lavaen and flying close to the face of the massive creature. The lavaen swatted at the raven with her other paw. At first, the raven evaded the lavaen, ducking and diving around the lavaen's face like a mosquito. But then, with a loud thwack, the lavaen hit the raven hard and sent it smashing into the rough walls of the underground cave.

The bird fell to a ledge halfway up the wall, its body still.

Jena's eyes widened, and a sob escaped her chest. She watched the raven for a moment longer, waiting to see if it would shake its head and stand up. Nothing.

Even the raven couldn't help them against this foe.

Jena frantically thumbed through the pages in her head for a spell, something that would stop, or at least distract, the lavaen.

Fire was no good. She lived in lava. Nothing else seemed to fit either. Jena shook her head, trying to clear it of her clawing fear for Bree.

If Nate were here, he might have been able to summon a water demon. That particular type of demon might have had a trick up its sleeve for a lavaen. Or maybe even a fire demon could have talked to her, like it did with the last one. Argus could have distracted the lavaen while she found something in the book that might help.

With four of them, they might have been able to trick the beast. Or at least survive.

The lavaen curved her enormous neck around, and one of its red, glowing eyes looked directly at Jena over her shoulder. *You made a serious error of judgment coming here, little creature. I will kill your friend and then I will kill you.*

She snarled, showing off sharp white teeth that were each bigger than Jena's entire torso. Jena could only stare at the creature, her mind whirring, trying to figure out how to fight back.

"You've got it wrong. We mean you no harm. We don't want your gold or your gems. We just need your lavaen stone," Bree desperately shouted up at the creature.

The lavaen roared, lifting off from the ground again, her wings outstretched and her hand clamping even tighter around Bree's body. *That's worse! You mean to steal my most precious possession? A stone that was birthed from my body, that is made of the same things that I am made of. It is everything to me. You will never have that from me.*

The lavaen shook the hand holding her prisoner, and Bree was knocked violently back and forth like a child's toy. She went limp in the lavaen's fist.

Jena only just managed to hold in her scream. She couldn't tell if Bree had fainted or been knocked out. She wouldn't allow it to be anything worse. Jena swallowed hard and forced herself to focus. "We're sorry. We didn't mean to offend you," she said, trying to distract the lavaen. "We were told it would help us in our quest to battle Lothar, the king-in-waiting."

I don't care about the politics of humans. You're all pathetic little insects compared to me.

"You'll care about it when Ignisia is overrun with monsters from the darkness," snapped Jena.

"*I* am a monster from the darkness. Would you get rid of me?" The lavaen snarled and tightened her grip on Bree, who was still limply lying over her hand.

Jena didn't answer. She was too busy reaching down to the Hashishin knife at her ankle. Her heart was pounding erratically, and she felt like she couldn't breathe. But she was going to do everything she could to save Bree. She glanced to one side to see if the raven was awake, but it was still lying inert on the rocks.

She needed to distract the lavaen, maybe get her to drop her sister. Climbing higher on the lavaen's back, Jena looked around for a soft spot to stab the enormous lava creature. Scales covered most of her, and Jena had a feeling the knife would just bounce off the thick pieces of bone and skin. But there was a softer piece just next to the lavaen's neck. She reached up and slammed the knife into the lavaen's neck skin.

But it just bounced off again. The lavaen's hide was too thick, even for the Hashishin knife.

The lavaen snarled. *Stop that,* she said. *It scratches.*

"Then stop hurting my sister!" yelled Jena.

I'll do what I like. Now get off my back. The lavaen shook herself, and flicked Jena off.

She landed on a section of rock nearby, grunting with the effort of softening her landing. The rocks were hot, and she screamed, pushing herself up to standing. She shoved the knife back in its holder and turned to face the lavaen. Before she could even think about her next move, the lavaen picked her up in her other paw, holding her aloft next to Bree.

CHAPTER 13
NATE

"How much further?" asked Nate. He was hauling himself up the barren mountainside behind Argus, the afternoon heat surrounding them both like another layer of skin. Behind them, Remus struggled to put one foot in front of the other, the demon buzzing behind him, barely visible in the afternoon sun, periodically searing Remus from behind to remind him to hurry.

Nate's heart was pounding like a drum at the crescendo of a war song, and he was gasping for breath at the bruising pace Argus was setting. None of it mattered. They had to get to Jena and Bree before something bad happened.

"We've almost caught up." Argus pointed to a spot near the trail. "They stopped here, and not long ago." He paused for a moment, then strode on ahead.

Nate stopped by the place Argus had indicated, unable to see the evidence that seemed so clear to Argus, then continued on after the mercenary. "How are we going to defeat an insane lavaen in her own lair?"

"I don't know," said Argus, almost under his breath. His

hands were so tightly clenched they were almost white. His eyes were wild.

Nate glanced behind him at the demon as it harried Remus up the mountainside. "The fire demon will help." A fire demon had drawn the lavaen away last time.

Argus shook his head, clearly frustrated. "A demon can't do anything against a lavaen. It's like setting a breeze against a storm."

"It worked before."

"But why? It didn't make sense at the time, and it still doesn't. A fire demon shouldn't have been able to convince a lavaen to turn back." Argus threw a scorching look over his shoulder as he stormed ahead. "We can't rely on a fire demon a second time."

Nate looked back at the fire demon streaming along behind him. "Is that true? You won't be able to help us against this lavaen?" He felt the demon's fire reflected inside him, in the ancient burning flames that hid at his core.

The demon buzzed forward before answering. "The big one is correct. I do not have the power to defeat this particular lavaen. She is not the same as the last one. It is the power of the Firecaller that commands the beast."

"Firecaller?" Nate repeated stupidly. Out of habit, he looked around for the ghost mage, wanting him to confirm whether it was true. The old man wasn't there.

"Of course, master. As I keep saying, you command the fire creatures. *All* of us." The demon spoke the words in a low voice, so Remus couldn't hear. Nate was grateful the demon had the sense to keep his words from the shrinking mage.

A screech echoed across the mountains, carried on the faint wind that brushed past them. It rattled a flock of crows, and they rose up out of a barren tree, squawking at the disturbance.

"We need to hurry." Argus turned and ran up the path in long determined strides.

Nate took off after Argus, trying to keep up. Thoughts of Jena and Bree facing the lavaen on their own had him sprinting after Argus, despite the heat that blanketed the landscape.

Beside him, the demon kept pace easily. "Master, you have the power to defeat it, and you will know how when you meet the lavaen." The creature buzzed, flaring brightly for a moment, then returned to a distant haze.

Nate glared at the creature. "I don't need more riddles. I need actual help."

The demon didn't respond, and returned to Remus, like it felt him about to try something.

Soon Argus turned off the main path and stopped outside a small cave. "This is it," he said, turning to Nate. "It'll be dark."

"I'll create a fire to see by," said Nate. His powers tended to be all or nothing, but he'd been practicing. He held up his hand, and moments later, his entire arm, up to his elbow, was engulfed in flames.

Argus jerked back, a look of horror on his face. "Does it hurt?"

"Feels like a warm blanket around my arm." Nate glanced back down the mountain. The demon and Remus had fallen behind. "We don't have time to wait for them."

Argus gave a sharp nod. "They can follow behind us."

Nate lifted his arm and walked into the tunnel. The eerie glow lit the long narrow passageway, creating deep shadows and flickering flame-colored rocks. At first, they stepped cautiously over the rocky surface, trying to get a sense of the tunnel. Peering into the distance, Nate couldn't see anything but rocks and more darkness. "How far is it from here?"

"I'm not sure. I've never gone the entire way." Another reverberating roar pierced the silence, shaking the loose rocks over their heads. "We need to hurry."

They ran as fast as they could down the darkened tunnel, Nate awkwardly holding up his arm for light. The temperature rose, and Nate wiped at the sweat forming on his forehead, trying to keep it out of his eyes. He stumbled when he heard a familiar voice echoing in the cavern ahead of them.

Jena.

He ran faster, his heart pounding. When a light appeared in the distance, he thought he was seeing double because of the heat. But the end of the tunnel grew larger and larger, like some deadly creature speeding at them, determined to cause harm.

They ran toward it, faces grim.

Nate slowed as they approached the end, the bright light beyond hurting his eyes and making it impossible to see what was happening. The smell of sulfur permeated everything, and the heat made it feel like they were voluntarily running into a campfire. Nate's flames rose in reaction; it was like he was burning from the inside out.

He felt compelled to move toward the end of the tunnel, his legs moving of their own accord. The magic crackling in the air felt familiar; fiery and thrilling. He was drawn to it, fascinated by it. For a moment, he forgot what they were doing here, and allowed himself to soak in the glorious feeling of the powerful flames he sensed inside the cavern.

Jena yelled again, the sound indistinct. But her familiar voice was enough to knock Nate out of his stupor. He shook his head to clear it and pulled at his shirt where it was sticking uncomfortably to his skin. He was standing at the edge of a cliff, with nothing but lava below him.

Heart pounding, he stepped back. He'd been about to step over the edge because of the compulsion. Beside him, Argus moved to the edge as if he was in a stupor. Nate grabbed the mercenary, pulling him back and shaking him. Argus blinked as he recovered from the spell. "What in the Flames?" he said.

"Some kind of spell," said Nate. He peered over the ledge. They were on an outcropping high above the lair. Lava bubbled in pools at the base of the cavern, and fires burst out of multiple vents. Flickering firelight covered everything. There was a path of sorts leading down to the base of the cavern, but it was more a narrow gathering of rocks that barely earned the name.

In the middle stood the biggest lavaen Nate had ever seen. Her enormous ebony scales—the size of dinner plates —reflected the firelight, and the fiery cracks in her skin were packed with boiling lava. She so perfectly matched the colors of the lava and the volcanic rocks in her lair, she almost melted into the background. Large ebony claws scratched at the rocks beneath her, and her cold black eyes stared down at her hands. She was beautiful, sleek and powerful.

The lavaen screeched in the enclosed space, and Nate covered his ears to keep them from bursting. Fire and blood pounded through his body, and for a moment, he saw perfectly leaping flames, dancing in formation. The magical fires in his core leaped up in response to the lavaen, whispering love poems to such a perfect fire creature.

He clenched his fists into tight balls and forced himself

to concentrate on staying in the here and now. If he lost himself in the fire, he'd never be able to save Jena and Bree.

"She can't be a real lavaen," Nate whispered to Argus. The lavaen was a massive flame he could see as clearly with his eyes shut as he could with his eyes open. "She's enormous."

Argus nodded, his face glowing red in the lava light. "She is. And meaner than other lavaen."

Nate wiped his sweaty hands on his pants. She turned slightly and Nate inhaled sharply.

"Look," he said, pointing. Argus nodded grimly. The lavaen was holding Jena and Bree, one in each hand. Jena was struggling to get free, but Bree was limp, her eyes closed.

"What do we do?" Nate asked. He couldn't make a decision right now. The power of the fire and the lava and the lavaen combined was so immense, all he wanted to do was bathe in it. The dark fires in his belly were thrumming with heat, and he wanted to ignore everything else, his friends, the rest of the kingdom, and just immerse himself in the violent crimson flames.

Which meant they needed a plan of Argus's making rather than Nate's.

"I'll create a distraction, while you use your Firecaller tricks," said Argus.

"I don't have any Firecaller *tricks*," said Nate, his mind fizzing with flames.

Ignoring his words, Argus reached into an inside pocket of his leather vest, and pulled out the small fire ruby, tossing it to Nate. "Use this if you need it."

He stepped onto the narrow path that led down to the lavaen's lair.

"Wait, Argus. I don't—"

But it was too late. Argus was running down the dubious path on the outer wall of the cave, toward the ground level.

Nate looked down at the fire ruby in his hand. He immediately felt the pull of the ruby's magic trying to draw him down into its power. He'd been enthralled by the rubies that Argus had given him when they'd first met, only able to escape when Argus had slapped him.

It was a struggle not to fall into their power a second time.

The tiny gem had worked for them against other dark creatures, including the first lavaen he'd ever seen. They'd survived that time, although it had felt more like an accident.

The second lavaen they'd come up against, they'd also survived—mainly because his fire demon had persuaded it to leave. And it had taken Bree's horse in punishment.

He'd also had help that time. *The ghost mage.*

Where the hell was the old man now? He'd seemed so desperate when he'd told them what was happening. Why did he only appear when it suited him?

Nate swallowed hard and tried to concentrate on the fiery beast in front of him. It was up to him to distract her while Argus did...whatever he was going to do. By the Ashes, he was a *Firecaller*. That must mean something.

It would be fine.

They'd figure it out.

Probably.

Maybe.

His hand clenched tightly around the fire ruby. Nate watched as Argus jumped across the rocks, avoiding the lava pools and bursts of fire. He landed facing the lavaen, his expression set. He glanced up at Nate and nodded once, then turned to the creature. Without hesitation, he started waving his arms in front of her. "Hey!" he yelled. "Let them go, you great noxious beast!"

Nate stood frozen for a heartbeat, his mind locked in place. What in the Flames was Argus expecting him to do? He stumbled to the very edge of the cliff, his heart dropping with the stones that tipped over the side and tumbled to the lava pools below, sizzling as they landed. His insides were churning. The flames in the cavern were calling to him, telling him he was home. This place was where he belonged. He didn't belong with the humans. They were puny sacks of meat, so easily killed.

He was more powerful than any of them.

The heat of the fires burned his skin and sweat dripped down his face, blurring his vision. He wiped one arm across his eyes, trying to clear the moisture. He felt feverish. The voices of the fires echoed in his head, repeating themselves. He was cocooned inside a great fiery sea of power, driven by the lavaen in her own home, with her objects of power around her, and the fire ruby in his hand. He was floating in waves of fire, like water gently lapping at his skin, warm and glowing.

Except he knew he was forgetting something important.

Tendrils of power curled out from his body and sought the fire creature in front of him. His magic reveled in the flames that surrounded her, the power that emanated from her very soul. A rumbling noise sounded deep in the lavaen's chest, and her heartbeat thundered like a drum.

What was he supposed to be doing? Why was he here?

He watched, hypnotized, as the fire creature leaned toward Argus. *I do so enjoy fresh meat.*

Argus pulled his sword out of his scabbard and stood

ready, holding his weapon steady. He looked tiny next to the lavaen, his small face red with reflected color from the hot pools of lava.

Then, as if to show her power, the lavaen turned slightly and ignored Argus, holding up Jena. She sniffed Jena's hair delicately, the sensitive nose twitching. "You smell strange. Like smoke and magic. You will taste delicious as well."

Nate held his breath. *Jena.*

He felt dizzy, his vision blurring as his connection to the lavaen's fire wavered. Then it settled back, and he was cocooned in the depths of the fire once again.

Energy swelled around the cavern. A fireball slammed the side of the lavaen. Nate felt the fire surge.

The lavaen laughed. "I'm immune to fire, you silly girl. You'll have to try harder than that." She smiled, and her large teeth glinted in the light of the flames.

Jena renewed her struggles, batting her fists against the tough scaled paw of the lavaen, crying out in rage when her efforts achieved nothing. She let off another couple of smaller spells, but each of them bounced off the lavaen's hard scales.

Nate watched her, transfixed. A pained breath of air pushed out his mouth.

There was something he was forgetting...

CHAPTER 14
NATE

T he lavaen roared, a pain-filled bellow that echoed around the room. She screamed again, its eyes glowing red. Her tail lashed, whipping the air, and her vast body shifted from side to side.

Argus had wedged his sword between the scales on the lower back of the lavaen and was chopping at them as best he could.

The pain echoed inside Nate's body and pushed him away from the power center. Behind him he heard Remus whining and the buzzing of the fire demon as they emerged out of the tunnel and onto the ledge next to him. The familiar feel of the demon's fire was enough to wedge him a little further from the cocoon of the lavaen's fire magic.

He turned, looked at Remus's shrunken body and sweat-covered face and fully remembered why he was here. He had to save them.

Jena. Argus. Bree.

"You're smarter than you look," said Remus. "This is the safest place to be in a fight against the lavaen. She's a complete bitch."

Nate didn't have time to get angry. He'd punch Remus later for sending Jena and Bree to the lavaen when he clearly knew they'd fail. Right now, he was fighting with the memories of the red rage that had engulfed him when he'd fought the mercenaries. It was making him hesitate about what to do to save Argus from being her next meal.

He couldn't control the flames. His power was too new, too uncertain. He could just as easily kill them all if he let that ancient power free right now. He had to think of another way. His hand tightened on the fire ruby. Maybe he could use the ruby to control the lavaen? It seemed ludicrous. He certainly didn't feel strong enough to control her by himself, no matter what the demon and the ghost mage said.

Nate swallowed hard, wishing he had the ghost mage to help him. Wishing he had any ideas other than letting loose a power he couldn't control...

"How about you and I just leave them to it? We could disappear right now. I could help you with your little Lothar problem. You could help me. We'd both get to live." He peered down at the lavaen. "Unlike that lot. It's a great pity, but they're already dead."

Nate stared wide-eyed at Remus for a long moment. Then he looked to the demon that was burning next to him. "Whatever you do, don't let him escape," he said. "Burn him if necessary."

"Yes, master," said the demon.

"No! You idiot! Don't—" Remus squealed as the demon burned his arm.

The lavaen screamed again, knocking Nate out of his frozen uncertainty. If he did nothing, they would all die anyway. Nate held onto the ruby and focused his attention inward.

The ruby's full power surged up and into his body like it had just been waiting for the opportunity. It blazed inside him, filling the crevices of his soul. It tried to overpower him, to draw him into its very center and keep him there. He fought to maintain control, reminding himself that he wasn't fighting for himself. He was fighting for Jena, Bree and Argus.

Nate gathered the magic of the fire ruby together and searched for the lavaen with his mind.

She wasn't difficult to find. The lavaen was like a bright, shining ball of fire, blazing as brilliantly as the sun. Her magic hit him in the chest, and for a moment he flapped and gasped like a fish in the bottom of a boat. She was very different from the other lavaen he'd faced. Bigger, more powerful, stronger. He was like a speck, a tiny dot against the lavaen's fiery power. How was he supposed to do anything against that?

A buzzing light appeared next to him as he struggled against the feeling of nothingness. "Master, focus. She is tricking you with the brightness of her power. Using it to mesmerize you. She does not have the substance to destroy you." The demon flickered next to Nate's eyes, making him blink and unlocking him yet again from the lavaen's thrall.

Nate shook his head, trying to reset his mind. He managed to get his breathing back under control, and his focus returned. The ancient fires inside him burned brighter and he began to see how he might control this beast after all. "Thank you, demon," he whispered.

"You must save your friends. They hold the key to your path," said the demon.

Nate nodded. He'd save them, but not because they were part of his 'path'. They were his *friends*. "Let the women go, lavaen," he said, standing tall at the edge of the cliff. His mouth dried out as the lavaen turned to glare at him, but he stood his ground. Driving down to his core of molten fire, careful not to use too much of the dark flames that scared him, he wove his power and the fire ruby magic around the lavaen's, encasing it in tendrils of brilliant fire under his influence.

Who are you to command me? The lavaen's voice echoed inside his head as she leaned her long neck toward Nate and sniffed. Dark eyes that seemed to see into his very soul glared at him. She didn't seem to sense his power surrounding hers. Not yet anyway.

"I am the Firecaller. You must do as I command." His hands shook, but he clenched them tightly, so it wasn't visible. The fire ruby burned in his hand, and he wondered if it would leave a mark.

He didn't know if the bindings he'd placed around the lavaen's power were strong enough. He didn't know if she was about to burn them all alive. He just had to keep it together long enough to get them out of here.

The lavaen roared again, at first like she was amused, but ending with a high-pitched scream. She'd found his bindings. Nate felt her bashing at the fiery magical ropes he'd put around her power. They held... so far.

What do you command, little man? The words were barely audible, so heavily were they coated in her angry snarl.

"Let the women go. Let us all go free."

I answer to no one.

Even to Nate's ears, that statement sounded hollow. His power surrounded them both, getting stronger as each second passed. "You answer to *me*."

His flames were becoming so powerful, Nate was beginning to worry that he might not be able to control them. His whole body was rock hard with the tension of making sure his ancient magic did what he commanded and didn't escape to destroy and demolish everything in its path. Including his friends.

You want me to starve? The lavaen's voice became soft, cajoling. *The Firecaller was never so harsh before.* Soft tendrils of magic snaked around him. The creature was attempting some kind of mesmerizing magic on Nate.

For a moment, the lavaen's scales seemed brighter, her eyes more innocent.

Jena's harsh scream broke the spell. The lavaen was squeezing her tighter as she worked her magic. Jena's Hashishin knife was in her hand, but she couldn't get the right angle to stab the lavaen.

Nate sent a warning push of power through the bonds. "Don't toy with me, lavaen."

"Nate, get out of here," Jena yelled at him from where she was dangling awkwardly from the lavaen's claws. "She's too powerful. You have more important tasks to perform. Your journey can't end here."

Bree lifted her head momentarily from where it had been lying limply against the lavaen's hand. She was starting to come around again.

Nate tightened his grip on the creature's energy source. "Let the women go, and we'll leave you in peace."

The lavaen looked down at Jena and Bree as they swung in the air, trapped by her paws. She appeared to consider her options, then opened her big, scaled palms and let go.

"No!" yelled Nate, moments too late, his heart in his mouth.

Jena and Bree screamed as they dropped, each landing with a sickening thump on the rocky ground below. Neither of them moved. The lavaen looked up at Nate, her eyes swirling with satisfaction. *Yes, master,* she said mockingly.

Argus roared, sprinting toward Bree, his heavy boots thumping on the hard surface.

"You are not to touch either of them again," said Nate, feeling sick. He hadn't protected them enough. He'd let the lavaen follow his orders and still harm Jena and Bree. "You will not harm a single hair on their heads. You will stay exactly where you are, lavaen, creature of fire." Nate's voice reverberated around the cavern, filled with raw power. His anger and fear blended together until he couldn't tell one from the other.

"She'll kill you all, if you don't watch out," said Remus with a cackle. "She's trickier than a thirsty rattlesnake. You need to stay up here if you're going to survive this encounter."

Nate glanced at the demon. "Watch him. Make sure he doesn't go anywhere. We might need him."

"What could you possibly need me for?" asked Remus.

"To use as a trade." Nate had the satisfaction of seeing the shock on Remus's face as he realized what Nate meant.

He ignored Remus's spluttering reply and raced down the uncertain path, straight to where Jena lay next to the lavaen's massive hind leg, the burning-hot fire ruby clutched in his hand. The ancient fiery magic inside him lapped at his soul, pushing to escape, dancing with the power of the fire ruby and the lavaen's fiery presence. It wanted to be free, to dance in the heat of the lava that surrounded them. Everything was tumbling out of control. He was controlling the magical bindings around the lavaen by the skin of his teeth.

He shoved the fire ruby into the pouch at his waist, and crouched down beside Jena, reaching out to brush the hair away from her face. She opened her eyes, and he let out the breath he'd been holding. She was alive. The fires inside him settled for a moment, and the bindings around the lavaen tightened again. The creature screamed behind him, but he ignored her.

He picked up the knife Jena had dropped and gave it to her. "Can you stand?" he asked, touching her arm carefully. He knew she hated to be touched, but he needed to help her up.

She nodded and allowed him to pull her to her feet, although she seemed unsteady. He peered at her face, trying to decide if she was okay to walk on her own. The magic swirling inside him made it difficult to focus and he was having a hard time keeping his attention on Jena. The fire ruby was burning him through the leather of his pouch.

"I'm fine," she said, pushing away his hands. When she swayed, he grasped her again, holding her until she was steady. All the while, the flames inside him crackled in time with the beating of his heart.

"Thanks," she said, moving away again like he was too hot to touch. Even now, she was protective of her scars. Nate let out a breath.

He stepped closer when she hesitated and gently pushed her toward the path up to the ledge, whispering against her ear, "Get out of here. I don't know how long the creature will be under my control."

Jena hesitated. "Where's Bree?"

"Argus has her. Go. I need you out of the way so I can use my magic." The fire ruby was pulsing now, pumping in time to the blood in his veins. The fiery magic in the cavern was overwhelming. He felt like he was on the verge of releasing all his ancient magic. They'd end up dead if he couldn't hold it in for just a little while longer.

Jena nodded unsteadily, and then ran up the path, slipping and sliding her way to the top. The lavaen watched with the glittering eyes of a predator. Nate sent a burst of his magic at the lavaen, wanting her to focus on him, not Jena. She looked down, her blazing eyes gleaming with fiery energy. He became ensnared in the lavaen's eyes, the deep red depths calling to him and for a long moment, he just stared up at her.

His magic was still entwined with the enormous creature, their powers fighting for control. It felt like he was standing on a precipice, high in the air. Like perhaps it could go either way; she could just as easily turn the tables and have him under her control. Part of him wouldn't mind, he knew she wouldn't hurt him. She *couldn't* hurt him.

But she could still hurt his friends, and he was sure she would, given the chance. She was angry and bitter, like she was acting from human emotions rather than the primordial need of a lavaen. She was razor sharp, her beady intelligence helping her think her way through this situation. He had no idea who she had been as a human, but she was truly magnificent as a lavaen.

It made her very, very dangerous and Nate worried he wouldn't be able to maintain the upper hand for much longer.

The thought sent a shiver of fear through his body. A creature as powerful as a lavaen, inside her own environment, and thinking clearly without the usual lust for the fiery magic of the lava to consume her...

It seemed like a deadly combination. They needed to get out of here. *Now.*

All he had to do was drag his eyes away from her swirling hypnotic irises.

CHAPTER 15
NATE

With a strength of will he hadn't been sure he possessed, Nate dragged his gaze away from the lavaen's—for now, at least. His magic swirled around him, eager to expand beyond the tight bindings he had around the lavaen. He ran to where Argus was crouching next to Bree, holding her limp hand.

Nate bent down, afraid of what he would find, and put a hand over her heart, waiting for a beat. He let out a breath when he felt the gentle thump.

"She's bleeding from a head wound," said Argus, half watching the lavaen behind Nate.

"You'll have to carry her." Nate glanced up. The tunnel entrance was high overhead. The ruby in his pouch was pulsing painfully, his fiery magic thrumming along his body in discordant bursts. He didn't know how much longer he'd be able to hold the lavaen to his will.

"I was afraid to move her. Her injuries—" Argus glanced at the congealing blood on the side of Bree's head.

"We have no choice. I can't hold the lavaen forever. We can heal her when we get back to the tunnel."

What's the matter, little man? purred the lavaen, making Nate jump. *Can't lift a puny little woman? Would you like some help?*

"Just do what you're told," growled Nate, pushing more power at her, holding her tighter in his fiery grasp. "Don't worry about us."

The creature roared suddenly, the sound echoing around the room. Nate jerked backward and almost slid into the lava surrounding them.

"Careful, master," murmured the fire demon from nearby. "You are immune to much of the fire these creatures can throw at you, but you are not immune to lava."

"What are you doing?" said Nate with a scowl. "You're supposed to be guarding Remus."

"Jena sent me down here. She insisted you needed my help."

Nate and Argus shared a look. They had to get out of here. Argus hefted Bree into his arms. She hung limply; her face pale and her long, blonde hair matted with blood.

"Get her back up to Jena," said Nate, his voice cracking. The heat was overwhelming. His control was wavering. He didn't know if he could stand up to the lavaen on his own. He turned toward her. "You will not touch them. You will not even look at them."

The lavaen snarled at him but made no other move.

Nate watched as Argus carried Bree across the rocky cavern in front of the lavaen, ignoring the beast. She narrowed her eyes to angry slits, teeth glinting in the light from the fires. He tightened his magical bindings, and she glared back over her shoulder at him. Fire surrounded him, and for a moment he lost himself to the flames. He gasped for breath, reminding himself over and over what he was doing.

Jena. Bree. Argus.
Jena. Bree. Argus.

Meanwhile, Argus didn't even falter, just kept putting one sturdy foot in front of the other. He made it to the bottom of the path, and hesitated. He glanced back at Nate, giving a small nod, then stepped onto the path. He trudged upwards, trying to hold Bree steady as he found his footing with each unsteady step, focusing as if his life depended on it.

Which it did.

Jena crept partway down the path, glancing between the lavaen and Bree as she went. Remus stood at the top like a statue. As soon as Argus made it to Jena, he stopped, shaking his head and refusing to let Bree go. Shrugging, Jena walked backward in front of Argus and helped him find the best places to put his feet.

They were almost at the top when Argus tried to step over a larger rock and slipped.

Nate's heart jumped into his throat. Argus threw his weight forward, dropping Bree onto the path, and tried to scrabble with his free hand. The rocks he had dislodged fell and splashed into the lava pools below.

But Jena somehow managed to not only grab Bree and hold her on the path, but also drag Argus back onto it as well, all the while muttering some kind of spell under her breath. Nate let out his breath. She'd done it. She was so much more than she thought she was.

He didn't take his eyes off them as they crawled their way up the rest of the path, half-dragging Bree between them. When they made it to the ledge where Remus was waiting, Nate let out a relieved breath. They'd all survived this encounter, even if they were a little worse for wear.

He turned back to the lavaen. He wasn't so sure he was

going to make it out of here. Not when the lavaen was watching him so closely with her intelligent eyes. His fiery magic was weakening. His vision was blurred. This lavaen was powerful, that much was clear. She was fighting him, pulling at the magical bonds he'd put around her. She was magnificent. A creature of fire and power. And she'd probably be the death of him.

Alone at last, Firecaller, said the lavaen, her voice echoing uncomfortably inside Nate's head. Her eyes swirled and her body undulated in reaction to the flames around them.

"I'm not your enemy," said Nate. "It doesn't have to be like this." He stared up at the lavaen, the flames in her eyes captivating his attention. He wished it could be different.

I wasn't looking for trouble. It was your friend who tried to steal from me. The lavaen growled, a sound made worse by the unpleasant echoes in the confined lair. The hairs on Nate's arms rose up, but he couldn't look away.

"Master, you must leave," said the fire demon urgently, buzzing next to his ear. "There isn't much time."

Something snapped inside Nate's head. He blinked and looked away. The demon's gravelly words had broken the spell the lavaen had been quietly weaving around him.

He started to run. The demon was right. He had to get out of here. He followed Argus's path, trying not to feel sorry for the lavaen. She'd been about to kill Jena and Bree. She'd rip him apart given half the chance. She didn't need his pity.

But the smoky smell of fire and ash that lingered around her body was like a perfume to Nate, calling to him. Her flame-filled eyes watched him closely, and her whole body reflected the glow from the lava pools that surrounded them. He'd had problems with being fire-enthralled before, but a creature whose very essence was fire was almost more than he could handle.

"It won't be for much longer," said Nate, torn between comforting a creature he was drawn to, and the safety of his friends. "I do not take pleasure in this. But you gave me no choice." He was almost there; he could see Jena waiting in the shadows at the top of the path. He risked a glance back at the lavaen.

He jumped when he realized she was right behind him, standing on her back legs, following his path up the side of the lair with her brilliant, fiery red eyes. *There is always a choice,* said the lavaen. *You chose to enslave me, and I do not forget. I do not forgive.*

"I'm sorry," he whispered. He could feel the pain it was causing the lavaen to fight against his powers. "They're my friends."

They tried to steal from me, said the lavaen, before licking her lips. *You'll make a mistake. Then I will have you for my dinner.*

Nate shuddered. His magic wanted to turn back to the lavaen, to bathe in her fiery essence. Instead, he forced himself to keep running up the uneven path. He slipped and only just caught himself in time. Up ahead, Jena was helping Argus carry Bree into the tunnel. Remus had disappeared, probably already inside. Nate reached the top of the path and stopped, turning to look back at the lavaen one last time.

She stood watching him, her enormous head almost level with his. There was a moment, a connection, and he felt longing in his heart. The lavaen was beautiful. She filled his newly expanded senses with fire and energy.

A whisper of sadness rolled up inside him. "I wish

things could have been different," he murmured, only for her. "We could have been allies."

He turned away, toward his human companions, allowing his bindings around the lavaen to drop and his magic to fall away. His grip on the fire ruby loosened. He didn't need it anymore.

Just as he reached the entrance to the tunnel, he saw Jena and smiled. He let his concentration on the lavaen go and looked forward. He'd survived another encounter with a lavaen, this time using his powers. It was more than—

Sharp claws wrapped around his waist, and he was lifted in the air. His breath was knocked out of his chest, and he gasped, seeing stars. The lavaen drew his face up to her own—so close he could see the individual strands in her irises—and peered at him. *Such a puny creature. How can you control me so?*

Behind him, Nate could hear yells from Argus and Jena, but all he could do was gaze into the eyes of the fire creature. His control over her was gone, but he knew she couldn't harm him. He felt it in their connection. He also felt her frustration and her anger at this restriction. She wanted to destroy him completely for daring to control her.

Just as quickly as he'd been lifted, she put him down. Nate turned to tell the others he was fine. He immediately saw why she'd lost interest in him.

"No! Argus, Jena, get back!" Nate yelled, but it was too late. Argus and Jena had both rushed onto the ledge to save him, and now the lavaen had them trapped.

The creature reached out with one large taloned paw and plucked Argus into the air. Argus's yell of pure rage and pain reverberated through the cavern, mixed with the lavaen's scream of triumph.

Nate rushed forward and tried to protect Jena from the lavaen.

With her other paw, she reached out and flicked a claw at Nate, knocking him over.

His head hit the rocky outcropping behind him. He felt a blinding burst of pain and rolled to one side. He couldn't stop himself as he tumbled over the ledge. He slammed into the side of the lavaen and then everything went black.

CHAPTER 16

JENA

J ena screamed as the lavaen clutched Argus right in front of her.

The same instincts that had made her run out after him were now telling her to run back inside the tunnel with Bree and Remus. Argus dangled in the air, his angry bellows punctuating the cavern and echoing around them.

When Argus saw Jena, his eyebrows caved into an angry scowl. "Get back inside the tunnel, you idiot!"

Good advice, tiny man. Or she will be my next treat. The lavaen dropped back into a crouch at the bottom of the cavern, watching and waiting to see what their next move would be.

Jena ignored the lavaen and Argus. The mercenary was squirming angrily in the lavaen's clutches, attempting to use his strength to escape. She had no doubts that he'd get himself free; he was harder to kill than a cockroach.

She was more concerned about Nate. The lavaen had knocked him with a flick of a talon and he'd disappeared over the ledge. If he was still dazed, then he couldn't protect himself.

She peered over the edge of the outcrop, squinting down into the cavern, hoping he hadn't fallen into one of the many lava pools. She let out a breath. He was sprawled on the rocks below. She watched for a few moments, trying to catch his eye.

Except he wasn't moving.

Her heart leaped and panic set in. Had the lavaen killed him? Was this all for nothing? Had they lost the only man who could challenge Lothar for the crown?

But then he moved, his eyes flickering open. He put one hand to his head as if it hurt. Jena let out another relieved breath. At least he was alive. That was a start. He shook his head like he was trying to clear it and then pushed himself onto his hands and knees. He still seemed stunned, and she desperately hoped he was okay.

She saw the moment Nate realized what had happened to Argus. Eyes wide, he stared up at the lavaen with her prize in her hand. He pushed himself to his feet, moving like an old man.

"I'm coming down," she yelled, not caring if the lavaen could hear her.

He glanced at Jena and shook his head. "Stay there," he yelled.

She shook her head right back at him. "I can help."

"Look after Bree. I'll save Argus." His words were partially drowned out by Argus yelling at the lavaen to let him go.

Jena hesitated, and Nate took that as agreement. He stumbled on shaky legs toward the lavaen. Jena watched, held frozen, her whole body tensed for... she didn't know what. Should she ignore his instructions and run down there after him? Or stay with Bree?

She glanced over her shoulder and saw Remus standing at the entrance to the tunnel. He still seemed to be caught up in the statue spell she'd cast, but she didn't know for how much longer. She'd risked her life putting that spell on him. She'd pissed off Remus in a major way, but she didn't regret it. It had been the only way she could convince the demon to go help Nate. Remus's eyes blazed at her, and she knew he was plotting how best to kill her. Now that Remus knew she could cast mage spells, he wouldn't let it rest. She'd have to deal with that later, once they were out of this mess. *If* they made it out of this mess.

She definitely couldn't leave Bree with him. It would be just as dangerous as being down there with the lavaen.

The hairs rose all over Jena's body. Nate was using his power, attempting to gain control over the lavaen again. She watched him, wishing she could go help. What if he needed a distraction, or she could have helped save Argus by using a spell?

The lavaen roared, smoke and fire spurting toward the roof. Jena could feel the creature's rage, all directed at Nate.

"Let him go," he yelled. "He means you no harm." He was standing directly in front of the lavaen, his whole focus on the creature.

Lies! snarled the lavaen.

The lavaen held Argus in the air, peering at him like he was some kind of insect. She shook him until he rattled, then picked him up by one of his legs with her other paw, dangling him over the lava as he twisted and turned, trying to get free—but also not fall into the bubbling pool below him.

Jena sucked in a breath, only just holding in the scream

that wanted to break free. She took a step toward the lavaen, then stopped. What could she do against this creature? Nate was the one with the Firecaller powers swirling around the heated cavern. She hoped it was enough.

Frantically, she flicked through the pages of the Book of Spells. What else could she do? A wind spell? Not strong enough. A statue spell like she'd used on Remus? The lavaen was too big. A rockfall? No, she could hurt the others. She let out a low growl. Everything seemed wrong or too insignificant against a creature like the lavaen.

There was nothing she could do that would be more powerful than Nate's ability to control the lavaen. If he could just figure out how.

"Leave him alone, lavaen," yelled Nate, and this time his voice boomed with power.

Jena held her breath, but the lavaen ignored Nate. She continued to dangle Argus upside down, giving him another rough shake. Blood dripped from a wound on his head.

He doesn't look so heroic now, does he? said the lavaen, her eyes glittering.

"Put him down!" yelled Nate, his whole body vibrating with anger. "*Carefully.*"

Your control is slipping, Firecaller. I can feel it. Save yourself and leave your friend to me.

Nate hurled himself up the side of the lavaen's body. He flung a fireball at her head, then another. The demon swirled around the lavaen's head, adding another dimension to the attack. The lavaen tried to flick Nate away, but he was too fast. He climbed up the side of her body and onto her back. She roared again in response.

Jena held her hands out in front of her and created another fireball, just in case Nate needed her help. The last fireball she'd thrown at the lavaen had been useless, but perhaps it could be a distraction?

She held herself ready at the top of the cavern, feeling stupid. Nate had asked her to stay where she was, and he was right, she couldn't leave Bree alone with Remus. But it meant that all she could do was wait for the right moment to throw her fireball and try not to look too closely at Argus dangling from the lavaen's talons.

The lavaen reared up onto her hind legs, trying to shake Nate free, but he clung to her back, holding tight to her scales. Jena wasn't sure it was doing anything positive for the situation, but at least he was trying. Jena threw the fireball she'd formed at the lavaen. The creature didn't even notice as the blazing fire hit its flank. The fireball dropped into the lava and flared briefly before disappearing into the swirling heat. The lavaen shook her body, the ripples flickering down her side, and Nate fell toward the ground. He landed near the lavaen's rear leg, and Jena softened his landing using a quick air spell.

The lavaen gave a roar of triumph, her brilliant eyes glittering in the flickering light. In one long, scaled forearm, she held Argus up high near the ceiling. He dangled limply, and Jena could only hope that he was okay. She held another air spell ready in case the lavaen dropped him onto the rocks, so she could cushion his fall.

"Don't you dare hurt him," yelled Nate frantically.

His whole body was shaking, but the flare of power that he'd been using seemed to have disappeared. Jena hesitated. Should she form another fire spell? Or hold on to the air spell? She couldn't decide which would be better. Holding her breath, she prayed to the gods that the lavaen would spare Argus.

Except of course she didn't.

The lavaen started whispering words, unintelligible via the mental link she used to communicate with them all.

"Stop that," yelled Nate, but even from her perch high above, Jena could tell his words didn't have a ring of power behind them. He'd lost his focus and no longer had the lavaen under his control.

The voice in her head grew louder, and Jena could make out words. They were in old Utugani, the language of the gypsy folk she'd been raised with, but the version only used at official ceremonies. How did a lavaen even know the old Utugani ceremonial language?

Jei caten thei hava a cruften, jey hele biden, jey hele siden. Jey du felder i unden timer. Jei caten thei hava a cruften, sa shell det bide.

Cruften?

It had been a long time since her adoptive mother Elsa had forced her to learn the verbal language, but she recognized that word.

Curse.

The lavaen was cursing Argus.

"No!" yelled Jena. She tried to perform a blocking spell to protect Argus from the magic, but the curse had already been uttered. Argus was glowing red in the cave, his expression one of agony.

The lavaen held her prize between her fingers for one second longer.

And then she let go.

Argus plummeted to the rocks below, and Jena only just managed to send the air spell in time to cushion his landing.

Without thinking, she started running down the path. She didn't know what she was going to do, but she couldn't stay at the top, just waiting to see if the lavaen killed them both. All she knew was that she couldn't just stand still and watch a moment longer.

"Jena. Stop! Stay up there," Nate yelled at her, his voice panicky. "I can't do this if you're down here too."

"You need help," she yelled back. "She cast a curse. I can't—"

"Stay with Bree. *You have to stay with her.*"

It was the desperation in Nate's voice that finally made Jena stop. She glanced at Argus. He lay unmoving, his body glowing a terrible blood red. The lavaen screeched from behind Nate. The creature's wings unfurled behind her, pushing the heat out through the cavern in a wave.

Jena took a step backward, leaning into the rock wall behind her, grateful that she wasn't closer to the enormous creature. She backed up the path again, desperately wishing she'd never listened to Remus about coming here. She was going to make him hurt when this was over. She caught him staring down at her from the entrance to the tunnel, his eyes glittering in the reflection of the fires in the cavern. Maybe she'd make him hurt *before* this was over. It was his fault that Argus was cursed. That Bree was hurt. That Nate was down there with the lavaen, desperately trying to save the situation.

But Remus didn't matter right now. Nate and Argus were still in danger. They had to get out of here before she could enact any of her revenge fantasies on Remus. As she climbed back to the top, Jena kept her gaze tightly on Nate. He was waving his hands in the air, trying to distract the lavaen away from anyone else. His fire demon was swirling around the head of the creature. The demon buzzed up the length of the lavaen, whipping around her head, going in and flicking burns on her body. In a human the same burns would have created a massive open wound and agonizing pain, but her thick scales protected the lavaen and it simply left small, inflamed patches on her hide that she barely seemed to notice.

Just as Jena arrived back at the tunnel entrance, the lavaen roared, snapping her huge teeth at the demon. But the small fire creature was too fast for her jaws. Rearing up onto her hind legs, forearms out full length, the lavaen swung angrily at the small fragment of light darting around her face.

It was enough of a distraction for Nate. He moved quickly, sprinting to where Argus lay on the floor. He crouched low beside the mercenary, and Jena watched closely, trying to figure out from his reaction if Argus was alive.

Behind her she heard the noise of someone waking. Bree.

She turned—too scared to know the truth about Argus just yet—and rushed back to her sister inside the tunnel. Jena's heart was pounding, and fear raged through her body. Was Argus okay? If he died, it would be because of her and Bree. Because they'd listened to Remus, believed what he'd said.

Remus stood to one side, still as a statue, his air of smug satisfaction gone. He was covered in dirt and had a scratch down one side of his forehead, like he'd crashed into a low-hanging rock. She glared at him, wishing she'd never met him. They should have gone straight to the Utugani, just like Argus had said. She had to swallow down the sob rising in her throat. "Stay back, you disgusting ash-gatherer. We'll deal with your treachery later."

Remus gave a tight grimace, his lopsided eyes tilting even further to one side. "My treachery? You'll suffer *my* wrath, girl. I know your secret. I know you've been casting *mage spells*. That'll get you killed every day of the week."

"Not if I kill you first," growled Jena, taking all her fear and rage out on Remus. She wanted to burn him to cinders right here and now. Her silver flame flickered to life in her palm, and she turned fully to face him. His eyes widened, and some of her vengeful thoughts must have shown on her face, because he didn't reply.

Next to her, Bree moaned.

"You're lucky she's more important to me than you," spat Jena. She turned back to Bree. If the possibility of Argus being fatally hurt was killing her, it was going to destroy Bree.

Bree's eyes opened. She looked up at Jena blearily. "What happened?"

"We're in the lavaen cave," whispered Jena, her voice hoarse.

"Where's Argus?" Bree whispered, her voice hoarse.

CHAPTER 17
NATE

Nate knelt next to Argus's limp body, trying not to look too closely at his wounds.

He could feel the magic buzzing discordantly around the mercenary and tried not to think about what the lavaen had just done to him. He knew the beast had cast some kind of spell—and he couldn't figure out how that was possible. He touched a shaking hand to his friend's chest to see if his heart was still beating.

Nate let out a tiny, relieved breath.

There was a thready beat. Unsteady and thin, but there. Argus's face was pale, and he was so limp he was almost part of the rocks beneath him. But he was alive, and that was all that mattered.

Behind him, the lavaen roared, still distracted by the demon darting around her face. He didn't know how long it would last; she could decide at any time to ignore the demon and come after Argus again.

Nate squinted up at the tunnel. He just needed to get Argus up to Jena and Bree; surely they'd be able to heal him? Bree had healed them after the Riders attacked near the Forest of Ghosts. Jena had the Book of Spells inside her head. Between them they were powerful enough to save Argus.

They had to be.

Because Argus would die if he didn't get help. He could feel the spell boiling around the edges of Argus's body. It was trying to push him away, the buzzing vibration along his skin getting more insistent the closer he got to Argus. But he ignored it. Grasping his arms under the big man's armpits, Nate made sure he had a tight hold. Then he pulled, hard, straining against the sagging bulk he was trying to drag.

Argus didn't budge. Not even a little bit. He also didn't wake, or moan about being moved. His body was completely slack, like an enormous sack of potatoes. Nate's heartbeat picked up, and he tried again, trying not to let panic set in. He glanced up at the lavaen, terrified she would notice what he was doing.

The lavaen's eyes were on the demon as it buzzed around her head. She was taking swipes at it, trying to knock it out of the air.

Nate took a deep breath and pulled again. This time he managed to drag Argus a short distance, taking a gasping breath before giving another painstaking heave. Nate's breath was now coming in panicky gasps. What did Argus's lack of reaction mean? He buried the thought and dragged Argus again, using all his strength, his breath rasping in his chest. He pulled the mercenary another few feet and felt as exhausted as if he'd just dragged him halfway up the mountain. He looked up at the ledge where Jena and Bree were waiting for him. It seemed like they were further away than the stars. Nate stopped and squeezed his eyes shut, trying to block out the lump he could feel pushing against his chest.

He couldn't carry Argus to safety. The mercenary was too heavy.

For a moment, Nate stood there, frozen, despite the heat. It felt like lava was burning inside his stomach. Acid rose in his throat and the heat of the cavern was suddenly too much. He felt claustrophobic, like the air in the room was wrapping itself around him, tighter and tighter. His muscles clenched, and his thoughts spun inside his head, off kilter and desperate. He stumbled to one side, only keeping his balance because he was holding onto the dead weight of Argus's body.

He took another deep breath, trying to focus. He glanced around him, but there weren't even any stray ghosts about to give him terrible advice. Not even the damned mage ghost, who'd conveniently disappeared when Nate needed him most. Every way he looked, there were only bad choices.

He couldn't drag Argus to safety on his own, and even if he could somehow manage it, he wouldn't be able to do it without the lavaen noticing. She'd never leave him be, and right now he couldn't feel any of his new power inside him —he'd depleted it when he'd tried to control her the first time.

He couldn't protect them both.

She might leave Nate alone because he was the Firecaller—although there was no guarantee of that—but she wouldn't leave Argus alone. She'd proved that already.

Nate looked up at the tunnel again, trying to figure out what to do. He needed help. There was no way around it.

Just then, Jena strode out of the tunnel and stood on the ledge. Their eyes met. He didn't want to call Jena out into the lair again. He wanted to keep her safe, to protect her. But he had no other option. He couldn't do a normal mage spell, but Jena could. It would take up precious time they didn't have, and it would probably draw the lavaen to them. But it was their only hope of saving Argus.

He gestured for Jena to come down, and she nodded. She turned to look over her shoulder, said something, and then raced back down the path. Nate could only admire her courage. She hadn't even hesitated.

He turned back to Argus, putting one hand on the big man's arm. Argus was limp. His arms were sunken into the ground, his face a gray waxy color. It was almost as if...

Nate touched one hand to Argus's chest. There was still the faintest beat, but it was fading fast.

The demon burst into the air next to him. "Master, we must take him into the Edges. Right now. Death hovers over him."

"But—"

"No arguments." The demon buzzed and flared brightly... and then Nate and Argus were inside the place in between the living and the dead, where the demons lived.

"You can only be here for a minute or two, master. But the big man has even less time. The lavaen has put a curse inside him. She is stealing his essence, pretending to fight me to give her spell more time. You need to put the big man into the fire ruby to protect against her spell, and to give him more time. Time runs differently inside the fire rubies."

"How did she—? I can't—I can't p-put him into a fire ruby," said Nate, his brain stuttering to a halt as he tried to take in what the demon had just told him.

"If you don't, he will die in this cavern. It is your only hope."

Nate stared at the demon like it had just grown an extra

head. "I don't know *how*," he said desperately. It was like someone who'd never seen water before being told to 'just swim across the ocean'.

"Then figure it out. I cannot tell you how, only that it is within your powers. And if you do not do it, your friend will die, and Lothar will win."

Bile rose in Nate's throat, burning his mouth. "I don't —" He swallowed. The demon didn't care about his fears. It wouldn't even argue with his low estimation of his abilities.

And it said he could do this.

Nate pulled the fire ruby from the pocket where he'd placed it. It glowed gently in his palm, and he had to force himself to keep moving, to avoid the thrall that affected him so easily with these rubies.

"Just concentrate," said the demon.

Nate glared up at the glowing ball next to him. "It's not that easy."

The demon moved closer to Nate, and then it was inside his head.

He wanted to scream, but everything was frozen. The demon didn't hesitate. It forced his eyes wide open, made him look down at the ruby, and closed his hand over it. The power inside the ruby flared to life. There was a strange fog coming out of the tiny jewel, and it flowed out over Argus. The fog moved until it covered Argus, and then it somehow tightened, contracting until it looked more like a layer of material wrapped over him.

For a moment, it hovered there, and then it tightened again.

Nate gaped as Argus's body was contorted by the mist into a smaller shape, twisting and turning him in the air, jerking him backwards. And then, as quickly as it had appeared, the mist shot back inside the fire ruby, taking

Argus with it. The fire ruby glowed brightly, as if Argus's energy was making it light up from the inside.

Nate just stared down at the ruby. Argus was inside there. Dying slowly from a lavaen's curse.

The demon slid out of Nate's body and shuddered like it had just touched something slimy.

"What now?"

"You have twenty-one days to find a cure for your friend's curse. Or he'll die. The fire ruby will dim, as Argus's life force disappears."

Nate opened his mouth to argue, but the demon disappeared, and moments later, so did the Edges. The heat of the lavaen's lair hit him like a punch. Nate staggered, trying to orient himself back to this world.

A touch at his shoulder made Nate jump, and he turned, jerking his hands high, ready to throw fire at the lavaen.

"Watch it! It's just me," whispered Jena, ducking down in front of him.

Nate let out a breath. He still didn't understand what had just happened.

"What just happened? You went... fuzzy... for a bit before I got here. Where's Argus?"

Nate opened his hand and showed Jena the fire ruby. "He's inside the fire ruby. He was cursed by the lavaen. The demon said it was the only way to save him. I don't know how, but we have to find a way to end the curse, and quickly."

"He's in there? In the ruby?" Jena looked incredulously down at the small jewel.

Nate nodded. "It was the only way."

"What are we going to tell *Bree?*" Jena's expression was horrified.

CHAPTER 18
JENA

J ena's throat constricted as she tried to inhale the heated air in the cavern. It felt heavy and metallic, and burned her lungs as it went down, like it was air she shouldn't breathe. She and Nate were running across the rocky floor of the lavaen's cave, dodging bubbling lava pools and trying not to stumble on the rocky surface.

Jena could feel the scarred skin across one side of her body stretching painfully in the heat, and her knife strapped to her leg was warm where it touched her skin. What would happen to her skin if the lavaen's flames hit it? It would be many times worse than burning in a campfire, of that she was sure.

The enormous fire creature loomed next to them, black scales glinting with the reflection of the lava. She was up on her hind legs, peering into the tunnel as if she was trying to see how easy it would be to pluck Bree out of there. Jena shuddered. She'd told Bree and Remus to stay back out of the way, but if Bree didn't listen... Jena forced the thought away. She just had to focus on running.

The lavaen hadn't noticed them yet. Maybe she thought they'd still be trying to get Argus to safety. Or maybe she just figured she had them trapped and wanted the others as well.

Maybe she was right.

Jena jumped from one rock to the next, her concentration fuzzy, and almost lost her footing. The lava loomed next to her. Nate caught her elbow and pulled her backwards. She glanced at him and knew he could see the fear in her eyes. She'd been too preoccupied to even cast a spell to save herself.

"We need to hurry," whispered Nate. "I don't know how long we have before she notices us."

Behind them, the lavaen roared, and Jena flinched. The sound shook the entire cavern and set loose rocks from the ceiling. Jena ducked, shoving her hands over her head, trying to avoid the falling debris. The small pieces of rock plopped into the lava pools, sending droplets of lava in arcs toward them. Jena used a quick air spell to push the droplets away from them both, then kept running.

Kept hoping.

The lavaen roared again and this time Jena turned her head. Black eyes stared down at her, malice in their depths; it was like looking at her own death.

"She's seen us!" Her voice cracked as she tried to warn Nate.

He glanced back as well. "Keep going. Don't stop." He kept running but moved directly behind her as if to shield her from the lavaen. He was the Firecaller and had an affinity with fire creatures—maybe it would work.

Or maybe it wouldn't. This fire creature had a mind of her own.

But they had no other choice. They just had to keep

running. Jena could feel Nate just behind her, his breath gasping just like hers.

One foot in front of the other. She chanted the words inside her head. *We're almost there.* If she said it enough times, eventually it would be true.

The bottom of the path was just a few feet away. *So close.*

When she reached it and started up, she glanced over her shoulder. Her breath caught. The lavaen was right behind them, watching intently, as if she was just biding her time. When she caught Jena's eye, the lavaen leaned down toward them, taking a deep breath.

She was going to blast them with fire.

Jena let out a scream, half rage, half despair. She tried a blocking spell, but it was weak at best. She'd used up too much of her power on the fireballs. One blast of the lavaen's fire would kill them both. There was nothing they could do to protect themselves from that kind of fire. Her legs kept moving, and Nate was just behind her on the rocky uphill path, but it felt like a useless act of defiance.

The lavaen was about to cover them in deadly flames.

Jena let out a tiny sob, then swallowed it back down, determined not to show her fear. She forced herself not to wince, or cry out, or even stop—when all she wanted to do was crouch down with her hands over her head, as if that would save her.

She hadn't expected them to fail this early in their quest. Argus was already gone, maybe forever. They were about to join him. Bree would be the only one left, and she couldn't fight Lothar alone.

What had made her think she could take on this creature? Take on Lothar? Half a sob stuck in her throat, and she stumbled. The only thing that saved her was Nate grabbing her from behind, his strong hands holding her steady. He murmured something unintelligible, something comforting. She leaned in closer to his solid strength and took a deep breath, bracing for the burn of the lavaen's flames.

But instead...she heard a single, determined caw. *The raven.*

It survived.

A spark of hope flared in Jena's chest. With a loud caw, the raven swooped down, raking its claws across the lavaen's delicate snout. The beast roared, her head tipping back in obvious agony. Jena's heart thudded as the lavaen reached up for her nose, momentarily forgetting her deathly fire breath.

Jena didn't think; she just ran, her hand still linked with Nate's, dragging him behind her. The raven was buying them time, and she wasn't going to waste it. She felt the air shift as the lavaen stretched out and swatted at the bird. She glanced over her shoulder in fear, but the raven dove, dipping around the lavaen's head, easily staying out of reach.

The lavaen bellowed, rising onto her hind legs, trying to swat at her minuscule attacker.

"Come on, it won't distract her for long," urged Nate.

Jena nodded grimly. They pounded up the uncertain path toward the tunnel entrance. The heat made the air feel thick, like running through syrup. Her body had run out of puff, her legs were screaming, and her vision blurred. Getting to the top felt impossible.

But Jena wiped the sweat from her eyes and kept going. She focused on one step after another, trying not to stumble. With her gaze locked on the tunnel entrance, she blocked out the caws and growls behind her.

Just as they arrived at the top, the screech of the lavaen

made Jena flinch. She stumbled, and only Nate's grip kept her on her feet.

"Keep running," gasped Nate. "Just keep running."

Jena nodded and ran as fast as she could into the tunnel, welcoming the darkness and cooler air. The lavaen's growls echoed behind them.

Jena let out the breath she'd been holding.

They'd escaped the lavaen—by the skin of their teeth.

She ran as far as she could, but soon it was too dark to see. She stumbled to a stop, her breath heaving, and bent over with her hands on her knees. Her pounding heart was all she could feel. Relief flooded her body, making her dizzy.

After a moment, the darkness became overwhelming, and Jena flicked her fingers. A small silver flame appeared in her hand, providing light, but also creating strange shadows that danced over the nearby rocks. She glanced back at Nate. He stood motionless, staring down at the fire ruby in his hands, almost as if he were enthralled. She took a step toward him, but he spoke before she could get closer.

"I should have stopped him from going back out," he said.

Jena walked closer and put a hand on his arm. "We thought you were in danger. We were trying to save you."

"I should have been able to keep the lavaen under control. Argus would have thought I still had her under my power." Nate looked like he'd aged ten years in the time they'd been inside the cave.

"Did he say that? Do you think Argus blames you?"

"No. *I* blame me. This is my fault. I don't know how to be the Firecaller."

"It wasn't your fault, Nate. The *lavaen* hurt him; not you." Jena willed him to believe her.

Nate nodded, but she could see he didn't take any

comfort from her words. Before she could say more, the raven's caw echoed along the walls, distracting her. She let out a long breath. The raven was okay.

The tunnel brightened, and a demon appeared as well, illuminating the harsh expressions on their faces. The demon buzzed around Nate's head, clearly communicating with him.

"We have to keep moving," said Nate. "The demon says the lavaen is leaving the cavern and will probably search for us on the mountain. If we're going to escape, we need to be fast."

Jena nodded. "I hope Bree and Remus aren't too much further," she murmured, peering into the darkness. They were already deep inside the tunnel. "I told them to go further in, but I didn't think they'd go this far."

Nate narrowed his gaze, searching ahead of them as well. "Maybe they're waiting on the mountain end? It would be dark in the middle."

Goosebumps rose along Jena's arms. Her intuition flared. "Something's wrong."

Her breath lodged in her throat and the flame in her hand stuttered, then flared. Why would they have gone all the way to the other end? Remus had still been under her statue spell. He shouldn't have been able to go this far—unless he broke the spell.

"Let's get to the other end before we panic," said Nate. He sounded just as worried as she felt. "It'll probably be fine. They'll be there, waiting. Maybe they didn't like the dark."

"If Remus has done anything to Bree I'm gonna…" She couldn't even finish. She'd rip him apart if he hurt a hair on Bree's head.

She'd only left them alone because she'd been desperate

to help Nate and Argus. Remus had still been under the statue spell. She'd given him a slightly wider radius to walk in as she'd left, so they could move down the tunnel, but it should still have kept him mostly immobile. Maybe she'd messed up? Jena's breath came in shorter gasps. Had she accidentally let him go?

"Let's just get to the other end," said Nate again.

Jena nodded jerkily. "Maybe they're just waiting down there. Maybe it's fine." Even to her own ears, the words sounded hollow. Nate clearly didn't believe it either.

It was a long, silent trip back through the tunnel. Water dripped around them, and the weight of her thoughts made Jena's breaths uneven. The demon's unsteady glow meant they had to watch each step on the rough ground, but she didn't need her flame.

As they jogged the final stretch, Jena fought her fears. Would Bree be waiting for them at the end of the tunnel? Was her worry for nothing?

What if Bree wasn't there?

She couldn't let herself think about it. She had to just keep going, keep hoping, just as she had inside the lavaen's cavern. She couldn't break down now, before they even knew what had happened.

When the light at the end of the tunnel became visible, Jena sped up to a sprint. Her whole body ached, and she felt like she'd been pounded by ten lavaens, but she ran anyway.

She ran as fast as she could toward the light.

CHAPTER 19
JENA

Jena burst out of the tunnel, even the late afternoon sun hurting her eyes after the darkness in the caves.

She squinted around as best she could, but couldn't see the white of Bree's hair.

They weren't there.

The raven burst out of the tunnel behind her and swooped up into the sky. The demon buzzed into the light just after the raven. Nate came through last, holding his hand over his eyes to shield them from the burn of emerging from the cave into the sunlight. He looked around, the hope visibly dying on his face when he saw the same barren landscape as Jena.

She growled, her anger overpowering the fear. If Remus had done anything to hurt Bree, he was going to regret it. She would burn him slowly over an open fire. She'd peel off his skin using a spoon. She'd—

"Jena, look!" said Nate urgently.

He was pointing to a rock, where something was smeared in reddish-brown—was that blood? Jena clenched her fists until her nails were painfully digging into her skin. If that was Bree's blood, she was going to kill him, then bring him back to life with dark magic, and kill him again.

She squinted at the rock, unable to make out what the scribbles said. "What does it say?" She moved closer, her senses sizzling. Someone had performed magic on this spot.

Nate peered at the words. *"I have Bree. See under rock."* He scrambled behind the rock and came out holding a small glowing orb.

"A message globe? Why was he even carrying that?"

Nate's expression was grim. "He's the kind of person who'd plan for any possibility. I'm guessing it's how he's survived this long."

"They're usually imprinted with the name of the person they're for," said Jena. "Thornal used them sometimes. Just say your name."

Nate leaned close to the orb. "Nate," he said. When nothing happened, he spoke again. "Nathaniel."

The orb lay dormant. Nate looked over at Jena. "Maybe it's for you?" He held out his hand.

Jena didn't want to hear what Remus had to say. She hesitated, staring at Nate.

"We have to know what's happening," he said.

She switched her gaze back down to the glowing orb. How was it that something so ordinary could seem so ominous? "Jena," she whispered reluctantly.

The orb glowed brighter. Then Remus's voice spoke, the sound coming from inside the glowing ball. *"I have your sister. You'll never find her. I have magic you've never even heard of that will keep her hidden. The only way to get her back is to save Argus from his curse and bring him back to me. I will exchange Argus for Bree. You have my vow as a mage that I will honor this trade. I will keep your sister safe for three weeks until the coronation. If you haven't returned Argus to me by then, I will kill her. Do not waste precious time trying to rescue Bree, or I will kill her. The only way to get your sister back is to save Argus and return him to me."*

The orb brightened for a moment, then burst into stars.

Jena and Nate covered their eyes, trying to avoid being burned by the lights, but they were magical rather than real. Jena crouched down, fighting the urge to bring up the contents of her stomach. "I shouldn't have left them together. I should have known he'd be able to get out of my spell. He's been researching ways to get out of spells for the last half-century."

"He was probably planning to kidnap you and took Bree instead."

"That doesn't make it better. At least I could have tried to—"

"You have the Book of Spells inside you, Jena. If he'd taken you, it would have been far, far worse."

Jena felt a sinking sensation in her stomach. "We shouldn't have come here. We should have listened to Argus when he warned us about Remus." She knew she'd regret traveling up this mountain until her dying day.

"Maybe." Nate's hand tightened around the fire ruby in his hand. "But we're stuck now." He stared down the mountain. "I believe him when he says we'd never find Bree."

Jena swallowed hard. She wanted to scream and argue, but she knew he was right. This mountain was Remus's playground. He knew every nook and cranny. There was no way they'd find him.

"What about Argus? Would he know? Can you talk to him?"

Overhead the raven cawed twice, urgently. It swooped back down, heading straight for Jena. She wished she could avoid what was coming next, but instead she lifted her shirt from her stomach, and the raven smashed itself into her skin, the pain of it making Jena wince. Immediately, images of the lavaen flying overhead filled her vision. "It's the lavaen," she said. "We have to hide."

They moved as one toward the tunnel entrance. "She's going to look here first," said Nate, stopping abruptly.

"Where do we go, then?"

"Down."

"How do we get down the mountain without the lavaen killing us?" asked Jena. "We can't let that happen. Bree is counting on us to rescue her." The thought of Bree waiting the three weeks, expecting them to come for her, and it never happening was enough to break Jena's heart.

"The demon can help with that, I think," said Nate. "It can sense the lavaen, because it's a fire creature as well. We just hide whenever she's near."

Jena narrowed her eyes and peered down the mountain. "Maybe I could do a spell to make us blend into the rocks a little? A camouflage spell. I use it when I'm hunting. We wouldn't be completely invisible, but if we knew when she was flying over and slowed our movement, we'd be fine."

"Sounds perfect," said Nate. "Do it quickly before she gets here."

Jena saw the spell clearly in her mind. She often used it when she was hunting for rabbits for the stewpot. "Hold on to everything you want to be camouflaged and grab my hand. It won't last long, maybe an hour or two, and we'll be visible if we move. When the demon says she's coming, we stay completely still. Understood?"

Nate nodded, but as he had nothing but the clothes he was standing in and the fire ruby in his palm, he just reached out his hand to Jena. His hazel eyes watched her carefully, and she knew he was thinking about her usual aversion to touch. She gripped his hand in hers, and the warmth of his palm eased her nerves.

There was something about Nate, and everything they'd experienced together, that made her feel... more settled. She took the first deep breath that she'd had in a while. "Okay, I need to touch the earth, so we both have to crouch down."

She started the spell, holding the thought of hiding in her mind. It had to be crystal clear, or it wouldn't work. She touched one hand to the earth, feeling the grains of dust and dirt on her fingertips. Nate's thigh was almost touching hers as they crouched next to each other, heat emanating from his body. She whispered the words under her breath, and the air hummed. The wind swirled in a mini-tornado around them. The currents caught at their clothes and their hair, twisting and pulling.

She closed her eyes, and the spell built in strength. It grew around them slowly and steadily. As she used her magic, she became aware of the power emanating from Nate; his Firecaller abilities were a tangible presence on their own. She could almost reach out and touch the blazing magic that was burning around him. It made the possibility of their survival seem more real.

Jena opened one eye, and looked down at her body, while continuing to mutter the words of the spell repeatedly. She could feel her power swirling around them. The wind was almost visible, it was moving so fast. Her hand where it touched Nate's was glowing.

Nate's eyes were closed, but he was also faintly glowing, and his body seemed to pulse.

"Did it work? I can't tell." He opened his eyes and frowned down at his arms. "I don't see any difference."

CHAPTER 20
JENA

She gave a small half-smile. "It worked. You're glowing."

Jena brushed off the dust from the windstorm. "I don't know exactly how long this spell will last. I've never done it on two people at once before. We need to move, and fast."

Nate looked skeptically down at his arms. "Are you sure?"

Jena gave him a look. "The only way to know for sure is to test it. Let's go," she said. They didn't have any time to waste.

The little demon buzzed down beside them, its glow dimmed out in the daylight. "Master, the lavaen is about to pass over us."

Jena stopped walking and looked up. She saw a large shape flying in wide circles in the sky above them. The lavaen seemed impossibly huge, her scales reflecting brilliantly off the low afternoon sun. She flew in lazy circles, wings reaching wide across the sky, waiting for her prey to come out of the mountain. According to the Book of Spells, lavaens had amazing vision, and could spot things on the ground from high above.

Jena stood still, holding her breath. They both craned their necks, watching the lavaen, ready to run if she swooped in their direction. But she just continued her lazy sweeps, looking for all the world like she was cruising the sky for no reason.

"She thinks she's going to get us," said Jena.

"Yeah. Without your spell, we'd be sitting ducks."

The lavaen glided off down the mountain, and they both let out a breath.

"We'll be fine if we stick to the shadows of the rocks," said Jena.

"Come on, we need to get moving."

"Where?"

"I need the rest of my gear from Remus's house." Nate glanced at the setting sun. "It's almost dark, and we need to stop for the night and make a plan."

"I'm not staying at Remus's place." Jena shuddered.

"I don't think Remus will be there," said Nate. "But I don't think we should, either."

"There will be a cave or something similar we can stop in," said Jena. "Once we have our bags."

It had seemed a long way on their walk up, but it was even further going down. Darkness would soon cover the mountain, and Jena didn't want to be out in the open at night. It added an extra edge to her footsteps as they trudged down. The raven scratched to get out again, and she lifted her shirt so it could fly free of her stomach.

Jena was constantly glancing up at the sky, waiting for a bellow of recognition, and the sharp claws of the lavaen against her skin.

The raven cawed over her head about halfway down the

mountain, but Jena ignored its summons. It cawed again, swooping low and blowing a wingbeat of breeze over her scalp. She didn't want to let the raven back onto her skin, they needed it in the air helping the demon.

She just kept going, one step after the other. Slowly, bit by bit, they crawled down the mountain, like creatures afraid of the sun. They were almost to the ground when the demon buzzed down beside them. "It's coming your way, Master."

Moments later, the lavaen screeched overhead. They froze, eyes wide. Jena didn't even dare to look up.

"She's angry. I don't think she's seen us," whispered Nate, searching the sky. It was late afternoon, and the light was turning into that golden twilight glow.

Jena let out a breath that turned to a gasp when the lavaen flew low and fast over the rocks where they were hiding. The creature swooped a few feet over their heads, and Jena had to hold in her scream. But the lavaen's claws didn't rake her back. She just flew onward, clearly trying to flush out the prey she couldn't see.

"It's working," said Nate with a relieved grin.

They continued creeping down the mountain, stopping and holding their breath every time the demon warned them the lavaen was about to do another increasingly angry sweep. The sun sank lower in the sky, until the afternoon was almost gone. Jena's heart stopped pounding, and exhaustion set in, hanging around her neck like an unwanted dinner guest.

As they came closer to Remus's cabin, another violent screech echoed up the mountain, this one more like a bird but louder and deeper. They both froze.

"That wasn't the lavaen, was it?" whispered Jena. They

were out of sight of the cabin, but it was close, just over the next ridge.

"I don't think so," said Nate, frowning. "We're both tired. It was probably nothing. A bird, or something." But he didn't sound convinced.

"I think I've heard it before," said Jena, wracking her tired brain for the memory. "I just can't think where." The sound was fragmented, as if she were hearing it from two different places at once. She looked up into the sky. The raven was gliding overhead; it was projecting what it could hear back to her. The bird dove toward her. It swooped over their heads, strangely silent in the air, before circling twice around her head. She lifted her shirt, and the raven dove back onto her skin. Immediately, it sent images of red eyes and black muscle and flames. She shivered.

"There's something up ahead. I'll see what it is." She ran in a low crouch toward the lip of the path, using the cover of the rocks to hide from whatever was in the valley where Remus's house was sheltered.

Peering over an outcrop, she stilled. Prickles of awareness flowed along her arms.

Outside Remus's house was a murghah. Flame snorted from its nose, and its eyes glowed red in the afternoon light. Jena ducked back down. Was it the same one they'd encountered in the village? Or a different one? The thought that there was potentially a second murghah roaming Ignisia sent goosebumps over her skin. Nate arrived a moment later, crouching his tall frame down beside her.

He opened his mouth to speak, and without thinking, she put her hand over his lips. Both the murghah and the lavaen had excellent hearing.

She gestured for him to look over the outcrop for himself. He nodded his understanding. Except he didn't move, just watched her face. Jena blinked, then looked at her hand over his mouth.

She quickly pulled away from him again. Since when was she comfortable enough with Nate to do something like that?

Nate said nothing, just turned to peer over the rock. She heard his soft curse as he saw the murghah standing beside Remus's crooked house.

Jena shook her head, trying to focus. The murghah were powerful, and Lothar had been controlling the last one they'd met on their travels. Was he controlling this one too? It seemed likely. Usually, the murghah lived in the darkest corners of the earth during the daylight hours, only coming out when it was dark, and then only reluctantly. If this shadow creature was roaming during the daylight hours, it meant Lothar had likely sent it.

How could they possibly defeat such a man? On her stomach, the raven rolled and then pecked her, wanting to be free again. "Again? You only just came back onto me."

It pushed images of the murghah into her head again, and she knew it was telling her that was the only reason it had come back so soon. "Okay, fine. We need you in the air, anyway." Wincing, she lifted her shirt, and the raven burst free in a rush of wind and feathers.

She peered out over the rock again, this time paying more attention. The main part of the murghah's body looked like a large black stallion, with red eyes and stomping feet. But attached to the stallion's back, like a strange growth, was the top half of a woman. Her black silk dress glinted in the sun—was it even a dress? Maybe it was part of the creature too? Jena didn't know.

The murghah's hair draped over her human face as she searched the area around Remus's cottage with eyes the same burning red as the murghah's other set of eyes, on its stallion head. Jena fervently hoped Remus wasn't there. They didn't want his soul to be sucked out by this creature, not before he'd told them where Bree was.

"Come out, Remus. We have much to discuss. My master would like to know how your side of the bargain is progressing." The murghah's voice was gravelly, almost like she was gargling the words. It took Jena a moment to decipher what she'd said. Remus had a bargain with Lothar? Except the murghah wasn't acting like they were partners. More like Remus was a slug underfoot. Had Lothar forced Remus into an alliance?

What had happened to Remus's protection that Argus spoke of? Had Lothar broken through and forced the shrinking mage into a bargain?

Jena cursed. So many questions, and she had answers for none of them.

The raven had found a perch near the roof, and Jena picked up more of the woman's muttered words through their link, although distorted by the bird's mind. "I'd prefer to gnaw his head off too, my beauty. But he's made a deal, and Lothar intends to honor it. For now."

Jena pulled Nate back down by his shirt. She motioned for them to go back the other way.

Nate shook his head. He leaned in close to her, whispering the words: "We need to save Remus from that thing."

She shook her head, speaking against his ear in the same way he had. "Remus made a pact with Lothar. It's not here to kill him."

Nate paled. "Then we need to get the flames out of here."

CHAPTER 21

NATE

Nate swallowed over his parched throat.

His skin was stretched tight across his face, and his eyes felt like they'd been rubbed raw with sand. His whole body was heavy with fatigue. Except they had no other choice but to crawl back the way they'd come, and head west along the ridgeline. Neither spoke, knowing they had to keep as quiet as possible until they were far enough away from the murghah.

He glanced overhead.

The twilight was dimming, and the lavaen was still out there searching for them, too. Nate's head ached from using his unfamiliar Firecaller magic to try to control the lavaen. He had scratches and bruises all over his body, and his chest tightened every time he felt the shape and heat of the fire ruby nestled in the pocket of his trousers.

He'd been looking forward to getting to Remus's cottage. The shrinking mage might be a double-crossing ash-dweller, but at least there would have been shelter and food. He'd even vaguely hoped they'd find him there and could convince him to change his mind about Bree.

Instead, they had to keep moving—without their gear, which was even worse.

"Where are we going?" asked Jena eventually, turning to face him. Ash covered her face, and her eyes were missing their usual spark. She'd already been through so much today.

"We need to find shelter," said Nate. He put one hand over his eyes, trying to see an outcrop of rocks or a darker section that might indicate a cave. "We just have to head away from Remus and hope we find something."

"I think I can help." Jena lifted her face and closed her eyes. Moments later, the raven appeared in the sky above. Her gaze locked onto the bird, and then it took off along the edge of the mountain range, skimming the rocks and low-lying trees.

"I've told it to find us a cave or some kind of shelter for the night along this ridgeline."

Nate breathed a sigh of relief. He didn't think he could climb up again. They kept trudging along the faint path that Jena had found, Nate occasionally looking behind them just in case. He also kept checking the sky, and it occurred to him that this was what it was like to be an animal with too many predators. It wasn't a good feeling.

"You're fine," said a voice beside him.

He flinched, then turned to glare at the ghost mage walking to his left. "Where were you when we needed you?" he whispered.

"I can't always control when I can come back into this world," said the ghost mage sadly. *"But I wouldn't have been much help, anyway."*

"You could have prevented what happened to Argus." He knew he was being unfair, but the horror of having Argus slowly dying inside the fire ruby was taking its toll.

But the ghost mage didn't seem to take offense. *"Prob-ably not, son. I'm more of an observer and advice giver,"* he said with a twist of his mouth.

"Yeah, even when I don't want your advice," grumbled Nate.

The ghost mage gave him a look. *"I heard that."*

Nate just glared back. The ghost mage had been haranguing him like a fishwife since the Forest of Ghosts. He wasn't saying anything that wasn't true.

The ghost mage stared up at the raven, then at the path ahead. *"I cannot stay any longer right now. Just keep following the raven. It will lead you where you need to go."*

"But—" The ghost mage was gone before Nate could ask him anything more. Typical.

The sun had disappeared behind the mountain, and the dim early evening light was making it almost impossible to see where they were going. How would they find shelter among the barren rocks and scrubby bushes?

Nate's vision was blurring, and he could feel a blister forming on one of his feet. Up ahead, Jena had stumbled a couple of times and only just kept to her feet. Her face was almost grey. She'd been exhausted and sore before this latest trek. They all had been. Now it was just the two of them, and their frayed emotions were making a terrible situation even worse.

What if he fell and lost the fire ruby from his pocket? Once he went down, he wouldn't be able to get back up.

Jena halted. The raven was swooping overhead, flying in a formation designed to get their attention. Jena pointed to an overhang just ahead of them. "Over there. We can rest there."

Blinking quickly to see better, Nate let out a relieved

breath. They stumbled over the rocks, both desperate to find somewhere to hide and rest.

Jena stopped at the entrance to a small cave. Nate peered in over her shoulder but could only make out darkness. The fire demon, which had been zooming around in the sky with the raven, buzzed past Jena's head and entered the cave, lighting it for them. It was dry and clean, and most importantly, empty.

"All clear," said Nate, relieved. They were unprepared and unable to battle another creature right now. A rabbit could take them on and win. He sat heavily on a large rock at one end of the cave. His feet throbbed, and his head felt like it had splinters running through it. There was a knot in his chest the size of an orange.

Jena looked around their small sanctuary. "It's safe enough for now. At least they can't see us from the sky in here."

"Has the camouflage spell worn off?" Nate looked down at his hands.

"Only just," replied Jena. But Nate saw the truth in her eyes. They'd been walking out there like sitting ducks for much longer than he'd realized. He sank further into the rock, glad he hadn't known until now.

"You don't think the lavaen will start searching the caves?" asked Jena. "She's pretty angry."

Nate shook his head. "No. This cave is too small for her."

Jena sat down heavily, leaning back against a rock. Her burn scars stood out on her face, her hair was knotty and covered in ash, and her dark eyes were dim. She didn't even look like the same person he'd met in the Forest of Ghosts. Her usual vibrancy was gone, replaced by blankness.

He didn't blame her. She'd lost her sister to Remus. Argus was hurt. Half their traveling team was gone. It made him want to scream and rage. Instead, he stood. "Get some rest, Jena. I'll sit by the opening as lookout," he said. "I'll wake you for the next shift. Then we'll figure out what to do in the morning."

Jena nodded wearily. She took off her outer jacket and balled it up. Then she leaned to one side and curled up in a tight ball, closing her eyes. He doubted she'd sleep, but at least she could rest.

Nate walked unsteadily to the cave's entrance and carefully positioned himself on the ground, making sure he couldn't be seen from outside. If nothing else, he could at least give them some advance warning of a threat.

He took out the fire ruby and rubbed it absently with his thumb. The glow enthralled him, as it always did, and he had to blink a few times to look away. The light outside the cave was darkening, and it was almost full night. The demon had said that the bright glow would fade as Argus slowly died inside. He peered down at the fire ruby. Was he imagining it, or was the ruby a little less bright than before?

He couldn't bear the thought, and put the fire ruby back in his pocket.

Sighing, Nate shuffled about on the rock, trying to get comfortable.

Eventually he gave up, accepting the edges poking into his back, and instead listening to the sounds of the night outside their cave. He had so many thoughts screaming for attention, he couldn't even concentrate on any of them.

"Nate..." said Jena quietly.

He looked up. Jena was still lying with her eyes closed.

She hesitated, clearly reluctant to speak. She took a breath, then blurted, "How are we going to find Bree?" Her voice cracked.

Nate took a breath. "Right now, we need to get some rest," he said. "Tomorrow we'll figure out a plan."

She gave a tiny nod and let out a long sigh. "I'm so tired," she whispered. "I'll just take a quick nap and then take my shift. You must be tired too."

"I'm fine," lied Nate. He was just as tired as she was, but he knew he wouldn't sleep. Everything felt as if it was spiraling out of control. He didn't think he was going to have any more of an idea of what to do tomorrow either, despite what he'd said to Jena.

Nate stared off into the outside world through the entrance of the cave, and tried to figure out how in the flames they were going to get out of this mess.

CHAPTER 22
JENA

J ena tried desperately to fall asleep.

She was exhausted and sore and knew it would help. Her wound from the fire hawks was playing up again, despite the healing magic that Bree had worked on it before—her mind skittered away from finishing the thought.

She curled her hands under her chin, trying to find a comfortable position. The ground was too hard, and despite shifting and turning, she just couldn't do it.

Despite her best efforts, she kept thinking of how they'd blithely walked up the side of the mountain to the lavaen's lair. How she'd thought she could handle anything. If she'd known what would happen, she'd never have left Remus's cabin.

Miara would be unsurprised to learn that Remus had betrayed them. She'd told Jena and Bree to be wary, but they'd arrogantly assumed they'd be able to deal with anything. Jena had gotten cocky, and Bree was paying the price. Her hand clenched into a fist and she tried to push away her thoughts. If she was going to rescue Bree, she needed a clear head, and some sleep. She scrunched her eyes shut and tried to force her body to relax. Everything was sore. Her arms and legs felt like they were made of rocks. All she wanted to do was sleep.

But she couldn't.

Somewhere, in the distance, there was a drip, drip, drip. Her heart beat in time to the drops of water, and for a while, she just lay there, counting the drips.

She swallowed a few times over her parched mouth and thought longingly of a drink, but she knew the waterskin was empty.

Opening her eyes, she looked around their small cave. At the opening, Nate was staring off into the distance, a small orange-red flame idly flickering across his fingers. She watched his fire for a moment, mesmerized. He was getting better at controlling his power. She felt a small beat of hope that she quickly quashed. Just because he could hold a flame in his palm, didn't mean he'd figured it out.

She blinked and kept searching. Near where she lay, at the back, was a tunnel. The dripping sound was coming from there. Maybe there was a stream or even a puddle that she could fill their waterskin from?

Standing quietly, she glanced at the front of the cave again. Nate looked so melancholy, she didn't want to interrupt him. She'd just go fill the waterskin and be back before he even knew she was gone.

Except...

That was a dumb thing to do.

"Nate," she whispered.

He jumped a mile at the sound of her voice. The flame in his hand flickered out, and he turned to frown at her. "By the Flames, Jena. Don't frighten me like that."

"I didn't mean to scare you," she said. "I'm thirsty, and I

can hear a drip further into the cave. I'm going to fill the waterskin." She held it up in her hand, as if to prove what she was doing.

He hesitated, then nodded. "Don't go far. Yell if you need me."

"I'm not a child," said Jena, annoyance flaring. Did he think she couldn't take care of herself? That she hadn't taken care of herself her whole life? "I don't need your permission."

He scrunched his eyes shut, rubbing one hand across his face. "Sorry, I know you're just as capable as I am. Probably more. It's just... we've only got each other now. And Argus and Bree are relying on us."

Jena's anger died off just as quickly as it had appeared. She felt the same weight on her shoulders. "I'll be careful," she said, almost like a vow. It was a promise to Bree as much as to Nate.

The entrance to the tunnel was small, only coming up to her shoulders. The rocks were rough but had damp moss growing along the sides. She could hear water dripping in the distance.

Taking a deep breath, she ducked her head and crept down the narrow enclosure, her shoulders hunched. The fire demon appeared behind her, and its glow lit up the tunnel.

"You're coming too?" she asked.

"Yes, Fire Mage," was all it said, before buzzing in front of her along the tunnel.

She blinked at the honorific it had given her, but she was glad of its presence.

It was sticky and humid in the confined space, the moisture in the air making her feel even thirstier. The dripping in the distance became louder, and her dry throat rippled painfully.

She crept along, crouching low, her outstretched hand following the uneven surface of the rocks at her side. The farther she went, the thicker the air became, until it was a struggle to breathe in the humidity and heat.

She was soon rethinking her decision to crawl down the tunnel.

Small beads of sweat ran down her face and neck, and she wiped a hand across her forehead. The wound on her side ached. Only the sound of water up ahead kept her going. Through the demon's flickering light, she could see that the tunnel was even narrower up ahead. This had been a stupid idea.

Just when she started thinking it was a dead end, she saw something up ahead, a widening in the tunnel. It looked similar to the entrance of the lavaen's lair.

Jena froze. She flashed back to the terrifying moment when the lavaen had grabbed them. Nothing she had done had helped; all her spells had been useless against the beast of fire.

Forcing herself to take calming breaths, Jena tried to control her thoughts. Should she head back? She was alone in a dark cave. Finding water didn't seem as important as it had before.

"What's the matter, Fire Mage?" asked the demon. Its light bounced unsteadily over the rocky walls of the tunnel.

"Just—I just..." She couldn't even think of a reason for stopping. "I'm just scared, okay?" she blurted. "What if there's another lavaen in there?"

"There is no lavaen. I would tell you if there were."

She let out a slow breath. She was tired. That was why she was letting her fears get the better of her. "Thank you."

She crept forward until she was at the edge of the tunnel. Cautiously, she peered out from behind a large rock, keeping a wary eye out for danger. The demon buzzed gently beside her, unconcerned.

The enormous cavern was taller than the lavaen's lair, with massive rock formations covered with glittering blue gemstones around the walls. Glowing pinpricks of light in the ceiling marked thousands of tiny glowworms.

In the far corner of the cavern's ceiling, there seemed to be another opening; she could see the faint glow of what might have been the moon. In the middle, toward the back, was a pool of water that flowed under a large rock to one side.

The dripping came from a point above the pool. Water drizzled down the rocks in a tinkling waterfall, then spilled over an outcrop and disappeared into the pool of water. She couldn't see anyone or anything in the cavern.

She tried to swallow, but her mouth was too dry. Without thinking, she scrambled over the rocks to the pool and eagerly dipped her hand into the water. The cool liquid felt like silk through her fingers, and it slipped easily down her parched throat. The demon followed, buzzing above her head as she drank from the surprisingly sweet water.

"We are not alone," it said.

Jena looked up. Her stomach lurched. She knew it. "A lavaen? You said you'd let me know!" she whispered fiercely. Her breath caught in her throat. All this for a sip of water?

"No. A creature of a completely different flame."

Jena frowned. Another fire creature? She looked around cautiously, trying to understand the demon's description.

"Where is it?" she asked hoarsely, her eyes darting

around the cave. At least she had the demon with her. Maybe it would help her escape this new beast.

"You will see soon enough." The demon buzzed over to the other side of the cave, its erratic light throwing brightness into the shadowy corners of the immense space. The blue gemstones made the demon's light glitter and glow.

From her position in the center of the room, Jena had a better view than she'd had from the entrance. At the far end, just below the opening high in the roof, there was an outcropping of rock, a perfect place for anyone who wanted to stay hidden.

At first, she could only see a heat haze, humid air rising from the rocks. But as she watched, the outline of a creature emerged from the shimmering air. It focused in and out of her vision, sparkling in the demon's light. Larger than the lavaen, this new creature was translucent; ripples of shape and color appearing and then disappearing, as the surrounding light murmured and changed.

It opened one eye, and Jena gasped. Like the center of a fire so hot it had turned blue and white, its eyes were so fierce and beautiful she couldn't look away. As she watched, the blue spark in its eyes spread to the rest of its body, and soon the creature was ablaze, blues and purples and greens burning across its back like a moving, water-colored cloak.

The creature stood and slowly walked on four legs toward Jena, its long neck reaching out gracefully. Jena took an involuntary step back before she could steel herself to stay still. It was like a cross between a dragon and an open flame—only much larger and far more magnificent. It had strong front legs, with larger back legs, like a dragon, and its body was a mix of scales and flickering flames that looked almost like fur that would be soft to touch. The creature's head was around three-quarters of the way up to the roof of the cavern, and it had large, translucent wings tucked snugly onto its back. Its coat of flames burned brightly in the dark cave.

"By the Flames, what is that?" she whispered to the demon as it buzzed back to her side. She couldn't take her eyes away even though the creature was twice the size of the lavaen, and looked like it could kill her with one swipe of its enormous forearm.

"It's a shimagni."

"A what?"

"A shimagni. It's very rare. Humans seldom see them."

Jena didn't know what to say. She just stared as the shimagni moved closer. She skimmed through the Book of Spells in her head to find a page with more information on this beautiful creature.

There was nothing. It was the first time she had ever come up empty. If they were so rare, perhaps no other mage had seen one? The thought made her heart skip a beat.

"It doesn't seem too angry with us," said the demon, buzzing around her head.

Jena glanced at the demon. "You expected it to be?"

"It was a possibility. That's why I came with you."

The demon's words momentarily startled her. They weren't known for their loyalty to the human realm. "Thank you," she said.

Ideally, it would have warned her that this creature was in this cave in the first place, but demons were capricious creatures, and whatever help it gave her was entirely at its own volition.

"I serve my master, the Firecaller," it said, as if that were the most normal thing in the world. "You are important to my master."

"Is that something demons usually do? Serve the Fire-caller?" She'd never heard of that kind of loyalty from a demon.

"Not all Firecallers. This one is special."

Jena was about to ask more, but movement from the shimagni reminded her of her current dilemma. She'd ask more later—if she survived.

Right now, she needed to focus on not being eaten by this enormous fire creature. She swallowed hard as the shimagni leaned in closer. Its flames were a dizzying array of pinks, blues, purples, and greens. She couldn't help being transfixed.

"Remember to be very polite to this creature; they take offense easily," said the demon in a low voice, meant only for her.

Jena nodded, unable to do more. The shimagni's eyes blazed with fire, and its teeth glinted in the cave's darkness. Jena's breath stilled; she tried not to move, in case the creature considered it impolite.

Or decided that she was easy prey.

"Who are you that you dare to break into my sacred abode?"

Jena jumped. The voice had appeared in her head, causing a faint buzz. It was a feminine voice, sweet and fluid, but with a sharp edge. The shimagni glared down at her.

"I... Uh..."

The fire creature snarled, the flames in its eyes burning brighter. She reared higher, looming over Jena, showing her long pointed teeth.

"Bow to her. Bow low and she might forgive you," said the demon beside her.

Jena flicked a frightened glance at the demon, and then

bowed low, hoping that the creature wasn't about to slam one of those enormous paws into her back and end her life.

She couldn't die yet—she had to save Bree.

CHAPTER 23
JENA

"I ask again. Who are you, that you dare to break into my home and disturb my sleep?" The creature's words burned into Jena's mind as it waited for her answer.

Jena pulled herself up from her bow and peered up at the shimagni. Her whole body shook as she tried to think of what to say. "Uh...Um... I'm so sorry. I didn't mean—"

"You travel with the Firecaller." The shimagni interrupted her garbled words.

Jena cleared her throat, trying to regroup. "Um. Yes. Yes, Nate is a Firecaller," she said, her voice breaking in the middle.

"The water demon also told me of this man. He is not just any Firecaller. He is the Firecaller. The water demons are all buzzing about it."

Jena frowned. Water demon? She glanced at the pool of water in the center of the room.

"Yes, child. It inhabits that pool at certain times. You should be more careful with water in caves."

"I didn't think—I was so thirsty..." Jena trailed off. Her

voice sounded harsh and loud in the cavern next to the musical beauty of the voice inside her head. "I should have known better." A water demon had captured her on their travels to Remus, and she'd only survived because of Nate. She shuddered at the memory.

"Is that what drove you to disturb my sleep? Thirst?"

"I'm so sorry. I didn't see you. I would never have disturbed you if I'd known," said Jena, thinking how very true that was. The shimagni was enormous, twice the size of the lavaen. She looked like she could kill Jena with a flick of one enormous front claw. Waves of heat came off the creature, like an actual fire was burning over her flanks.

Would it burn her hand to touch its skin? Something inside Jena desperately wanted to reach out and touch the blue-flamed scales, just to see what it was like. She moved closer but didn't dare to put out her hand.

"What is your name, creature of fire?"

She blinked. "Jena," she croaked, thinking furiously. What did she mean, 'creature of fire'?

"Jena. And your companions?"

"Nate, the, ah, Firecaller. The demon, here." She gestured toward the demon. "And also... we have... our friend Argus. He's inside a fire ruby." Jena tried not to let the tears well up again. They burned at her throat, aching to get out. They would save Bree and Argus. It would be okay.

"Argus? The slave of the mage Remus?"

Jena looked up swiftly. "You know Argus?"

"I keep watch on the mage Remus, and know all his familiars. What happened to Argus?"

"My sister Bree and Argus fell in love, which broke Remus's spell. Argus is a free man now." Jena looked back toward the tunnel that led to the cave where Nate was still sitting, oblivious. He had the fire ruby with Argus inside, carefully hidden. "Or at least he's free of Remus."

The shimagni settled back onto her haunches. *"I am glad to hear it. He did not deserve to live under Remus's spell."*

"No, he didn't. Remus is an awful little man." Jena took a breath. "Only problem is that Argus found love and freedom with my sister Bree, but then the lavaen cursed him, so now he's in a worse position than before. And then Remus kidnapped my sister," she said, the words tumbling out of her as if she'd been spelled. "He wants us to free Argus from the curse and then come back and trade him for Bree. If we can't break the curse, it will kill Argus, and then Remus will kill Bree."

Jena took a couple of ragged breaths as she thought about her sister. Was Remus looking after her properly? Or did he have her in a cave somewhere, surviving on bread and butter with a pot in one corner? What would happen if they couldn't save Argus? Nate couldn't even control his powers. She couldn't use hers without risking execution. They were only two people. They wouldn't—

The shimagni moved closer and Jena's gaze caught on the swirling fires, twisting and turning in a soothing pattern over her body. The blue and purple flames captivated her attention, absorbing her panic and easing her jumbled thoughts. She took a deep breath, and her heartbeat slowed.

"So, Remus kidnapped your sister? Tell me more. When? How?" The shimagni's voice had changed. It was more reassuring, focusing her attention back on the present.

Jena gave her head a small shake. "Are you doing that? Affecting my thoughts?"

The shimagni smiled, showing two long rows of sharp

teeth. *"You seemed to be upset. I was just helping you calm down. I can only do it for creatures of fire, like yourself."*

For a moment, Jena battled the urge to tell this creature to stay out of her thoughts. She didn't need to offend her any more than she already had. Except... "Wait. Creature of fire? What does that mean?"

"Only that you are a Fire Mage, and as such, you are more attracted—and susceptible—to my kind."

"Fire Mage?" The demon had called her that too, but she'd ignored it. "What makes you think I'm a mage?" Jena looked around nervously. She didn't like that this creature had already guessed one of her secrets. Was this a trick to get her to admit it?

The shimagni tipped her head to one side. *"Can it really be that you don't know? Interesting."*

"Don't know what?" Jena tried to keep her face neutral.

"You're not just any mage, Jena. You're a powerful Fire Mage, who can manipulate fire more easily than most. Not in the same way the Firecaller uses fire, of course. He is partially made of fire. You simply use it to your will." The shimagni sniffed the air in front of Jena. *"I can smell it on you, clear as day."*

Jena stared up at the shimagni, trying to decide if she was telling the truth. She flicked through the pages of the book in her head...and landed on a page at the back. One she'd skipped over many times.

Fire Mage. Ice Mage. Air Mage. Earth Mage.

They were all listed there. Not common traits, but ones that had been seen before. More powerful than a normal mage, often hunted for their skills. They rarely lived to old age, because their powers drew attention. She tried to breathe and found the air in the cave suddenly thicker.

"You really did not know?" The shimagni peered closer to

Jena's face. *"It is surprising. One with your talent is usually so full of themselves it's hard to get a word in edgeways."*

Jena gritted her teeth. "No, I didn't know. I've had to hide my mage powers all my life. I only know what my master told me."

Which turned out to be not much, given that he'd also secretly been her grandfather.

"Perhaps we can help each other, Fire Mage. I have some need of your skills. And you need my knowledge."

"Maybe," said Jena cautiously.

She knew better than to make a deal with a strange creature she'd only just met in a cave.

"But first, tell me what happened with your sister."

Jena sighed. "We were battling the lavaen, and while we were distracted, Remus overpowered Bree somehow. He says we'll never find her. We have until the coronation to break the curse and bring Argus back so we can swap him for Bree."

"He really wants his slave back, doesn't he?"

"I guess."

"He must need Argus for something important," said the shimagni thoughtfully. *"I wonder what it is?"*

"It doesn't matter why he's done it," said Jena fiercely, forgetting to be polite. "We just need to get her back." She drew in a shuddering breath, trying to regain her equilibrium. All she'd wanted was some water.

The shimagni's blue flames shivered across her back, and her eyes blazed.

"Child, understanding motivation always matters. It helps unravel the mind of your opponent, so you may think like them, and anticipate them.

"I know Remus very well, which is why I know where he might have hidden your sister."

CHAPTER 24

JENA

J ena's heart stuttered. "Where? Can you take us there?"

"I will send the water demon to look for you. Some places are not easily accessible."

A tiny burst of hope speared Jena's heart. "You think it will find her?"

"I do not know. But we can at least check."

The shimagni closed her eyes, and her flames shimmered the colors of water, deep blues and greens. A moment later, a water demon emerged from the pool, a glowing blue creature made of running water.

"Yessss, Rottthhhhell?" it said, rolling its words like running water.

"I need you to search the mountain caverns where the mage Remus hides his treasures. We're looking for a woman."

"She looks like me, but without the scars, and with white-blonde hair," said Jena.

The demon looked at Jena, water dripping from its strange flowing form. "You travel with the Firecaller," it said. It glanced at the fire demon buzzing around her head.

"Yes, I travel with Nate." Jena hoped that admission would help them. The demons seemed to like Nate, and the fire demon next to her had practically admitted it would do anything for him. "He wants to find her as well."

The water demon glowed brighter for a moment, then disappeared.

"Does it know where to look?" said Jena. "You didn't tell it anything."

"It knows. It helps me keep watch on Remus."

Jena tipped her head, frowning at the shimagni. "Why do you keep such a close eye on him?"

"I like to make sure he does not take things too far."

"He's already taken things too far," she said fiercely, unable to keep the pain from her voice. "He enslaved Argus. He tried to kill me and my sister by sending us to the lavaen. He's kidnapped Bree. And we think he's working with Prince Lothar. I'd say that's much farther than he should have gone."

The shimagni growled, a soft sound that reverberated through the room, making Jena shiver. The flames on the creature's body had returned to an almost invisible blue.

A tightness clenched along Jena's scarred skin, and she wished she were better at keeping her mouth shut. She'd offended a creature she had no wish to upset.

"The news of your sister and Remus's associations with Lothar are both new to me. I was unaware he was acting so outrageously. But Argus always seemed lost, and somewhat content to be under Remus's spell. It did not seem so bad to leave him there. Perhaps I was wrong."

Jena nodded, thinking fast. "He wouldn't have met my sister if you'd helped him escape. And he wouldn't have been able to save Nate from Lothar's assassins. Sometimes things happen for a reason."

The shimmering creature bowed her head in a graceful gesture of acknowledgement. *"Perhaps. You are also assuming I would have had the power to help him escape. Remus is a powerful mage, despite appearances."*

"He's cunning and devious, more like."

"Yes, he's those things as well." The shimagni tipped her head, swirling eyes considering Jena. *"Why did he allow you onto his mountain? He has many protections in place."*

Jena hesitated. "He thought Nate had the Book of Spells. He thinks there is something in the Book that will reverse his shrinking."

"The Book of Spells? That's ridiculous. The Guardian would never entrust it to someone else."

Jena swallowed. "The Guardian is dead."

"The Guardian is dead? When? How?" The shimagni lowered her long neck down toward Jena. *"The prophecies have begun. Who holds the Book?"*

"Um…" Jena glanced around the cave, trying to find inspiration for what to tell this creature. The shimagni leaned even closer. A wave of humid air, smelling of ash, brushed over her. She squirmed, trying not to meet those beautiful eyes, but unable to resist. A strong desire to tell the truth washed over her. She pressed her lips together, but the words slipped out. "I hold it."

The shimagni blinked, then gave a sharp nod. *"I smell its power around you. But it is not quite as it was. You really have it?"*

"Yes," whispered Jena, still caught in the creature's fiery gaze.

The shimagni stared down at Jena for several heart-beats. *"It is inside you. You are the Book of Spells,"* she said.

Jena tried to breathe normally. In a very short space of time, the shimagni had gathered her deepest secrets. How was she going to survive in Flame City without giving herself away?

The shimagni seemed to see her thoughts. *"Do not worry. I have a special skill. I can draw the truth from other fire creatures. You had no hope of resisting me."*

"Will you tell anyone?"

"I have no desire to see you hurt, child of the book. Who was the guardian to you?"

"He was my master. He saved me from the slave markets then freed me." Jena tried to hold in her next words but couldn't. "He was also my grandfather."

"That explains it. Thornal was a powerful fire mage as well." She nodded, as if satisfied to have things explained. *"Thornal was a great man. He will be missed."*

This creature knew Thornal? Another whoosh of ashy breath blew the hair off Jena's face. She tried to hold herself steady in the presence of the enormous fire creature, but it was getting harder.

When the shimagni reared up on her hind legs, and flames burst out in bright blues and purples across her body, it took all Jena's willpower to stay still. Only the sense that it wasn't for her benefit kept her in place. Jena stood transfixed as the creature lifted her head to roar at the ceiling, a long keening cry that seemed sad and joyous at the same time.

"Jena! Get ready to run. I'll distract it," yelled a voice from the corner of the cave.

Her attention had been so focused on the shimagni that she jumped at the words. She turned and saw Nate, one arm outstretched like he was about to cast a spell.

Jena held up her hands. "No, no, Nate. She won't harm us," she said frantically. "I don't think," she added under her breath, glancing back up at the creature.

"No, I will not harm you, Guardian of the Book of Spells." The shimagni looked over at Nate. *"Nor you, Firecaller."*

Nate took a step backward, as startled at the voice in his head as Jena had been at first. He lowered his hand.

"She's a shimagni. A very rare, very special fire creature." Jena smiled up at the shimagni, hoping she didn't take offense at her description.

"Thank you, Guardian." She bowed her head.

Jena blinked. "Oh no, I'm not the Guardian. I'm just looking after the book." Jena shook her head, taken aback at the suggestion.

"You hold the book. That means you are the Guardian. You do not think your master wanted the book either, do you? The Book needs a protector. It has found you."

"Thornal was a powerful mage. I can't protect the Book of Spells like he did!" Jena felt a cold sweat break out over her body at the thought of trying to protect the Book of Spells from the Mage Council or Lothar.

"You are a Fire Mage, greater than you think. But he would also have helped you. Sent someone along to provide for you."

Jena thought of the raven. "He gave me *some* help, I guess." The raven pecked her stomach, and she winced.

"And the book protects you."

"Maybe." There were many times she'd found a spell because the Book was in her head. And she could feel its power lying dormant inside her.

Nate moved to stand beside Jena. He put an arm around her shoulders. "You're the Guardian, Jena, whether or not you like it," he said with a grin.

"The Firecaller is correct. But then he does not fully realize what a Firecaller is, and I fear his duty is much worse than yours."

Nate's face paled. "What?"

CHAPTER 25

NATE

"What do you mean?" asked Nate, his whole body tensed for an answer he wasn't sure he wanted.

He glanced at Jena, but she looked as confused as he felt.

The enormous creature loomed over them, her body glowing with fire. When he'd first entered the cavern, all he'd seen was that another enormous, flaming monster was attacking Jena. He'd flashed back to the lavaen, and his instincts had taken over.

Now he could see more clearly that the creature was nothing like the lavaen. Even her movements, although graceful, were slow and soothing. Blue and green fires burned over her body, and he felt the urge to reach up and touch the flames, just to see if they burned.

"The Firecaller of the prophecies will sacrifice much to save Ignisia from the darkness that has fallen over us."

The words floated inside his head, similar to the ghosts who spoke to him, but the shimagni's voice was gentler, like water flowing in a creek. "What makes you think I'm the Firecaller of the prophecies?" Nate said. He wasn't keen on the idea of sacrifice. It sounded painful. "There could be someone else."

"Think of the prophecies. I'm sure you both know them. The guardian is dead, and the Book has been burned."

"Demon beasts have taken wing against us," whispered Jena. "And the raven, it's the Guardian's mark. It flies free, and travels with me."

"Lothar's family name—his father's—is Rosenthorn. He wishes to crush the Throne of Flames, to put it out and destroy our legacy."

"But they never go out. It's impossible," said Nate, feeling like the sands were shifting beneath his feet.

"Nothing is impossible. They have already been partially extinguished. Lothar controls the Flames. That's why he's so desperate to find you; it's a massive drain on his powers. Once he is confirmed as King, I believe he will destroy the Flames completely."

Nate's head started spinning. "Is he really that powerful?"

"I do not know. He certainly thinks so."

Nate thought of Lothar's arrogance when they talked in the Flame Echo. "I'm sure he thinks he can do it. But would it be possible?"

"The prophecies seem to think it is. And they came straight from the Great Mage himself. Only a Firecaller can save Ignisia and push back the darkness."

Mages were made to memorize the prophecies during their training, and Nate knew them just as well as the others. "I'm more likely to die trying than save Ignisia," he said. "I can't use my power properly. Lothar's been honing his for years. He's got all the advantages."

He scrunched his eyes closed for a moment, trying to

control the feeling that everything was spinning out of control. He had felt so sure when he'd confronted Lothar, so positive that this was the correct path. But now everything had fallen apart. Remus was a disappointment, Argus was locked in a curse, and they might never see Bree again.

Nothing seemed certain now.

"What if I don't want to be part of the prophecies?" he whispered into the echoing silence. "What if I don't want to be king?"

"Then rule like someone who never wanted the crown," said the shimagni. *"Rule for the people, instead of the power."*

Nate shivered. When he opened his eyes again, the shimagni had leaned in closer and he blinked to focus on her.

"There can be no doubt the prophecies have begun," she said. *"The demons have chosen."* Her gaze flicked to the demon hovering between Jena and Nate. *"Is that not correct, demon?"*

"It is correct, my lady," said the demon. "The fiery crown has been forged."

Images of the demons crowding around him on the Edges instantly filled Nate's head. He could still feel the heat and energy of it, the demons pushing to be nearer to him in a frenzy of power. "What could you possibly know about it?" Nate muttered, looking around the cave, trying to push away the images, to slow the sudden pounding of his heart. "You live in a cave."

Jena moved closer. "She knows more than you're giving her credit for," she said softly. "She's a shimagni, a powerful fire creature. I can feel her magic swirling around us, even if you cannot. She also keeps an eye on Remus—we should listen to her."

Nate peered up at the enormous creature in front of

him. "Why do you watch Remus? Who is he to you?" he asked suspiciously.

The shimagni hesitated, the flames on her body dulling to a soft pink glow. *"He was once my true love."*

Nate blinked. Of all the answers he had expected, that was not one of them. "Your true love? Remus?" Too late, he realized he should have kept the surprise and disgust out of his voice. "I mean—"

"Do not fret, I understand. But when we were both much younger, he had more character, more nobility." The shimagni paused. *"Although he has always been arrogant and somewhat ruthless."* A flicker of pink flames swept across the shimagni's body, and she ruffled her wings. *"Once upon a time, they seemed more acceptable traits to me."*

Nate gazed up at the powerful creature in front of him, waves of shimmering fire floating across her flank like nothing he'd ever seen before. He couldn't picture her together with Remus. "How is it you were in love with a man?"

"I was once a woman of your world. I was a witch, and I was in love with a mage."

Jena's small intake of breath must have been audible to the shimagni, and the flames stirred again, lighting her body to a deep orange. Nate glanced at Jena and then back at the shimagni.

"It was an illegal pairing, and we kept it secret. I would have done anything for him, until I walked in on him and his other lover." Red flames burned across the shimagni's flank. Her gleaming eyes blinked. *"Still, I would have taken him back. We demanded he choose between us. He became angry and said he would punish us both. He cast a hasty spell and turned us both into the one creature the fates determined we most resem-*

bled. I became a shimagni, and the other woman became a lavaen. The one you encountered."

"The lavaen?" Nate's mind whirled. How was that even possible? Remus was more powerful than they'd realized.

"She was not always the dark creature she is now. She was a talented witch and tried to resist the pull of the lavaen's soul for many years. It has turned her mad, the mix of lavaen and woman in one body. It is how she cast the curse on Argus—no ordinary lavaen could have done that. I was luckier. My shimagni self exists in harmony with my human self."

Nate shivered. He had disliked Remus, but he hadn't known just how terrible he was. "He's shrinking now. He'll die soon."

"Yes, that pleases me, too." The shimagni gave a small shake of her head. "It was the lavaen. She saw what he'd done faster than I did and cast a shrinking spell in reply. I layered it with an eternity spell moments before I turned. He will never break that spell now. Her madness holds it locked in place."

"That explains a lot about what happened," said Jena, her voice cracking in the middle. "No wonder she reacted so badly when we said we knew Remus."

"Yes, that would have been like a bloodstone to a dragon, I'm afraid."

Nate let out a long breath. His heartbeat relaxed again. The shimagni radiated calm, despite the flames that burned across her skin. It was difficult to ignore. "So, what do you know that might help us, shimagni?" he said.

"You are on the path of the prophecy, I know this for a fact. Thornal protected the Way by putting the Book of Spells inside Jena's head. Your power is bursting to get out. It will not end until you have fulfilled the fates one way or another. There is much more at stake than you realize."

Nate took a deep breath, thoughts spinning. There had already been so much at stake, he didn't need more. "What do we do? We have to save Argus before he dies, and then save Bree, but we also need to get to Lothar before the coronation."

"Go where you think you must. Do what you think you should do. You are the ones inside the prophecies, not me. But know this: your time is limited. The prophecy swirls around our kingdom like a beast waiting to strike, and if you do not play your part, we are all doomed."

"No pressure," muttered Jena under her breath.

Nate shot her a look—he'd been thinking the same thing. "What if I'm not the right person?" He swallowed, feeling a lump in his throat that was rapidly expanding to block his chest. Despite the dangerously enthralling creature before him, he could only concentrate on the dread.

They kept saying he was the Firecaller from the prophecies, but he didn't feel any different. He didn't feel special. It terrified him to think that the safety of the kingdom was balanced precariously on his shoulders.

The shimagni in front of them leaned in, her long shimmering neck curving elegantly toward Nate, until her head was inches from his. She looked at him with fiery eyes and time seemed to stand still. Nate couldn't look away and he couldn't blink. All he could do was look into her ancient eyes. *"You are the one from the prophecies. This much I can tell you right now."*

Nate swallowed over a suddenly dry throat. "Then do you know anything that might at least lead us in the right direction?" he asked.

The shimagni hesitated.

"Tell us," said Nate.

"The lavaen, the one who cursed Argus, was an Utugani witch."

Nate glanced at Jena, and she gave a small nod.

"They like their curses. And if she cast an Utugani curse, one of the elders might know a way to undo it," said Jena, albeit a little reluctantly. She was clearly unhappy about visiting the people who had raised her and then sold her.

Nate paused, thinking uncomfortably about Argus's family; Eldrin would have told them by now that Argus was coming home. What would they say when they found out he might die of a curse? How much more devastating would that be?

"Go with your gut. That is all you can do." The shimagni gave a fatalistic shrug, and the waves of flame on her back turned into a swirl of royal purple and deep blue.

Nate locked eyes with the enormous creature, and for a moment, was lost in her fiery gaze. Could they really afford to delay going to Flame City? Lothar had the power to destroy the whole kingdom with his machinations, and Nate was the only one who could stop him.

But Argus was their friend. And if he died, Bree would die too. "Let's go to Argus's family." His stomach churned. What if it was the wrong decision?

But it was the only decision he could make. He owed it to Argus and to Bree.

"Excellent. Now you must rest here with me for the night. It is warm in my cavern."

Nate bowed. "Thank you...uh...shimagni," he said.

"Call me Rothell. That was my human name." The shimagni blew a tiny piece of fire onto a nearby wall sconce, and the wick burst into flame. The fire then carried from one to the next until the entire room was lit by evenly spaced wall sconces above their heads. They gave off a friendly, flickering light that in turn lit up the bright blue gemstones that grew naturally in the walls around them.

The effect was stunning, and Nate paused a moment as he took it all in.

He blinked and realized that Rothell was still staring at him, waiting for his reply.

Nate bowed his head. "I am honored, Rothell."

"You are both exhausted," she replied, moving her gaze between Jena and Nate. *"You need sleep."*

Nate wanted to deny it. He wanted to keep asking questions, to find out everything he could from this creature, someone who finally seemed to have some answers.

But Rothell was right.

He glanced at Jena and caught her swaying where she stood. She looked as exhausted as he felt, black smudges under her eyes, and lines at her mouth that Nate didn't remember seeing before. They both needed sleep. "That sounds perfect."

"Come, Jena, I can be your pillow and keep you warm."

Jena let out a sigh. "You can't read minds, can you?"

Rothell chuffed out a laugh. *"No, child. That is not one of my powers."*

"Good. No offense."

"None taken."

Jena moved toward the shimagni, who had curled up her front legs in such a way that it created a little cocoon of warmth. Jena hesitated, then climbed over one foreleg and sat down, leaning back into the warmth. "This is much better than our previous bed," she said with a sleepy half smile.

Rothell looked down at Nate. *"You need sleep as well, Firecaller."*

Nate nodded wearily and climbed over her foreleg as well, settling down near Jena. Not touching, just close in case she needed him.

As he closed his eyes, he considered the enormous fire creature. He wasn't sure why he trusted Rothell, why he was so comfortable with crawling up to sleep next to her, or why it seemed so natural to do so.

But he was.

He closed his eyes, telling himself he'd just sleep for a couple of hours. Then they'd ask more questions and figure everything out.

CHAPTER 26
JENA

The sizzle and smell of food cooking made Jena's nostrils twitch. Her stomach rumbled, and she swallowed over a dry throat, her mind fuzzy. All she knew was that she was lying on a soft, uneven surface that was keeping her warm.

Opening her eyes, the first thing she saw was a large, scaled foreleg, and the gentle sway of a coating of flame over the scales. She smelled ash and sulfur, and heard the relaxing hum of someone else's breathing.

She felt relaxed and rested, and for a moment, couldn't remember where she was. She just knew she was safe for the first time in a long time. She heard the cawing of her raven somewhere high in the cavern, but when she peered up into the shadows, it stayed hidden in the darkness. She'd let it off her skin last night moments before she succumbed to sleep, so it could keep watch.

She looked over the leg and saw Nate tending a small fire near the cavern's pool not far away, the smoke swirling up toward the roof. And just like that, Jena's memories of the previous day's events came flooding back. Her hands tightened into fists, and she tried not to let panic overtake her again.

She watched Nate as he shoved the sharp end of a stick through a medium-sized fish and started roasting it over the flames, turning it slowly. They'd lost most of their supplies when they'd run from Remus yesterday, so he was obviously making do with what he had.

Nate looked up, saw her watching him and smiled. "Good morning. Fish for breakfast, courtesy of Rothell. She lured it to the surface, and all I had to do was pluck it out of the water."

"Smells amazing," Jena said. She sat up slowly, stretching her sore muscles. Despite the stiffness, she felt completely refreshed. "I feel so good. I hope you got some sleep too?"

"I only just got up not too long ago," said Nate sheepishly. "I'd intended to get up much earlier, but Rothell's magic kept us sleeping. She's the reason you feel so good." He glanced upward and nodded at Rothell.

Jena stood, climbing out of the warmth of Rothell's forelegs. She turned and bowed at the shimagni, like she had the previous day when the demon had told her to bow to save her life. "Thank you, Rothell. I appreciate your hospitality."

Rothell smiled, showing her sharp teeth, but managing to look pleased. *"I'm happy to help you both on your journey toward the prophecies."*

Jena winced at the reminder, but nodded again. "I'm worried about my sister. Did the water demon come back with news?"

Rothell peered down at Jena, her eyes softening. *"It returned while you both slept. It searched all Remus's usual hiding places but couldn't find your sister. No sign of Remus either. We must assume he has her securely hidden somewhere."*

"Then we have to get to the Utugani as soon as possible to find a way to free Argus," said Jena. Her stomach tightened at the thought of Bree in Remus's hands. "We have to get Bree back."

"As soon as we're done with breakfast, we can leave," said Nate.

"I will help you, Firecaller. I will fly you both to the Utugani campsite to save you time."

Jena glanced up at the shimagni in surprise. "You let people fly on your back?"

"Not usually. But sometimes the circumstances require it."

"Thank you, Rothell. That would be wonderful." She'd been dreading the walk down the mountain, especially with the wound in her side. Part of her knew she should be worried about flying on a shimagni, but it was so much better than walking, she could only be grateful.

Rothell stood up abruptly on her hind legs. *"I am going to stretch myself. I have been sitting still all night, and it has taken its toll. If you will excuse me?"*

"Of course," said Jena, hoping Rothell wouldn't be long. They needed to leave as soon as possible. Not that she was going to say that to Rothell's face.

Rothell stretched upwards, reaching out her front paws to catch onto the rocks overhead. She pulled herself upward into the topmost section of the enormous cave. She spread her wings and stretched out her neck, while holding onto the rocks, looking like an insect crawling along a stone wall. As soon as she reached the hole in the roof, she disappeared outside. A rhythmic thud-thud sound showed she had launched herself into the air and was flying overhead.

Jena stared up at the hole in the ceiling for a moment,

wondering how many people had ever seen anything like that in their lives. "You think we're right to trust her?" she asked Nate as she sat down next to him in front of the small fire. Nate seemed just as rested as she felt.

He glanced up from watching the fish, surprise on his face. "We trusted her enough to sleep in her arms all night. She didn't hurt us then; I don't think she'll hurt us now."

Nodding absently, Jena put her hands out to capture some of the warmth she'd lost when she'd crawled out of the safety of Rothell's forelegs. Nate was right. She'd slept like a baby curled up to Rothell.

The burned skin on her face tingled in reaction to the fire blazing in front of her. Funny how the flames on Rothell's body hadn't affected her. It had felt warm and soothing to be inside those flames. Was it because of what Rothell had said? That she was a Fire Mage?

She glanced back at Nate. "Do you think it's true? About your role as Firecaller? And about me being a Fire Mage?"

"I don't know," said Nate, heaving a sigh. "Part of me wants her to be mistaken. It's a heavy burden if she's correct."

"The prophecies have always been vague. No one was ever sure precisely what they meant," said Jena hesitantly. But even as she said the words, she knew Rothell was right. The prophecies had started. There were too many things that lined up. And when she looked at Nate, she saw he knew the truth as well. "We'll just get through this as best we can," she said staunchly, as if he'd spoken. "It's as Rothell said. We're the ones inside the prophecies, so our choices are the ones that matter. It's not about making the best choice or the right choice, it's that they're our choices."

"You don't think there's a correct decision?" Nate frowned at her. "One right way to do this?"

Jena shook her head emphatically. "I've seen too much with Thornal to think there's ever just one way to achieve something. He'd do crazy things; things that seemed to go against everything that made sense in the world, and they'd work out. Sometimes because he'd researched it, but sometimes just because he believed they'd work."

"But he was a powerful mage. He'd been practicing magic for decades."

"I had the sense he was always like that. That it was part of who he was."

"What if I can't do the same thing? What if my decisions are the wrong decisions?"

"But that's just it. Because they're your decisions, they're always the correct decisions."

Nate blew out a breath of air, switching the stick into his other hand like it was getting heavy. "Let's hope you're right," he said softly.

"I can take a turn with the fish," she said, holding out a hand. "I'm pretty good at turning a stick."

Nate shrugged and gave it to her. "If you like."

Jena held the makeshift skewer in one hand, turning it slowly and staring into the flames. The fish sizzled and the delicious smell made her stomach rumble again. Nate put his hands closer to the fire, staring intently at the small blaze in front of them. Slowly, the flames started burning toward him, their flickering drawn to his hands like moths to a light.

"Nate! Stop it, I'm cooking," Jena said with a grin. The flames had moved so close to Nate that the fish Jena was holding was hanging over open air. A tiny bubble of laughter burst out of her unexpectedly.

Nate let the flames go with a whoosh of movement, and

they returned to their natural position. He stared at her. "I'm not sure I've ever heard you laugh before," he said.

Jena eyes widened and she immediately dropped the tiny grin that was still lurking at the edges of her mouth. She leaned forward and hid her face behind a fall of her hair. "It's amazing what a good night's sleep can do," she muttered, but she was just as surprised as he was.

She really was more relaxed than she'd been in a long time. There had seemed very little to actually laugh about for a while now, but even before Thornal's death, she'd always held herself back from spontaneous laughter. It usually felt too much, like maybe she would be asking for trouble if she ever felt happy enough to laugh like that. She didn't even know what it was about Nate stealing the fire that had tickled her funny bone so much.

Nate cleared his throat. "You didn't even blink at the idea I can call fire to my hands," he said, changing the subject. He could see her discomfort, which made Jena want to hide even more.

She forced herself to look at him. "I lived with the most powerful mage in the kingdom from the age of twelve. I've seen a lot of magic in my time."

Nate blinked as if it hadn't occurred to him before now. "He did magic in front of you?"

"All the time. He wasn't supposed to, but he didn't care about the old rules."

"I'm realizing that no one in power seems to care about the rules that the rest of us think we have to abide by," muttered Nate.

His eyes were like dark pools, the shadows on his face—created by the fire—adding to his mage tattoo and making him seem remote and jagged. Except she knew he wasn't at all distant. He was brave and kind and thoughtful. He was becoming less and less like the selfish mage she'd first met back in the Forest of Ghosts. Maybe it was who he'd always been, but he'd hidden it behind the careless attitude.

They were both changing, even if it wasn't visible to anyone else.

She wasn't sure who they'd be at the end of this journey. Maybe the kind of people who could take on Lothar and win? Or perhaps they wouldn't even be *alive*. It was a chilling thought and stripped away the last of her mellow mood. She opened her mouth to answer, when the light inside the cave dimmed.

A whooshing sound made Jena look up.

Rothell had returned to the cave.

CHAPTER 27

NATE

Rothell settled herself near the fire, her flames swirling contentedly across her body.

"Did you have a good flight?" asked Nate awkwardly, feeling like his words were inadequate for the situation.

The shimagni dipped her head and puffed smoke from her nose. *"The air was fresh, and my wings were strong. It was a perfect flight."*

He looked up at her, stretching his neck to see her properly. He considered pinching himself to make sure he really was sitting here with such a creature.

"We need to get going," said Jena. She was still holding the fish over the fire, turning it slowly. "We need to get to the Utugani and see if they can break Argus's curse."

"Yes," said Nate, turning his attention to Jena. "We definitely need to get moving, but we should eat—and I'd like to hear what else Rothell knows." He turned back to the shimagni. There had to be something she could tell them that would tip the scales in their favor. He just had to ask the right questions.

"I do not have all the answers you seek, but I will do my best." Rothell smiled, her large teeth showing in the fire-light. The lines of her body shimmered, and Nate's eyes watered just looking at the multitude of colors hazing across her body. *"You may eat your meal while we talk."*

Jena pulled the fish away from the fire. "I think it's done."

Nate watched as she placed the stick on a rock and rummaged at her ankle. When she pulled out an ornate Hashishin knife, with its red ruby in the center, he couldn't help a tiny gasp.

She used the knife to cut off a piece of the soft charred flesh and then handed it to him.

She glanced up and saw his expression. "It's the knife they used to kill Thornal," she said defensively. She glanced down at it. "I washed it afterwards. There's no blood on it."

"How did you get it? Did the assassin leave without their knife?"

Jena shook her head slowly, clearly trying to decide how much to tell him. "No. I killed the Hashishin. None survived the attack."

Nate didn't say anything, just took another bite of his fish.

"Does that upset you?" asked Jena, her eyes flashing.

He shook his head. "No, of course not. It just reminds me you're more powerful than you realize, just like Rothell said."

Without replying, she cut a piece off the fish for herself and bit into it, closing her eyes for a moment as if to savor the taste.

She set the remaining section of fish on a stone between them, along with the Hashishin knife.

His piece of fish smelled amazing, and he took another

bite. It had lots of small bones, but given it was the first thing he'd eaten for almost a full day and a half, it tasted like the best fish he'd ever had.

He caught Jena looking at him strangely as they ate, and he could only assume she'd expected him to react more to the story about the Hashishin knife. But he didn't feel outrage, he just felt... respect. He was impressed that she had overcome the Hashishin who'd attacked their home.

As far as he was concerned, that was that. He even used the knife to cut off another piece of fish, just like it was an ordinary blade. He felt the pull of the fire ruby in the hilt, but managed to stay in control.

Jena watched him, a slight frown on her face.

Once he'd eaten a few bites, Nate took a deep breath. "You should know that I am only ever impressed by your powers, Jena. It was a shock to find out that you were a mage, I'll admit that, but only because I'd never questioned the old laws before. Now that I've met you and know you, I can see clearly that they're idiotic rules that need to be changed."

Jena took a shaky breath. "Thank you," she whispered.

Nate turned to the shimagni. "Rothell, what else do you know about being a Firecaller? What does it mean?" It was the question that had been plaguing him the most, ever since he'd accepted what the ghost mage had told him about his powers.

"A Firecaller is a very rare type of human who can control fire. It's not just because of an affinity with fire or a connection to it. They're partially made of fire."

Nate shook his head, rejecting her words. "But I can't control fire. Not properly. It controls me." He paused, trying not to let memories of burning flesh and terrified screams force their way into his head. "I can call fire demons, but that's not making fire do my will." All of a sudden, the remaining charred fish in his fingers didn't seem so tempting.

"You have not tried, Firecaller. I am a fire creature, and I will do your will. The lavaen, she is also a fire creature. She would have recognized you instantly. She could not have hurt you, whatever happened to the others. And if you'd known how to wield your full powers, you could have ordered her to your will and she would not have been able to hurt anyone at all."

The words hit so hard that Nate felt like he'd been punched in the stomach. "I should have been able to save us all," he whispered hoarsely. "It really is all my fault." Argus's imprisonment in the fire ruby weighed even more heavily on his shoulders.

"It's not your fault," said Jena, leaning forward. "Don't say that. We shouldn't have listened to Remus. It was our fault, mine and Bree's." Her eyes were bright with the reflection of the fire.

The shimagni snorted out a breath of hot air that blew the hair off Nate's face. *"Enough with the dramatics, both of you. She is a cunning creature, the lavaen. There is no way of knowing what might have happened. She could have tricked you in any number of ways. You went into that confrontation without the full information on who she was, and what she could do."*

"What if I go back and demand she reverses the curse?" Nate asked. He glanced at Jena as he asked the question; she leaned forward, her expression hopeful.

"You could try. But like I say, she's unpredictable and cunning. And you don't have full use of your powers yet. There's no way to guarantee that Jena wouldn't end up cursed as well. It is better to move forward, rather than backward in this case."

Nate deflated a little. "So if I can't look back, what else

can I do? What else should I *know*?" He didn't even know the right questions to ask, let alone know how to wield anything. His hands were clammy, and his heart rate had sped up again.

"Sometimes a Firecaller is called forth by the fates when our world is out of balance. They are given the tools they need. But they can be a savior or a destroyer, depending on their actions."

Nate couldn't suppress his shudder. He certainly didn't feel like a savior. It felt like he'd accidentally climbed onto a powerful, unbroken stallion and told to ride like the wind. "How do I save everyone?"

"The Great Mage was a Firecaller. That's how he created the Royal Flames." The shimagni smiled, and her enormous eyes glowed in the cave. *"The same fire burns inside you. They are yours to use as you will. You need only ask."*

Nate leaned forward and tried not to throw up the fish he'd just eaten. "I'm nothing like the Great Mage. He was powerful, all-knowing. He created Ignisia, gave us the Flame Throne. I can't do anything like that."

"Power has to start somewhere, Nate. It doesn't come into this world fully formed. The Great Mage would have started as you have. He would have had to figure it all out, the same way you will."

Nate stared at Rothell, horrified. "The Great Mage was much older than me when he founded Ignisia and the Flame Throne. He'd had an entire lifetime to learn his craft. I don't have the luxury of time. Lothar is going to take over Ignisia in *three weeks* if I don't stop him. And he wants to do it by *killing me*. I don't have time to learn everything about my powers."

"Then just learn one thing. The one thing that will allow you to control the flames."

Nate stood up and started to pace in front of Rothell and

Jena, his hands tightly clenched. "I ask for a tiny flame and the flames create a forest fire. I don't control them. *They* control *me*."

"You have the power within you. You are resisting it."

Nate felt the anger he'd been suppressing rise to the surface. "I don't know how to do any of this!" He waved a hand toward the outside world. "It's not a matter of resisting. It's that no one can tell me how. Everyone thinks I should have some kind of instinctive knowledge, but I *don't!*" He tried not to look at Jena as he yelled his greatest fear into the cave.

The shimagni leaned her head down to be closer to Nate, her eyes glowing with sympathy. *"I can only tell you what's inside you. I am not a Firecaller; I do not know precisely how it works. There hasn't been a Firecaller for many, many years. There is no one alive who can tell you how to use your powers. But it is always the same for every Firecaller."*

"But we have no time; we have to save Argus and Bree, as well as stop Lothar in *three weeks*. Everyone is relying on me, and I don't know *anything*." Nate gave a frustrated growl. "I never asked for any of this."

"No one asks *for something like this, Firecaller,"* said Rothell, her voice like a growl. *"Do you think I* asked *to be turned into a fire creature? I make the best of it. I do what I can. I move forward, live my life."*

Nate stared wide-eyed up at Rothell. "I'm sorry, I didn't mean—"

"I do not need an apology. But you need to understand there is nothing you can do to change who you are. You cannot give it away, or force someone else to take up the mantle. You are who you have always been. Either you think you are up to the task, or you do not. There is only what you believe about yourself and the choices you make."

Nate swallowed hard against the instinctive need to reject her words. He knew she was right. "Then it's up to me to figure it out," he said, resignation making his voice gruff. He took a breath. "What else do you know about my powers?"

"For a start, you have far more potential power than Lothar."

Nate let out a frustrated noise. "That only counts if I know how to use it."

"It is imperative that you find a way to learn, Nate. For all our sakes. Lothar is a powerful opponent."

Nate took a breath, trying to ease the thrumming in his chest. "I'll do my best. That's all I can promise."

The shimagni sighed out an ashy breath in response. *"That is all we can ask."*

"Do you really think Lothar can destroy the Flame Throne?" Nate couldn't quite get his head around the idea. "Flame Echoes burn in every town and village in the kingdom—the magical ricochet would be devastating. Surely he knows that?"

"Your cousin believes he is on a moral crusade and will stop at nothing. You must be careful."

Nate put a hand to his head, trying to ease the headache that had appeared. "How do you know this? Are you sure?"

"I speak the truth." The shimagni growled in the back of her throat.

Nate held up his hands in apology. "I didn't mean to offend you. I just don't understand why he'd destroy the Flames. They're the beating heart of Ignisia. They power our magic, keep the mages in line, and hold our enemies at bay."

"His mother raised him with the belief. He blames the Flames for King Harad's disastrous reign. He sees the destruction

of the Flames as the only reasonable solution to the succession issues."

"Lothar must be powerful if he can hold the Royal Flames in his thrall and convince everyone that he's the next in line." Nate swallowed nervously, thinking of his own hit-and-miss magic.

The shimagni moved her head so she could look down at Nate with one shining eye. Her scales shuffled across her back, and her wings shuddered. *"He has a number of tricks and potions at his disposal. He is extremely sharp. He isn't as innately powerful as you, Firecaller, but he has spent many years perfecting his craft. Researching ways to augment his magic, gathering objects of power. You have spent your life avoiding your powers. It will be difficult to overcome his machinations."*

Nate winced, thinking of his years as a salt mage. "I didn't do it on purpose. I was told I was a useless mage so many times in my childhood, it was impossible not to believe it." An image of his austere grandfather popped into his head. The old man used to loom over him as he tried to accomplish the most basic magic spell expected of young mages and was visibly disgusted at his failures. If anyone should have known about Firecallers, it was his grandfather.

"There is no point in regretting the past. We must plan for the future."

"So what *are* our plans for the future?" asked Jena, her face tight with worry. "How do we save Argus and Bree, as well as defeat Lothar? In the next three weeks."

Nate's doubts were pushed aside when he saw the fear in Jena's eyes. He wanted to wipe away her worries, to tell her everything was going to be fine. And if he was going to do that, he needed to step up, to regain the determination he'd felt after confronting Lothar. He was the Firecaller from the prophecy, dammit, and people were counting on him.

Jena was counting on him.

He took a breath. "First, we travel to the Utugani, see if they know anything about Argus's curse. Then we plan for our meeting with Lothar." Nate peered up at Rothell. "Are you okay to leave soon, Rothell?"

Rothell bowed her head. *"We leave as soon as you're ready."*

CHAPTER 28

NATE

"We can go right now," said Nate, looking to Jena for agreement.

Jena was standing next to him, her clothes dirty and ripped, with a determined expression on her face.

It wasn't like they had anything to pack. They'd lost everything when Remus disappeared—they couldn't go back to his house in case the murghah was still there. Rothell kept saying that Nate had the power to control the dark horse and its rider, but he didn't know how. Not yet. What if he couldn't do it? What if his power wasn't as strong as they kept telling him it was? It seemed too dangerous, especially when they had to save Argus and Bree.

He sighed. They couldn't risk it. Which left them with very few rations and no change of clothes.

"The sooner we leave, the sooner we get there," said Jena. She looked down at her shirt. "And the sooner I can get some more clothes."

Nate grinned. "And maybe some soap?"

Jena rolled her eyes. "What I wouldn't give for some soap."

He looked around the cave one last time, trying to memorize the details. It had been a safe sanctuary, even for such a short amount of time. It would have been nice to stay here longer, to let Rothell protect them from the outside world. But they didn't have that luxury.

The prophecies were in play, and they had to make their move.

"You sure you're okay with this?" he asked Jena. He knew she was worried about going to the Utugani. She nodded silently. She'd make sure she was fine, because it was what was best for Argus and her sister.

Nate dreaded meeting Argus's brother Eldrin again and having to tell him what had happened. He kept thinking of Eldrin's huge grin when he'd recognized Argus, and how pleased he'd said their father would be to know Argus was still alive. It was going to be difficult.

But they had no choice. It was the only hope they had right now. Someone at the Utugani camp had to know how to undo an Utugani curse.

"I have something that will help you, Firecaller." The shimagni dipped one transparent paw into the bubbling pool. The fire went out around the paw as it searched the depths, eventually emerging with a black stone in her padded palm. The stone burned darker than night, and emanated power. It smelled of earth and stone and sulfur, and it sizzled in the damp atmosphere of the cave.

"What is it?" asked Nate, his gaze locked on the small round object in the shimagni's paw. The fires inside him burst into life, and he took an involuntary step closer. He started salivating with the stinging taste of it on his tongue.

"A lavaen stone."

"That's what Remus sent us up the mountain to get," said Jena indignantly.

The shimagni nodded. *"He was right. Although she would never have given her stone to you."*

"How is it that you have one, then?" asked Nate. His insides burned, screaming with desire to take the stone and use it. To burn everything and everyone around him.

"She owed me a debt and repaid it with this stone. It was her first, so it is even more powerful."

Nate couldn't move his gaze from the stone. It called to him. The flaming power inside him tried to claw its way out. "What does it do?" he whispered unevenly, as his inner fire launched itself again and again at the barriers he was holding against it.

"It calls to you, I know. Resist until you need it, because this power will change you. But it will help you defeat Lothar, and give you the power to overcome his dark arts."

Nate closed his eyes and shook his head sharply, trying to clear the inferno raging inside him. "Thank you, but no. I can't be around that stone. It's too powerful. It would drive me insane holding myself back from being enthralled all the time." Even now, without being able to see the stone, he could feel it so strongly with his other senses that it seemed like his eyes were open. Squeezing his eyes even harder, he clenched his hands until they hurt and pushed down on the fiery power that raged inside him.

A cool hand touched his temple, and immediately the pain eased and the overwhelming pull from the lavaen stone became bearable. He opened his eyes to find Jena standing in front of him, her dark eyes watching him closely, her hand gentle on his forehead. The lavaen stone throbbed from inside her clenched hand. It wasn't gone, but its power was somehow dampened.

She gazed up at him calmly, waiting for him to settle. "I'll carry the stone, keep its power hidden from you, if you like." Shadows flickered across her face in the uncertain light from the shimagni's flames.

"Thank you," he whispered. He closed his eyes again and let the coolness of her hand provide the comfort he needed in the humid heat of the cave. She was protecting him from his own powers. He wished he didn't need it, but he did. He took a few deep breaths and tried to focus like the ghost mage had taught him.

After a while he opened his eyes again. "How do you do that? Block its power?" He watched her closely, trying to understand how she could do something that was so foreign to him.

"It's actually just a quiet spell from inside the Book of Spells," she said softly. "Not often used, but powerful in its own way."

Behind them, the shimagni gave a shuffling laugh. *"And you say you're not the Guardian, little one."*

Jena's wide-eyed gaze flicked to the shimagni. "It's a simple spell. Not like the magic of the powerful mages of Flame City." She removed her hand from Nate's forehead and took a step away, as if that would take back what she'd just done.

"You underestimate your powers, Child of the Book. Thornal chose well when he passed his responsibilities on to you." She tipped her head to one side as if considering them both, her flames swirling over her body in a strangely hypnotic pattern. Her eyes were mesmerizing, blazing strong, holding the power of fire in their depths.

Where the lavaen had been angry and irrational, the shimagni radiated calm and a soothing sense that everything would be all right.

"The prophecies are in good hands." Her body was shimmering and almost translucent. Her flames were dimmed down, but her eyes shone with light.

Jena stared at Rothell like she'd just grown an extra head.

"Thank you," said Nate.

"Before we leave, there's one last thing we need to do." Rothell ambled over to the closest wall of blue crystalline gems and used her sharp teeth to bite off a small piece. She grabbed the tiny blue jewel in her front paw and took it back to where Jena and Nate were standing. *"Here, Jena. Hold this to the wound on your side. It will complete the healing."*

Jena looked up at Rothell in surprise. "How did you know?" she said.

"These stones are healing stones, and I am connected to them, from living inside this cave for so many years. I can tell when someone is in pain."

"Thank you," said Jena as she held the gemstone to her side. She closed her eyes for a moment. "I can already feel it healing."

"It won't take long," said Rothell.

Nate watched Jena as she held the gemstone to her side. He hadn't realized she was still in pain from the fire hawk wound.

After a couple of minutes, Jena opened her eyes. She pulled up the side of her shirt and revealed unblemished skin. "It's gone. The wound has completely healed."

"This whole cave is filled with healing crystals?" said Nate as he looked around at the thousands of growing crystals.

"I am the guardian of the cave and its healing crystals. I do not let just anyone use them."

"No one would ever be hurt or sick."

"They can only heal someone with magic, and they must be used very specifically, otherwise they can become poisonous. Their use is very limited."

"Thank you, Rothell. I am in your debt," said Jena.

"I have a feeling that a few weeks from now, the entire kingdom will be in your debt," said the shimagni. *"Come then, let's go. Climb on my back."*

They gathered next to Rothell, shuffling awkwardly, both hesitant to take the first step. Nate cleared his throat. The reality of the situation hit him. They were going to climb on the back of a flying creature and travel through the sky. She was large, maybe too big for them to actually ride like a horse. How would they stay on?

Rothell grinned down at them. *"I will not break. I am strong."*

Jena glanced at Nate and gestured for him to go first.

Nate hesitated, wondering how his life had come to this. Climbing onto Rothell's back seemed like a terrible idea. Except... he knew he had to do it. He nodded grimly, then stepped forward. He climbed onto Rothell's bent leg, pulled himself up and swung a leg over her broad back. It was a strange feeling, like sitting on a breath of air, warm but insubstantial. Rothell's body shimmered and sparkled under him, almost as if he was inside a mirage on the horizon. Nate shook his head at the thought. He'd never experienced anything like it.

What he was realizing was that not only did it look like Rothell shimmered and moved unnaturally when you were looking at her from a distance, she also did it when you were sitting on her back. Rothell wasn't always completely solid, and it really messed with his perspective.

Nate forced himself to focus. They didn't have time for

him to freak out about traveling on Rothell. Grasping the closest back ridge, he turned to look down at Jena and gestured for her to follow him. He leaned down to pull her up, his warm fingers touching her ice-cold hands. Jena tightened her lips together and climbed onto Rothell's back, right behind him. She put her arms around his waist, the only sign that she wasn't as confident about this idea as she seemed.

"Everyone ready?" asked Rothell.

"As we'll ever be," said Nate, hands tight on the ridges of Rothell's back.

"Hold on while I climb." She leaped up and grasped the rocks, the same way she had when she'd flown earlier. Nate made a garbled noise and clung to the neck ridge he'd grasped. Behind him, Jena gave a startled squeak and clung even tighter to him. The neck ridges acted almost like a seat as they climbed vertically, keeping them in place despite the angle. After moments of what felt like red-hot terror, Rothell climbed out of the hole in the top of the cave and sat for a moment on an outcropping.

"Everyone still okay?" she asked. *"Sometimes that can be a little scary for passengers."*

"You've had other people ride on your back?" asked Jena incredulously.

"Only in extreme circumstances."

Nate glanced over his shoulder at Jena, who was extremely pale, her eyes open wide. She looked how he felt. Terrified.

"You're sure the lavaen isn't still searching for us?" he asked.

"She's back in her lava pool, plotting revenge. She will not bother us."

He swallowed twice before forcing the words out of his

mouth. "Then we're good. Let's go." They had no choice. And if Rothell said she could keep them safe, he believed her.

Rothell's wings expanded out on either side of them, and Nate gasped. Her wings were enormous, but thin as gossamer, and looked like a starry sky. They were the most beautiful thing he'd ever seen.

The shimagni's powerful hind legs launched them into the air, and her wings spread even wider, catching the air currents and making them twist and turn through the morning sky.

Nate squeezed his eyes shut, half expecting to hit the side of the mountain as they flew past. When he opened them again, he could only see clouds and blue sky.

Out in the light, Rothell's body was translucent, shimmering with all the colors around them, reflecting the light. It made her almost completely invisible. Nate tightened his grip and tried not to look down. It was a disconcerting experience, like they were flying on nothing. The powerful flames inside him rose toward the surface as panic took over. They were holding on for their lives.

How had he ever thought that this was going to be okay?

Nate clung to the ridge in front of him, small flames licking at his hands. Behind him, he could hear Jena breathing heavily, as if she were trying to stay calm.

Just like he was.

And then, the world dropped out from under them.

Jena screamed, her hands clutching Nate's waist, as they swooped through the clouds. It felt like he'd left his stomach somewhere high above them. Nate clung desperately to the neck ridge, his fingers going white with the pressure. The shimagni dove low before climbing back up to cloud level, her euphoria pouring through their minds, a bright golden stream that lifted Nate's spirits, even as he was terrified of the flight. As they dipped into a turn, Rothell's enormous wings spread out on either side of them, and the landscape below swooped by, too fast for them to see anything more than a blur of color.

"I won't let you fall, humans." Rothell's voice was warm with humor inside their heads.

Rothell took them higher into the sky, her powerful wings pounding the very air around them into submission.

Soon they were flying high above the ground, Rothell simply using her wings to glide through the air currents.

The wind whipped uncomfortably across his face, his fingers burned from holding on so tightly, and Nate's heart was trying to pound its way out of his chest.

It was the worst and the most amazing thing he'd ever experienced.

CHAPTER 29

JENA

J ena clung desperately to Nate's waist, not caring that she was closer to another person than she'd been in a long time—maybe ever.

She clenched her stomach muscles and felt the raven scrunched up on her skin. When it scratched a claw in painful protest, she wasn't surprised, but she didn't let go.

Rothell's enormous wings beat through the air, creating a thrumming noise that would probably block out the sound of Jena screaming, if she accidentally fell off the shimagni. She tightened the grip of her legs around Rothell's back.

"No need to grab so tightly to me," said Rothell. *"I will not let you fall. See how evenly I am flying?"*

Jena peered around through half-opened eyes. They were flying above the western edge of the mountain, the rugged beauty of the entire range spread out before her like a jagged blanket.

Her breath held in her throat, and she blinked several times. Never in a thousand years could she have expected to get this kind of view of the world. It was beautiful. Everything was so much smaller than on the ground. It no longer looked like separate trees, mountains, and fields—it was a patchwork quilt of different colors and shapes that went on forever.

Between the beats of Rothell's wings, Jena started to look for familiar landmarks. She thought she saw some natural flame echoes that might have been the ones where they saw Lothar. Was that the mountain pass they'd been traveling through when they met Eldrin? Rothell's enormous wings were carrying them so much further than they could ever have managed on foot.

Wind whipped through her hair, and it was only because Nate was a barrier that she could keep her eyes open to peer around.

She almost couldn't comprehend how far down it was to the patchwork landscape below. But she did know that if she fell off Rothell's back, it was a long way down.

It was frightening to know that the smallest slip or accident on her part could send her plummeting to her death.

But it also felt... *exhilarating*.

It was starting to seem... safer. Rothell was flying steadily, and they hadn't fallen off. As long as they were careful, this was a once in a lifetime experience. Who else had even *seen* a shimagni, let alone ridden on the back of one?

Jena tipped her head back and laughed.

What a thrill!

Who would have thought that flying so high would be exciting rather than terrifying? She'd been prepared to survive the experience with stoic determination, not to feel this amazing sense of freedom and wonder.

"*This is how I feel every time I fly, Jena. Can you imagine how wonderful it is to be a shimagni? I cannot help loving Remus still, in a little corner of my heart, for allowing me to experience this life."*

Jena sobered at Rothell's mention of Remus. It reminded her of their mission and the a small fire ruby hiding in Nate's shirt pocket, beating in time to his heart.

"How long to the Utugani hearth?" she yelled to Rothell, trying to be heard above the sound of the wind, and Rothell's beating wings. Her words were whipped away too fast for Nate to hear, but somehow the shimagni knew what she'd said.

"Not long, although I flew the long way to avoid the Murghah, as Nate requested."

Jena watched the view below, her excitement dulled by the reminder of their duty.

"We can't meet it again. Nate's not ready." Jena shivered. She had to believe they'd be able to help Nate with his powers. He was their only hope. He wasn't ready yet, but he would be. She was determined to fight every moment they had left.

She closed her eyes and tried to recapture her enjoyment of the flight. The cool wind buffeting her face, the feeling of moving faster than she'd ever moved before. Perhaps Rothell would—

A screech in the sky above interrupted Jena's thoughts.

Her heart stuttered and her eyes flew open as a cloud of black smoke materialized into a lizard-like creature with leathery wings and flame-colored eyes.

It was still far enough away that she had to squint to see its details.

What kind of creature could it possibly be? She searched the section on beasts in the Book of Spells and found an identical drawing of the smoke-covered creature above them.

It was an ash-fang, a creature Jena had heard of but never seen. It must have been dragged from the depths of the mountains by Lothar, just like the Murghah.

Smoke coiled around its body, constantly moving in strange hypnotic swirls.

"Watch out for its acidic ash and sparks," yelled Jena. "Don't let any fall on you."

According to the book, the ash left a trail of destruction as it burned through skin and plants alike, and the sparks lit anything they touched with an unstoppable fire.

Any living thing was destroyed in its wake.

Jena stopped worrying about falling and started worrying about the creature attacking from above.

"I will attempt to outfly it," said Rothell, but she didn't sound sure.

The ash-fang screeched like it had heard her words, and a spray of ash, sparks and smoke spewed from its mouth, dropping quickly toward them.

Rothell tipped to the side, Jena and Nate clinging to her back as she evaded the attack. The ash fell inches from Rothell's outstretched wings.

What would happen if the acidic ash touched her delicate wings? Jena didn't want to find out.

"No, you won't be able to do it. It's small but fast, and the acidic ash is too unpredictable. It can also appear and disappear at will," said Jena. "Nate will have to control it." She leaned to one side and slapped his arm.

Nate looked back over his shoulder and shook his head. "I don't know how," he yelled, the wind sucking away his words.

"You have to," Jena yelled back, glaring. She pointed at

the ash-fang, then at the three of them. "We won't make it if you don't figure it out."

"I'll try," he yelled, his expression grim. The raven tattoo on his face seemed to shimmer.

Jena looked up. The ash-fang's dark shape was moving toward them in the open sky.

"Now, Nate. You've got to do it now!"

Jena felt the flames of her magic curling around her and prepared to throw whatever she could at the dark beast... except she knew it wouldn't work. The beast used fire to *heal* its wounds, so her flaming balls of fire wouldn't hurt it. They might even make it more powerful.

The only one who could affect the ash-fang was Nate. She clenched her hands tighter around his waist, willing him to believe in himself.

She watched as he lifted one of his arms, gazing directly at the beast that hovered nearby. She felt the power of his magic shift the surrounding air. Goosebumps rose along her arms in reaction.

Overhead, the ash-fang swerved, screeching. The creature swept its dark wings in a powerful beat, then pulled away. It swirled in and out of existence, becoming smoky and insubstantial for a few moments before returning to reality.

Nate swore. "I thought I had it, but then it disappeared for a second and I lost it. When it turns to smoke, it's like it's not there anymore."

The creature screeched again and its magic pulsed through the air.

Nate gasped in pain. A low hum vibrated around them, raising the hairs on Jena's arm.

The fire ruby in Nate's pocket pulsed.

Jena leaned forward, all her energy focused on Nate.

"It's...It's pulling at me. I don't know if..." Nate pushed the words out, every syllable threaded with agony. He put both hands to his head, as if trying to contain the pain.

Jena gasped, clutching him tighter and grabbing the neck ridge in front of her to keep them both on Rothell's back.

"Rothell, he's not holding on—don't do anything crazy," yelled Jena, terrified the shimagni might try another roll.

"I will fly steady, but you must get him to control the ash-fang. This creature could destroy us all," said Rothell, her voice calm inside Jena's head.

Jena leaned close to Nate's ear. "You're the *Firecaller*, Nate. You can do it. You *have* to."

Jena hoped her words were true. If Nate couldn't win against this creature, they were all lost.

Nate growled, his body tensing, his movement knocking Jena backward. Overhead, the ash-fang's hum became louder, the sound heavy in the air.

Nate swayed, hands clamped to his head.

"It is attempting to confuse Nate's powers. I cannot stop it." Rothell's voice was angry.

"Nate! Do your worst, let out your core," said Jena. He didn't seem to hear her. "Defeat it, for all our sakes!"

She muttered a wind spell under her breath just in case, but it was like a breeze against a storm. She couldn't let go of Nate to build a fireball. She desperately tried to find another spell inside the Book of Spells, but anything involving fire would be useless, and nothing else seemed to fit.

Nate was their only hope. Except he looked like he was about to implode.

He felt hot to the touch, growling in an undertone that

vibrated through Jena. His hands pressed to his head as if to block something out, and the only thing keeping him on Rothell's back was Jena's desperate grip.

Perhaps if they let Rothell do some acrobatics? She shuddered at the thought.

"Nate, please," she screamed, desperation carved into her voice. "You have to let go, just like last time."

She clung to his waist, refusing to think about what would happen if he couldn't unleash the fire.

She could see ash dripping from the creature as it flew closer, and she shuddered. What if it landed on Rothell's wings?

An unstoppable fire sounded very, very bad.

So far, it seemed more interested in using its magic against Nate, but that could change at any moment.

And suddenly, as if he finally understood that they were about to die, a burning heat burst out from Nate.

The tremendous blast of energy jerked Jena's body back. The air filled with crackling magic, the sheer force of Nate's fire billowing around them. Even the shimgani shifted under them, her skin rippling in reaction.

As Jena watched, Nate transformed.

He glowed, a fiery light emanating from his skin. The static energy became stronger until it was almost too painful to hold on to him.

Jena gritted her teeth and didn't let go. Her old burns screamed in agony, but she refused to let him fall.

Nate roared, a sound that seemed to emerge from the very depths of the Edges.

Burning power emanated from his body.

Lifting one arm, Nate shot a bolt of fire directly at the ash-fang.

It hit squarely in the chest—but instead of hurting it, the fire made it swell.

The humming grew louder, and Jena swore she saw amusement in its flame-colored eyes.

Nate's fire gave it more power, not less.

Jena's heart pounded so hard she could barely breathe. They were going to die.

Again, Nate roared, and this time Jena heard pain in the sound.

"What else can we do? It's not working–"

And then Jena felt something shift, as though someone were drawing on the heat in the very air. It became even harder to breathe. The cold became colder.

At the edge of her vision, the ash-fang faltered, dropping a few feet before righting itself.

"You are mine, creature. You will do my will." Nate's voice boomed.

The ash-fang screamed, flicked itself high into the air, and disappeared into smoke.

It reappeared directly above them. Jena let out a startled sound and held onto Nate more tightly.

The beast opened its mouth, releasing ash and sparks that floated down toward them.

Jena summoned the same wind spell as before, pushing the deadly mist away. It fell harmlessly to the ground.

Heart pounding, she pressed close to Nate. "We can't keep holding it off like that. You have to get it under your control."

Nate held out his hands again, but this time didn't throw fire. She could almost feel the fire inside him churning as he pulled on its heat for power.

He swayed in her arms, but his hands were steady.

"You are mine," roared Nate, his voice echoing around them.

Goosebumps prickled Jena's skin as his magic flared around them like a thick blanket of power.

The ash-fang screeched and pulled away, flying higher as if trying to escape his reach.

It screeched again, faltering in mid-air as if trapped. It vanished into smoke, then reappeared. Nate trembled violently. The ash-fang screeched again, and then pulled itself higher, and higher still.

Then it disappeared into smoke... and was gone.

Jena searched the skies, waiting for it to return. She kept the wind spell ready, but it didn't come back. The creature had escaped.

She glanced at Nate, wanting him to drag it back, to force it to his will.

But Nate was glowing orange, shuddering so hard, Jena thought he might fall off.

His body sagged like a half-empty sack of potatoes. She only just held on to him.

And then he went boneless.

That was the only way she could describe it.

His glow disappeared, and his whole body collapsed to one side.

It happened so quickly, so unexpectedly, that she couldn't keep him upright. He slipped from her grasp and slid off the side of the shimagni.

Jena screamed.

CHAPTER 30

JENA

Jena reached out to grasp at him, but she touched only air.

Nate was already tumbling, plummeting through the sky below them, mercifully unaware of what was happening.

"Rothell!" Jena yelled, even as the shimagni turned and matched Nate's fall. Jena clutched her neck ridges as Rothell dove into nothing. Nate was tumbling so fast, it seemed like they wouldn't be able to catch him, but Rothell curved under him, reaching out as he fell past, and snatched him out of his terrifying fall.

She grasped him in both forepaws, holding him safely against her chest.

Only then did Jena breathe again. The flight no longer seemed thrilling. She felt like she'd been blasted with so much fear in the last few minutes that her heart might never settle down again.

"We're almost at the Hearth. I will carry him until we arrive."

"Hurry, Rothell," Jena said. If the ash-fang came back...

She couldn't help frantically searching the surrounding air, trying to spot the deadly creature. If they didn't have Nate to control it, they'd be dead. Every wisp of cloud looked ominous, and Jena no longer felt safe—even with Rothell.

She let out a shaky breath and accepted that maybe they wouldn't be safe until Lothar was gone from their lives. At least Nate had used his powers to scare the ash-fang off. That was progress, right?

Except Nate had been knocked out by his own magic.

Jena leaned forward, trying to glimpse him cradled in Rothell's arms. She could only see his legs, dangling from Rothell's forelegs.

Was he okay? Rothell hadn't spoken since her words just after she caught him.

Jena shook her head, trying to banish the doom-filled thoughts threatening to overpower her. She clung to the neck ridge in front of her, leaned close to Rothell's body, and hoped the flight would be over soon.

To distract herself, she flicked through the Book of Spells, trying to find something that would destroy the next creature that dared to attack. She couldn't find anything that would help, especially against a fire-breathing, flying beast like the ash-fang. Mage power had always felt so all-encompassing, so powerful.

The raven shifted against her skin, and pictures of Thornal using his magic in various ways flicked into her head. "There's a spell for everything," he used to say. And it wasn't always the spell you thought of first.

Perhaps that was it? She was using her powers too literally. She needed new ways to fight these beasts. She flicked through the Book of Spells with that in mind, considering each spell from a different angle, trying to see how she might have used it against the ash-fang, now that the heat of battle had passed.

Eventually, the shimagni began to spiral downward toward a large river that wound between an enormous forest and grasslands. If she weren't so worried about Nate, Jena might have been more in awe of the landscape, all laid out below them like a green and blue tapestry woven by a master. She'd never seen anything like it.

They were flying toward a large grassy area near a fork in the Flaming River. It had everything a traveling hearth might need, all in one place. It brought back memories of her own childhood with the Utugani, the freedom of roaming the landscape, living off the land... and the terror of being pushed onto a burning campfire, and sold by her jealous stepbrother before she'd properly healed.

The scarred skin on her face became tighter than usual, and her fingers wedged into Rothell's back ridges so firmly they turned white. Her breath was ragged, and she had to remind herself to breathe deeply.

She was no longer a child, and no one in the Utugani could hurt her. Not anymore.

Thornal had never asked her about her burns, and she'd never told him anything. She'd hoarded the secret of how it happened close to her chest, afraid to tell anyone, until she'd met her sister in the Forest of Ghosts. Even then, she'd only told Bree and Miara the bare facts.

She'd kept everything else squashed inside: all the hurt and betrayal—the secret fear that maybe she'd deserved it, just as Otis had said—until it was buried so deep it no longer touched her.

Now it was all rising to the surface, leaking out and making her feel like a frightened kid again, scared and alone. Her eyes locked on the patchwork of earth below them. Childish whispers ran through her head, saying she hadn't been good enough. She'd done something wrong. That's why Otis had hurt her; that's why Elsa hadn't protected her.

She shook her head sharply, trying to shake it off. They *couldn't* hurt her. She was a powerful mage. She'd burn the campsite to the ground before she let anyone hurt her again.

She needed to focus on Nate and their quest to save Argus and Bree. They were her family now. She couldn't let these stupid memories get the better of her.

But everything was all mixed up in her head—fear for Nate, childhood memories, and the devastation Eldrin was about to feel when they told him Argus was locked inside a fire ruby, a victim of a curse.

Jena squeezed her eyes shut. She needed to stay focused if she was going to get through the next few hours. Pushing everything back inside, she concentrated on breathing steadily, in and out, and on ignoring the pain that was clamoring to escape. Not just ignoring it, actively squeezing it back into the tiny box where she'd hidden it all these years.

When she opened her eyes again, the small dots on the ground quickly grew bigger, turning into people and tents and caravans as they flew closer. She took a deep breath... and felt better.

"I will land away from their encampment. We need Nate to be conscious and able to talk before we go to them. He has asked to be the one who tells them the news of Argus."

Jena nodded, even though Rothell couldn't see her. Nate had been traveling with Argus for a while now. It made sense that he'd want to be the one to talk to the Utugani. And she sure as ashes didn't want to do it. The people below became larger until she could almost make out the individual faces. Jena searched for Eldrin, but he wasn't among the people coming out of their tents to stare up at them as they came closer. She didn't know if it was a relief or not.

Rothell landed lightly on a grassy patch away from the campsite and placed Nate on the ground. He was still unconscious. Jena slid down Rothell's side to the ground, rushing to where Nate was lying prone at Rothell's feet.

She crouched beside him and reached out to smooth the hair from his face. He still looked deathly pale. She whispered an energy spell and gave him a small jolt through her fingers.

He groaned and opened his eyes, their cool hazel color startling against his ashen skin.

"I never want to travel that way again," he said, slurring slightly.

CHAPTER 31
JENA

"Were you awake while we were flying?" asked Jena, trying to hold in her shudder at the thought.

She touched his neck and arms, checking to see if he was wounded.

Nate weakly batted her hand away. "I'm fine. I just used up too much power on the ash-fang." His voice sounded distant, like he was talking down a long tunnel.

"You need something to eat and drink, and quickly, before Argus's family arrive." Jena eyed him fearfully. He had dark smudges under his eyes, and tight lines around his mouth. He seemed...off. Something was wrong, and she didn't know what it was.

Nate nodded, holding his hand over his eyes for a moment, then rubbed them. "What have we got?"

Jena grabbed the water pouch Rothell had found for them and gave it to Nate. He took a long swallow, spilling water down his chin.

"There's also some fish from breakfast." Jena handed

him the bundle wrapped in leaves and hovered while he unwrapped it. He was shaking, and his face was still grey.

"I don't feel so good." Nate's voice was confused. He dropped the bundle of fish and started to shake. Jena crouched back down beside him, touching his forehead. His skin was cold and clammy. Her heart sinking, Jena quickly scanned the Book of Spells to find more information about Firecallers, and the aftereffects of their powers.

"Rothell, do you know anything that might help?" she said desperately.

"I do not know enough about Firecallers. Search the Book of Spells. There will be something that will help him in there." Rothell leaned closer to Nate and took a sniff. *"He doesn't smell right."*

"I can't find anything useful in the Book," said Jena. "Not for something like this."

"There must be something. Look again."

Jena bit her lip against the sharp retort she wanted to make. The shimagni was right. There must be something. And hadn't she just told herself that she needed to think outside the box? She'd meant it in relation to fighting creatures like the ash-fang, but it could work here too. She flicked through the pages, desperately trying to find something that might help.

Nate lifted his head, the sweat on his forehead making his hair wet. "I don't know if I've ever told you..." he said in a hoarse whisper. "I see ghosts... Something about being close to the Edges." He took a gasping breath.

"It doesn't matter that you see ghosts. Just save your energy," said Jena, keeping her voice soothing, despite her panic.

"It matters...there's a ghost mage. He's been following me. He says...look for the spell on page 157...Book of Spells."

Jena frowned. It wasn't the weirdest thing she'd ever heard, but it was still strange.

Nate coughed as if his insides were trying to get out. "He says you have to hurry."

Jena hesitated a moment longer but then checked the page. She didn't have anything else to lose. It was an energy healing spell, like the small one she'd just used on Nate, but much bigger and way more powerful, using energy from the Edges.

Usually for when someone was dying.

Her heart skipped a beat. "He definitely says page 157?" she said, trying to stay calm.

Nate paused, his brows raised. Then he nodded. "Yes, that's the one."

"We can trust this ghost?"

"Yes. Think so... He told us... what Remus had done." He paused as if listening. "Says to be quick."

Jena felt her blood run cold. "He's sure? It's the only option?" She'd never had to use the spell herself, but she'd seen Thornal do it once. It was complicated and could easily go wrong. What if she couldn't get it right?

"He says be quick, or...." Nate swallowed hard. "Or he says I'll die." His eyes looked up at her, the whites showing his fear.

Jena nodded to herself. If Nate was dying, she had to use the spell quickly.

She had no choice.

She took a deep breath and stood. Reading the instructions carefully, she made sure she understood everything she had to do. Chanting low, Jena concentrated on saying the words exactly right. Opening her mind, she sought the energy from the Edges that no-one—except maybe Nate—could see.

She started chanting louder and louder, bringing the energy all around her into her body. It pushed back at her, almost knocking her over. She planted her feet wide to make sure she didn't fall. She held her hands cupped in front of her and, still chanting the words of power, pushed everything she captured into her hands. Soon, there was a glowing ball, sizzling and bucking between her palms. The energy was trying to escape her control, pushing, battering at her defenses until she wondered if she could really make it do what she needed.

Invisible hands started to claw at her, scrabbling to get back from the Edges, trying to use her to reenter this world.

Her breath came in short gasps, and she had to focus to keep them at bay. She stepped closer to Nate, who was watching with shadowed eyes. Pushing her hands to his chest, she thrust the power she had pulled from the Edges into Nate, hoping that she'd done it right, and hadn't just made it worse.

Then everything went black.

JENA GASPED, feeling as if hands were still clawing at her throat, choking her. She battered against her attackers but only encountered empty air. She closed her throat on the scream that threatened and made herself look around.

Nate was lying next to her, his face pale, his eyes closed.

"Is he okay?" she asked Rothell who was looming next to them.

"I think so. His heart is beating, and I can't sense anything wrong with him. He no longer smells strange."

Jena nodded, trying to remember what happened after

the spell last time Thornal had done it. "I think the spell takes a while to take root. How long have I been out?"

"Only a minute or two. The Utugani warriors are gathering nearby."

Momentarily panicked, she tried to sit up. Her head spun, and bile rose in her throat, her breakfast along with it. She vomited onto the ground beside her, then lay back down again, closing her eyes.

"You are still very weak. You will need to rest." Rothell's voice was soothing inside her head. *"It was a powerful spell."*

"I don't think we have time to rest, not if the Utugani are coming." She didn't open her eyes, and her words were barely a whisper. "Do you really think Nate is okay?"

"He is fine. It is simply the aftereffects of the spell."

"How do you know?"

"You saved his life, that much I know. He used his powers, but maybe too much at one time. Or maybe the ash-fang did something with its own magic. I do not know. But whatever happened, it drained him dry. I felt it. He was dying, and you saved him."

Jena leaned back in the grass, trying to stop the spinning in her head. "What now?"

"You need food and rest. You need to ask the Utugani for help. But first you must talk to their warriors and convince them we are friends and not foes."

Jena took a few deep breaths. At least Nate wasn't dead. She sat up, slower this time. "What if they won't help us?"

"It is your responsibility to make sure they do. If you are to save Argus and your sister, you need their help."

"What if we can't undo Argus's curse?" Jena couldn't help the plaintive tone in her voice. Everything was going wrong.

"There will be a way to undo what has been done. There always is."

Jena glanced up at Rothell. "What about Remus, the shrinking mage? He never found a way to undo what had been done."

"Ah, but there was a way. He could have reversed the spell he put on us. Then the witch could have undone her spell. But he chose not to do that. He was arrogant and self-righteous; and he thought he could find a way around it. Now it is too late. She is no longer human and he is trapped."

Jena thought she heard a trace of satisfaction in Rothell's voice.

CHAPTER 32
NATE

Despite their hard faces, the tense lines around the mouths of the Utugani men were easing, and the rigid stances they had adopted at first had relaxed. Their knives had been returned to their leather pouches, and they'd stopped looking at the shimagni behind him every two minutes. Best of all, they were now making eye contact with him.

So far, so good.

Nate swallowed and tried to push down the nausea that was threatening to overwhelm him. He just had to last a little while longer. Rothell had said they needed to eat as soon as possible after the spell Jena had performed, but first, they had to convince the men in front of them that they weren't a danger to the hearth. The Utugani were suspicious, and rightfully so.

These were dangerous times.

He flicked a quick glance at Jena. She was maintaining a quiet and solemn presence, ignoring the surreptitious glances the warriors kept giving her scarred face.

Did she notice? Is that what happened every time she

met someone new? He'd seen the way Remus had looked at her, but he'd just assumed it was because Remus was awful. Some people thought burn scars meant you were cursed, marked by the fire that ruled the kingdom. Is that what the Utugani thought too? Would they even let them in?

It made him want to tell them off, to give them a lecture on not staring. His stomach lurched, and everything spun around him for a moment. Jena gave him a worried look, and he tried to smile at her, to show her he was fine. He was pretty sure it looked more like a grimace.

He took another deep breath, trying to maintain a facade of easy affability. It wasn't easy. On top of everything else, he felt guilty for not being able to return Argus to his people in one piece. The fire ruby felt like it was burning a hole in his pocket. He didn't want to be here, about to give them bad news.

The eldest Utugani warrior had leathery skin, the deep lines revealing the years he'd lived. He wore a shirt and trousers in brown and green, and he had a patch covering his right eye. He caught more with that one eye than his companions did with two. The one-eyed man watched as Nate and Jena replied to the questions hammered at them by the younger, stronger men who bracketed him.

"We need proof of who you are before we go to the Utugan," said the man on the right, his green shirt blending with the green of the valley.

"If we could speak to Eldrin, he would tell you we are friends of Argus's. We must speak to Eldrin or the Utugan." Nate held still, trying to coerce them to agree by the power of his thoughts.

"It won't work, you know. You're not using the right spell." The ghost mage appeared at his side, and Nate jumped

slightly. He tried to keep his face from showing the annoyance he felt when the ghost mage appeared like that. He saw the one-eyed gypsy watching him thoughtfully and kept his face blank.

"The good news is that these fellows seem to be coming around to your point of view without the need for a coercion spell. You've argued our point well."

Nate nodded, then stopped, realizing too late what he was doing. The young Utugani warrior in front of him frowned, and he inwardly cursed. He focused again on the older man in the middle.

"I can tell you things about Argus that no one else would know. Things he would only have told a friend. Would that help?"

"What kind of things?" The old man paused; his one eye clear as he looked at Nate.

"Argus used to be a flame guard," said Nate.

The old man shrugged. "That's not a secret."

"He's loyal and brave. Has his own honor code that he follows religiously," said Jena.

"Doesn't everyone?"

"He recently rescued Eldrin from a water demon," said Nate. "We were there. We helped him."

The old man shared a look with one of the younger men.

"He has a scar on his elbow. He once told me he got it when he was a kid, when he and Eldrin were mucking around with play swords," said Jena. Nate glanced at Jena. He hadn't heard that story.

The old warrior frowned. "I was there for that one. Argus didn't even cry, not once."

Jena gave a tiny smile. "I can see he hasn't changed."

"Now, tell me who *you* both are," said the old gypsy. He waved his hand. "Other than a friend of Argus."

Nate cleared his throat. "My name is Nate. I'm a mage. I was also a salt collector until recently." He paused, trying to think what it would be best to tell them. "Argus helped me escape from assassins, then he took an arrow for me. I owe him my life twice over. More probably."

"Argus was always brave," agreed the old gypsy. "Nothing has changed in that." He dropped his gaze to Jena. "What about you?"

"I'm Jena. My sister Bree and I, we've been traveling with Nate and Argus. We were going to the shrinking mage's home to get help with our quest." Jena's eyes filled with tears. "Argus and Bree, th-they...fell in love." Jena swiped at her eyes, trying to wipe away the moisture.

There was so much more to the story, but Nate managed to keep his mouth shut. He also noted that Jena had avoided telling the old warrior who she was. She also didn't mention she'd been raised with the Utugani people.

"You know, that's where Remus underestimated Argus," said the ghost mage. *"The old fool always misunderstood love. It explains the mistake he made with the lavaen and the shimagni as well."*

Nate had to concentrate hard on keeping his gaze on the older warrior, and not looking at the ghost mage. It was harder than it should have been. His stomach was making strange noises and everything around him was blurry.

The old one-eyed Utugani let out a breath. "My name is Seban. You may enter the camp. But you will need to set up to one side, away from the main hearth." He glanced at Rothell. "That creature is too large to be let loose among our people."

"But–" One of the younger men protested.

Seban held up a hand and silenced him. He gestured with his head, and the man on his right—the green shirt warrior—turned without another word and ran toward the camp. Going to warn the others about what was happening, Nate assumed. He let out a breath. They'd done it. The world spun a little around him, but he couldn't help his relieved smile.

"Thank you," said Nate. "You won't regret trusting us. Argus is our friend."

"Come. Follow me, I will lead the way." The two remaining warriors turned and walked away, Seban nodding at Jena and Nate. Nate gestured back to Rothell, who stood up and followed them with her graceful four-legged amble.

As they came closer to the camp, he realized that the green-shirt warrior hadn't just gone to warn the others. He'd gone to fetch the Utugan and Eldrin. The two men were striding across the field of grass toward them, both frowning.

Nate swallowed. The moment was here. He had to tell Eldrin and his father what had happened. How Argus had been cursed and might die because of him. They slowed and stopped, Rothell waiting quietly behind them.

Eldrin looked just the same as before; big and broad shouldered, his long strides eating up the distance between them. Striding next to Eldrin was an older man who was obviously their leader, the Utugan. He looked so much like Argus, it hurt to look at him. Tall, strong, broad shouldered. Long blond hair and a big beard that hid half his face. He was nothing like the cheerful Eldrin, and everything like the stoic Argus. He was wrapped in the ornate furs of the wild bears they revered, the brown and silver coat glistening in the late morning sunlight. He had

223

a large bear tooth pierced through the fleshy part of his ear.

Eldrin arrived first, his bright eyes moving from Nate to Jena. "What's happened? Where's Argus?" he asked, looking around. "Where's Bree?"

Nate took a deep breath but waited until the Utugan arrived before answering. "Eldrin, I'm so sorry," he said, looking at Eldrin and then his father, his chest tight. He had to force the words past his lips. "We fought a lavaen, only a day past. The creature cursed Argus. He's inside this fire ruby, held in time, so we can save him before he dies." He held up his hand with the fire ruby again. "But we don't have long, and we don't know *how* to save him. We need your help."

Eldrin sucked in a breath and his face paled.

Beside him, the Utugan took a step backward, his hand half raised as if to deny the news. "No," he said, his face creasing with denial. "He's coming home. Eldrin told us he's coming home."

"We were betrayed by Argus's master, Remus," Nate continued, trying to say it all at once. "He tried to kill Jena and her sister Bree." He gestured to Jena, who nodded. "When Argus was cursed, Remus kidnapped Bree to use as a bargaining chip. If we're going to save them both, we need to find out how to break the curse."

"You saw it happen? He's truly inside this stone?" asked Eldrin. His face seemed calm, until Nate looked into his eyes and saw the wild storm raging there. Eldrin reached out as if he planned to take the jewel, but Nate pulled his hand out of reach.

Nate swallowed hard. "I'm the one who put him inside the fire ruby, to extend his life long enough for us to save him." He looked away, unable to bear the look in Eldrin's eyes any longer. "I'm sorry, Eldrin. I should have protected him better."

"Argus is a grown man," said Eldrin, still looking at the fire ruby carefully, as if he might see Argus's face inside it. "Not a child in need of protection. But what help can we possibly give when you have such magic?"

"We need to find out more about the curse, and quickly," said Jena. "We believe the lavaen was once an Utugani witch. Is there someone in your hearth that might know about Utugani curses?"

"I don't understand how something like that could happen, but..." Eldrin glanced at his father, and then back at Nate. "We might have someone who can help."

Nate took a step closer to Eldrin. "Then we need to speak to them urgently. There's not a moment to lose, if we are to save him."

Eldrin nodded solemnly and held out a hand, grasping Nate's shoulder. His eyes were darker than they'd seemed previously, but his face remained impassive. "Thank you for coming to us," he said. He looked at Jena. "We will help you save them both."

The Utugan stepped forward. His face was pale, but he gave no other sign of emotion after his initial outburst. "You may enter our hearth, you and your creature," he said in a gravelly voice. He glanced warily up at Rothell, who was looming behind them. "We will discuss the curse once you are settled." He glanced around. "You have no supplies?"

"We lost everything when we fought the lavaen," said Nate. He thought longingly of a change of clothes and his bedroll. He didn't have either anymore. Even a piece of Jena's terrible jerky would have been a blessing at this point.

"Then I will send someone with food and other things you might need. Come." With that, the Utugan turned and left. His strides weren't quite as long and confident as they'd been when he arrived. Eldrin nodded sharply at Nate and followed his father.

Nate just watched them for a moment, trying to control the nausea that was still churning in his stomach.

"We'd better go, too," said Jena. She turned and gestured at Rothell and then started walking.

Nate put the fire ruby back in the small pouch where he'd been carrying it, then slipped it into his shirt pocket. Then he trudged across the grassy meadow into the Utugani Hearth.

CHAPTER 33
JENA

"*I make them nervous. I can smell it.*" Rothell's body swirled with violets and blues. Her tail swished about anxiously, making the flames in their small hearth burn higher. Jena shifted away from the brighter fire. She was unrolling the small canvas shelter the Utugani warriors had brought them when they first arrived—along with wood for a fire and food for their aching stomachs.

Jena stopped what she was doing and put one hand on the side of Rothell's neck, running it soothingly over the shimagni's soft scales. "They'll get used to you," she said softly. Rothell leaned closer and hummed like a cat.

"That's why we're here, and not in the main part of their camp," said Nate. He was next to the fire, adding more of the chopped wood. They'd just devoured some of the fresh berries and delicious apple cake the warriors had left behind, and Jena felt like maybe she wasn't about to keel over.

They were using the fire to heat some water so they could have the hot tea they'd been given as well. Nate still looked tired, his skin pale and dark circles under his eyes, but thankfully he didn't look like he was about to faint.

The guard with the green shirt—Davos—had shown them where to set up their hearth, but they hadn't talked to anyone else since then. It was a spot on the far edge of the camp, away from the main hearths. Davos had said it was so Rothell could stretch out, but Nate was right—it was more likely so that she didn't scare the rest of the Utugani.

The Utugan had said he would give them time to set up and then they could talk.

"We should be talking to someone, finding a cure for Argus," Nate said roughly. He was clutching Argus's fire ruby. He stood and walked a little way toward the main Utugani camp, and then back to their small hearth, his impatience palpable.

The flames in the fire followed his path, leaning in his direction wherever he went. Jena didn't think he was even aware of it.

"They said they needed to gather more information," said Jena. "For now, our best option is to wait." She hoped she was right. Surely they hadn't forgotten about Argus?

What made her nervous was that the Utugani people in the main camp were distracted. Something was happening —a lot of people were moving about, anxious expressions on their faces that had nothing to do with the shimagni that had just appeared in their midst. They seemed to be organizing and... packing up? Except it wasn't the right time for them to be leaving this campsite; it was far too early.

Nate stalked back and poked at the fire with a stick, this time more aggressively, accidentally knocking a larger piece of wood off the top. Sparks flew into the sky around them, and Nate's face was momentarily lit up like a demon's. Jena shivered, despite the warmth of the day.

When they'd first arrived, they'd been busy. Nate had lit the fire, while Jena had dragged over a couple of logs to sit on—with help from Rothell—and they'd prepared and then eaten their meal.

But now they only had the shelter to put up, and Nate was getting antsy about saving Argus. They needed to start actively doing something about the curse. They'd waited long enough. "Come on, help me finish the shelter," said Jena. "Then we'll figure out what to do next."

Nate grumbled under his breath but took the other edge of the woven material and helped to pull it out. Together they worked to put it up, using poles and ropes to keep it in place. They'd been on the move for so long, always doing something, having a goal in mind, that waiting for someone else to come to them felt unnatural. She completely understood Nate's impatience, but she didn't know what to do about it. They had to wait on the Utugan—that much she remembered about Utugani camp protocols.

Just as they were putting the finishing touches on their shelter, still wondering if they were doing the right thing, Jena sensed movement and glanced up. Seban stood on the far side of their small fire, his expression stern. The lines on his face were harsh in the early afternoon light. There were two Utugani warriors standing at attention not far off, both holding sharpened spears.

Jena shifted uncomfortably. They didn't look welcoming in the slightest. She smiled, attempting to look like someone the Utugani could trust. "Good afternoon.... uh... Seban. Do you have information for us?"

"Come. The Utugan wishes to speak with you." Seban

looked sternly from Jena and Nate to Rothell, then turned and strode away toward the far end of the camp.

"That was awkward," said Jena, pushing the last wooden peg into the ground. She picked up the bedrolls they'd been given and threw them inside the tent.

"At least the Utugan is going to see us. Hopefully he's going to have some information," said Nate.

"Did Seban look like someone who was going to be helpful?" Jena shook her head. "Something is going on." She looked up at the shimagni, wondering how the enormous creature would fit into the Utugan's tent.

"I will wait here," Rothell said softly. *"Call me if you need me."*

"Come on, let's go. We don't want to keep him waiting," said Nate. He touched the shirt pocket where he was keeping the fire ruby, as if reminding himself why they were on this quest. Then he turned and strode off in the same direction as Seban, his long legs eating up the head start the guard had gained.

Running a little to catch up, Jena joined Nate as he walked through the camp after Seban. She looked back over her shoulder at Rothell sitting serenely by their campsite. She wished the shimagni could come with them. At least then she'd feel safer. Things could still go either way with the Utugani, especially if the Utugan decided that Argus being inside the fire ruby was their fault.

She knew how capricious the Utugani could be.

In the family one minute, sold as a slave the next.

She hardened her expression and pushed away her old insecurities. They wouldn't help her now. And she was no longer the scared young girl. She was a powerful mage. Let them try to hurt her.

In the distance, standing by a large pot over a campfire,

she saw an old woman watching them, a satisfied smile on her face. Jena nodded briefly, but her nerves were tight at the thought of meeting with the Utugan. She rubbed her scarred hand, smoothing the bumpy skin between the fingers of her other hand.

At the entrance to the Utugan's tent, two guards glared down at them and didn't move aside. Seban had already gone inside a moment earlier.

"Are we allowed in?" asked Nate. "We were told he wanted to speak with us."

One of the guards reluctantly pulled aside the hides and gestured for them to go inside.

Jena ducked her head under the heavy material, entering the large cave-like room. Enclosed lanterns lit the space from several corners. Thick woolen rugs and leather hides covered the floors, and wildflowers poked out of metal urns. Large, colorful pillows were scattered across the room, along with low woven chairs. The Utugan was standing in the middle of the tent, his features stern. Seban stood to one side, his sharp one-eyed gaze watching them closely, while another older guard stood by the entrance.

A young girl—no more than twelve or thirteen—with tanned skin and long dark hair moved closer to offer them a steaming lemon drink and small chunks of bread and cheese on a wooden board.

"This is my youngest daughter, Ellie," said the Utugan. "She's the light of my life."

The young girl blushed and glanced at Jena and Nate. "He likes to embarrass me," she said.

A flicker of unease crossed Ellie's face when she saw the burns on Jena's cheek for the first time. Jena's uneven skin contracted and tightened, a reaction that made her feel even more awkward. She hated it when new people reacted to her scars; the instinctive reaction was always pulling away, a blink of fear and horror. It made her self-conscious, and somehow it was worse this time because she was back with the Utugani where it all began.

But Ellie was too practiced at receiving guests to falter for long. "How do you do?" She smiled sweetly, her initial flicker of reaction wiped away. Jena made herself relax, smiling back and holding out her hand in greeting. Jena wondered if it would be rude to ignore Ellie's hand, but Nate had already taken it in a firm handshake. She put out her hand and tried to ignore the frisson of fear she always felt when someone she didn't know touched her scars. The young girl shook both their hands, and then with a curtsy to her father, slipped out of the tent.

They were alone with the Utugan and his two guards. The Utugan sat down in one of the low chairs covered in furs and gestured for everyone to sit down as well. His eyes were set deep in his face, and he looked tired. He seemed older than he had just a few hours earlier.

Jena was certain it cost him to be sitting here, acting as if nothing much had happened. But much like Argus, he seemed like a man who was used to doing things rather than thinking about them. And given that he was the leader of all the Utugani, he wouldn't want to show weakness, even to unknowns like Jena and Nate.

Nate moved closer and Jena followed, both sitting down across from the Utugan.

"So, do you have new information about the curse?" asked Nate, leaning forward eagerly.

CHAPTER 34

JENA

The Utugan frowned.

He opened his mouth to reply when a sudden clamor rose at the entrance to the tent, as the guards tried to keep someone out. Jena turned to watch as Eldrin pushed the tent flaps aside and marched into the room. "Father, I insist on being here for this meeting," he growled at the Utugan. "You can't keep locking me out of everything."

The Utugan's expression shifted as he looked at his son. He gave a resigned sigh. "We are on the precipice, Eldrin. We cannot falter. Our people must survive what is coming."

Eldrin frowned, his eyebrows nearly meeting in the middle. "I know, Father. That's why I'm here. I can help. There is no need for you to carry the burden all on your own."

"I'm trying to protect you, Eldrin. You only just returned to us. You escaped from a *water demon*. You need rest. You did not ask for the mantle of leadership."

Eldrin strode closer, until he was standing next to his father. "No one asks for it. It's just what happens," he said.

He looked older and more serious than Jena had ever seen him. "I can help you."

"I—I am... not used to... getting help." The Utugan cleared his throat. "Come, sit with us, Eldrin. We have much to discuss."

Eldrin took a seat next to his father, his expression stern. But then he winked at Jena. She let out a relieved breath. Having Eldrin here was going to make this much easier.

"We need to talk about many things," said the Utugan, his words brusque. "But first, you need to tell me what happened to my eldest son and how we can save him."

His expression was haunted, and Jena's heart clenched. His pain was her responsibility. Eldrin had come back to his father with the news that Argus would be returning home, and now he'd been taken from him again.

"I'm so sorry," she blurted. "We allowed ourselves to be tricked by the Mage Remus. We should have known better." Her guilt hung like a heavy travel cloak around her, uncomfortable and tight, choking her at the neck. If she'd been more savvy, if she'd just thought about it, she'd have realized it was too dangerous, that Remus wasn't on their side.

Argus and Nate wouldn't have had to come save them, and they'd be having a very different conversation right now. She'd been blinded by her arrogant confidence in her own powers.

"My son was a grown man. I do not blame you for his..." he gestured toward the fire ruby that was now in Nate's palm. "...current state. But I do plan to help ensure his safe return."

Jena could only stare, her fears about what the Utugan would say wiped away with one short sentence. "You should—"

"You cannot tell me what I should or should not think. It is not your responsibility. Now, how long does my son have?"

Nate cleared his throat. "He has approximately twenty days, give or take a night. We need to fix the curse and heal him, and we need it now."

Jena tried not to think about her sister, trapped by Remus, maybe for the next three weeks. If he hurt her, Jena wouldn't rest until she made the shrinking mage pay. At least she knew he was keeping Bree alive until they brought Argus back to him. Once Argus was out of the fire ruby, they'd rescue Bree in a way that didn't involve Argus becoming Remus's slave again.

"I have talked to our elders, and they have never heard of a witch being turned into a lavaen," said the Utugan, with a glance at Eldrin. "It is an extraordinary story."

"All we know is that she was turned into a fire creature by her lover, the mage Remus."

The Utugan raised his eyebrows, then shook his head briefly, like the crazy antics of witches and mages were unsurprising to him. "As I said, it is not something our elders know about." He hesitated. "Small, harmless curses are common among the Utugani, but a curse such as this takes much more power and a great deal of expertise. The only person who might have known more—my sister— died many years ago."

"I'm sorry for your loss," said Jena. The Utugan had seen more death than most in his life—his wife, his eldest son, his sister. No wonder he didn't want to lose Argus, too. "Is there anything you can tell us based on the smaller curses? Anything that might help?"

He shook his head. "Powerful curses are a whole different type of magic. They take years to perfect. Our hearth's knowledge of powerful curses died with my sister."

Jena's heart sank. She'd been so sure they'd find more information here with the Utugani. "Is there anyone from a nearby hearth who might know? Any of the other traveling families?"

"We could waste many days searching for other hearths and still find no answers. I'm sorry I do not have better news."

Jena glanced at Nate, who was staring down at the fire ruby in his hand. Was he even listening? Their whole plan was being turned on its head, and she wasn't even sure he was paying attention. "Do you have any suggestions? Anyone else who might be able to help instead?"

The Utugan leaned forward, his face betraying his anxiety. "I am sorry. I want to help you, but the answers do not lie within our hearth."

Eldrin cleared his throat nervously. "I might know someone." He glanced at his father. "When Argus and I were Flame Guards and lived in the capital city, there was an old Utugani witch who used to sell potions and spells. I cannot guarantee she knows how to undo what has been done, but if she's still there, she could be your next best option."

Jena glanced at Nate again. He was staring intently at Eldrin, his face rigid. "Then we need to go to Flame City," he said. "For Argus, but also to confront Lothar."

"Eldrin told me of your plan to confront Lothar," said the Utugan with a nod at his son. "I can more easily assist you with that."

Jena stared at him in surprise. "You can?" She was so used to thinking of it as a fool's errand, she was genuinely surprised that someone would offer help.

"Lothar has become a problem for many in Ignisia." He nodded toward the outside campsite. "For the protection of my people, we're packing up and moving to our Hidden Hearth in the mountains."

"What have you heard?" asked Nate, leaning forward.

"He destroyed an entire village south of here. There were no survivors. Terrible beasts are roaming; a black-winged horse, wolvans. Even a lavaen. The Flame City is suffering at his hands with stories of roaming guards arresting innocent people. I never thought I'd wish for King Harad back, but I do."

Jena's skin prickled and her burns seemed to harden. She hadn't realized the effects of Lothar's creatures were being felt everywhere across Ignisia. It was a reminder that confronting Lothar was about more than just revenge for Thornal's death; it was about the entire kingdom. People were already suffering under Lothar's rule. "What else can you tell us?" she asked.

"The prophecies foretell of someone who will revolt against Lothar. We would do everything in our power to help that person." He looked significantly at Nate, like he was already sure who he'd be helping.

Jena swallowed. Another person talking about the prophecies. Both Miara and Rothell had said they were in motion, and now the Utugan was confirming it too.

Outcasts unite, the Flames burn bright, and the Way will continue. The line from one of the prophecies came to mind. Nate's flames certainly burned bright.

"How much do you know about the prophecies?" asked Jena.

"We know them, the same as you do. We also have our own ways to foresee the future and protect our people. We believe Lothar will turn against the Utugani people next, and I must stop him from decimating our hearths."

"*We* must stop him," said Eldrin with a glare at his father.

The Utugan nodded at Eldrin, giving him a placating half smile. "We'll pack up and leave first thing tomorrow for our hearth deep in the mountains west of here. My—" He glanced at Eldrin. "—*Our* priority is keeping our people safe. We need every able-bodied man and woman to protect the elderly and the young at our Hidden Hearth. We must move quickly, before the coronation. There is a reckoning coming for Lothar, but I do not wish to be caught up in the backlash."

"A reckoning?"

"As is stated in the prophecies."

Jena glanced at Nate. How much did Nate believe in the prophecies? Thornal had made Jena learn them forwards and backwards, but she wasn't sure how much she trusted them. Especially because everyone seemed to think they were in the middle of them. "What help can you give us on our journey?" said Jena, ignoring the frisson of fear.

The Utugan gave a humorless smile. "For a start, we can provide you with travel rations and clothes," he said with a glance up and down each of them.

Jena looked down at her stained travel clothes. He was right about their need for basic supplies. She was sore, dirty with ash and blood, and had multiple rips and holes in her clothes. "Thank you," she said gratefully.

"I will send two of my most trusted guards with you, to guide you on your way. And we have contacts in the city who will be useful."

Jena let out a breath. She'd hoped for a group of Utugani fighters to back them up against the entire Flame City Royal

Army. Plus, the Hashishin. And the Royal Guards. And all the mages.

Actually, when she thought about it, she could understand why he wasn't sending his people to be slaughtered alongside them. "Thank you," she said softly. "We appreciate any help you can give us."

"I've also got your horses here, waiting for you. Nicely rested and fed on the juicy grass in this valley," said Eldrin.

"Thank you, Eldrin," said Jena. She smiled at him gratefully. "Although we might need you to look after them for us a bit longer. Rothell has said that she will carry us to the Flame City."

Nate rubbed his eyes as if they were sore. "We need to prepare to leave. If you can't help with Argus's curse, Eldrin's witch in Flame City is the next best place to find the answers we seek," he said. "We cannot delay."

The Utugan nodded and stood. "We leave at dawn tomorrow. Our warriors will be ready to leave with you once they have helped with our preparations." He paused, a determined expression on his face. "I must protect my people at all costs." Eldrin stood up next to his father, his expression more serious than she'd ever seen it. It gave her goosebumps along her unscarred arm. Everything felt more real all of a sudden.

Jena and Nate stood as well. "We'll help you pack up before we leave," said Jena. If they were going on a suicide mission, at least they could help others survive.

"I can help carry their supplies to this new camp." The shimagni spoke into her head from her position outside. Jena jumped slightly—she hadn't realized Rothell was listening in. "Rothell says she can carry supplies."

The Utugan blinked but was quick to mask his surprise. "Thank you," he said with a regal bow of his head.

239

Jena rubbed her arms, looking around the tent. Ellie had returned and was sitting in one corner, her large eyes taking in everything. Jena was glad for her sake that her father was focused on taking his people to safety. She just wished she and Nate had more of a plan for how they were going to save Argus. It still felt like they were making things up as they went along.

And yet again, they'd been told that it was up to Nate to save Ignisia from Lothar, but they still had no idea *how*. A Firecaller who hadn't been trained properly and a servant girl with the Book of Spells illegally in her head.

Not exactly auspicious.

Nothing like the heroes of the prophecies.

CHAPTER 35

JENA

J ena folded one side of the small tent into another and laid it on the ground.

Next to her, Nate was bringing in his half, as they'd been shown. They folded the two halves yet again and ended with a neat pile. Together they carried it to the covered wagon, where it was all being packed.

They'd been folding and collapsing and carrying for several hours, and every muscle in Jena's body ached. Nate looked as exhausted as she felt. But they'd promised their assistance for the move, and everyone was working just as hard as they were to pack for their departure at dawn the next morning—including the Utugan's mother, who they were currently helping.

"Here you go, Catarina, this is the last of it." Jena felt awkward using her first name, but the old woman had insisted when they'd been assigned to her.

"Thank you. I can manage from here. It's almost all done. Go back to your hearth and eat your dinner. You deserve it." Catarina leaned on the handle of an ornate cane, her gnarled hands strong despite her age. Her long grey and black hair was pulled back into intricate plaits and knots and tucked out of the way beneath a richly patterned grey and blue scarf. Her lined face was flushed from the effort of packing, but the smile she gave them was relaxed and easy. The old woman had worked just as hard as they had. She must be just as exhausted, yet she didn't show it.

"Thank you," said Jena, rolling her aching shoulder muscles. "You're going to stop soon, as well?"

"Very soon. I have a couple more small things to sort out. Your hard work for me is appreciated. I've enjoyed getting to know you both," said Catarina, nodding her head formally.

"It's been an honor to help you, and get to know you as well, Catarina." Jena realized she meant every word. As they'd folded and packed everything from linen and towels to hammers and mallets, she'd ended up talking to Catarina about her life, including her childhood with the Utugani and Elsa, the Utugani woman who'd found her as a baby. She rarely talked about it, but something about Catarina's kind face seemed to make the memories spill from her lips.

The people she'd met here were friendly, loyal and hardworking. She was having trouble matching them with her memories of her foster brother Otis and the small broken hearth where she was raised.

"What are you thinking about so seriously?" asked Nate, glancing at her as they walked back to their small hearth. His hazel eyes seemed to see right through Jena to the scars on the inside.

She took a ragged breath. "The Utugani who raised me. You've heard me talk about them. They were nothing like the people we've met here."

"Every people—every race—has good and bad. I'm sure

there are some good people here, and some capable of doing very bad things."

"Argus insisted the Utugani are an honorable people. Perhaps he was right."

"Think of it like this: at least your own family isn't trying to kill you."

Jena looked up into his face. It wasn't self-pity. He was trying to cheer her up. She smiled, a ghost of a curl on one side, and he grinned back like he'd won a medal.

He cleared his throat. "The ghost mage has been badgering me about what we're going to do when we get to Flame City. Rothell has said she'll fly us to the outskirts, so we could be there this time tomorrow."

A chill went along Jena's spine. They could be there tomorrow? She hadn't thought about how fast Rothell could fly. "She doesn't mind?"

"She said it's important, and she's right. There's a lot riding on this. On us."

"What about the Utugani guards?"

"I think we just ask for one guard and get them to show us the way to this witch. We don't need more than that. We undo Argus's curse, rescue Bree... and then confront Lothar."

Jena's heart rate notched up. How were they going to do all that in the time they had? "So we focus on Argus first, then Bree?" If they didn't get to Lothar in time, what would happen?

Nate nodded, his eyes becoming serious. "One at a time. It's the only way to get things done and not freeze with fear," he said. "Rothell has said she'll help as much as she can. She feels responsible for Bree's kidnapping."

"That's silly. She wasn't even a part of it."

Nate shrugged. "She's Remus's self-appointed watchdog. She vowed to not let him harm anyone else. We also really need her help, if she's offering it."

Jena hesitated, and then nodded. He was right. It would take far too long to ride on horseback to the capital city.

"He won't stop hunting for us just because we have another problem now," said Jena, a warning in her voice. "We're going to have to confront Lothar at some point soon. The coronation is in three weeks."

"Which makes it even more important to break Argus's curse as soon as we can."

"Then it's settled. We have a destination and a time-frame. We just need a plan."

"We have to find out more first," said Nate. "If we're part of the prophecy, we need to find out in what way."

"It might be easier said than done," she said softly. "The Utugan didn't seem to know more than Miara or Rothell. Everyone seems to be positive it's started, but no one wants to give advice on what we should do."

"We'll find a way." Nate casually bumped shoulders with Jena. It was a gentle movement, but Jena tensed, waiting for the usual reaction. But she found she didn't mind Nate touching her; he did it so gently that her scars weren't affected, and her fears stayed hidden. They continued to walk, shoulders side by side.

Leaning into Nate's strength felt decadent but also necessary to her peace of mind. She savored it for a moment longer. "What if it's not us?" she whispered. "What if they're wrong?"

Nate stopped and turned so he was facing her. He carefully put a hand on each of her arms and looked into her eyes, his tawny gaze serious. "It doesn't matter if we're part of the prophecies or not. We need to ignore the prophecies and just concentrate on saving our friends. Then saving the kingdom. The rest of it is..." he waved a hand like he couldn't even think of what it could be.

"It's all so vague. We don't have any concrete plans." She had a niggling sense they were forgetting something.

"We have enough." He let out a sigh. "I think we both have to get used to this being a fly-by-the-seat-of-our-pants type of quest. We just do what we can and hope it's enough."

Jena nodded. She didn't know why she felt so uneasy. "I guess so," she said. He was right. Worrying about how little they knew wouldn't change anything.

The truth was, she probably wouldn't make it past their journey to Flame City. She was a woman who could cast mage spells, had the Book of Spells inside her head and a mage tattoo on her skin. Just one of those alone would be enough to convince another mage to execute her—all three guaranteed it. The fact she was heading to the capital city, to the one place with the most powerful mages in the kingdom, only made it more likely. She was determined to make the rest of her life mean something. She would help Nate free Argus and save her sister. Then she would make Lothar pay for Thornal's death.

Her nervousness was just because she was living on borrowed time.

She had to focus on their tasks. She didn't know how they'd achieve them, but they would. She was determined. Then they would destroy Lothar and put the true king—Nate—in his place.

No matter how much the true king resisted the notion.

"I know this all seems crazy," said Nate. "But we can do this. We have a destination, and someone else who might help. Plus, a shimagni to take us there. We're going to save Argus and Bree. I just know it."

Jena noticed he didn't mention Lothar. "I hope you're right," she said, trying not to think about Bree and where Remus might have her trapped.

"Of course I'm right," said Nate with a grin. "And now, let's go eat. I'm starving."

CHAPTER 36
NATE

They headed back to the campfire in companionable silence.

Nate had been extra careful when he'd touched Jena; he knew how sensitive she was about it. But he felt strangely pleased that she'd let him. It felt like he was making some kind of progress in their friendship.

He didn't know what was going to happen when they left the Utugani, but he was glad he would have Jena with him. Between the two of them, they'd rescue Argus and Bree.

Maybe they'd even beat Lothar at his own game.

When they arrived back at their small camp, they found Rothell resting beside a small fire—one of the warriors had come and lit it for them not long since.

Jena went over to Rothell and rubbed one hand along her neck. The shimagni made a vibrating sound, almost like a cat's purr.

"You look like you've had a long day," said Nate.

"I flew to their secret hearth as many times as I could," she said tiredly. *"I think it was helpful to them."*

"I'm sure it was," said Nate with a smile. He sat down next to the small fire, holding out his hands. "I don't suppose they left us any more food?"

"Not yet. They said they'd come back."

Nate made a face. He should probably be glad of any food at all, but he was hungry right now. But even if they did bring more, they had no pots or pans to cook with, and nothing to eat alongside it. Even worse, the smell of a rich, meaty stew being cooked in the main Utugani hearth was wafting their way.

"Do you think we should ask Catarina if she has any spare food for us?" said Jena. "We did help her."

"The Utugan said he'd give us supplies. I don't think he meant for us to starve," agreed Nate, his stomach rumbling.

Jena nodded. "Let's go find something to eat," she said determinedly. She glanced at Rothell. "What do you normally eat? Is there something we can bring back for you?"

"I am fine. I do not eat as regularly as you do. I will not eat for another week or so."

Nate stood and made sure their fire was burning low enough not to spread. He saw a flash of movement out of the corner of his eye.

"Jena," he whispered, catching her attention and nodding his head toward the young woman who'd just arrived.

Her long, dark hair fell in waves out of a yellow scarf. She wore a long skirt and a brightly embroidered shirt, traditional clothing among the Utugani. She was holding a snugly wrapped baby in a woven sling across her front and a bowl of steamed rice in the other hand. To Nate, she seemed somehow very proud and completely uncertain at the same time.

The woman strode up to where they stood beside their fire. Without saying a word, she held out the large bowl of rice to them. Jena stood up and took the gift, smiling encouragingly at their visitor.

The young Utugani woman glanced at the shimagni, then looked at Nate with solemn eyes. "Argus is my cousin. They say you know him, and that he saved your life?" she said. She had the same intensity as Argus, and a way of tilting her head that reminded Nate of the ex-mercenary.

A wave of guilt hit him in the chest. It was his fault that Argus wasn't here, reuniting with his family. Meeting Argus's cousin only made it worse.

He swallowed hard. This was his punishment for not protecting Argus better. "That's true," he rasped.

"Can you tell me the story of how he saved your life?" Again, the woman glanced at the shimagni. Rothell shimmered in the half-light of the fire, her eyes glowing and swirling with color.

Startled, Nate glanced at Jena, then back at the young woman. "I don't think—"

"They need to know, Nate. This is important," said Rothell.

Nate jumped in surprise as Rothell spoke in his mind. He glanced back at the shimagni, and she gave him an encouraging nod. He focused back on the young Utugani woman in front of them.

"I'd like to know more about how he spent his life. It's been so long since I saw him," she said. Her baby in the wrapped sling snuffled in its sleep as if agreeing.

Nate hesitated a moment longer. "I guess… yes, I can." He gestured for her to sit down on one of their nearby logs.

"We have little in the way of food or drink," said Nate apologetically. "We had to leave our supplies behind." Even as he said the words, Nate heard the chatter of young children and looked up. Two more women, each with two children clinging nervously to their skirts, walked toward them, a determined set to their jaws. "We heard you might tell us the story of Argus's bravery?" said the one with long wavy blonde hair, her hand stroking the matching blond hair of one of her little boys as he hid his head in her skirts. "He was our friend when we were children. We'd like to hear the story of how he saved you." She held out a bowl filled with steaming stew. Nate's stomach rumbled.

The other woman, with darker olive skin and long, mahogany colored hair that matched her brown eyes, held out a platter of fruit and a flask of drink. "We bring gifts for your campsite." Her two boys both had matching hair and skin, and their large dark brown eyes watched Jena and Nate carefully.

Nate took the offerings with a smile and placed them to one side of the campfire. "It will make a delightful change from fish," he said, and motioned for the women to sit next to their first guest. "I can't offer you proper fireside hospitality, I'm sorry. We have no other supplies, including plates and mugs."

The dark-haired woman nodded to the elder of her two sons, who ran off, presumably to find plates.

Instead of moving toward the proffered seat, both women stared up at the shimagni. The shifting, blue and violet glow from Rothell's body was reflected on their faces, making it difficult to read their expressions. They all seemed fascinated by Rothell, but were still cautious.

"She won't hurt you," said Nate, still standing on the other side of the campfire.

The blonde woman's eyes sharpened, turning them to dark jewels in the firelight. She was a stunningly attractive woman. "I am not afraid. I simply wish to assess my surroundings."

"A wise sentiment," said Rothell softly in all their heads.

The women jumped, and the youngest with her baby stood, stepping backward over the log.

"I mean you no harm. Please do not be afraid."

"She is here to protect us, not harm us. You are wise to be cautious, but it is not necessary around Rothell." Nate smiled up at Rothell as he spoke.

The three women shuffled and glanced at each other, before sitting back down on the log, ruffling their skirts to hide their nerves. The little blond boys peeked out from behind their mother, curious eyes on the shimmering beast in front of them.

The little dark-haired boy arrived back, gasping big breaths—Jena suspected he was afraid of missing something good—and holding several plates and some mugs for tea.

"Oh good. You can have something to drink while you listen to Nate's story," said Jena, smiling down at the young boy. He all but ignored her and stared over her shoulder at Rothell.

Nate held back an amused smile, while Jena poured liquid from the flask for their guests. With a creature like Rothell around, it was hard to compete for attention. One boy whispered in his mother's ear, and she shook her head sternly.

"It is all right. He may touch my side. I will not harm him."

This time all three women and all four children stared up at Rothell with matching expressions. No one moved.

"See, I told you," said the little boy to his mother. "She said it was okay."

"Come stand with me," said Jena, holding out her hand

to the boy. "My name is Jena. I'll be your guide." Jena looked to his mother for permission, the same as the boy.

She gave Jena a stern look, but at her son's entreating face, she relented. "Fine. But do not get too close."

The boy inched forward, one hand in Jena's and the other hand outstretched. "My name is Blane," he whispered, not taking his eyes off Rothell.

"Nice to meet you," said Jena softly.

Everyone, including Nate, watched with fascination as the young boy walked bravely up to Rothell, and reached out with one pudgy hand. When his palm touched her leg, he let out a tiny gasp. "It's soft. Like a deer pelt," he murmured.

The other three boys moved away from their mothers and came forward too, almost like they were compelled. Nate had a feeling most people reacted to Rothell that way. Almost as one, they touched their hands to the shimmering skin on Rothell's flank.

"It feels... like a cloud," said the oldest boy. "It's so soft."

The dark-haired woman stood. "Like a cloud you say?" She walked cautiously over to Rothell. "With your permission," she said, bowing her head and holding out her hand hesitantly.

"Permission granted," replied Rothell in all their heads. Her eyes wandered over to the other two women. *"To all who are here."*

The woman with the baby stayed where she was, but the striking blonde woman stood and strode over. She touched Rothell's body and let out a soft exhalation of breath. "It's so soft. Not at all what I expected." She looked up at Rothell's head. "So beautiful."

Rothell nodded regally, like she got compliments like

that all the time. *"Now, shall we have something to drink and listen to the story?"*

Jena jumped into action and set out the offered food on an overturned log, pleased that the distraction of Rothell had eased some of the tension around their campfire.

The children each grabbed handfuls of sweet forest berries, then settled close to their respective mothers, who cradled cups of tea in their hands. Jena piled a plate of food for both herself and Nate, and placed Nate's plate next to where he'd been sitting.

He nodded his thanks and took a deep breath. She could see he was nervous and wondered how much of the story he was going to tell them.

CHAPTER 37
NATE

J ust as Nate opened his mouth to say the first words, several more visitors walked into the circle of their campfire.

Shy expressions and strong features were common among the new arrivals. Each had an offering of food, and they were all women. Nate hadn't spent much time among the Utugani, but he hadn't had the impression that the women were the leaders. It had always seemed like such a warrior-led society.

And yet here they were. Some were older and some younger, but all claimed some kind of kinship or friendship with Argus. One of the last to arrive was Catarina, Argus's grandmother, on the arm of her young granddaughter Ellie. They'd both smiled at Nate and Jena, then sat down next to the women at the front who'd made room for them.

Nate counted almost two dozen women around their campfire, even as more visitors trickled in. Each time, they brought more food with them, and each time, Jena and Nate welcomed them in. Soon they were helping themselves to the feast they had provided and murmuring in low voices to each other. Most of the women had moved closer to touch Rothell's hide—the shimagni had to be getting sick of the attention by now.

"I'm willing to put up with it, if it helps us in our quest," said Rothell, presumably only in his head.

Nate gave her a nod that he hoped conveyed his thanks.

"Are they all telling the truth?" Nate asked Jena in an undertone at one point, as he chewed on a particularly delicious bread roll. "Were they all close to him?"

Jena looked around the campfire, taking in the faces in the flickering light. "Utugani are very close to each other. They spend a lot of time together, and family is more than just your parents. It's the wider community too. He could easily have had the connections these women are saying he did."

"Why is it only women and children? Where are the men?"

"I wonder if the men even know they're here?" said Jena, amusement on her face.

"I'm sure they'd notice this many women missing from the hearth." He paused. "Maybe."

Nate lifted one hand and rubbed at his chest, trying to soothe the uncomfortable tightness. Argus had missed out on seeing his family, on hugging and kissing them, swapping stories and living with them again.

And it wasn't just that he'd missed out this time. There was a chance that he'd never be able to do that again. The pressure to save Argus felt like it was suffocating him.

Unable to stop himself, he put his hand in his pocket and pulled out the fire ruby, staring down at it. He was sure it had dimmed even in the short time since he'd put Argus in there.

"We should be trying to break the curse, not wasting

time telling stories," he whispered to Jena. He clenched the fire ruby in his fist.

Being in their midst, meeting Argus's family, was breaking Nate's heart. The campfire was becoming increasingly crowded. The women were laughing and joking, eating their food and waiting for him to begin. He pushed aside his fluctuating emotions. Nearby Jena simply watched him, holding herself motionless, like she didn't want to spook him.

"We can't travel this late in the day," she said softly. "And it would ease their hearts to hear about Argus." Jena gestured around her. "You'd better tell the story."

Nate looked around at the women in various stages of eating and talking. He caught the eye of several who were obviously waiting for him to start. "No pressure," he muttered. He slid the fire ruby back into his pocket, wishing it didn't feel like it weighed more than a boulder from the nearby river.

"None at all," agreed Jena. She seemed far more relaxed than she'd been since they'd landed with Rothell. Everything had happened so quickly they really hadn't had a chance to catch their breath.

But he didn't have time to worry about that right now. He had a story to tell.

He strode to one side of the campfire, placing the shimagni behind him, her violet and blue translucent body rising up off the ground, and providing a glittering backdrop. It would allow them to listen and watch the shimagni at the same time.

"Thank you for visiting us and thank you for your kind gifts of food. We've eaten better tonight than we have in many weeks."

There were murmurs from the crowd, many nodding their heads and accepting his thanks.

"You're here to listen to the story of Argus, and how he saved my life. He actually saved my life, not once, but three times in the short time I've known him, and I can only thank you, his family and friends, for his great deeds." Nate paused and looked around the faces at the campfire.

"Well done, you're a natural at this," said Rothell approvingly.

Nate took a deep breath, then continued. "The first time Argus saved me, he was only just in time. Deadly assassins had surrounded my house..." Nate continued to talk, weaving the story of their trip into the story of Argus, so they would understand what he meant to them. He told them how Argus had been freed by his love for Bree, and how it was only because he was free that he'd been able to go save Jena and Bree. When it came time to describe how Argus had been wounded and had ended up in the fire ruby, there were tears running down the faces of many in the audience.

It was true love that had saved him and cursed him at the same time.

Nate's gaze went to Jena; she watched him with dark eyes that glittered in the firelight. He knew she felt guilty for her part in putting Argus in danger. He wished he could convince her it hadn't been her fault.

Silence filled the hearth when he finished. "We brought him straight here to his family, hoping to get help." He left out meeting the ash-fang, trying not to alarm them. He nodded to show he'd finished. "We have to break the curse and save him." He swallowed hard, feeling like he should do something more right at this moment. Telling stories seemed frivolous when Argus and Bree were trapped.

"This wastes nothing. We need these people on our side. Telling them this story is how we pay for the help they're giving us." Rothell's words inside his head were sharp. He flicked his gaze to her and gave a quick acknowledgement.

His audience started chatting to their neighbors, talking about the story they had just heard. Nate had stuck to the truth as much as he could, and Argus had come out as the hero he was. The low murmuring was strangely soothing, and Nate let out a breath, relieved to no longer be the center of attention.

In small groups, the visitors started leaving, thanking Nate and Jena for their hospitality as they left. Many were even brave enough to farewell the shimagni, who nodded graciously every time.

"You're a natural storyteller, mage," said Catarina. Her smile was wide and her eyes shone. They were the same blue as Argus and Eldrin's.

"Thank you. I was only stating the truth. Argus's actions speak for themselves." He bowed respectfully.

"He was always a good boy, my grandson. Thank you for making him come alive for us again. We will do everything we can to help reverse the curse and get him healed." The old blue eyes filled with tears, but they didn't overflow. Catarina had pounds of self-control.

"Thank you."

She nodded. "It does you credit, young man." She looked at Jena for a moment. "Your sister is still trapped by the mage Remus?" she said, her eyes narrowing.

Jena blinked quickly at the blunt question. "Yes. He kidnapped her while we fought the lavaen."

"And she loves Argus?"

Jena hesitated, then nodded. "Yes, she loves him."

Watching the regal old lady take in this information,

Nate wondered for the first time if the Utugani would have tried to prevent Argus and Bree from getting married if they'd arrived as they'd planned. Argus was of the royal line. There were probably rules about who he could marry.

Catarina's eyes glinted with her unshed tears. "At least he has love to keep him warm inside his fire ruby prison," she said, then shuffled away, taking the arm of her granddaughter, Ellie.

Jena watched Catarina walk away. "They're a tight knit community," she whispered, her voice uneven. "I'd forgotten what that was like."

"They all love him," agreed Nate. "I could feel it, too."

"And because of us, he's cursed, maybe dying. I'm surprised they're able to look us in the eye, let alone come out here and talk to us." Jena gripped her mug of hot tea in both hands.

"Silly humans. They know you are his friends. You are his best hope for being saved." The shimagni's voice rumbled in their heads.

"Let's hope so." Nate wished he could be so certain.

"Do you doubt me?" The shimagni's voice sharpened, and her shimmering scales darkened to deep purple and midnight blue.

"No, I don't doubt you," said Nate, holding out his hands in supplication. "But you're the one they came to see, not me."

"They left with a story told with heart and truth that will stay with them, whatever happens. You gave them something special, Nate, and I believe it will stand us in good stead with the Utugani."

"I hope you're right," said Nate.

CHAPTER 38

NATE

"*Of course she's right,*" said the ghost mage, appearing beside Nate.

Nate jerked to the left, surprised by the sudden appearance. "What are you doing here? Is something wrong?" He looked around quickly to see what might be happening.

The ghost held up his palms. *"No, no, son. It's all fine. I just thought we needed to plan for Flame City. You're heading there tomorrow, and you don't even know what you're going to do."*

"Who are you talking to?" asked Jena looking around.

"A ghost has just appeared," said Rothell.

"You can see him?" Nate looked at Rothell in surprise.

"I cannot hear his words, but I can sense him. He was a powerful mage when he was alive."

Nate glanced back at the ghost mage, who shrugged. He didn't deny what Rothell was saying.

"Tell me about these ghosts you see," said Rothell, her neck curving down closer to Nate's face. The firelight flickered across her face and danced in her eyes.

Nate glanced at Jena, but she didn't even blink. She was too used to magic to be worried about anything he might say. "I've seen them since I was young. I help those I can, but many of them are tricksters and time wasters."

Rothell blinked. *The ability to see ghosts is not a Firecaller ability I have ever heard of, but perhaps it was not considered the most useful of your skills.*

"It's not always the most convenient skill to have," agreed Nate. "They turn up in all sorts of places and they generally only want one thing."

"Your help?"

"Yes. They want me to help them accomplish whatever made them stay behind rather than going past the Edges and into the beyond." He glanced at the ghost mage, who scowled back at him. "The ghost mage is the only one who has never asked me for anything."

"He's different from the rest?"

"Yes. He keeps helping *us*. Or he's telling me off," said Nate, thinking of the ghost mage growling at him for leaving the Forest of Ghosts without the others. "He can follow me in a way that no other ghost has ever been able to. There's something special about him, I just don't know what it is."

"If you want to know more, ask him."

Nate glanced at the ghost mage. "Will you tell me more about who you are? Why you're special?"

"I'm not important, son. You don't need to know," said the ghost mage, his body shimmering.

"Do you even know who you are?"

The ghost mage scoffed as if that didn't even deserve an answer.

"What if I said I thought it was important that we know who you are?" said Nate. His stomach churned as he spoke.

261

The ghost mage crossed his arms over his chest and glared. *"We don't have time for these shenanigans. We need to plan your next move."*

Nate looked at Rothell. "He won't tell me."

"Then describe him to Jena. She will tell you more of him."

Nate looked between Rothell and Jena, frowning. "But—"

"Jena will help you decipher the puzzle," said Rothell with an air of finality.

Jena shrugged. "I know many of the old mages. Thornal used to trade potions and ingredients all the time. I'll probably recognize him from your description."

"I'm not important. Knowing who I am won't help you," said the ghost mage, but there was an edge of desperation in his voice. *"Don't do this."*

Nate cleared his throat and looked the ghost up and down. What harm could come of finding out which crazy old mage was haunting him? Even the ghost's desperation wasn't that uncommon. Ghosts always had ulterior motives, and they never wanted you to focus on the things they thought were unimportant. "He's old. Tall and thin. Pale skin, gaunt."

Jena rolled her eyes. "That's more than half of them. What else?"

"Stop this. It's better if you don't know," said the ghost mage.

Nate peered at the ghost for something distinctive. "Blue eyes, kinda intense when he's annoyed." The ghost mage glared. "Which is a lot."

"This is your problem, Nate. You don't listen." The ghost mage stormed away from the campfire. Nate watched him go, wondering if the ghost was right. Perhaps there was a good reason he didn't want to be named?

"Any distinctive markings?" asked Jena. Her eyes were locked on his face, her hands clenched at her sides, like she was trying to control a powerful emotion.

The ghost mage stomped back into view and crowded close to Nate. *"You need to stop this here and now. What you're doing is going to wreck everything,"* he growled.

Nate stared at the old mage, and a chill went down his spine. He knew nothing about this ghost. He'd gotten into the habit of trusting him, but ghosts had always proved, again and again, that they couldn't be trusted. What if he was working for Lothar? What if that was why he was hiding his identity? "He's got long white hair," Nate blurted. Peering closer at the ghost mage, he tried to see the details he'd been ignoring. The ghost stepped back and scowled.

"His beard is white and partially covers a scar running down his chin," added Nate. "That's pretty distinctive."

The old ghost mage looked like he was in pain as he stomped away again.

Jena's face had gone pale. "Anything else?"

Rothell shifted slightly behind Jena, her eyes blazing as she watched. Nate glanced at her, wondering why the shimagni was so invested in the identity of the ghost mage. Could he really be working against them? But why did he help save them so many times? What did all this mean?

The ghost mage wasn't even a proper mage. He wore dirty old robes and—Nate snapped his fingers. "He doesn't have a mage tattoo. He wears mage robes, which is how I knew he was a mage, but no tattoo. At first that used to bug me, because I thought he'd been practicing magic illegally. But when you told me the Guardian could take his tattoo off as well..." Nate shrugged. "I figured it's more common than I realized."

Jena's gaze became even more piercing. "Nate, did you ever see Thornal in real life?" Her words were urgent, and she was giving Nate a strange look.

Nate shook his head, frowning. "No. I always embarrassed my grandfather. He'd never have introduced me to the Guardian." He blinked, looking at Jena. She was looking at him like she'd seen a ghost—

"Wait. You think *Thornal* is the ghost mage?" he blurted, his stomach sinking. "The *Guardian*?" He sat down heavily on a nearby log, feeling dizzy. He glanced over at the ghost mage, who was angrily pacing nearby and ignoring Nate.

Jena nodded. She took a ragged breath. "Thornal was tall. When I first met him, he seemed impossibly tall, and I always felt like I was looking up at him from such a distance. His eyes were this deep blue, but they would change with his moods, like the weather changes the surface of a lake. He had a scar running down one side of his face, and he refused to tell me how he got it." She sniffed, clearly trying to think of other details about Thornal.

"He liked to wear these old faded black robes that no other mage would be seen dead in. I tried to get him to buy new ones, but he always refused. Said he preferred the anonymity that his old robes gave him. But wherever he went, people always knew who he was. He was never mistaken for anyone but the Guardian."

Nate listened to her description with growing alarm. "You mean the Guardian of the Book of Spells, the greatest mage of his time has been following me around? Telling me what to do?" he said, stunned that it was the Guardian who'd been haranguing him like a fishwife. His throat felt tight. He tried unsuccessfully not to think of all the times he'd been rude to the ghost mage.

This was why the ghost mage hadn't wanted to be named.

Jena looked at Nate, her thoughts making her blue eyes darken like the shores of a lake. Nate wondered how he hadn't figured it out by himself.

They were the same exact blue as the ghost mage's eyes.

CHAPTER 39

JENA

J ena turned to Rothell. "Is it true? Is that what you think?"

Rothell nodded regally. *"Yes, I believe it is Thornal."*

"He's really here?" she said to Nate. She peered around Nate, as if Thornal would pop out from behind him.

Nate cleared his throat, still looking like he'd just eaten a bad lemon. "He's here. He's been helping us." He pushed his hand through his hair and stared down at the flames in front of them. "He told me what Remus had done and made sure we would get there in time to save you."

He hesitated.

"What is it?" said Jena impatiently.

"He's here looking after *you*," he said, staring hard down at the ground, like he was fitting a puzzle together. "It's not about his own quest at all. That's why he never asked for anything like the other ghosts. He's here to look after *you*."

"He's not dead?" Jena asked, her chest filled with a sudden—completely irrational—hope.

Nate glanced quickly back up at her. "I'm sorry Jena. He's definitely dead." He shook his head. "But they're usually tied to the Edges because they want to finish something in this world before moving on. They always ask me for something, but the ghost mage never did. I couldn't figure it out until now."

She put one hand over her mouth, trying to hold in her emotions. "He told me he knew about his death for a long time before it happened. He must have prepared for it. He must have done this to himself."

"I've never heard of someone becoming a ghost on purpose before. It always just seemed to happen accidentally when they died."

"He was a powerful mage. He would have figured it out."

"I'm positive it's because he's helping you."

"You don't know that for sure," said Jena. "Ask him, right now." She started pacing around the campsite.

Her emotions were all over the place. She didn't know if she was happy or angry about this new development. She'd loved Thornal, but since his death she'd found out how much he'd lied to her about everything. Tears threatened to fill her eyes, and she halted abruptly to swipe at them angrily with one hand.

He was silent for a moment. "He says to ask him anything."

Jena felt like her chest was being ripped open, and she searched for the question she most wanted to ask. "Why are you still here, Thornal?" Her throat felt raw, and she swallowed hard.

"He says it was for you. *You* were his purpose," said Nate, ducking his head to get Jena to look at him. "He couldn't just leave you when he died. He was the one who led you to the Forest of Ghosts, and your sister." Nate's words, softly spoken, hit Jena hard.

"He made me burn down the house and leave it all behind," she said, her voice hoarse.

"He's sorry for the necessity. But he couldn't leave anything for his enemies to find and use. He had no choice."

Jena nodded jerkily. She'd always understood that—it had just hurt to destroy their home.

"He's been protecting you, that's why he stayed in the Edges. He didn't want to leave you on your own," said Nate, clearly trying to convince her of Thornal's good intentions.

Jena didn't know how to react. "So, he knew? That he was my grandfather?" Her stomach roiled.

"Yes. At least, he guessed."

More tears welled, and this time she let them roll down her face. She didn't know why she was so upset to learn that Thornal was Nate's ghost mage. It was confusing. She felt happy but also like she was being torn apart. "Tell him that this is far worse than if he'd just told me when he was still alive," she said, her voice hoarse.

"He says he's sorry." Nate moved to stand in front of her.

"Then why didn't he tell me all of this?" The words burst out of Jena. She didn't want to say them, they revealed too much of the hurt she'd experienced since finding out he was her grandfather. But she couldn't seem to help herself.

Nate waited a moment, his gaze on the ground, clearly listening to Thornal's answer. He looked up at her and took a breath. "He says he couldn't tell you at first. You were too... wild and angry. You'd had too many terrible things happen to you. You needed a gentle return to everyday life." Nate's eyes were filled with compassion as he repeated things she would never have told him otherwise. "He says that later it became impossible. He worried you'd think he had lied to you. He didn't want to lose your trust. You never quite lost that wildness, and it made him afraid of losing you."

Jena felt like she was going to throw up. Emotions that she couldn't even name boiled inside her. Some of the wildness that Thornal was speaking about burst into her chest. There were too many truths happening here. Too much emotion. She looked around and wondered what would happen if she just ran away? Left Nate to save Argus and Bree by himself, to deal with Lothar on his own.

Behind her, Rothell shifted her leg closer, and Jena felt the warmth of the shimagni at her back. Her emotions calmed, and for the first time, she was glad of the creature's effect on her. She gave a quick glance back at Rothell and nodded.

Then she focused back on Nate. Of course she wasn't going to run. She'd never forgive herself if she didn't save Argus and Bree.

Nate took a step closer to her, then hesitated. "Are you okay, Jena? Do you want me to continue?"

She stared up at him—into his familiar face, with his dark, compassionate eyes and his raven tattoo slashed across his face—and nodded once, sharply.

Nate spoke slowly as if reciting the words: "He says he couldn't protect your parents: his son Primus and his daughter-in-law Dalaphine. He found out too late what the Mage Council had done, and he couldn't save them. It was like a knife to the heart finding out they'd been murdered." Nate swallowed. "He says it was—and still is—his life's greatest failure. It broke him, and he never recovered. His second greatest regret is that he didn't know his two beautiful granddaughters had survived the attack. But as soon as he found out that you and Bree were still alive, he made sure you were both safe."

"He didn't *trust* me. He thought I'd overreact, do something stupid. Or did he think I wasn't smart enough to survive on my own?" Jena felt a little hysterical as the possibilities whirled in her head.

Nate took a step closer, holding out his hands, palms up, as if soothing an animal. "He says he knows you're strong and didn't need his protection. But he wanted to be here." Nate glanced behind him.

"Is that where he is? Behind you?" Jena peered over Nate's shoulder but could see nothing but shadows. She swallowed hard over the lump in her throat and tried not to be resentful that Nate could see Thornal when she couldn't.

Nate nodded. He moved closer again and put both hands gently on Jena's upper arms, almost like he was trying to prepare her for what he was about to say. She should have felt uncomfortable, but she needed the comfort right now. And it was *Nate*.

"He says you're the most important person in his life, and he wishes he could have stuck around to be here for you now. But that wasn't his path. He could only prepare you as best he could." Nate's dark brown eyes were intent on hers, like he was trying to will her into accepting Thornal's words.

Jena's shoulders trembled, and a rushing noise filled her ears. Blindly, she put her arms around Nate's middle and buried her face into his chest. All she could think about was the overwhelming grief that was flooding her body. She shook as she sobbed, tears flowing down her cheeks.

Nate just shifted his arms around her and held her while she cried.

Jena let it all go, all the grief that she'd been holding tightly inside since the assassins had murdered Thornal right in front of her. She hadn't cried since, not once. She'd just done what he'd asked, traveled on her own to the Forest of Ghosts. She'd pushed all her emotions down where she couldn't feel them. And now she was making up for it, wracking sobs escaping her body. It felt horrible and cathartic all at once.

Eventually, her crying eased, and Jena became aware that she was still tucked inside the warmth of Nate's arms. She lifted her head and pulled back but remained within in his embrace.

"Thank you," she mumbled toward his broad chest, noticing the wet stain on his shirt. She moved awkwardly backward out of his arms, embarrassed that she'd lost control in front of him. She wiped her hand across her eyes and tried to act like nothing had happened.

"Any time," he said with a faint smile in his voice. "Thornal says you're strong, Jena. He says that you've been forged out of adversity for the quest we're on."

Jena didn't say anything. What could she say? Her past was in the past. No one could change it or mend it now. Saying it had made her who she was today was true, even if it felt like a justification.

"How is it you can travel with us?" he said, talking to Thornal. "None of the other ghosts I've ever met have been able to do it."

Nate paused as if Thornal were speaking.

"What did he say?" she asked impatiently.

"That he left his tattoo and his ashes with you," said Nate, a puzzled frown marring his face.

Jena lifted her shirt and showed Nate the raven tattoo on her stomach, which shimmered under the light of the campfire. "You've seen it attach itself to my body?" she said. Seeing it there on her body still seemed unreal after all this time.

Nate leaned forward, reaching out his hand as if to touch the raven on her stomach. At the last minute, just as his fingers were about to touch the inky tattoo, the raven moved on her skin, fluttering its wings. Nate froze.

"It moved on your skin," he said.

The blue-black raven opened one tattooed eye and peered at Nate.

"Yeah," Jena said, a slight blush crawling up one side of her face.

The raven moved restlessly, and Jena realized it hadn't been able to fly free all day. It pulled itself from her body, flinging itself into the air like it had been released from a prison. Perhaps that was how it felt to the raven to be stuck on her body?

"By the Flames," he said breathlessly. "This is unbelievable. It's *his* tattoo? On *your* body?" He looked like his head was spinning, and he was struggling to fit this kind of power together. "I just thought he'd created some kind of magical tattoo to protect you."

"He did, in a way. The raven did it the first time to warn me about some soldiers on the road. At first, I thought it was just my master's familiar helping me," said Jena. "Then Miara said that it was possible for mages to take their tattoos off, and for them to come alive—and I knew it was his tattoo."

"No wonder me moving the flames of the fire didn't seem like a big deal," he said. "There's nothing you can't do. You're the granddaughter of the most powerful mage in Ignisia, and the daughter of a mage and a witch. Of course, Thornal taught you mage work."

"Not just any mage work," said Rothell softly. *"Fire Mage work."*

"But I did nothing to earn the raven. It was a present from Thornal." *Her grandfather.* The thought bounced around in her head like a noisy unwelcome guest.

"I've never seen anything like it before. I didn't know it was possible." He touched his own face tattoo, like he was checking to see if his tattoo had started moving too. "And that's how you've been staying with us, Thornal? Through the tattoo?"

"What's he saying?" said Jena impatiently, when Nate took too long to respond.

"He says it's a combination of the raven and the ashes you're carrying. He saw his own death and used the fore-warning to attach part of his soul to the raven. It pulls him with us wherever you go." Nate paused, as if listening. "The ashes amplify the spell. He says it's not perfect, there have been gaps where he's not been able to find us, but... he did it all for you, Jena."

Jena put her hand to the little bag of ashes that was hanging from a leather string around her neck. It had always made her feel safe having the ashes close to her heart.

"Tell him... Tell him thank you. And also, he's not off the hook for not telling me about it before he died. For not trusting me." Jena blinked back more tears.

Nate nodded, his expression sympathetic. "He says he's sorry. He should have known better. But he's going to help us find a cure for Argus and rescue Bree. And then help us defeat Lothar."

CHAPTER 40

JENA

They woke before dawn the next morning to help with the final move of the Utugani Hearth.

Rothell disappeared to help fly several more loads of supplies—and a couple of brave warriors willing to go on her back—to the hidden hearth, while Jena and Nate quietly packed up their meagre supplies, both thinking about the revelations of the night before.

"Does Thornal have any suggestions on what we should do next?" asked Jena.

Nate shrugged. "He says he can't interfere with our decision making. It might affect the prophecy."

"How is that helpful?"

"He'll offer suggestions," said Nate wryly. "We just don't have to take them."

"Ha. He'll love that," said Jena with a grin. "Nothing bugs a mage more than being ignored."

"He did say that he agrees with what we've decided," said Nate.

Jena let out a snort-laugh. "I wonder what he'd have done if he didn't?"

"Carefully suggest something else?"

"He's used to being in charge. I don't think he'd be careful about any suggestions he made."

"No, he's not been careful with me since he first turned up," said Nate with a wry twist of his mouth. "He's growled at me more often than not."

"What did you do when he did that?"

"Just ignored him."

"Now that you know who he is, what will you do?"

Nate made a face. "I don't know. It makes him harder to ignore, knowing he's the Guardian."

Jena grinned at Nate, the skin on her face stretching at the unaccustomed feel of it. "He can't do anything about it, if we choose to ignore him still."

"I'll be shaking in my boots, knowing we're not listening to him."

"Like he said, the prophecy is about us, not him. We have to make our own decisions. Do this our way."

Nate made a face. "Who do you think the Utugan will send with us?" he asked, changing the topic.

Jena hesitated, glancing around the busy campsite nearby. It was still a way off from dawn, and the fires made all the people shadowy and dark around them. "I don't know. Someone who's not afraid to fly, hopefully," replied Jena as she tied off the top of her new backpack. The Utugan had been true to his word, and they had sufficient supplies, changes of clothes and food to last them a while.

"We're finished here. We may as well get some breakfast before we leave," said Nate. "While we wait for Rothell to return." The warrior who'd brought their supplies had told them to take their fill from the communal pot of porridge in the central hearth.

As they walked into the main hearth, they were greeted

by several people with a smile and a wave, a very different reception to the one they'd received just the day before. "Your storytelling skills served us well," said Jena with amusement. "I think some of these women have a crush on you now."

Nate gave her a funny look and kept walking. Jena shrugged. It was true, although the thought of him finding a wife made her stomach twist uncomfortably.

Despite the early hour, and the darkness still surrounding them, the central hearth was a busy hub of activity, with people moving in and out as they finished their packing and took their last meal before their long trek. Nate and Jena lined up and dolloped their porridge into spare bowls, the delicious smell of various spices added to the mixture making Jena's mouth water.

She sat down on a nearby stone and put the first spoonful into her mouth, letting out a groan. It was exactly the same as the porridge she used to eat as a kid. It brought back memories of sitting next to her adoptive mother, Elsa, early in the morning, talking quietly about the day ahead. She shivered. Those memories had all been marred by the memory of being pushed into the fire, and then being sold by Elsa's son Otis, the small hearth's leader.

She rarely let herself think about the before times.

As they sat eating, Jena considered the people around them. Aside from those who were eating, most were still working hard to break down the hearth. Even the youngest children were helping their parents by carrying items or running messages. Close by, a group of men worked together around one of the bigger tents. Their movements were fluid and sure as they pulled it down.

"One, two, three, lift," shouted the leader. They all grunted their replies as they hefted the heavy poles.

"They work together well," she said to Nate.

"They have to," he replied. "They wouldn't survive if they didn't."

"My hearth fought all the time, about everything. I can't imagine them being able to organize something like this."

Nate shrugged, his mouth full of porridge. "Hmhn."

Jena snorted at him before looking back to where the men had gotten the tent half folded. "Argus told me the people I described from my hearth weren't like other Utugani hearths," she said thoughtfully. "He said a proper Utugani leader wouldn't have sold a young girl. I didn't believe him back then. I told him I did, but I really didn't. Turns out he might have been right."

"You were speaking from your own experience," said Nate, his dark eyes burning with flames for a moment. "That's all we can do. My family—my grandfather and my aunts and uncles—sent me away as soon as they could. It was painful, and I thought I'd done something wrong. But now I think it was because I reminded them of my mother, and it was too much for them. They might not have done the right thing, but that doesn't mean they were all bad." He paused. "Well, some of them were. But mostly they're not." He grinned.

Jena gave a small half-smile. "You turned out well, despite it all."

"I do my best," said Nate, with a mocking bow of his head. "There was a time when you would have said I'd turned out like a rotten piece of fruit."

"You've since shown your true character," said Jena, her grin getting wider.

"And you turned out well for someone who didn't know what the Utugani were truly like."

"I had an old mage who pulled me back into line," she

said. Thornal was the only one who'd seen something more in her than rage and bitterness. Of course, now she knew that he'd also recognized his son and daughter-in-law.

"You would have figured it out eventually," said Nate softly.

Jena shrugged. She wasn't so sure. "Maybe."

A throat cleared behind them. "May we join you?"

Jena turned and looked up into the pre-dawn darkness, squinting her eyes. It was Catarina. Beside her was a large woman with graying red hair and a bright scarf.

At first, Jena smiled, not recognizing the second woman. Then it hit her like a punch to the face; something about the way the woman tilted her head. Or maybe it was how she walked?

"Elsa?" Jena croaked out the name, her throat closing on any other words. She struggled to take a breath. Pain slithered its way along her burned skin, like a sly old friend.

The woman nodded jerkily. "Yes, it's me, Jena."

Jena shook her head in denial, closing her eyes and trying to shake away the memories and the ghosts, to unsee the person who was standing in front of her. She opened her eyes again, but Elsa still stood next to Catarina, a pleading look on her face.

"Jena, I'm so sorry," she whispered, tears flowing down her cheeks. "Please forgive me."

Jena couldn't help it. She sneered. Every bitter thought rose to the surface. Every hurt, every scared feeling she'd felt when Otis had sold her to strangers. Every kick she'd received, every harsh word while she was a slave. It all came back to her and surrounded her as she looked up at the woman who'd raised her.

Who hadn't protected Jena from her son.

Elsa had let Otis sell Jena. Had let him push her into the

fire, had let him hurt her. She wanted nothing to do with this woman.

"What is she doing here?" Jena glared at Catarina.

"I recognized Elsa from your description earlier, my dear. I thought you should mend your broken relationship."

"Mend our relationship...?" Jena looked back and forth between the two old women, trying to remember what she'd told Catarina about her life. She must have left out the most important part. "She *betrayed* me. She doesn't get to *mend* anything."

"Everyone deserves the opportunity to explain their actions," said Catarina calmly.

Jena felt like the air was whooshing out of her lungs. "How do you explain burning a child?" she growled. She gestured to her face. "How do you explain selling her before she'd even healed?" Jena's words were furious and raw. She felt like she was back in that moment when everything had disintegrated around her. When the one person she'd thought loved her and would always protect her didn't even have the guts to stand up for her.

"I didn't—It wasn't—" Elsa looked like a fish on a hook, her mouth moving but no sound coming out.

Jena's breathing was short and sharp. She couldn't get quite enough air into her body. Just as everything was going blurry, she felt the warmth of Nate's large hand on her back. Her skin rippled at the touch, but she let him nudge her forward until she was leaning over her knees. She immediately felt better. Jena concentrated on the trampled grass on the ground, trying to ignore the feet of the women just in front of her.

"I can see I should have warned you," said Catarina. "But I know Elsa. She has a kind heart. And she wanted to see you again."

279

"You're assuming *I* wanted to see *her*," muttered Jena. Nate's hand warmed her back, the heat spreading across her rib cage and down into her stomach. She concentrated on that warmth, rather than on the woman in front of her.

"Is there somewhere more private we could go?" she heard Nate ask as if from a long way off.

She knew he was trying to help, but Jena shook her head frantically. She didn't want to go anywhere else. Elsa had betrayed her. She could still feel the deep cracks that had formed inside her when they'd sold her. She'd buried them deep, covered them over with time and determination, but they were still gaping valleys that would never heal.

Nate rubbed her back and leaned down to whisper in her ear. "Better to do this in private, Jena, than where everyone can watch. I'll be right by your side the whole time."

She didn't answer, every part of her rejecting the idea of talking to Elsa. She stayed curled forward, comforted by the act of hugging her own body. She didn't want to go anywhere with this woman. This was her worst nightmare come true, the reason she'd been so scared about coming here.

"A wound that's ignored will fester," said Catarina, her elderly voice wavering.

"This wound is well past festering," muttered Jena against her knees. "It rotted and died long ago."

Elsa made a tiny noise of distress. Jena clenched her fists, hating the part of her that wanted to make Elsa feel better. To tell her it was fine.

It wasn't fine. It would never be fine. "You sold me into slavery," whispered Jena, her voice hoarse. "You deserve nothing from me."

CHAPTER 41

JENA

Nate rubbed one hand over her back, as if trying to soothe an anxious horse. He kept his touch light, but she was so overwhelmed with what was happening, she didn't move away.

He kept quiet. He seemed to know there was nothing to say.

Catarina didn't have the same knowledge. "If you don't want your personal information aired out in front of everyone, I suggest you do as Nate suggests and accompany us somewhere private." Her voice was stern, like she was talking to a recalcitrant child.

Jena looked up and glared at Catarina. "We're not talking about some innocent act that could be forgiven. These burns"—she gestured at her face and body— "directly resulted from this woman's neglect. My life as a *child slave* was because of her. If you're expecting some kind of joyful reunion here, you're going to be disappointed." Her voice was a low, angry hiss. To think she'd actually *liked* Catarina after spending time with her yesterday. Not anymore. Not after this piece of meddling.

"I simply want you to face your demons," says Catarina, her lined face concerned. "They hold you back from your true potential."

Jena lifted one hand and ran her palm along the lumpy, burned skin on her face. Could she sit and listen to Elsa talk about how sorry she was? How she hadn't meant for it to happen? That she hadn't known what her son was doing? It was all bullshit. Lies pulled from the ashes. She had let Otis do what he wanted, without protecting her, which made her just as guilty.

Except... did she have a choice?

Jena glanced around her.

People were staring, some frowning, wondering what kind of argument they were having with Catarina. They'd protect the Utugan's mother with their lives if it came to that. It didn't matter if Jena was in the right, or that it should be her choice whether she talked to Elsa.

Like it or not, Catarina was a powerful member of the Utugani Hearth, and they needed her help. Jena couldn't go against Catarina's wishes, no matter how much she wanted to. She glanced at Nate. There was nothing but concern in his eyes. He wouldn't expect her to do anything against her will, but they both knew they needed the Utugani if they were going to save Bree and Argus.

Her hand rubbed over the knotted scars on her neck. The skin, even after all these years, was still sensitive. But it was a reminder that she was strong. It was a reminder that she was a survivor. That she never gave up. It was a reminder that she had survived worse than a conversation with an old lady.

She took a deep breath and lifted her head. Looking up at Elsa, she nodded. "Somewhere private, then."

"My... my wagon is just over here." Elsa gestured to one side of the hearth.

Jena looked where Elsa was pointing and experienced another jolt. The wagon was almost identical to the traveling wagon they'd lived in when she was a child. Even in the pre-dawn darkness, she could make out the forest green paint that covered the wooden side panels, accented with a brown trim. Flowers grew in containers on the windowsills, although the curtains fluttering behind them were an unfamiliar pattern. A grey horse chewed on grass on one side.

She hesitated for a moment longer, desperately not wanting to be reminded of her old life. But she'd survived worse. It was just bad memories. She could overcome that. Couldn't she?

Jena slowly followed the two older women, one foot in front of the other. She had to concentrate on every step. The comforting warmth of Nate's hand on her back kept her going, and she took a breath, then another. She could do this.

Probably.

As they got closer, she took in more of the details of the wagon. The intricately carved trim on the eaves of the roof was different to Elsa's old wagon, and the steps were a darker wood. Wordlessly, she followed Elsa and Catarina into the cramped interior. It was so similar to Elsa's old wagon that she stopped, stunned. She recognized the rug on the floor and the pictures on the walls. Was she dreaming? Lost in a memory, as she had been earlier? She pinched her arm. No, still awake.

"Please, sit down." Elsa's voice was pleading, begging her to be kind. Jena saw the small bench and table attached to the wall, and remembered sitting and playing cards, eating and joking with Elsa. She also remembered lying on that same table, screaming from the agony of the burns on her face and neck. Her mouth hardened. It was easy to be sad afterwards. Regret was a wonderful thing. She stayed standing, even when Elsa and Catarina sat down. Nate stayed behind her, supporting her, but not touching her. A solid presence that was the only thing keeping her sane.

"Where's Otis?" she said, deliberately taunting. She wished he would appear so she could show him what it was like to fight an adult.

"He's... He's dead, Jena. Killed."

Her eyes darted to Elsa's. "Who killed him?"

Elsa sighed. "He picked one too many fights. Someone landed a punch that sent him to the other side."

"When?"

"A few years ago, now." Elsa looked sad at the idea of Otis's death, but Jena couldn't feel anything but disappointment that she'd not been the one to cause it.

"He got what he deserved."

Elsa opened her mouth to speak, then closed it. She nodded. "I suppose he did. He was my son, but he wasn't a good man. I'm sorry, Jena, for what he did to you. For what it's worth, I tried to protect you."

Jena sneered. "No, you didn't. You don't get that salve to your conscience. You knew what he was. You let him bully me, you let him burn me, then you stood by while he sold me to the first available merchant. That's not protection." Jena spoke clearly and precisely, making every word count. "That's collusion."

A mottled red flush spread up Elsa's neck and onto her face. "I didn't know what had happened until it was too late. I didn't *let* him sell you, Jena. He told me you'd run away, and I believed him, because..." Tears filled Elsa's eyes, one escaping down her cheek. She reached up to wipe it away.

"Because it was easier? Better than having to stand up to your jealous and irrational son?"

She swallowed. "You always seemed to do just what was required to push him over the edge—"

Nate interrupted with a growl. "She was a child! Don't put the blame on Jena. He was a grown man who picked on a young girl," he snapped, stepping forward to stand beside Jena. "If that's why we're here—so you can lay the blame on Jena—we're leaving." Nate put an arm around Jena, and she took a gasping breath, leaning into his chest, grateful he was there with her. He was warmth and comfort in a situation that had somehow escalated until it was even worse than her nightmares. She'd thought she could handle anything, but she wasn't ready to hear Elsa blaming her for how Otis had treated her.

"Oh no. No, no, no," said Elsa, her voice wavering. "I wasn't blaming Jena. I didn't mean it like that. Otis just wouldn't see reason with her. Looking back, I can see he was jealous. He'd been my only child for so long. I spoiled him. I know I did. And he took it out on Jena. My sweet baby Jena."

Jena stared at Elsa, unsure how to take her words. Tears had filled the old woman's eyes again. "When he burned you..." She took a ragged breath, the sagging skin of her lined face jiggling as she shuddered.

Jena glared at Elsa, silently refusing to be moved by the old woman's remorse. Catarina sat silently beside Elsa, her dark eyes wide, her lined face pale. She clearly hadn't been expecting this level of emotion. Jena glared at her too. This was her fault.

Elsa gulped and took a deep breath, wiping away her

tears with a hand covered in silver rings. "When he burned you, I thought you were going to die. I still don't know how you survived such burns. But you did. It was then I realized he would kill you. I couldn't bear it, so I tried to back away, to make it seem like I loved you less than I did. I was trying to protect you."

Jena sneered. "You just helped him convince everyone I was bad luck, that *I* had caused all the problems at our campsite, not him." Jena paused, her stomach roiling, her throat thick with emotion. "And you convinced *me* that you didn't love me anymore. I didn't know what I'd done wrong." Her voice cracked on the last few words, and she wanted to take them back. They held so much pain, they showed too much of what she'd gone through. She didn't want this woman to know how badly she'd been hurt.

"I loved you! I did. He lied to me. I would never have let him sell you. Never." Elsa took a deep breath. "I don't expect you to forgive me, but please believe me. I loved you. I still do."

Jena shook her head, refusing to give in. "You *let* him. You wanted his lies because they were easier than the truth, the truth you knew in your heart." Jena fought to stay afloat in the emotions that were fighting for control inside her. Mostly, she felt pain and devastation, emotions she'd thought she'd buried long ago. She wanted to throw her fists and cast fire spells all around her, destroying everything in the small wagon. It was so familiar it hurt. "You knew what he was, what he did to me. If you'd really loved me, you would have known he was lying. You would have *protected* me."

Jena said the words like a mantra, repeating what her adult self knew to be true. But there was also another tiny part of her, an echo of that scared and lonely child, who heard the declaration of love and wanted to *believe*. Wanted to fall back into the arms of the woman who had meant so much to her.

But that part of her was small.

Insignificant.

Mostly, she knew the truth. That Elsa hadn't protected a vulnerable young child like she should have. That she didn't try hard enough. Elsa may as well have been the one to push Jena into the fire, because she'd allowed Otis to become so bold he thought he could get away with it.

She may as well have been the one to pocket the gold that Otis had taken for Jena—by the ashes, she probably *had* pocketed some of it, even if she'd been unaware— because she'd believed what Otis had told her without questioning him.

Elsa was weak.

Elsa didn't deserve her love.

CHAPTER 42

JENA

And perhaps that was it. The answer she'd been searching for all this time. It felt like an old wound had opened up inside her, gaping and painful, but she finally understood enough to heal it.

"You didn't deserve my love," whispered Jena. "You're a coward. That's why you let it happen." She shivered, the hairs on her arms rising in reaction. As a child, she'd never properly seen the flawed woman who stood in front of her now. "It was never my fault. It was *yours.*"

It was as if she was seeing Elsa for the first time. Now, as an adult, she could see that Elsa had always been that way. She hadn't liked conflict. She would always take the easy road, the path of least resistance. She'd let Otis get away with bullying the younger members of the group because to stop him would have been too much.

Memories resurfaced, things she'd buried long ago. He'd picked on all the kids, but Jena was the only one who'd stood up to him, who'd defended herself as well as the others. Elsa was right. She'd always known how to anger him, because she'd been trying to deflect his erratic temper away from the other kids.

After he'd sold her, Jena had curled up in her corner of the kitchen at night, wondering what was wrong with her. Why she'd been so easily discarded by her Utugani family. Why Elsa hadn't stood up for her when Otis sold her.

Why Otis hated her so much.

She'd always thought Elsa would keep him from truly hurting her. Instead she'd ended up a slave in a stranger's house, flawed and broken, scarred down one side of her body. She'd blamed herself, assumed that it was something about who *she* was.

Who would want someone so disfigured?

Certainly not Elsa.

Definitely not the Utugani.

"I never wanted to hurt you," Elsa insisted. "Please believe that I wouldn't have let him sell you. I would have stood up to him."

"You didn't stand up to him when he pushed me into the fire."

Elsa's gaze shifted away, the lines on her face deepening in sorrow. "He—he said it was an accident."

"But you knew it wasn't."

Elsa looked back at Jena, her tear-filled eyes beseeching. "Not until long after. He let it slip once you'd been gone a few months." She reached out with one hand, then dropped it. "By then it was too late. You'd left me." Elsa's voice was almost petulant, and Jena saw a moment of anger in her face.

Jena's wrath flared in response. "So you blamed *me*? You were upset with *me*? You knew what Otis was like, but you believed him when he said I'd run away?" Jena rubbed her forehead with a trembling hand. The old woman had believed Jena had deserted her. She felt as if her head was exploding. "You thought I'd run away by myself, when I hated to sleep with no one else in the wagon? When I feared the dark?"

It had been the result of constant bullying from Otis, and maybe even from the long-forgotten knowledge that there should have been another little girl sleeping nearby. She should never have been alone. She should have grown up in the comfort and safety of a home with a sister who looked just like her.

"I didn't think. I..."

"You didn't *want* to think. You believed Otis because it was easier," Jena practically snarled out the words. "I had to learn to survive, scared and alone, in the household of a stranger who paid Otis a pittance for me to be the lowliest of the slaves in his home. I was kicked and shoved and spat on, given the worst possible tasks. I was expected to keep waking up each day and continue on with no hope of ever being free again. It made me strong, but by the Ashes, it was soul-destroying. And you are directly to blame for that. *You*, Elsa." Jena knew she was ranting, but she couldn't help it. She needed Elsa to know and understand what had happened to her, what she had done. It wasn't enough to be sorry. She had to *understand.*

Jena had seen herself as damaged and unwanted. It had formed her, made her wary of others and afraid to love.

"I didn't—I wasn't—" Elsa gave Catarina a beseeching look, as if begging the older woman to believe her inarticulate denials.

Catarina just watched Jena, the lines on her face deeper than they'd been before.

"I was a *child slave.* I had no one who cared about me, no one to look after me. I was only valuable for what I could do as a servant, how much water I could carry or how many floors I could scrub. And when they needed money, they sold me at the markets, like I was a horse or a goat."

Elsa gasped, and even Catarina blanched at Jena's words.

Her words couldn't even explain how bad it had been. Jena had been terrified, standing up on the slave block. It had been worse than when Otis had sold her, because back then, she hadn't realized what it would be like. When Thornal had bought her, and she saw he was a mage, she'd been sure he was planning to experiment on her or turn her into a frog for one of his spells.

It had only been luck that Thornal had turned out to be her savior. He'd been the first person to care about Jena since Elsa. But because of Elsa's betrayal, she'd held her heart close to her chest and didn't give an inch to Thornal. It had taken years before his unruffled disposition allowed her to believe he might not throw her away, too. Even then, she'd never been entirely sure he wouldn't one day change his mind.

But if the problem was Elsa, then... it changed everything. Maybe Jena wasn't to blame. Maybe she wasn't as damaged as she'd thought. Maybe Elsa had still loved her, in her own way.

"I'm so sorry. I didn't know." Elsa's voice wavered as she spoke. Her face was blotchy, and tears ran down her face. She looked like she'd seen a ghost. "I never thought..."

"You only thought about yourself, and what it would mean to you."

"I wish I'd left you in the forest where I found you," murmured Elsa as she dabbed at the tears on her face.

The words were whispered softly, but they pierced a knife right through Jena's flesh, all the way to her heart. She choked out a sound, her throat strangled with emotion. Just when she'd started thinking that maybe Elsa had loved Jena in her own way...

"That's enough," growled Nate. "We're done. Catarina, I'm sure your intentions were good, but we're not taking any more." Nate's warm hands turned Jena and ushered her to the door. Jena tried to take comfort in his protection of her, but all she could think was that she'd been right after all.

Elsa wished she'd never even met her.

There was noise behind them as Elsa pushed her bulky frame to standing and took a step toward them. "No! *No!* Not because I regret knowing you, loving you, Jena. It's because Catarina tells me your sister had a much better life than the one I gave you. All you had from me was pain and suffering." Elsa took a sobbing breath. "I'm sorry, Jena. So very sorry."

Nate hesitated by the door. Jena lifted her head and peered cautiously at Elsa. Tears were flowing down Elsa's face. She seemed sincere. But was it real?

Taking a breath, Elsa went to a small cupboard above the kitchen bench, pulling out a carved wooden box. Opening the lid, Elsa drew out a chain with a silver amulet in the shape of a raven. She held it out to Jena. "This is yours. I was going to give it to you when you were a little older. But I never had the chance." She dropped the amulet into Jena's hand.

The power hit her immediately, compelling and...familiar. The potent magic swirled over her, insistent and forceful. Jena recoiled back and almost dropped the necklace before she steadied herself.

"Jena?" Nate's questioning word was accompanied by a gentle touch on her shoulder. He was right there, ready to defend her. It gave her the strength she needed to continue.

"It's fine,' she said, taking a deep breath. She balanced out her reaction and pushed the magic away. Then she looked down at the silver raven in her palm. It was her father's amulet; she was sure of it. It was supposed to protect her, as the wooden owl amulet had protected Bree. The design was intricate, with the wings outstretched, reminding her of the raven that curled around her stomach, and the small carved raven Thornal had given her. Her tattoo shuffled against her skin in response.

The dark eyes of the raven amulet seemed to understand her, and she somehow recognized the piercing gaze. That night, or some part of it, skittered across her mind. She felt rain, heard howls in the distance. The kiss of her mother, the brush of her father's hand. The heavy silver placed on her chest. She'd fought it. Somehow, she'd known their parents were leaving them, and she'd fought it.

Even then, she'd struggled against the way things had to be. She'd battled against the inevitable. And look where it had gotten her. On an impossible mission to fight a powerful enemy, with a skill that would probably get her killed.

"I have to think," said Jena, her mind whirling painfully. "This is too much." She'd expected it to be difficult to be here among the Utugani, but she hadn't expected it to be this bad. She never thought she'd meet Elsa again.

And to be given this piece of her father, along with the memories of that night... Her mind felt overly full, swirling with confusing emotions. All of a sudden, the wagon felt cramped and suffocating. The eyes of everyone on her was too much, too pointed. With a moan, she pushed past Nate and ran out of the small, cramped wagon.

She ran without thinking, trying to escape the pain. She thought she'd overcome the feelings of being sold, of being deserted by the woman who raised her. But she'd just buried it deep down. The wound inside her chest felt like an enormous fizzing fracture, gaping and wide and waiting to envelop her whole. It was just as bad as it used to be when she was a child. As much as she wanted to believe it was all because Elsa was shallow and spineless, there was a ragged and bruised part of Jena that still believed she was to blame. That there was something wrong with her.

So she ran as fast as she could until she couldn't run any more, until her breath came in loud gasps and she was so dizzy she saw stars. She was near the river, a spot along the edge that was protected by trees and grass, and a distance from the Utugani camp. She collapsed onto the ground and pulled her knees up to her chin, wrapping her arms tightly around her legs. It was like she was trying to physically hold in all the emotions, trying to control the tide that was threatening to break loose.

Moments later, Nate sat down beside her, still trying to catch his breath. He said nothing at first, just breathed heavily. And then he stayed silent, waiting for her reaction. She shuddered, and he put a gentle arm around her, lending her some of his warmth. Her skin shivered, but it wasn't unpleasant. She leaned into him.

"It's a lot to take in," he said eventually.

"Yes."

"She seemed to mean what she said. She wasn't lying." Nate said the words softly, tentatively. "She loved you."

Jena shook her head immediately in rejection of his words. "She should have fought harder. She should have protected me more. I was just a *kid*. She was an adult, and she let me take the brunt of Otis's rages."

"You're strong, Jena. You stand up for what you believe in, but not everyone can do that. Sometimes people just want as few waves in the pond as possible."

Jena stiffened. He was defending Elsa?

She tried to pull away but wasn't strong enough. "You think it's okay what she did?"

"Of course not. I don't mean—" Nate tightened his arm around her shoulder. "I'm not absolving her. What happened to you wasn't okay."

"She let Otis hurt me," she whispered brokenly, her voice raw. Her words seemed to echo across the water.

"She should have looked after you better," said Nate carefully. She could feel the rumble of his words against her skin. "And I wish with every bone in my body that I could have been there to protect you from everything that happened. I'm just saying that she seemed sincere. I think she really loved you. And I don't think she had any part in Otis selling you. He lied to her about it, and she believed him."

"Because it was easier."

"Probably. She's not like you. She's not brave or determined."

"I don't feel brave," she whispered. The words poured out of her. Jena tried to hold them in, but she couldn't. "I feel like I'm back there in my childhood, wishing I'd been a better person, so they'd have kept me."

She felt rather than saw Nate's sharp intake of breath. "None of it was your fault. Otis was a bully and a worm, and probably an expert at manipulation. You were just a kid. You shouldn't have had to go up against an adult like that. It was never your fault they sold you. *Never*." He said the words so vehemently it was like an oath.

Jena took a breath, startled by his fierceness. Why did

he care so much about how she'd felt as a child? "Thank you," she whispered.

"You dropped this," said Nate, holding out the silver raven amulet.

Jena felt the jolt of magic as it landed in her palm, and she almost dropped it again. The amulet overwhelmed her senses, and this time, she couldn't dampen them down. The crack inside her expanded unexpectedly until it finally broke, like an earthquake erupting inside her body.

She clutched the silver raven to her chest, trying to take strength from the familiar feel of her father's magic. But it wasn't enough. Heat rushed up her body, her face crumpled, and painful tears fled down her cheeks. The dam she'd been trying to hold back finally broke. Gasping sobs racked her body. Everything felt broken and uneven. Her skin was too tight, and her scars ached. The raven moved uncomfortably.

It was all too much.

She turned instinctively to Nate, scrunching herself up against his solid, warm chest. He held her as she cried gut-wrenching sobs that felt like they were breaking her apart.

CHAPTER 43
NATE

Nate held Jena long after her sobs had ceased. He knew touching her was a risk, but he couldn't help it. Not when she was hurting so badly. And every time he touched her, she let him stay a little longer.

He thought he'd been doing the right thing by picking up the amulet that she'd dropped from her nerveless fingers as she'd fled the wagon, but it seemed to have tipped her over the edge. Yet another thing he didn't get quite right.

Except... maybe she'd needed to let the emotions out? Her sobs had been raw and powerful, but until now they'd been pent up inside her. Maybe now she would be lighter? More at ease?

On the inside, at least.

He'd guessed some of what she'd told them back in the wagon, but it had been shocking to hear her spell it out. She'd been a child slave, the lowest of the low. Sold for a pittance because she dared to stand up to her foster-brother. Nate had always known that she was tenacious and brave, but now he knew just how strong she really was.

She was fire and determination and fury.

He peered down at her. She looked more relaxed; her face was pale in the pre-dawn light, but peaceful. She was so still and silent he thought she might have dozed off. He tried to hold himself as still as possible, to let her rest.

He couldn't imagine being sold to a stranger by the people who were supposed to take care of you. His family had sent him away, but they'd never disowned him. They'd always made sure he had a bed and food and people to look after him. He really wished he could have been there with her, to protect her from Otis. He wanted to magic away the pain she'd experienced as a child.

"Thank you," she said after a while, her voice low and raw. She pulled back out of his arms, and he reluctantly let her. Her eyes stood out on her ashen face like dark pebbles in a stream. He knew that every moment of touch against her skin was a big decision for Jena. When she'd let him comfort her, she'd granted him something precious.

"Anytime," he said, and he meant it like an oath. He hoped she couldn't hear what he was really saying. He'd faced assassins, flames and death. But he couldn't quite bring himself to tell her how he felt about her. Not yet.

She sighed. "You always seem to catch me when I'm at my worst." She looked away across the river, as if she wished she were anywhere else right now. Her long hair billowed down her back, and Nate had to rein in the impulse to run his fingers through it. "Your worst is other people's best," he said with a small smile. "You're allowed to be broken. You're still the strongest person I know."

She scowled at him, her eyebrows drawing down over her serious eyes. "I mean it. I appreciate you being here with me."

"Right place, right time." Nate pushed down the other

words that were clamoring inside his head, trying to be heard. It wasn't the right time to be asking for more. She needed a friend. Someone to help her through this. Not a fumbling idiot, saying he wanted to be more than friends and companions on the road.

He cleared his throat. "Do you feel any better?"

She nodded. "It was just too much all at once." Her skin was blotchy from crying, and her scars ran down her face like a river, but she had never seemed so beautiful as she grappled with her past and tried to make sense of this new reality.

"Catarina meant well."

"I didn't tell her who gave me the burns, or what Otis was really like. She thought it was just a silly misunderstanding."

"I know you don't want to hear this, but Elsa really seemed like she didn't know anything."

Jena sighed. "I meant what I said. She knew what Otis was like, she knew *me*, and she still believed him. That hurt far worse than anything Otis ever did." She touched the scarred side of her face as if to emphasize her point. "She didn't stand up for me."

Nate heard the undercurrent. Her younger self had wondered what she'd done wrong, just like he had at the same age. She'd blamed herself.

"You weren't the problem. They were," he said firmly.

"She survived something that not everyone could." Thornal's voice was soft. *"She's stronger because of it. And she's more Utugani than Elsa or Otis combined."*

Nate's heart lurched into his throat as soon as Thornal spoke. He'd forgotten the ghost mage for a moment. He swallowed hard, and forced himself to continue the conversation, to help Jena, despite the mage next to him. "Jena—"

A distant scream broke the tranquil setting, and Nate jerked back, turning to look behind them. "What was—"

More screams filled the air, and Nate and Jena both scrambled to their feet. They stared at each other, eyes wide, for half a breath.

"It sounds like it's coming from the Utugani camp," said Jena urgently. "Come on."

Together, they sprinted back the way they'd come. Dawn was spilling over into the surrounding landscape, and Nate saw smoke slithering up into the sky in the distance. A roaring screech filled the air near the camp, and he ran even faster, pushing his body to the limit. His heart was pounding, and he felt like he was going to be sick. More smoke filled the air around them as they got closer, and Nate's breath hitched.

Something was attacking the camp at the worst possible moment.

Was it another creature sent by Lothar? Or something completely unconnected? It had to be aimed at Nate—who else would attack the Utugani like this? He'd known Lothar was after him. That he would do anything to kill Nate before the coronation. And still he'd blindly lumbered his way into the Utugani Hearth, bringing his troubles with them. He should have known better.

It was his fault they were all in danger.

He sprinted in a direct line for the campsite, his thoughts bashing around inside his head. Screams and the sounds of the unknown beasts attacking filled the air. If only they'd never visited the Utugani. If only Catarina hadn't meddled. If only they hadn't run so far.

All he could think about was the young kids he'd watched playing around the tents this morning. The women and shy young children who'd listened to the story of how Argus had saved him.

He heard a familiar screech from the air—Rothell had entered the fray. It didn't make him feel better. It meant that whatever was attacking the Utugani was something that Rothell didn't think they could handle on their own. Beside him, Jena was gasping for breath, but she didn't let up any more than he did. They'd made too many friends in a short amount of time to be anything but desperate to help.

They burst through the trees and into the clearing to find the mostly broken-down campsite in total chaos. At least ten large, winged creatures that looked like a mage spell gone wrong—somehow mixing a giant flying insect with a lion—were zipping around in the air above the camp, ripping anything that looked breakable with their enormous claws, and pulling the camp apart.

Luckily, most of the tents were packed down, but there were still belongings and equipment in piles waiting to be packed for transporting, hearth fires with their breakfast still bubbling and far too many wagons parked nearby. People were running about, dodging the flying creatures, as they tried to protect themselves, their children, and their possessions.

"What in the Fiery Flames *are* they?" asked Nate.

He'd never seen anything like it. They had six hairy legs with paws like a lion's, and wings that flicked them about like flies. They had the head of a lion and blank golden eyes that seemed to see everything and nothing at the same time.

Utugani warriors were throwing spears, but the creatures seemed to know exactly when to move to avoid being hit.

"Barker lions," said Jena, her voice breaking in the middle.

"What does the book say about them?"

"They're—they're..." Jena took a shuddering breath and started again. "They rarely attack by themselves. They're carrion animals, they usually take the dead and dying left by predators."

"Does that mean something else is here too?"

"Maybe. Or maybe Lothar is forcing them outside of their normal instincts, like he did with the murghah and the ash-fang. The murghah didn't want to be out in the sunlight when she attacked us the first time. It was burning her hide, but she did it anyway."

Jena looked at him, her eyes haunted. They both knew this was their responsibility. They'd drawn these creatures here, putting the Utugani in danger.

"How do we kill them?" Nate asked grimly. That was all they could do.

"Fire. Lots of fire," said Jena. "I need to get to the main campfire and use a spell to gather up the flames and throw them, see if that works."

Nate nodded. Jena's mage skills were above and beyond anything he was capable of. "I'll summon a demon. But I'll need to stay here, out of the way, to do it."

Jena nodded once, then hesitated like she wanted to say more.

"Take care of yourself," said Nate softly. He didn't want to separate, but they had to help the Utugani.

Jena blinked, then nodded again sharply, and took off.

"You'll need to use your flames. There are wolvans here, too. A demon and the shimagni won't be enough." Nate jumped—the mage ghost was always sneaking up on him.

Correction: Thornal, the Guardian, the most powerful

mage of their time, kept sneaking up on him. It made him shudder just thinking about who had been following him around.

Nate shook his head, trying to be polite, despite the fear surging through his veins. "I can't use my fire. It's too dangerous. What else can we do?"

"Son, we don't have time to argue. You can do this. You don't need to be afraid of your powers. I can help you." Thornal gave him a stern look, and gestured for him to get a move on, like he expected Nate to just do what he said.

But Nate still remembered what happened last time. "Like you helped me in that mercenary camp? I went berserk and killed everyone there! What if I hurt the Utugani? Or Jena?"

"It doesn't work like that."

Nate studiously ignored Thornal—even though he was the guardian—and crouched down behind the closest wagon. He closed his eyes and demanded that a demon come forth. Moments later, it was there, glowing softly in front of him.

"Yes, Master?" it said.

"I need you to fight those creatures in the air, kill them all—except the shimagni. Don't hurt anyone else except the barker lions."

The demon's eyes lit up. Usually, Nate didn't let them do anything as exciting as killing.

"As you wish, Master." It took off.

Nate crept along the edge of the wagon, wondering if he should summon another demon. He briefly considered summoning *hundreds* of them, like he had on the mountain, but the thought of being surrounded by so many demons again was even more overwhelming than using his Fire-caller magic. It had also depleted all his other magic, leaving him vulnerable. He wasn't ready to go that route just yet.

"You don't need to summon the demons. Not this time. Just use your own powers."

"I can't—"

Screams rent the air, terrified and raw.

"The wolvans are attacking."

Nate didn't hesitate. He ran toward the sounds of the screaming, looking around for some kind of weapon as he went. He grabbed a broom that had been left lying on the ground, desperately wishing he had a sword or a knife.

He turned the corner on one of the last tents still standing and almost tripped over a bloodied pile of flesh. It was an Utugani warrior, his body almost torn in two. Nate recognized him immediately—it was Seban, the one-eyed Utugani warrior who'd been on guard duty when they first arrived.

Nate felt the porridge he'd eaten less than an hour ago rising from his stomach. He swallowed hard and forced himself to keep going. There were two other dead warriors with similar wounds. Ahead of him, three more men battled an enormous beast that almost looked like a wolf— but a wolf from someone's nightmares. Enormous, bigger than the three warriors put together, its fur was ragged and unkempt, its ears bitten and frayed and its eyes glowed red, like it was possessed by a demon. Except Nate knew it wasn't. They were just... focused. Once they had a target, they kept going until either the target was dead, or they were.

One of the warriors tripped over a rope from the tent, falling backward onto the ground, and the wolvan didn't hesitate. It struck out with one paw, its claws ripping into the man's chest.

The man—a guard from the Utugan's tent—cried out in pain, then went horribly silent. The wolvan snarled, but the other two men didn't look away. They knew they'd be dead if they tried to help their fallen friend. They just kept hacking at the wolvan with their spears.

Nate hesitated behind them, remembering how Argus had saved him from wolvans when they first met. The big man hadn't even *tried* to fight them. Their only plan had been to distract and run.

Wolvans didn't stop; they didn't listen to reason, and they were stronger than ten men put together.

The entire camp of people would all be dead if Nate couldn't figure out a way to save them—and Jena and himself. Jena was powerful, but not against so many attackers. The Utugani warriors had only their physical weapons. He was the wild card, the one of them with something more to offer. He knew it, but it was the last thing he wanted to do.

"You must use your powers, Nate. And fast. More people die every second you delay."

Everything inside Nate rebelled at the idea.

"It's the only way these people will survive. There are too many dark creatures. I will help you control the flames."

Fighting his own instincts, which shouted that he couldn't control an ant, let alone the powerful flames inside him, Nate closed his eyes.

He had no choice.

He would have to let the flames free.

CHAPTER 44
JENA

J ena desperately scrambled around near the main campfire.

One of the barker lions had already destroyed it, and everything was scattered about in pieces. The porridge pot lay on its side, the stones were no longer in a tidy circle, and the wood itself had burned low and was mostly out of flame.

She was trying to pull sufficient fire out of the remains to create an even bigger fireball than usual, so that it might actually kill a barker lion. She heard a buzzing sound and looked up to see a creature flitting menacingly overhead. She raised her hand and flicked a silver fire spell at it. The creature darted away, and the fireball whizzed by harmlessly.

Jena swore.

She muttered the words of another spell under her breath, trying not to draw too much attention, but knowing it was pointless. The secret of her mage powers was going to be obvious to the Utugani after this. What would the Utugani do to her once it was over? Would they refuse to help Nate's quest? Or would they attempt to execute her, as was mage law?

She didn't know the answer, but she knew she couldn't just leave them to their fate. She and Nate had drawn these monsters here to the Utugani Hearth, and it was their responsibility to defend them.

"Hey," yelled a voice behind Jena.

Jena turned and saw an Utugani guard with a long spear. He had blood dripping down his face and arms.

"You need to get back to the tent with the other women," he said. "It's not safe out here. Those things will rip you apart." He gestured toward the barker lions in the sky.

Jena followed his arm and stared at the creatures. Part of her wanted to do just that. To hide in the tent. To keep her magic hidden and not get herself killed trying to save people she didn't even know.

Except... "I'm more powerful than you think," she said. What was the point of having magic if she couldn't use it to save people? "And I'm safer out here than you are."

She turned away from the Utugani warrior, and her magic surged inside her. The remaining fire from the wood merged into one spitting ball of flames. Another barker lion was hovering nearby, distracted by three more Utugani warriors with spears. She didn't even hesitate, casting the fireball at the creature. The ball of flames hit dead center and burned through its body.

The creature gave a garbled screech, and then fell to the ground, dead before it landed.

The warriors turned to Jena, startled.

She swallowed, straightened her back, and stared back. For the first time in her life, she'd just given herself away to a group of people she didn't really know, and she wasn't sure what they'd do. Her blood pounded in her veins, and her mind blanked for a moment. If any of these warriors told the wrong person, she was dead.

No one would blame them if they threw a spear through her heart right now. A woman who cast spells was an abomination.

Instead, they nodded grimly, then ran off to help someone else. She turned back to the guard behind her, but he was following the other three warriors.

She stared after them, wondering what else they'd seen, that her powers didn't even faze them. Would they—

A piercing scream filled the air nearby, and Jena jumped, startled out of her thoughts. The noise and furor of the surrounding battle filled her senses again, and she looked around.

People were running between the remaining tents and wagons. Utugani warriors crept through the hearth, stalking the wolvans, their faces grim. They would all die if she couldn't do more to save them. She had to gather more flames.

She moved closer to the campfire again, muttering the same spell a second time, trying to draw more of the flames out of the dying embers.

A rush of wind pushed Jena's hair off her face as Rothell flew by overhead, chasing a barker lion, its high-pitched squeals panicked as she closed in on it.

Jena raised one hand to protect her eyes from the dust that swirled up. The air made sparks fly from the fire, and the flames surged higher again. She gathered the flames into her hands, creating another ball of fire. Then she looked around. Where best to use it?

The growl of a wolvan sounded nearby, and Jena moved quickly. Flame-filled hands held out in front, she raced toward a gap between a caravan and a tent and came up from behind on the wolvan. Up close, the creature was enormous, its back higher than a person, with long mottled fur and paws the size of Jena's head.

It could kill Jena with one swipe.

This close, it was smellier than she'd expected, like the stench of a wet, long-haired dog, only a hundred times worse. The thought of a pack of these creatures hunting her parents through the Forest of Ghosts made her feel sick.

She swallowed hard. The wolvan was fighting off six Utugani warriors, each with a spear. There were two more warriors lying dead nearby, their bodies torn apart. Jena tried not to look at their faces, scared it would be someone she knew. The remaining warriors were desperately guarding the Utugan's tent, where they'd met him yesterday. It felt like a hundred years ago.

Her heart stopped. Who was in there? The Utugan? Definitely his youngest daughter, Ellie. Maybe Catarina and some of the other children. She had no choice. She had to stop this creature.

She flicked through the Book of Spells, but it had nothing more to say on the wolvans than what was immediately obvious to Jena as she crouched just behind this one. Large, powerful. Focused on its target. No mercy, no thought.

She crept forward, trying to figure out the best way to use her ball of flames on the wolvan. Throw it toward its middle? Its head? It was hard to know where it would be weakest. It looked rugged and tough everywhere.

Before she could even throw the ball of light, the wolvan turned unexpectedly and leaped at her, jaws full of snarling teeth. Jena tripped and fell backward, landing painfully on her butt. Air whooshed out of her lips, and she had no time to think. All she could see was a mouth full of teeth, glowing red eyes and a beast so immersed in the hunt that it had lost all reason.

For a moment, time stood still, and she wondered if this was it. The moment it all ended. Then she lifted her hands, thrusting the sizzling ball of flames at the wolvan. There was no time to aim, no time for thinking. The wolvan tried to twist out of the way of the fireball, but she'd hurled it harder than usual, and the flames hit it square in the chest, burning through fur, skin, and then the bones underneath. The wolvan howled in pain, and the smell of sizzling fur filled the air.

But Jena didn't have time to feel relieved. The fireball hadn't stopped the enormous creature's aborted leap, and it toppled directly toward her.

CHAPTER 45
JENA

S he screamed out a barrier spell, using the surrounding air to create a shield around her body.

The wolvan's body slammed into the shield of air, sending a shock wave through Jena's body, but protecting her from the worst of its weight. The wolvan shuddered, then slid off the shield and fell to the ground, dead.

Breathing heavily, Jena scrambled backward, barely able to comprehend what had just happened. She looked up, and one of the Utugani warriors ran over to her.

"You are a brave woman," he said, helping her to her feet. He was the warrior who'd delivered their supplies this morning and told them about the porridge in the pot. He had a claw mark down one arm and was bleeding from a gash on his forehead.

Jena nodded and winced as she stood back on her feet, wishing she felt brave. Mostly, she just felt scared and worried that their efforts wouldn't be enough. Even now, her magic was a distant flame compared to what it had been. She'd used up too much on too little. "How many wolvans have you seen so far?" she asked, her voice uneven.

"Too many," he replied, his expression grim. "For every one we kill, another appears."

Jena looked up at him and saw the truth in his dark brown eyes. They needed to do something drastic, or they were all going to die.

"Do you wish to go into the safety of the tent? I will tell them about your bravery. My brothers and I will protect you as best we can."

Jena glanced over at the remaining warriors. They all looked exhausted, like they'd been fighting for hours. There was no safety in this situation.

Not even inside that tent.

"I'm far more useful out here," she said grimly.

He nodded in understanding. "You're probably right. Your flames saved us." He bowed and ran back to his position in front of the tent.

Jena hesitated for a moment, staring around at the devastation. Smoke and fire filled the air. Shouts and screams pierced the growls and screeches of the creatures that were still attacking the camp. She flicked through the Book in her head, frantically trying to find something that would help.

Nothing seemed quite enough.

They needed to change what they were doing. They wouldn't win if they continued to fight in the same way. It wasn't working, and it wouldn't suddenly change.

And that's when she felt it…

The terrifying warmth of a fire so big, it couldn't be contained.

Was it another creature sent to kill them? She didn't

think there was anyone strong enough to fight something that could produce that amount of power.

She ran down the space between the Utugan's tent and a wagon, looking for the source. Fear surged inside her; something far worse than barker lions and wolvans had just been unleashed.

Except...it felt familiar.

Could that surge of power be *Nate*? She'd felt Nate's Firecaller flames before. Maybe that was why she recognized it?

Her stomach churned at the thought.

He was on their side, but his power was untamed and unpredictable. He hadn't figured out how to control it. The last time he'd fully set it free, he'd killed an entire camp of hardened mercenaries. Jena had walked through the camp after Nate had burned it all to ash. She'd seen what he'd done and knew the power it would take to control magic like that. It was a level of control Nate didn't have, not yet.

If he unleashed his powers now, they could all die, right here, today. Everything they'd fought against, everything that had happened, would be for nothing. But if he didn't, what would happen? They'd all be dead, anyway.

He might be their savior, or he might be their destroyer.

Her breathing was ragged, and her thoughts stuttered to a halt as she tried to figure out what to do. But there was only one thing she *could* do. Despite her body wanting to run the other way, she ran toward the surge of power to see if she could help. Perhaps if she were there, he might not kill everyone in sight?

Rothell roared overhead as if she agreed, and another barker lion fell from the sky, dead. If it had just been the barker lions, perhaps they might have been okay, but Jena had glimpsed another wolvan as she'd raced away from the

Utugan's tent, and she knew there were more lurking in the shadows.

She rounded a corner of a brightly painted wagon and came face to face with a barker lion that had cornered three children and a woman against a tent. This close, the creature was twice Jena's height, with sinewy strength in its multitude of legs. Its wings beat lazily as if it had all the time in the world to kill its prey. The Utugani woman stood in front of the children, protecting them from the barker lion with nothing more than an old wooden broom. Her long black hair was flying everywhere around her face, and she looked like she was planning to protect the children with everything she had.

"Oy! Over here!" yelled Jena, waving her arms at the barker lion. It turned its head, the golden orb-eyes reflecting the fires in the distance. Its wings flickered uncertainly, like it didn't know what to make of her. Then it snarled, showing large, pointed teeth.

Jena muttered a spell under her breath, and a thundering wind flew toward the creature, buffeting it backward. It flapped its wings and used four of its six legs to hold on to the nearby wagon. When the wind eased, it simply snarled at her and turned back to the Utugani woman. It raised one clawed leg as if it were about to strike.

Jena flicked her fingers, and her silver flame appeared in her palm. She whispered another spell from the Book of Spells, and a line of flames burned out from her hands. She hit the barker lion in one of its strange golden eyes, and this time the creature screamed, stumbling backward.

The Utugani woman leaped forward and jabbed the broom handle deep into the creature's other eye. Her whole body trembled with the effort of shoving the stick as far into the creature's head as possible. The barker lion tensed, then shuddered and fell to the ground, dead.

It was a quick and dirty death, and it only worked because the barker lion had been distracted. But it was dead. Jena breathed out a relieved sigh.

"Take the children, run that way," she said, pointing in the opposite direction to where she felt Nate's flames. "Hide if you can."

"Thank you," whispered the woman, her eyes saying more than her words could. Jena recognized her from the night before; she was one of the women who'd listened to Nate tell his stories.

"Just go. Hurry." Jena gestured with her hand. Her heart was thumping madly in her chest. She was worried that her magic wouldn't be enough to save her a second time.

The woman gathered the children around her and ran.

Jena kept running toward Nate. With every step, she could feel the burn of his power getting stronger, brighter. He really was going to set it free. She wondered if he was doing it on purpose. She stumbled and almost fell, righting herself just in time. She could still hear the yells of the Utugani as they fought all around the campsite. The air was choked with smoke and fear. Rothell flew overhead, her magic scales shimmering. Flames burst from her mouth, and another barker lion screamed. But there were still so many of them in the sky.

Jena crouched low, trying to avoid being seen by any of the attacking creatures. She could probably fight off one or two of the barker lions, but she was afraid it would use up too much of her magic, and she had a feeling she'd need everything inside her to deal with Nate and his Firecaller powers. Was she making a mistake by returning to him? She didn't know. But he'd been there when she needed him, so she would do the same. She was following her gut, and it led her straight back to Nate.

If she helped him, and he could control his flames, then he could take on all these creatures by himself. She knew it. It would all be over.

A burst of flames went up into the sky just ahead of her, on the other side of a half-collapsed tent. Jena gasped as the heat burned her skin. She turned away, holding an arm over her face. Her scars tightened in remembered pain, and she almost growled with the effort to stay where she was.

Nate. It had to be. He'd released his Firecaller magic.

He might burn her to a crisp, just like the mercenaries. She could still smell the burning flesh. He wouldn't mean to do it, and he would be horrified when he came back into his real self, but it could happen.

She paused, trying to figure out what to do.

In the distance, a woman screamed in terror. A wolvan roared in triumph.

She had no choice.

Jena took a breath and ran on, directly toward Nate.

CHAPTER 46
NATE

Nate concentrated on his powerful core of magic, and let the flames rise to the surface, fiery and fierce.

They rose greedily inside him, hungry for the burn.

"Hold it steady, son. Don't let it go," said Thornal.

Nate couldn't help it. He growled. "By the ashes, what do you think I'm *trying* to do?" he said to Thornal.

The flames burned inside and outside of him, an inferno of heat and fire and devastation. The power was immense, burning everywhere around him. He was terrified he'd let go, that he wouldn't be able to control it after all. That he'd burn every man, woman and child from the Utugani campsite to ash. That he'd kill Jena. Eldrin. Even Argus inside the fire ruby.

Bile rose and burned the inside of his throat, and the surrounding flames flashed brighter.

"Just concentrate. Keep it controlled."

He swallowed hard. "I thought you said you'd be able to help," he muttered, his entire focus on his battle with the flames. "Not just offer idiotic suggestions."

His whole body felt like it was being ripped apart, his skin stretched tight over his flesh, his insides rubbed raw. The magic was coarse and unfiltered, but so, so powerful. The flames battered and pushed at his defenses, eager and confident they would gain control. The magic was practically strutting about like a rooster on a farm, preening itself and crowing at the sun, it was so sure Nate was about to let go.

The Firecaller magic wanted to burn everything and everyone in its path. Nate could see it inside his head. The image was so vivid. They would devour everyone, including Jena.

Especially Jena.

Somehow the flames knew she was important to Nate, and they focused their magic on her, as if burning her to ash would somehow give them more power. They surged in anticipation; the flames burned higher and hotter and more powerfully than anything Nate had experienced before.

They hadn't been this powerful when he'd let the flames kill all the mercenaries. They'd never felt like this before, and something inside Nate broke. He wasn't strong enough to control them. He should never have let them free.

Nate screamed, a raw, hoarse sound that was more like an animal than a person. It felt like the only way to express everything that was happening. The sound reverberated around him, its echoes bouncing off the wagons nearby. The flames seemed to lap it up, to enjoy the pain inside the sound.

"This is no time to lose control," said Thornal. He was pacing next to Nate, his worried face turned toward the rest of the hearth.

"No kidding," said Nate, his teeth gritted.

"Have you ever tried to knit?" asked Thornal.

"This is not the fucking time for your ridiculousness," growled Nate. The flames licked at his face, his arms. They softened, almost caressing him. It was like they'd changed tactics and had decided to seduce him instead of overpowering him.

"Humor me." Thornal's voice was grim.

"Knitting. Okay. Using pointed sticks?" Beads of sweat were dripping down Nate's face, and he knew he didn't have long. He couldn't believe he was talking about knitting with the ghost mage. He wished he were anywhere but here.

"Yes."

"Then no. I've never tried it. But one of my old nursemaids used to do it. I watched her."

"You need to do that. Knit everything together. Use the strands of magic to weave a greater, more cohesive whole. One that you control."

"That sounds great. But *how*?"

"I've never experienced Firecaller magic before, not like this. But even I can feel the strands. If you take a breath and stop panicking like a baby, you will too."

Nate desperately wanted to argue about whether he was acting like a baby, but Thornal was right. He needed to focus.

He closed his eyes and looked for the strands Thornal was going on about. Once he knew what to look for, they were obvious. Lines of burning flame within the whole. A pattern amidst the chaos.

He could knit them all together. Or at least, he could do something like it to get these flames under control. He doubted his nursemaid would call it knitting. He closed his eyes, and let his consciousness expand out, to the flames engulfing him, to the magic that surrounded him.

The strands were everywhere, crossing over, intersecting. He tried to pull them together, to fold them over each other, like his nursemaid used to do. But they resisted. They fought him. The strands didn't want to be woven together, constrained, or tied up. They wanted to burn uncontrolled through the whole campsite, devouring everything in their path. He snarled, pulling the sound from somewhere deep inside, and focused everything he had on controlling the flames. Dominating them.

He needed to create a woven blanket of flames. He needed to rule them in every sense, to make them bow to his superior power.

Except the flames kept fighting him. They pushed him away, fought against him with everything they had. Nate stretched and strained, pushing this way and that, but he couldn't quite force them into the pattern he wanted.

"Nate!"

The voice made him jump. Startled, he turned and saw Jena standing in front of him, small and fragile, the burns on her face and hands like a beacon to the powerful flames inside him. For a second, the flames surged, and he battled the urge to blast his fire at her, to burn her to cinders, to smell the glorious scent of newly created ash. It felt like he was breaking in two as he fought the craving. His whole body was tight with resistance; so tight, he thought he might break into a million pieces.

"*Hold on to it, Nate. Hold it tight!*" said Thornal, his voice desperate. He could tell how close to the edge Nate was. "*Tell her to run.*"

"No," said Nate, through gritted teeth. "I need to control this power. I can't let it control me."

"You can control it, Nate, I know you can," said Jena, her eyes full of confidence. She looked beautiful in the glowing light of his flames, brave and strong, her long hair flowing back off her face, her scars fully visible. "You're not your flame magic, Nate. You're the one who's going to save us."

"They're so powerful," he said, forcing the words out of his mouth.

"So are you," she said.

She looked so relaxed and sure, something inside Nate eased. The tension that had been gripping him softened. She was right. He was powerful. Not in the way his grandfather had expected, but it was there. "My grandfather always said—"

"You need to find your own magic, find *your* power, Nate. This isn't about anyone else, or any other power. Your Firecaller ability is unique to you. No one else can do it, except *you*."

Her words went straight to his heart, to the center of his being. She was right. He was the only one who could do this.

He relaxed his tight grip on the flames. Instead of using panicked control, he allowed his magic to become fluid, like the liquid metal the smithies used to create their swords. Strong, but malleable. The flames reacted by becoming more settled, calmer. Their blistering energy still crackled, but it wasn't so out of control.

"I feel it," whispered Nate. "I feel the flames. They're pleased I'm not fighting them anymore."

Jena nodded, like she'd known all along. "The Firecaller magic is inside *you*," she said. "It's a part of *you*. It's not an enemy to fight and overcome, it's a piece of *you*. Treat the magic like you would any other part of yourself, like your legs for holding you up or your hands for feeding you. Be grateful to the flames, not scared of them." Her eyes dug into his soul and forced him to listen to what she was saying.

Nate lifted his arms. It made sense now. He'd been so used to controlling and dominating the demons, to forcing them to do his will, he'd thought that was how it needed to work with the Firecaller flames. But he'd discovered the demons were more than creatures to be dominated, and now he needed to understand the flames inside him better.

He took a breath and delved deeper. He dove into the flames, no longer afraid of being consumed by them. At first, all he saw was bright white energy. Sizzling power that wanted to be set free. But then he saw the strands that Thornal had showed him, twisting and turning, flowing in a pattern that only they understood. He felt grateful that he could see something so beautiful and unique. Who else could be so close to such power and survive to tell the tale?

The flames reacted immediately to his gratitude. They curled themselves around him, the colors calming from angry reds and pinks to peaceful pastel oranges and yellows. He saw the connection immediately. Jena was right—they reflected his own thoughts and emotions. He'd been so scared and desperate, they'd reacted to that by flaring up. Now that he felt gratitude, they had calmed down and were more willing to do his bidding. He sent out feelings of love and acceptance to the surrounding flames, imagined wrapping them inside his arms, and telling them he'd always look after him.

And the flames became his. They melted at the attention he was giving them.

He let out a breath. He finally understood how to rule them: with compassion. It was the opposite of everything he'd learned about magic; against everything he'd expected from a power like the Firecaller flames; it opposed everything he'd thought he understood up to this point.

The flames surged higher, engulfing him, whispering to him. Loving him. It felt strange and off-balance, and part of him wondered if he could cope. He wasn't used to unconditional love.

He'd never had it in his family, and he'd never had it with his friends. The demons didn't love him. The ghosts only wanted to use him.

Then he looked down at Jena, who was watching him with her unwavering eyes. She was fire and strength and fury. And somehow, she was the only thing that calmed him.

With her here, he knew he could do it.

"Come on, let's go fight those creatures," he said to her. He'd tell her later that she was the only reason he'd been able to control the flames. That she'd saved them all with her confidence...and her beautiful eyes.

Jena grinned, relief visible across her face. "Damn right."

CHAPTER 47
NATE

ate ran back toward the main hearth, Jena close behind him. He was glowing, and it was visible even in the late afternoon light. But it didn't matter. They were all fighting for their survival.

A wolvan appeared around the corner of a wagon, and Nate blasted it with his fiery magic before it could even snarl.

"Well done, son, now go get the rest of them," said Thornal, moving with ghostly speed beside him.

"I'm working on it," Nate muttered under his breath.

He strode onward, his focus narrowed down to finding the remaining creatures before anyone else was hurt. Without warning, a barker lion swooped down and attacked from above. He lifted one hand and incinerated it. His flames flowed over him, pleased to be of service.

Screams broke out just ahead of where they were. "Come on," he said to Jena, and started running again. He didn't need to look to know she was right behind him. She never backed down from a fight.

"She's very independent. You're going to have to be careful with her," said Thornal as they stalked around a tent.

Nate didn't reply. He tried to ignore Thornal.

"If you're going to romance her, I mean."

He glanced to the side. "I understood what you meant. It's just not the right time to be discussing it," said Nate in an undertone. "In fact, I'd prefer not to discuss it with you at all."

"That's a very shortsighted attitude. I have many insights into her personality that would help you."

"Can you focus on the battle, please?" said Nate under his breath, as he scanned the skies overhead. "You're not taking this seriously."

Thornal didn't even seem to hear him. *"She deserves happiness. You both do. And finding someone to love would bring her that."*

Nate glanced at Thornal and tried to think what to say that would stop the ghost from discussing his attempts— or lack thereof—at romancing Jena. He had a feeling that nothing would work. His only defense was to ignore him and concentrate on saving people. He turned back to Jena to make sure she was okay and then ran around the edge of a tent.

He promptly staggered to a halt, forgetting everything else.

Instead of the neat and tidy main hearth where they'd eaten their porridge, they'd walked into the middle of a nightmare.

It was carnage.

There were bodies everywhere.

Blood. Flesh. Screams.

There were still people fighting, still resisting. Eldrin was battling one of two enormous wolvans alongside three other Utugani warriors, blood dripping down his face and one arm. Other Utugani warriors fought around the second wolvan, jabbing at it with spears, focused on bringing it down. Except the wolvans were stronger than four men. They were unthinking beasts who wouldn't stop until they were dead.

Nate didn't even hesitate. He ran right into the carnage. His flames surged up and out, twisting and burning, delighted to be released.

The first wolvan was about to swipe at Eldrin with one giant paw. Nate thrust out his arm, and his flames instantly burned the wolvan to ashes. Eldrin turned, his eyes wide with shock. Nate blasted the second wolvan, and it didn't even get to make a sound before it disintegrated. Ash and sparks rose around them, like a mini-tornado of death.

"Where are the rest of the creatures?" asked Nate, his voice cracking in the middle. Fire and heat surrounded him, and he could only just see his friends.

"I don't—I don't know," said Eldrin shakily. He glanced down at his body like he couldn't believe he was still in one piece.

"Where's everyone else?" asked Jena, looking around in a panic at all the bodies. "Where are Catarina and Ellie?"

"In the Utugan's tent," said Eldrin, gesturing behind them to the large tent. "They're all in there. We have our healers with them, working on the wounded. We were trying to lead these two away." He shook his head, his ash-and-blood-stained face devoid of his usual carefree expression.

"There are more creatures in the camp," said Nate. "We have to hurry."

"How do you know?" asked Eldrin, eyes darting around.

"I can feel them. I don't know exactly where they are, but they're close."

"Let's get them," said Jena. Her eyes glowed with the reflection of Nate's flames.

"I'm coming with you," said Eldrin. He nodded to the other surviving guards. "Stay and guard my father's tent. Help the others. We'll be back soon."

The warriors each gave him a quick nod and strode off to surround the tent. Eldrin turned to Nate. "We need to find every single one of these gods-forsaken creatures and incinerate them." His face was dark with anger; blood and ashes smeared over his skin.

Nate hesitated outside the Utugan's tent. Which way should they go?

"This way, son. I'll lead you to the nearest one," said Thornal, appearing beside him again.

Nate didn't even blink. He just ran after Thornal's ghostly image, followed closely by Jena and Eldrin, none of them saying a word. There was nothing to say. They rounded the corner of a large brown wagon and found a wolvan attacking a smaller wagon with a family huddling inside. It had its front paws up on the side and was attempting to push it over, snarling and snapping at the people inside.

Nate didn't even have to get close to the wolvan. He just sent out his flames, and it burned quickly, leaving only ashes and the faint smell of wet fur.

Jena opened the wagon door and spoke quickly to the woman inside, telling her to stay inside the wagon. It was safer than having them roaming the hearth, falling into harm's way.

"How many more?" asked Jena when she'd shut the

door. Her face was covered in ash, her eyes flashing with anger.

"I can feel maybe three or four more." Nate turned his head and saw Thornal walking off to the left. "This way, I think." He strode after the ghost, determined to do this quickly, and not just because it might save lives.

His eyesight was flickering, and everything was in hues of red, like he was seeing the world through the flames. They swirled around him, the magic going higher and higher. He was losing track of what part of him was a man and what was flame. He blinked a few times, trying to refocus.

He tried to express his gratitude, to pull the flames back into doing his will. But it felt like he was being consumed by them, and that maybe instead of doing what *he* wanted, he would do what *they* wanted.

And what they wanted was to *burn*.

Everything. Indiscriminately.

CHAPTER 48
NATE

He shook his head and sucked in a ragged breath, trying to think clearly.

He needed to take stock of their situation. There had been more wolvans at the campsite than he'd ever seen in once place. Even with Rothell in the skies, if he didn't have his Firecaller flames, they would never have survived this encounter. The good news was that the barker lions had suffered under Rothell's attacks, and only one or two still roamed the skies.

But there was another creature in the camp that was silently killing people. Nate could sense it. It was a fire creature that hid in the shadows, its flames burning inside its eyes. It was also smarter than the wolvans. It took its time and hunted its prey. Nate was determined to find and kill it, before it killed anyone else—but first he had to destroy the remaining wolvans.

"This way, son, keep up," said Thornal from up ahead.

They found another wolvan ripping a tent apart, its massive jaws clutching the material and shaking it until the tent poles fell over. Nate sent his flames rippling over its body, turning it to dust, sparks twisting and turning into the air above them. He pulled the flames back into his body just before they burned down the entire tent. He could sense people inside and knew his flames would have happily devoured them all. He was so close to the edge it scared him.

He swayed a little, his head spinning with fire and magic. "There are people in the tent," he said through gritted teeth, only just getting the words out. It felt like the flames were woven into every part of him, strong and powerful, and the balance of control was much finer than he'd thought.

Jena stared at him for a moment, worry clear on her face, but didn't say a word. She moved over to the tent, closely followed by Eldrin, and the two of them pulled back the heavy material. They discovered two women and three children huddling inside. They were shaking, their eyes wide with shock.

"I'll take them to my father's tent," said Eldrin.

Nate nodded. He didn't want them to be left alone either. "I'll kill the other wolvans. But be careful; there's another creature just as deadly roaming around. Don't deviate. Go straight to the Utugan's tent." He blinked rapidly, pushing away the flames, again and again.

Eldrin grabbed one of the smaller children in his arms and held the hand of another. Nate could see only hues of red over his face and body. He scrunched his eyes shut and opened them again. Eldrin hesitated, his face concerned, but the child in his arms was sobbing, and one woman looked like she was about to faint.

"I'll be back soon," he said, giving Jena a significant look. "Don't do anything stupid until I get back."

Nate figured he wasn't as good at hiding what was happening to him as he thought.

"Come on," said Jena. "Let's get the rest of them." She hesitated, searching his eyes. "Fast."

He took the lead again, following Thornal, who was flickering in and out in his vision as well. The flames were lovingly coating him in their burning magic, a swirling inferno that made it hard to think. Jena had been right; he could connect to them more easily when he worked with them. But now they were sliding into his head, changing the way he viewed the world.

At first, he'd simply enjoyed the feeling of destroying the wolvans, watching their bodies being incinerated under his burning flames, becoming nothing more than ash. The creatures had killed innocent Utugani people without a second thought, and it was nothing more than they deserved.

But now, his thoughts were filled with the desire to burn everything, not just the wolvans. The flames were pushing for control, and it frightened him. He wanted to see everything go up in smoke, to see his fire coating the entire hearth, burning and dancing and sparking and flaming.

He felt himself flickering between his own thoughts and the intense desires of the flames. They didn't think like people. They didn't discriminate; they didn't care who it was.

They just wanted to *burn*.

"Nate... Are you okay?" asked Jena. Her voice was soft and hesitant. Maybe a little scared.

Nate blinked and realized he'd been standing still for too long. He glanced down at Jena. Her eyes were wide, her expression concerned. The flames flickered inside his head and seemed to steady as he stared at her. He nodded, and following his instinct, grasped her hand in his. He needed the grounding feel of another person. But not just any person. He needed *Jena's* hand.

She tensed up, her entire body going still. Nate's flames roared inside him, like a predator sensing prey. His reality swirled, and for a second, he was more flames than person.

Then Jena relaxed, and the flames subsided. She tightened her grip on Nate's hand, and he let out a breath of warm air. The feeling of her skin against his helped to keep him grounded, and he could take another deep breath.

"Shall we go?" asked Jena carefully. She seemed to sense how precarious the situation was. He nodded again and led Jena down the closest gap between wagons toward the next wolvan, clutching her hand like he would drown if he let go.

"That's it, Nate. Get her used to being close to you," said Thornal approvingly.

Nate ignored Thornal's comment—it was so far from what he was thinking about it was almost laughable—and kept his focus on the next wolvan.

And on the warmth of Jena's hand in his, if he was honest.

But mostly on the wolvan.

They turned a corner, and there it was. The wolvan had blood all over its muzzle and was tearing apart the body of an Utugani warrior. Nate slammed his fiery magic into its chest without hesitation. The wolvan went up in flames, gone before it could even look up from its meal. Nate tried not to look too closely at the mangled body of the warrior.

Except he couldn't help it. He recognized the youthful face of the warrior who'd been with Seban on guard duty when they'd arrived. The green-shirted guard, who'd been so suspicious of them. Nate stumbled and caught himself on the nearby wagon. He felt numb. He knew who'd sent these creatures. Lothar wanted him dead, and he didn't care who else was hurt. Which meant Nate was the one who'd brought this trouble to the Utugani people. He'd known what Lothar was doing. How desperate he was. And still they'd come here, not even thinking of the consequences. Bile rose in his throat.

"One to go," whispered Jena. Her face was pale, her eyes reflecting the death and destruction.

Nate just felt cold, like he was detached from the world.

Even the flames couldn't seem to warm him. He knew he'd feel battered and bruised tomorrow. But right now, he couldn't feel anything. Even the Firecaller flames, which had felt so overwhelming and powerful not so long ago, couldn't reach him.

This was too much.

Too many people had died here today.

"This is all because of me," said Nate, his voice cracking in the middle. "This is because I didn't give in to Lothar and let him have what he wanted." The flames licked higher. They knew what would make him feel better. To *burn*.

Jena rounded on him, her eyes flashing. She grabbed both his arms. "No. Never that. This isn't your fault. Lothar is the monster, not you."

"We put these people in harm's way." He swept out one hand to encompass the entire camp. Innocent people who didn't deserve this.

Innocent people who might die because of Nate's flames, if Lothar's creatures didn't get them first.

"Lothar would have tried to destroy and kill everyone in this camp at some point, even if we'd never come here."

"But—"

"It's in his nature. It's what he does. And we're the only

people who can stop him." Jena said the words with such firm conviction, Nate was tempted to believe her.

He took a deep breath and tried to let the destructive thoughts go. Perhaps Jena was right. Maybe Lothar was to blame. He *was* the one who'd sent these beasts.

Jena looked up at Nate beseechingly, her brown eyes filled with fear—and compassion. "Nate, hold it together. You're the only one who has the power to stop Lothar. Without you, we're lost."

He took another shaky breath. His heart was pounding. His brain fizzing. The flames were lapping at his insides, waiting for their turn to burn everything in sight. He didn't entirely believe Jena, but it helped to have her say the words. "Then let's go kill the rest of these ash-dwelling monsters."

CHAPTER 49
JENA

The wolvans didn't stand a chance.

Not when Nate could destroy them with one blast from his magic. The last wolvan didn't even have time to look up before Nate burned it to ashes.

But Jena could tell that something bad was happening to Nate. He was paying the price for using his flames. His eyes... they weren't the same as before. The flames were consuming him, just like they were consuming the wolvans.

"Should we go back to the tent? Check on the others?" she suggested, peering into his flame-covered eyes, trying to figure out how close to the edge he was.

"There's still something else hanging around. Something dangerous," muttered Nate. "I can sense it. It's biding its time, waiting for the right moment."

Jena shivered. The wolvans were bad enough. "What's it going to do? Who is it going after?"

Nate shrugged. "Us probably."

"That's not helpful, Nate," growled Jena. His expression worried her. He looked... unconcerned. Distant.

Like they hadn't just seen half the camp destroyed by monsters.

"Thornal can sense where it is. Come on, we have to act fast," he said, more urgently this time.

She followed him between the wagons, still clutching his hand. She didn't know who wanted the contact more, but it seemed to calm both of them, so she didn't even consider pulling her hand out of his. Nate slowed down, and then stopped at the edge of a corner, peering out, searching the shadows. She could feel his body shaking through their connected hands.

"It's close," he whispered.

Jena nodded, too afraid to speak. She searched the Book for something that might help against an unknown creature, but all she could come up with were more fire spells. Her ability to think under pressure had burned up alongside the last wolvan Nate had destroyed. She felt too shaky, too battered by the assault on both her body and her emotions. All the death and destruction around her was too much. So many people had died here today it took all she had to just stay standing, holding Nate's hand.

And then she heard it.

A low murmuring, like several voices talking on the edge of her hearing. It was calling to her, telling her to come closer. She took a step forward without thinking, wanting to do whatever the voices said. Nate was a step ahead of her, moving in the same direction.

Her skin prickled, and the raven on her stomach clawed at her skin in warning. It made her steps falter. Whatever was calling to them wasn't a friend. It was probably the creature they were hunting. Even as she took another step forward, Jena frantically searched the Book of Spells for something to block her hearing, then muttered it quickly under her breath. The air thickened around her ears, dulling all sounds. The murmuring stopped, and she let out a relieved breath. She clutched Nate's hand tighter and tried to pull him back toward her. "Nate, it's using its voice to lure—"

Nate yanked his hand out of hers and walked toward the main walkway between the wagons. He didn't even look back at her.

"Nate, stop." Jena ran forward and tried to grab his arm to drag him back, but he was stronger than she was. He shook free and kept walking as if she were nothing more than an annoying insect. His magic pulsed around him, like the flames were trying to fight whatever was happening, but they couldn't quite overcome the murmuring either.

Jena searched the Book of Spells, trying to find something that would work for Nate. She hadn't expected an attack like this. The barker lions and the wolvans just used their superior strength, and flames and other physical attacks were the best defense. But whatever this creature was, it was using a unique power—something more subtle, and potentially more potent.

All she could think of was a spell that would block Nate's hearing as well. But she couldn't just thicken the air around his ears like she had her own. That was a self-spell, only for the mage who was casting it. It moved with her, and Nate kept moving away. It wouldn't stick.

Nate had moved too far out of reach for a Bubble of Air spell—he was already out on the walkway, and she needed to be touching him while she cast it. She peered around the side of the caravan, considering just running out and jumping on Nate's back. As long as he didn't try to burn her first, she could cast the bubble around both of them.

Except what about the unknown creature? What were

its other skills? Where was it hiding? What did it even look like? She had no answers, and it was frustrating. All she knew was that by running out there, there was a possibility she'd just end up under its power as well. That wouldn't save Nate, even if the action might make her feel better. The hairs on her skin were all raised, as if her body could sense the discordant presence of whatever monster was out there.

By the Flames, what *was* it?

She needed to think this through properly.

Where was the creature hiding? That was the first question to answer. She peered out again. Nate was walking reluctantly toward an empty area. Could it turn invisible? Was it a mage with a cloak? Maybe it was a trick, and the creature was hiding elsewhere. But when she turned sideways and glanced out of the corner of her eye, she saw it.

Something was flickering at the edge of her sight, like maybe it wasn't real.

She looked at it sideways again, and she saw it more clearly this time. The creature had a bony black head of a goat and large horns that curled off its long head, eyes that burned with flames, and a cadaverous person-shaped body clothed in ragged black robes. Its hands were long and thin, and it had a sneer on its strange animal-like face. She could feel the dark energy emanating from it in waves, thick and unpleasant. If she looked at it straight on, it disappeared into the shadows, like some kind of terrifying nightmare hiding in plain sight.

Its lips were moving, murmuring the words of whatever chant it was using to keep Nate stuck inside its magic. Nate took another step forward, enthralled, his flames flickering in his hands. His magic flared, and his flames momentarily burned higher around him. His magic was trying to fight the creature, but it wasn't working. Nate kept taking slow steps forward.

Jena reluctantly moved out from behind the caravan, desperately trying to decide what she should do. Jumping on Nate to cast the spell seemed like she might just get burned by Nate for her efforts. But if she couldn't jump on him, she had to disrupt things in another way.

She muttered the first spell she could think of, and a wind swept through the alley, making their clothes lift and the wagons shift. It was enough to cover the sound of the murmuring for a moment or two, and Nate looked back over his shoulder at Jena, his eyes normal again.

"Run, Jena," he said, his lips moving distinctly, making gestures with his arms. It only made her more determined to save them both.

And then the wind died down again, and his gaze shifted back to the creature in front of him. He took another step forward, even further away from where she crouched. The creature's eyes lit up, and its lips moved faster and faster, like it was amping up its chanting. Jena couldn't hold in the sob that was trapped in her throat.

She had to do something more.

If she couldn't block Nate's ears, then she needed something else. The opposite of what she'd done for herself. She flicked through the pages of the Book until she had what she needed.

Jena started murmuring under her breath, following the spell's words to the letter. Her magic flared inside her, expanding all around, becoming bigger and stronger. Nate took three more steps toward the creature, and Jena chanted faster. She didn't have much time.

And then suddenly, her magic hit the crescendo she was after. A loud boom of vibration, like thunder and lightning combined, echoed around all three of them. The sound echoed, and echoed again, creating a heavy vibration that Jena could feel even through the spell covering her ears.

The sound blocked the chanting from the creature, and Nate blinked, his eyes flickering with his flames again, then shook his head.

"Look at the creature side-on!" shouted Jena. "You can only see it sideways." Nate looked at Jena, and then back at the creature, which was standing only a few feet away. He narrowed his eyes and turned his head sideways. His expression hardened.

The creature tried to turn and run, but Nate was faster. He lifted one hand, his flames flying out of his body, and burned it where it stood. As Jena watched, its mouth opened, and it screamed in rage, the jaws filled with the sharp teeth of a predator. Flames covered its whole body, burning it so quickly it didn't even have time to take a step away.

Nate stood watching, the flames lighting up his face. He looked shattered, like he'd only just been holding himself together. He turned toward Jena, and all she could see was the wildness in his eyes, the flames burning so brightly it hurt to look.

Her heart stuttered.

Jena took a hesitant step toward him, not sure if he was in control. What if he blasted her with the flames, too? She wasn't facing the man she knew; she was facing the flames. She needed to be careful.

"It's okay, Nate. You did it. The last of the creatures is dead," she said slowly, keeping her voice low and soothing. She put her hands out, palms up, to show she meant no harm.

He nodded jerkily, but his eyes still burned bright, and he took a determined step toward her.

Jena's heart jumped into her throat. This was it. She could see it in his eyes.

He wasn't in control of the flames. They controlled him, and they wanted to burn. Her breath caught, and she froze in place, unable to look away.

He raised his hand; flames sizzled over his body.

CHAPTER 50
JENA

Jena backed up, heart pounding, still holding out her hands. "Nate. It's me, Jena. Remember me? We're friends."

There was no recognition on his face. Nothing. Flames were the only thing she could see in his eyes. His whole body trembled, and fire licked his fingertips.

He took a step toward her and held up his hands. The flames grew brighter and flared up to cover his palms. She could feel the dizzying power of his magic in the surrounding air, like the charged moment before a lightning strike.

This was it. Nate was going to burn her alive. He wasn't in control, and it would probably devastate him when he regained consciousness. But it was going to happen; she could see it in his eyes.

He was going to burn her alive, just like the wolvans. They hadn't stood a chance, and they were bigger and stronger than she was.

She pushed down a panicked sob.

"Nate, it's okay. It's not your fault." She swallowed hard. Tears streaked down her face.

He didn't react. Just took another step toward her, the flames licking his hands, turning his face an orangey-red color like a demon from the Edges. Her whole body tensed in expectation.

Would it be like when Otis pushed her into the campfire? Or would it be worse?

"Please, Nate," she said brokenly. "If you can hear me. Just try to come back to me. The flames are part of you, but they don't define you."

Nate took another step toward her. The flames over his hands burned brighter. There was nowhere to run.

"Please Nate. Please don't do this," she begged. She hadn't meant to. She'd wanted to make it easier for Nate.

But she didn't want to die like this.

She didn't want to burn again.

"Please, if you care for me at all, don't do this." Tears flowed freely down her cheeks. Her skin felt tight, and she shuddered.

Nate hesitated. He shook his head, and his hands lowered slightly. He stopped moving.

"Jena." Her name was rough and guttural, barely recognizable.

But Jena heard it. "Yes. Yes, it's me, Nate," she said, taking a slow step forward. Was it really Nate? "You can do it. I know you can."

The flames dimmed in his eyes, and his hazel gaze returned.

Jena's heart leaped.

He'd done it.

He was back inside his body. The flames over his hands went out, and he stared at Jena with wide eyes.

She took another hesitant step toward him, still watching carefully, just in case. Her heart pounded in her ears.

"I'm sorry," he said. The words were slurred and broken, as if he was forcing them out of his mouth. "Jena, I'm so sorry."

"Nate, it's okay. You don't—"

Nate reached out one hand, took a step toward her, then stumbled. He almost righted himself, gave her one last beseeching look...

Then collapsed to the ground, his body unmoving.

For a moment, Jena froze. Shock radiated out through her body.

Then she raced to his side.

"Wake up, Nate," Jena whispered as she knelt next to Nate's limp body. She placed her hands firmly on either side of his face, hoping the contact might revive him.

Nothing.

He was as still and limp as if...

She didn't want to finish that thought.

"You have to wake up," she said, louder and more forcefully. Tears blurred her vision as she leaned in close. He looked so *lifeless*. As if he wasn't there anymore. A sob worked its way up her throat. Was this the end of their journey?

Had Lothar won after all?

What would they—

She determinedly pushed away her panicky thoughts. Fear would get her nowhere. Putting her hand on his chest, she felt for the telltale rise and fall of his breath. Relief surged through her, and the tightness in her body eased as his chest lifted under her palm. It was shallow, but definitely there.

He was alive. Now she just needed to wake him up.

She touched his arm, and shook it lightly, as if that would somehow get through to him. His eyes fluttered, but he didn't wake. Even worse, his Firecaller magic felt... off. This close, the discordant hum of the flames coursing through his body was making the hairs on her arms rise. She was edgy and itchy and knew it was a reaction to whatever was going on with his powers.

It was like there was a lightning storm brewing inside his chest, fighting its way into the world. She shivered. If the magic was that strong from the outside, what was happening to him inside?

Had he used too much of it at one time? Or were the flames still fighting for control?

That had been one of his biggest fears about using his Firecaller abilities again. She tightened her grip on his arms and tried to lend him her strength.

He needed help.

What he really needed was Bree. She'd know what to do. But her sister wasn't here—she was rotting in a cell somewhere. Jena only just held in her sob at that thought.

They had to survive. Bree was depending on them.

She'd just find another healer. Someone from the Utugani must know how to help him. Eldrin had said there were healers in the Utugan's tent. She needed to get him to one of those healers.

It felt better to have a plan.

Jena grasped Nate under the shoulders and tried to pull him up to a sitting position, but he was surprisingly heavy. A creature howled in the distance, and her whole body tensed. There were *more* wolvans out there? A little sound, somewhere between a hiccup and a sob, came out of her mouth. What was she going to do? She couldn't leave Nate by himself, but he was too heavy to carry.

She looked around. "Hello? Someone help me!" She yelled the words into the surrounding air, desperation overcoming her fear of drawing in another wolvan. "I'm over here. I need help!"

She waited a beat for someone to appear. Smoke wafted around them, and the acrid scent of burning dog hair made her cover her nose with her arm. In the distance, she could hear crying and a tent canvas flapping in the wind. Further away, she heard another howl, and her whole body chilled.

Perhaps unsurprisingly, no one came to help.

She couldn't blame them. So many people were lying dead and mauled around the tents. What had once seemed a beautiful and peaceful hearth was now a place of nightmares.

Which meant she had to figure this out on her own.

With a growl, Jena pushed herself to standing, and put her hands underneath Nate's armpits. Placing her feet square, she pulled backward with a grunt. She put everything she had into dragging his inert body. Stepping slowly and unsteadily, she pulled him about two or three cart lengths, gasping for breath and struggling with every step. Arms screaming, legs burning, she set him back down on the ground, huffing out breaths. He was far heavier than he looked. His tall, lean body was solid muscle, and right now he was more like a sack of potatoes than a person. She looked down at his slack face, wishing he'd magically wake up.

She looked into the skies. Rothell was up there somewhere, maybe she could help.

Rothell? I need you. She said the words in her head, hoping against hope.

Another howl sounded across the camp. *I'm a little busy right now. There's a wolvan attacking me.* Rothell's voice was unconcerned but distracted. She had her hands full. There was no way Jena would tell her to leave a wolvan to its own devices and come save Nate instead.

No problem, she replied. *Stay safe, Rothell.*

She searched the Book of Spells, flicking through the pages, wishing she had an obvious solution. She needed a cart to carry him in, but there was no way to build a cart from magic. She'd even accept a second person to take his legs while she carried his top half. But she couldn't just magically call anyone to her, either. Well, anyone other than Rothell and Nate.

Jena looked down at Nate's unconscious body again. If she couldn't get help, and she couldn't make a cart, what *could* she do?

She could make a cart go *faster*, turn mud into honey, and even create a fireball, none of which were useful right now. Nate started tossing and turning on the ground, his face twisting as if he were in pain. The sense of urgency she'd been feeling increased tenfold, and Jena started flicking more quickly through the Book of Spells.

Maybe she needed to switch things up, like she'd done before. Turn her problem on its head. If she couldn't find something to help carry Nate at his current weight, maybe she could make him lighter, so he'd be easier to carry? A bubble or a bird to fly under him? The thought made her flick through the book another time, sure she'd seen something recently that might work.

"Yes," she said triumphantly as she found a spell for helping stonemasons build the stone walls of castles. It was supposed to be for stones the size of a head, but surely that would be fine.

The spell needed small stones, some mud and a spoken spell to work, but it would make Nate lighter for a short period—long enough for her to get him to the Utugan's tent. She reread the instructions and felt a flicker of concern, knowing that they were supposed to be for stones and not people. But one look at Nate's pained expression convinced her. She was running out of time and options.

She needed to get Nate to a healer. *Right now.*

Jena scrambled about in the dirt, picking up seven equal-sized stones for the spell. She made mud using dirt and a water flask she found nearby. Then she crouched over Nate and began speaking the words of the spell. Murmuring to herself, she sprinkled the mud and the stones evenly around his body, using the power inside her to infuse her words with the magic she needed. Nate groaned and his eyes flickered as the power rose around them, but he didn't wake. He was sweating, with wet patches on his shirt and droplets running down his face, like he was burning up from the inside. She could still feel the discordant power pulsing inside him, even as she used her own mage powers to create the spell to make him lighter.

She needed to hurry. She knew it in her bones.

She chanted the spell under her breath and then bent down to pick him up. She wormed her hands under his neck and knees, the spell swirling around her. Taking a breath, she hefted him upward, staggering back when she lifted him into her arms with ease. He weighed no more than a baby. She let out a tiny sob, grateful that the spell had worked. His tall body was still awkward to carry, but it was nothing compared to how heavy he'd been before.

"Now to get you to a healer," she muttered.

Jena staggered as his weight came back.

She immediately started chanting again, and strode toward the Utugan's tent, hoping she'd be able to make it the entire way.

CHAPTER 51

NATE

Everything felt broken.

Nate knew he wasn't dead, because even though his brain felt like mud, he was in too much pain. His head was pounding. It felt like someone was bashing him repeatedly with a mallet. His whole body was on fire, the flames inside him pushing desperately at the barriers he'd raised before he collapsed. They wanted to be free, to burn everything they could, to claim and destroy.

Except he wouldn't let that happen. Last time, he'd destroyed an entire enemy mercenary camp. This time, he'd be killing innocent people. Friends, new and old.

Jena.

The power pulsed through him, looking for an outlet, and he held steady, holding it close, not letting the flames take over.

"You can do it, son. Just hold it together."

He couldn't even reply to Thornal, he was so overwhelmed by his task. The flames were powerful, and they weren't responding to his attention like they had earlier. The desire to break free consumed them.

He burned. He writhed. He moaned.

Clamping down on the flames, he held himself in check. It was all he could do right now. He had to hope that the sensation would eventually subside, that he could eventually let go of this desperate hold he had over the flames. And if he couldn't, then he needed to get the hell out of here, away from everyone.

He wasn't going to kill an entire campsite full of people ever again.

The only thing that was keeping him from spinning out with fear was that in the back of his mind—a mere whisper of thought—he knew Jena was taking care of him. She was holding him; she was taking him to a healer. It calmed his desperation. It made him feel stronger and better able to take on the flames.

But it was a battle. A fight he'd never won before.

The flames were slippery. They existed in every part of him. They knew him inside and out. They whispered thoughts into his head to convince him.

What have these people ever done for you?

If you do not let us feed, you won't be powerful enough to fight Lothar, and everyone will die, not just these people.

You need to battle Lothar with our power. You cannot deny us.

We need to feed; we're so hungry.

Why would you deny us our only sustenance?

Don't you love us?

He could feel Jena's hands where she was carrying him. He could sense her heartbeat next to his—*thump-thump, thump-thump, thump-thump*—and it was the only thing that made him hold strong. He would never burn her. And he wouldn't burn all these other innocent people, either.

It had been bad enough waking up to all those dead

mercenaries. They'd kidnapped him, beaten him, been prepared to turn him over to Lothar, and it had still felt like he'd been stabbed through the heart. He'd killed a bunch of people he didn't know, and it had almost destroyed him.

What would it feel like if he let the flames go here?

Jena.

Eldrin.

Catarina.

The Utugan.

Ella.

It didn't even bear thinking about.

His hands curled into fists. He didn't need to think about it, because he would not let the flames free.

But it will kill you if you don't... You'll die with us. The flames whispered their last desperate plea. *You cannot hold this inside you.*

Nate shook his head, the burning inside his body getting worse. The flames weren't trying to trick him. He could feel the truth of their words. But it didn't matter. He wouldn't give up Jena's life for his own. He wouldn't hurt the rest of the camp just so he could live on.

He moaned. He burned.

He didn't want to die.

But he was determined to do what was right. What felt good.

Even if it killed him.

The flames burned harder, brighter inside him. Resisting his decision, pressing on him, pushing and fighting.

CHAPTER 52

JENA

J ena stumbled the last few steps toward the Utugan's tent. She was still muttering the spell under her breath, keeping Nate light enough for her to carry. The magic swirled around them both, kicking up dust and air, making Jena's eyes burn and her throat almost too dry to speak.

But she didn't dare stop her chanting.

Nate was heating up; his skin burned, and sweat dripped off his body. She could feel the battle raging inside him and wished she could help, but all she could do right now was keep repeating the spell. She was almost there.

The same warriors from earlier were standing around the Utugan's tent, spears at the ready. They looked bloodied and worn, like they'd seen a thousand years in the last few hours. But as soon as the closest man saw Jena, he broke formation and ran toward her. He was one of the warriors she'd saved from the barker lion. It was like finding a long-lost friend.

"He needs help from a healer. I have to get him to a healer," she rasped, not sure if her words made sense. As soon as she stopped chanting, Nate became heavy again. She staggered, unable to hold him.

"Let me," said the warrior, reaching for Nate. The warrior's face was smeared with ash, and he had a large gash on his left arm, the material of his shirt flapping in the breeze that was skimming through the devastated hearth.

Jena shook her head. She wanted to say no, to hold him close, but Nate was already slipping out of her arms. The warrior carefully moved her aside and grabbed Nate under the armpits. Another warrior grabbed his legs and between the two of them, they carried Nate inside the tent. Jena followed closely behind, peering anxiously over the shoulder of the closest man.

Inside the tent, it was chaos. There were people running around, wounded men and women lying on blankets and pillows, and others, including Catarina and the Utugan, tending them. Blood and flesh wounds from wolvan bites seemed to be everywhere. Limbs missing, gashes, and pain. Whimpers and moans mixed with quiet voices and grim commands. Even the Utugan's youngest daughter Ella was giving people water and wiping foreheads.

Despite the chaos, most people in the tent looked up at their entrance, many with widened eyes and fear on their faces. There was complete silence for a moment, and then they relaxed again. Catarina hobbled over and gathered Jena into a fierce hug, and she didn't even have the energy to avoid it. Everyone started moving again.

"I've been so worried," Catarina said when she pulled back. "We didn't know where you had gone." She was leaning on her ornate cane, her dress torn, blood dripping from a wound on her head. She was covered in ash, like most of the people inside the tent, and her face was even more lined than it had been before, if that was possible.

Jena looked away for a second, thinking about the last time she saw Catarina. It all seemed so long ago. Like years had passed instead of hours. "I-I ran out of the hearth. Sat down by the river for a bit with Nate. But when they started attacking... we came back."

"They just appeared out of nowhere. No warning." Catarina's eyes glazed over at the memory. "Elsa... Elsa didn't make it. A wolvan—" She swallowed convulsively and looked away.

Jena blinked, trying to focus her attention on what Catarina had said, but her thoughts skittered away. She couldn't deal with whatever was tugging at her right now.

"Nate's hurt," she blurted. "He needs help." She started shaking, her whole body only just reacting to the fear of the last hour. She couldn't deal with anything but his survival.

Catarina grasped Jena's shoulders. "Are all the beasts defeated?" she asked, almost as if she were afraid of the answer.

"Rothell is fighting a wolvan. It's the last one, I think. We defeated everything else."

Catarina let out a relieved breath. "Thank the gods."

Jena pulled back a little. "Nate needs help," she said again. She swallowed painfully over a lump in her throat. "I think he's dying."

Catarina glanced over to where Nate was lying nearby, then back at Jena. "What happened?"

"He used his flames to defeat the wolvans and... something else, another creature. But he's fighting the flames for control now. It's my fault. I convinced him to use the flames to save the hearth." Jena shook her head, trying to focus. "He needs a healer. A shaman. *Anyone*. Just someone who can help him fight the flames."

Catarina's eyes widened as if she knew exactly what that meant. "Can he win?"

"I think he's drowning," whispered Jena. "He won't survive without help."

Catarina peered around the room, at the people tending the wounded, and the guards standing at the entrance, then leaned close to Jena. "If the flames win, everyone here would be dead. *Everyone.*" Her voice wobbled on the last word, and she gripped Jena's arms tightly.

"I know. Can you help him? Can *anyone* help him?" Jena felt like she was asking the most important question in the world right now. So much depended on Nate. The indistinct murmur of hospital care around them seemed out of place for their discussion. Their eyes held for a second longer, heavy with foreboding.

Catarina's eyes swirled with secrets. Her face was old and lined, but somehow, she seemed more vital and alive than anyone Jena had ever seen. "I might be able to help."

Jena let out the breath she'd been holding. There was hope after all. "We need to work fast," she whispered, glancing over her shoulder at Nate. "We can't lose him." His eyes were closed, and his body shifted restlessly. He moaned and shook his head as if he were trying to say no to some invisible force.

Catarina nodded. "We can do this."

They both knelt on either side of Nate's body. He was tossing and turning, sweat glistening on his face and chest. The warrior who'd helped to carry Nate—the one she'd saved—was hesitating nearby. He was tall and strong, wearing the brown pants and forest-green shirt that was common among Utugani men. He looked uncomfortable but determined. "Do you need my help?" he asked.

"Can you get us water and a towel?" said Catarina firmly.

Jena looked at her in surprise. She didn't think water was going to save Nate. After the warrior had gone, Jena raised her eyebrows.

"Just to make him feel useful," said Catarina with a shrug. She leaned in close to Nate and put her hands on his chest. Immediately, Jena could feel the power of the flames even more. She swayed slightly in response.

Catarina glanced up, and Jena could see the fear in her eyes. "It's so much stronger than anything I've ever dealt with. I don't know if I can destroy them."

"We don't have to destroy the flames," said Jena, shaking her head. "They're part of Nate; it would destroy him too. We just have to convince them not to kill us all."

Catarina shook her head. "They're not exactly reasonable. They just want to get out."

Jena didn't question how Catarina knew all this. "We can't let them go free."

"What did other Firecallers do in the past? They must have been able to control this aspect of their powers."

It was a reasonable question, but Jena shook her head. "That's the problem. No one seems to know." Maybe they couldn't save Nate—and everyone else—after all. The thought made her breath come in ragged little gasps. Nate's hand was hot and sweaty in hers.

Catarina hesitated. "There is something in our culture..." Her words stuttered to a halt, and she looked at Jena, eyes wide.

"What is it? The time is now if we're going to save everyone." Jena tried to be patient with Catarina's reluctance—she understood not wanting to talk about her magic—but they were running out of time.

"It's a kind of collective memory that we've always used to help us. The Utugan, plus the women in the Utugan's family, are all connected to it. It's a secret, handed down from generation to generation. I could be thrown out of my hearth just for telling you about this." Catarina's expression was a mixture of fear and determination.

"Will it matter if I know about it if we're all dead?" said Jena urgently. "If there's a chance, we have to take it."

Catarina nodded, clearly resolved to continue. "You're right. I have to take the risk." She took a shaky breath. "I can look into the memories of all my ancestors, generation by generation, through this magic. One of my ancestors had dealings with a Firecaller. I... I believe—I hope—I can find out more about what Nate needs to do."

For a moment, Jena was too stunned to speak. "You have magic that remembers everything that's ever happened?"

"Only what our ancestors experienced. But yes. It's dangerous knowledge. Others would use it against us if they could. And as you know, it is not always safe for a woman to have magic." Catarina looked at Jena, her eyes keenly watching the younger woman's face. Word of Jena's fireballs against the barker lions had clearly made it into the Utugan's tent.

"Do it," said Jena quickly. She felt rather than saw the Utugani healers walking around behind them, tending the wounded. They were all innocent people who didn't deserve to die.

Catarina took a deep breath. "You need to protect me. I have no awareness of this world when I am inside the memories. Don't let anyone know what I'm doing."

Jena nodded. "I promise."

Catarina closed her eyes and went completely still. The

surrounding air seemed to thicken and power flared. The hairs along Jena's non-burned arm rose, and the raven tattoo on her stomach shifted uncomfortably. She didn't take her eyes off Catarina. She could actually feel the swirling magic, and it was like nothing she'd ever experienced before.

Catarina was so still—and for so long—that Jena wondered if she'd somehow transformed into a statue. Jena clenched her hands, trying to be patient. Nate rocked beside her, his low moans matching the noises from other injured people in the tent.

After what seemed like forever—but was probably not long at all—Catarina opened her eyes again. "I know what needs to be done. The flames want to be used, to burn. That will calm them back down to their normal level." Magic still swirled around her.

Jena leaned forward. "But we don't want them to burn anyone. And the wolvans and barker lions are all dead," she whispered urgently.

"We can give them another outlet. Instead of burning people, they could burn part of the forest."

"That doesn't seem fair. Any animals that weren't killed by the flames would be homeless. And the fire could rage through the entire forest, instead of just a little section of it."

"What's your idea then?" snapped Catarina. "Because I prefer the death of the forest to the death of my people."

"We just need to think of a different outlet," said Jena carefully, trying not to upset Catarina any further.

Catarina closed her eyes for a moment, as if she were concentrating on her inner magic again. "It doesn't have to be about burning some*thing*. It's simply about using the power." She opened her eyes. "If the flames are filtered through something—or someone—else, then it can turn their magic from flames to simple energy."

"Like what?" Jena was having a hard time imagining what else the flames could do.

Catarina looked around the room. "You said you helped your sister do healing magic on Argus?"

Jena frowned. "Yes. But Bree is the healer, not me."

"You're stronger than you think. You could use the same healing magic as Bree used to filter the flames and heal all these people."

Jena's eyes widened. "What makes you think I could do that?"

Catarina shrugged. "You have powerful magic. Even if my guards hadn't witnessed it, I'd still know. It hangs off you like a cloak."

Jena stared at Catarina, horrified. "Surely it's not that obvious?" she said. She was dead if it was.

"Not to normal people. But I've been dealing with magic since I was a child. I sense it more than others."

"More than other mages?"

Catarina hesitated again. "I don't know what mages know. I just know what I can sense."

Jena held Nate's hand tightly in hers. They didn't have much time. She just had to trust that Catarina knew what she was doing. She'd deal with everything else later. "How do we do it?"

"If you let me help, I can feed the magic through you. You just need to remember what it was like when you and Bree did the healing magic on Argus. Focus in on that energy. That should be enough. I have some experience with maneuvering magic that is not my own."

Jena wanted to ask more questions about the magic and how it was going to unfold, but honestly there was only one question she needed the answer to: "Will this work? Can we save everyone?"

"I can't guarantee anything, but I believe so, yes." Catarina nodded firmly.

Jena once again gazed around the room at all the people in pain, at the people tending to them. Heart in her throat, she nodded. "Fine. Let's do it."

"Come closer," said Catarina. "We need to be holding hands, as well as touching Nate." She leaned forward and grasped Nate's hand. He was still sweating and trembling hard. His eyes flickered as soon as Catarina's skin touched his. "Get comfortable. We need to work together."

Jena moved in closer and sat on the other side of Nate, opposite to Catarina. She reached out and touched his fingers, then whimpered and pulled back. "He's burning up. It's like touching fire." She glanced at Catarina, who was calmly holding his other hand.

"It's necessary. We both have to touch his skin, and it will burn. We need to control the flames, transfer their energy and then send the raw magic to you. You will then be able to use it to heal anyone inside this room, maybe even the camp."

Jena's eyes were like saucers as she looked at Catarina. "You're sure about this?"

"As sure as I can be. The old memories are sometimes a little faded, but..." She shrugged. "I'm fairly certain I have this one correct."

Jena looked at Catarina and traded a charged moment with the older woman. She had to trust that Catarina knew what she was doing. What other choice did she have?

Jena reached out and smoothed the sweat-soaked hair from Nate's forehead. His skin was burning, and it really was like putting her hand into the flames. She knew from personal experience what that felt like. But if it would help Nate—and everyone else in the camp—she'd do whatever it took.

She held out her hand and took Catarina's, then grasped Nate's hand with her other one.

Heat hit her palm, and it was like she was touching fire. Her fingers trembled, and she flashed back to being pushed into the campfire as a child, but she held steady.

"Let's do this," said Catarina.

CHAPTER 53
NATE

J ust when it seemed like the flames were going to consume him, their burning heat dimmed.

It came in waves, and he knew the next wave would flow over him again soon. There was no stopping the flow of flame magic.

The world spun around him. He was flying without being able to control where he was going. The flames were pushing and pulsing, but their ferocious power was... less. Not much less, but enough to make it bearable for the moment. He tried to open his eyes, but he was stuck inside the prison of his mind.

The only thing that kept him sane was Jena's presence close by. He didn't understand what was going on, but Jena was looking after him. She wouldn't let anything happen. He felt her hand on his forehead, and another familiar presence held his hand.

Bree? Was she helping Jena?

But then he remembered. Bree had been kidnapped. They were trying to save her.

So who was here helping Jena?

Then he felt another presence. Something he didn't recognize. It felt heavy, burdened and old. Much, much older than a single person could ever be. Magic inside magic, inside magic. More magic than was visible from the outside.

It reminded him a little of Jena, carrying her burden of the Book of Spells, as well as her own magic.

Except this magic was old. Ancient. Carried through the years, passed on from one person to the next. He didn't understand how it was possible, but he saw it. Maybe it was the flames inside him, giving him strength and vision he wouldn't normally have, but he felt connected to this new magic.

It is our Utugani memories, said a voice in his head. *Passed down through our leaders. We hold them steady and keep our knowledge for all the generations.*

He recognized the voice. *Catarina?*

I'm here with Jena. We're going to help you.

But how——?

Just hold the flames close to you until the time is right.

How will I know the time is right?

You'll know.

Just then, a surge of flame magic overcame him. He gasped, his whole body tensing. He pushed back against the flames, even as they begged him to set them free. They screamed at him, and it was all he could do to hold himself steady. He felt the touch of Jena's hand in his and he cried out, using every ounce of strength in his body to hold back the flames and give Jena and Catarina time to do... whatever they were going to do.

And that's when he felt it. Something was pulling at the flames, urging them to follow a path that neither they nor Nate had noticed before. There was a flowing magic swirling around in one corner of his mind, foreign to him, but somehow comforting.

Now? he asked.

Now, replied Catarina.

Praying that he was doing the right thing, Nate allowed the full force of the flames to follow the swirling tunnel of magic that led away from his core. The flames went greedily and hungrily, storming toward their only escape from their prison.

Nate gasped for breath, his whole body shuddering as the flames left his body. He tried to hold steady, to wait where he was for the flames to leave, but as they surged through the tunnel, he was compelled to follow.

Wait! Stop. It's dragging me out too.

Hold tight. Don't let that happen. If you leave your body, you may never get your consciousness back.

Nate tried to find purchase within his body, something to hold on to inside his mind. But the rushing sound became louder, the flames pulled at him, and it seemed like nothing was strong enough to keep him where he was. The flames wanted him to come with them, to enjoy the burn like they did, and they were going to make sure he wasn't left behind.

The burning, rippling desire inside the flames engulfed him as Nate was dragged down the swirling tunnel of magic. He'd lost all control; it felt like he was slipping and sliding, speeding up as he was pulled along in their wake.

His mind raced down the tunnel until he hit the ancient magic that was calling to the flames. It didn't burn like the flames; it was cold as ice, but vast and all-consuming. The flames were burning wildly, spitting and screaming for release, but he couldn't take his eyes off the swirling magic that held them so easily. This magic was more powerful than any he'd ever felt before, even his grandfather's. It was like a large group of powerful mages were surrounding him —stronger than the mage council, the most powerful group of mages in the kingdom—all towering over him, watching him without expression, without emotion. His magic felt small in comparison. The flames had simmered down, and were dancing prettily beside the towering ancient magic, as if they would never hurt a fly, and Nate almost growled at them.

Why did they act like that for this magic, but burn out of control for him?

Why could he never figure out how to control them?

Why was it like this every time he used his magic?

"You have much to learn, young Firecaller," said the ancient magic. It was as if all the mages in the entire kingdom were talking at once, all in different voices and accents. *"And no time in which to learn it. We give you this: defeating the dark prince is not only your task. It is a task for all Ignisia. Use the help when it is freely given. You are the cog in the wheel, the one who must make the quest turn, but you cannot do it without the spokes."*

"But how do I—"

"We cannot tell you more. You will succeed..."

Nate felt his heart skip a beat, even though he wasn't inside his body. He would succeed—

"Or you will die trying."

And there it was. The downside to this whole thing. If he didn't beat Lothar, he was done. There was no going back home, no chance of quietly hiding in another kingdom.

The flames swirled around him, as if they were trying to comfort him. They had calmed down, although they were still buzzing with energy, and they now seemed to see him again.

"What happens now?" he asked the ancient magic.

"We release the energy from the flames and save all our people."

A tiny gap opened in the surrounding magic. The flames seemed to sense that there was a way out, and without a second of thought, they dove through the gap and away from Nate.

Nate was again dragged after the flames. He scrabbled and scrambled and fought...but was unable to halt the flow of his connection to the flames.

And then he felt it. A warm hand on his forehead—fire magic that burned brighter than any other he'd ever seen. Jena was reaching out for him. She held onto him, held him tightly to her. His headlong tumble after the flames was halted, blocked by Jena's magic.

The flames sped onward, out the gap and into their release, and he felt it as the flames turned into pure energy. It was like bright light, power in its purest form. He didn't understand how it was happening, but as they transformed from flames into energy, the connection between him and the flames lessened. He flowed back into his body, back toward Jena, and he could finally take a breath again.

He could no longer feel the ancient magic, but the pulsing energy of his flames was still close by. For a moment, he panicked. What would happen to the energy? Was he supposed to do something with it? Then he felt Jena's fire mage magic grasp the pure energy and propel it around the room. It was no longer flame energy bent on destroying everything in its path. Jena turned it into healing magic, like her sister's, and spread it over everyone in the Utugan's tent—including himself—and healed their wounds. He felt the flame energy as it joined up flesh that had been ripped apart, as it stopped blood flowing where it shouldn't, and as it allowed breath to flow smoothly in the chests of several older patients. It was miraculous.

His magic—through Jena—healed all these people.

He didn't know what to think. He could only be grateful. His flames weren't always destructive. They didn't always cause death.

It was possible to channel them into something good. Something worthwhile.

He savored that thought until it was all he could think about.

And then everything went black.

CHAPTER 54
JENA

J ena walked through the devastation, her heart numb. She knew she should be helping to clear things up— and she would, soon. But for now, she needed time, space, to think.

Nate was sleeping inside the Utugan's tent, peaceful at last. The tent filled with wounded had been transformed into a tent filled with people who were healed. She'd been the conduit for that, and it had been... overwhelming. Powerful. More than anything she'd ever experienced before. It had given her a new appreciation of Nate's power. It was so strong, so overwhelming, so *feral*. She didn't know how Nate kept it inside and still walked and talked like a normal person.

Had it always been like that for him?

She shivered at the thought. Tried to distract herself by watching the Utugani clearing up the destruction in their hearth. Except that didn't work either, because the first thing she saw was the forest green and brown wagon that belonged to Elsa.

She'd forgotten about Elsa.

Catarina had told her what had happened to her old foster mother, but she'd pushed the information away, too focused on healing Nate to deal with it. But now her brain was free to feel the full impact of her death. By a wolvan no less. Her body was nowhere to be seen, but there was blood on the grass around the wagon. It took little imagination to picture Elsa lying there.

A tiny sob escaped Jena's lips. She didn't know how to feel. There was a giant lump in her chest, pressing down on her. She hadn't wanted to see Elsa again, hadn't wanted to speak to her. But she hadn't wanted her to die painfully either.

If Jena and Nate had never come to the Utugani hearth, this would never have happened. The guilt of that knowledge was pressing down on her, making her breaths come in little gasps.

Her feet moved, and she didn't know where she was going until she ended up beside the pile of bodies at the edge of the river. She'd known where they were taking the bodies, but until this moment, she hadn't wanted to be anywhere near it. Each person had been carefully covered by a blanket, and she counted more than thirty people in all who'd died here today.

Another sob escaped her. It was too much.

"He would have come for us, now or later; it makes no difference."

Jena jerked at the voice, just behind her shoulder. She turned to look at the Utugan. His face was haggard, and he looked years older than he had just yesterday.

"How do you know that?"

"We have ways of knowing these things. That's why we were leaving for the hidden hearth. But sometimes there is no way to outrun your destiny."

"How can you be so unemotional about all this?" said Jena, her voice raw. She gestured to the dead in front of them angrily. "He killed all these people."

The Utugan's face darkened. "Believe me, I am not unemotional. I feel every one of these deaths. These are my people, and this is a dark day in our history. But I do not want you to think that it was your fault. We were already in his sights. He does not like the wandering folk. We bring a different history to the land, a contradictory history. He wants to control what the people know, and he knows we would disrupt that. We have always been a target for Lothar. You being here simply made it happen faster."

Jena let out a slow breath. It didn't make it better, but it made lighter. "We have to stop him."

"Agreed. That's why I came to find you. We have emptied out the wounded—who are no longer wounded—from my tent. Rothell is helping to ferry as many people to the hidden hearth as will climb on her back. The rest will leave with me soon. But first, we need to talk with you and Nate."

Jena nodded. "Of course." She owed him that courtesy, and so much more.

"Follow me."

Jena walked behind the Uugan as he strode toward his tent. Everything had been tidied away, but there was no hiding the bloodstains on the side of the tent fabric. He held the flap open, and Jena ducked her head and went inside.

It was like it was a different room. Gone were all the patients and the medical supplies. The smell of blood and pain still seemed to linger, but there was nothing they could do about that. They hadn't brought back the large pillows or the comfortable chairs, or any of the things that had made this tent feel like a place that was lived in. Instead, there was a single large rug on the floor, and a small table nearby with glasses and a decanter of some kind of liquid. Nate was lying on a low bed made up of blankets next to the rug, eyes closed. She couldn't tell if he was asleep or just resting. Channeling the flames had been like attempting to control a roaring forest fire with only a glass of water, and it had left them all feeling sluggish, but especially Nate.

"We must leave soon. But this is a meeting that requires privacy," said the Utugan.

Jena turned as someone else entered the tent. Catarina nodded solemnly as she came in, and then Eldrin did the same as he entered behind his grandmother.

"Come, sit." The Utugan gestured for Jena to sit near Nate.

She went over to the bed and touched Nate's forehead. He opened his eyes immediately. The flames were gone, and his hazel irises stared back up at her. She let out a soft sigh of relief. "Hey."

"Hey," he replied. There was so much emotion in his gaze, she was lost in it for a moment.

Someone cleared their throat behind them, and he looked over her shoulder, eyes widening when he saw the others looking at him. He pushed himself onto his elbows, and Jena stood up and moved back to allow him to sit. He looked exhausted, but at least he was himself again.

"I'm sorry to do this to you so swiftly," said the Utugan. "But we wish to be gone from this place. We will take our dead with us and bury them at the Hidden Hearth."

Jena nodded. She understood the desire to leave the campsite. She could still hear the screams. "Why did you wish to have this private gathering?"

The Utugan sat down on the rug, and Catarina and Eldrin sat next to him. Catarina's arm was hooked through her grandson's, and the older woman looked as tired as Jena felt.

The Utugan motioned for Jena to sit as well.

"We would like to help you," said the Utugan.

"And we're grateful for everything you have given us," said Jena carefully. She sat down on the rug next to Nate's bed. Nate was sitting on the bed behind her.

"Of course. Yes. But there is something more we can do."

Jena glanced over her shoulder at Nate then back at the Utugan.

"Catarina told you one of our secrets yesterday," he said. He gave his mother a stern glance.

She just shrugged her bony shoulders. "It was either help, or have everyone die," she said, her tone determined. "I didn't have a choice."

The Utugan gave a small nod in her direction. "No point in keeping a secret if the entire clan is dead." He turned back to Jena and Nate, and his expression turned to steel. "But it is also our most closely guarded secret. As we have all survived our ordeal, I must now bind you to an oath of silence. Many covet our ancient magic. We cannot allow anyone else to discover it."

"Of course," said Jena, nodding. She understood keeping secrets. Nate murmured his agreement from behind her.

As soon as they agreed, Jena felt a tiny zing of power over her body. She blinked, glancing at Catarina.

"Just a tiny oath-binding spell," Catarina said, her expression unrepentant. "To make sure."

Jena frowned at Catarina but couldn't quite decide

what to complain about. She'd planned on keeping the secret to her grave. A spell forcing her to keep the secret wasn't going to change that. She glanced at Nate.

Nate just shrugged. "We agreed to it."

"You could have said you were going to do that first," grumbled Jena. "Given us warning."

Catarina shrugged. "You agreed to keep the secret. What more is there to know?" She hesitated, glancing at her son. "But there is more we can do for you, using our shared memories."

"The knowledge that gets passed on is important," said the Utugan. "It's been passed down through centuries of Utugani leaders. It means we might know a way to give you information that will help you defeat Lothar." He hesitated. "And maybe also tell you how to break Argus's curse."

"What?" The word burst out of Eldrin, and he glared at his father. "You had a way to find out how to break his curse, and you weren't going to tell them?"

Jena looked at Eldrin curiously. He obviously knew about the memories, but he didn't seem to know their capabilities. Did they keep it a secret, even from the next in line for the leadership?

Catarina shifted as if she were uncomfortable. She glanced at the Utugan but said nothing. The silence felt loud and seemed to last forever.

Finally, the Utugan cleared his throat. "Those memories, that knowledge, some of it's from a long, long time ago. It's the knowledge that people would kill for. That people have *already* killed for in the past. We must keep it hidden, for the sake of everyone." He swallowed hard over a lump in his throat. "It's not up to me to break that silence for the sake of one person, even if that person is my son."

CHAPTER 55
JENA

"I can't believe—"

"Eldrin, it wasn't his decision. It's a law laid down by the ancestors," said Catarina sharply. "We swear an unbreakable oath when we're given the knowledge of the memories. Your father didn't have a choice."

Eldrin looked like he wanted to say more but instead thinned his lips to a tight line.

Catarina looked around at everyone, her lined face solemn. "It takes time... and a large amount of energy to dig into the memories," she said. "There's no guarantee we'll even find what we need. This isn't something we take lightly. It's a heavy burden, carrying the ancestors' memories."

"For Argus, I think it's worth it," said Eldrin, his voice breaking.

His grandmother laid her head on his shoulder and patted his arm. "We all miss him, Eldrin. It's difficult for all of us."

"He misses you too," said Nate.

Jena's gaze flicked to Nate. She knew Argus had said

375

nothing of the sort. But Eldrin and Catarina seemed to take comfort in his words, and that was important.

"Do you really think the memories will help?" said Jena. "What could your ancestors possibly know about how to break a curse in the present day? Or how to defeat a man they've never met?"

"I don't know. But I will try," said the Utugan. He looked tired and weary, but the steel in his core shone through. "I owe you that much."

Jena nodded. "We'll take any help you can give us. Breaking Argus's curse and then confronting Lothar in the next three weeks is going to be hard enough."

"That's a lot," said Eldrin doubtfully.

"It's a task of monumental proportions," agreed Nate, leaning forward, his gaze intense. "But I refuse to give up on Argus, and we must stop Lothar. For the sake of everyone in Ignisia. Lothar will destroy the very fabric of our Kingdom if we don't. We need anything that could help."

"If we do not prevent Lothar from becoming King, this will only be the first of many attacks on our people," said the Utugan. "But I do not know if our memories will be enough to tip the scales in your favor."

"As Jena said, we will take any help you can give us." Nate shrugged.

The Utugan nodded as if this was the answer he'd expected. "Then we will help you. But in return, we would like to know more about Jena's powers. We will place the information inside our shared memories for future generations."

Jena blinked in surprise. "My powers? Not Nate's?"

"We have memories from the first Firecaller," said Catarina. "But we have never come across a woman who has such powers."

"That's because no woman was ever stupid enough to show herself before," muttered Jena, half to herself. She took a deep breath, wondering if she dared. Perhaps knowing some of her secrets would help? "I can explain a little more about my powers, I guess."

"Jena–" Nate leaned in with a whispered warning, "It's too dangerous."

Jena looked over her shoulder at him. "Half his warriors saw me use my magic. The Utugan already knows that I'm a mage. If he was going to do anything about it, he'd have done it already."

Catarina gave a sharp laugh. "The more I know you, the more I like you, girl."

Jena smiled at Catarina. "I think the Utugan is far more intelligent than most men," she said deliberately.

"You will get nowhere with such blatant flattery," said the Utugan, trying to frown over his obviously pleased expression.

"I mean no offense." Jena paused. She believed she could trust them with her secret. But if she was wrong, it could mean her life. "I will tell you something that could get me executed. You will have that power over me."

"We will protect that information as we protect the memories," The Utugan said solemnly.

"Thank you." She took a breath. "I was trained as a mage by the Guardian Thornal. If the mage council found out…"

There was silence around the room. Jena watched the three Utugani leaders and hoped she hadn't misread them. They all stared at her with a variety of reactions. The

Utugan looked curious, Catarina had an excited spark in her eyes, and Eldrin looked daunted. She swallowed hard.

"Your path leads to death," said the Utugan softly. "I suspected it, but to hear you say it out loud..."

Catarina leaned forward. "Bah, that's nonsense. There's no reason she can't be the first at something. Those old laws about magic are a bunch of humbug."

"There's more," Jena said. She partially lifted her shirt, and showed the mage tattoo on her stomach, the same one that covered half Nate's face. Catarina's eyes widened.

"A mage tattoo?" she said. "He gave you a mage tattoo?"

"Not really. He gave me his raven familiar. Which turned out to be Thornal's mage tattoo."

The raven, as if it knew she was talking about it, turned its head on her side, and looked at the Utugani.

The Utugan gasped. "Did everyone see that? It moved on her skin!"

"We saw," said Eldrin, his voice awed.

"There's more," said Jena.

The raven burst free from her skin in a flurry of feathers and flew around the room.

All three of the Utugani gasped. Their eyes were fixed on the raven as it swooped around the tent. Jena couldn't help the nervous twitching of her fingers as she held them in her lap. This felt like a big risk. She wasn't entirely sure why she was taking it, other than that they'd all just survived a battle together. They were connected now.

The raven landed on the rug next to her and preened itself, happy with their response. It was larger than average for a raven, and its feathers were a brilliant blue-black. He was a handsome bird, and he knew it.

"How? How is this possible?" The Utugan looked astounded.

"It's not my tattoo. It's Thornal's tattoo. I don't know the magic he used to remove the tattoo from his face, and I don't know the magic for how he made it come to life. But he somehow did all that and was able to pass his tattoo onto me."

"I've never seen anything like it," whispered Catarina.

She'd seen all the memories of her people across hundreds of generations, and she'd never seen it before? The thought was terrifying.

Jena took a ragged breath. "Maybe because there's another secret I hold. And this one is even more explosive than the last."

Catarina made a strangled noise, like she couldn't believe anything could be more explosive.

"I'm the granddaughter of Thornal."

"He had a granddaughter?" said Catarina glancing at the Utugan. "That can't be right. I thought his son died when he was young?"

Jena shook her head. "My father, Thornal's son, was killed by the mage council when I was a baby, because he had broken the mage law about marrying a witch. My parents successfully hid me and my sister before they were murdered."

Catarina gasped. "You're the daughter of a witch and a mage?" Her expression said it all. The tiny warding sign she gave said even more.

Jena winced. She hoped she wasn't wrong about these people. "I am. I only just found out about it, and I never met my parents. But it's true."

"No wonder you're so powerful," said the Utugan. "And no wonder no one has ever been able to do these things before. The mage law about witches and mages is followed very strictly." His expression was grim.

"It is. Which is why I need you to keep my secret like I'm keeping yours." Jena's whole body was tense as she waited. She could see their emotions flitting across their faces.

Surprise. Denial. Fear.

This was why she'd always kept her powers hidden; there was no way to know how people would react. Even those who seemed reasonable and kind changed when they realized someone was breaking old mage laws. She'd seen it happen before. And here she was, breaking more than one of those musty old dictates.

The raven was poking around next to her, as if it could sense some worms hidden in her pocket. Eldrin watched the bird as though mesmerized. The Utugan kept looking from her to Nate, a frown drawing his eyebrows together as if he was trying to do some kind of mental arithmetic to figure out how this could have happened. Catarina watched her with narrowed eyes, her lined face giving nothing away.

"That's a lot," said Catarina.

Jena set her shoulders, preparing for the rejection. As soon as they said the words, she'd have to make a run for it. She flicked through the Book of Spells for something that would distract them—but not harm them—while she ran. She didn't even know if Rothell was still in the camp. The shimagni might be halfway between here and the Hidden Hearth for all she knew. How else was she going to outrun a camp filled with Utugani warriors?

And what about Nate? Would he come with her? Her breath stuck in her chest at the thought.

Except he needed the help of the Utugani in his quest to overcome Lothar. Maybe it would be for the best if they separated? There were too many people who'd see her as a threat, or as some kind of abomination. It would put him at even greater risk.

Maybe by sticking by his side she was going to harm his chances of success?

As if he could hear her thoughts, she felt Nate move slightly so he was a warm presence just behind her, not touching, but close enough to provide strength.

Letting her know he had her back.

She let out a breath. She couldn't leave him. Not yet.

"By all the Flames, how are you still alive?" said the Utugan. He didn't seem to be angry.

"I'm very good at keeping secrets. And a fast runner," said Jena with a small twist to her lips. She was still ready for action.

"Then why tell us? Why expose yourself like this?" asked Catarina.

Jena leaned back slightly until Nate's knees were almost touching her back. It gave her the strength to keep talking. "This cause is important. We need your help. And I think being honest might help all of us work together better."

"Why is this so important?" asked Eldrin impatiently.

Jena took a breath. "I'm helping Nate, because I believe he's the true King of Ignisia. I believe we are making history right now."

The Utugan nodded, almost absently. "You're both creatures of legend. A Firecaller and a powerful female mage. I am honored to have crossed your paths." There was a long pause before the Utugan spoke again. "We will keep your secrets, Jena. Thank you for trusting us."

Catarina and Eldrin grinned, and even Jena was moved to smile. They'd passed the first step.

Now they just needed to find a way to save Argus and kill Lothar.

Simple as pie.

CHAPTER 56
NATE

"I regret this already," said the Utugan, his tone uneasy. He was watching his mother as she lay down on the rug, getting ready to access the memories.

Nate shifted uncomfortably at the obvious concern in the Utugan's voice. How dangerous was it, exactly? He peered at Catarina, searching for weakness, any sign that this was a mistake, but she seemed so strong and vital.

"I'm better at connecting to the memories we need, son," she said. "It makes sense for me to do it."

"Are you sure, Catarina?" said Nate. "This isn't worth your life." His palms felt sweaty, and the Flames had sparked to life in his chest. He didn't know why he felt so off-kilter.

"It will not cost me my life," said Catarina calmly, her voice steady. "I'm perfectly capable. I've spent more time with the memories than with my son. This is the best way." She closed her eyes and folded her hands neatly together over her stomach.

Discussion done.

Jena stood next to Nate, watching Catarina carefully. They desperately needed information to save Argus and Bree, and defeat Lothar, but he didn't want it at the expense of Catarina.

"You haven't done a trance in years," said the Utugan. "Not since you passed over the leadership to me. You've forgotten how much it affects your body. And now that you're..." He stumbled to a halt, realizing too late his mistake.

"Now that I'm an old lady, you think I'll fall apart?" growled Catarina, opening her eyes again to glare at her son. "I'm not dead yet."

"Of course not," he said. "That's not what I meant. I just—"

"Enough. I've decided. Let's get on with this." Catarina glared around the room, daring any of the rest of them to say something. Catarina turned to Eldrin. "You know what to do if anything goes wrong?" she said.

Eldrin nodded firmly. "Yes."

Catarina glanced at the rest of the group, her gaze landing on Jena. "Maybe you better sit next to me, girl. Just in case you're needed."

Without hesitation, Jena moved forward and took a seat next to Catarina. "I'll be right here. I won't let anything happen to you."

Catarina's expression softened for a moment. "You can't promise that, child. But I appreciate the thought."

Nate could only watch as Catarina closed her eyes and leaned back into the pillows. They were so quiet and tense, they could have heard a needle drop.

At first, nothing happened. Maybe Catarina really was too old? Maybe the memories were just too much for her now? Nate glanced at the Utugan, but he didn't seem to be worried, not about this part.

And that's when he noticed it. A buildup of power inside the tent. A thickening of the air, and magical sparks tripping off Catarina.

Her face started changing; her nose elongated into a snout. Thick brown fur appeared on her face, and within moments, Catarina's head had become that of a grizzly bear. Her long white hair had transformed into short brown fur, and fur-covered ears had appeared at the top of her head. Her black nose twitched like she'd scented something interesting. The rest of her body remained in human form.

Nate could only watch the transformation, stunned. It was the strangest thing he'd ever seen.

He glanced at Jena. She seemed just as shocked. He'd known the Utugani revered bears, but he hadn't realized how deep it went, that it was the basis of their hidden magic. It was totally different from his own magic, more rugged and earthy. But he could feel the power inside the tent, and it was just as strong as his own, if not stronger.

"How does this work?" Nate asked softly, wondering if Catarina could talk in this partial bear form. "Will she...just tell us what we need to know?" He couldn't imagine how she was going to talk with a bear's head.

"The memories will ask us questions about what we're searching for," whispered the Utugan, not taking his eyes off his mother. "Then give us any information they have. We can ask questions if we don't understand, but there is no guarantee they will know the answer. And we need to remember what she says, because Catarina won't remember when she comes out of the trance."

"She's getting hotter," said Jena, still holding one of Catarina's hands between her own. She was so close to

Catarina, she could probably feel the hot breath from the bear's mouth. Nate wanted to reach out and touch the fur, to see if it was real, or some kind of magical illusion.

"That's normal. It takes a lot of power to control and manipulate the memories. Especially the more ancient ones, like those that might know about controlling the Royal Flames. We don't often go that far back using the memories." The Utugan took a deep breath. "But she's right. This is important to all of us. We must do what we can to help."

They stood in silence, watching as Catarina's bear-face continued to move until it was fully formed. It looked like the bear was sleeping, then suddenly it opened its eyes. They were dark, almost black, and seemed to have secrets swirling inside them.

The bear spoke in a low, growling voice. "You seek answers from the memories?"

"Yes," replied the Utugan. "We ask for help with a curse upon my son."

"He is of the Utugan line?" It was difficult to make out the words; the voice was so low.

But the Utugan seemed to understand them perfectly well. "Yes."

"This is most grave indeed. What is the curse?"

"He'll die in less than three weeks if we don't help him." There was a catch in the Utugan's voice.

"Who cast this curse?"

The Utugan looked at Nate and then Jena.

"It was a lavaen," said Nate, not sure if that's what the bear-memories meant.

"But not just any lavaen," said Jena. "She used to be an Utugani witch."

"Such a combination has never been in our memories before. Who is this Utugani witch? Is she also one of yours?"

The Utugan shook his head. "We do not know."

"Tell us about this lavaen-witch," said the bear-memories.

The Utugan looked at Nate again.

"She was the lover of Remus the Mage, but he cast a spell and turned her into the lavaen. It happened a long time ago. Maybe forty or fifty years ago."

The bear-memories gave a low humming rumble. "There's a possibility we know who she is."

"Who?" asked the Utugan, leaning forward.

"Your older sister, Alessan, disappeared around the same time. She was a powerful witch and curse maker. It was known to your parents that she had a secret lover, but they did not know who. It seems possible it was Remus."

The Utugan shook his head emphatically. "That can't be right. She died."

The bear paused. "When she didn't return from a gathering trip, your parents presumed she was dead... but her body was never found."

"My parents always seemed very sure." The Utugan's face had gone pale. He looked shocked at this revelation about his sister.

"She would never have left for good without telling them," growled the bear. "Your mother was very close to Alessan. She grieved for many years. But it is too much of a coincidence not to be connected."

"Could this be true?" Nate asked the Utugan.

The Utugani leader's hands were clenched tightly at his sides. "She was much older than me. I thought my parents had confirmed her death. But perhaps not."

"The memories do not lie," snarled the bear, showing the tips of pearl-colored teeth.

"I'm sorry," said the Utugan, his voice breaking. "It's not that I don't believe you. I'm just shocked. It means that Argus was cursed... by his own family."

"Alessan loved her family. She would never hurt one of them knowingly," said the bear-memories.

Nate shook his head. "I don't think there's much of Alessan left inside the lavaen. The beast we met was full of rage and not much else."

"It saddens us to hear this. We will add it to our memories."

"Does this mean you can help with breaking Argus's curse? Do you know the curses that Alessan might have used?" asked Jena, still clutching Catarina's hand.

The bear-memories paused, as if it was conferring with other people—or memories. "We have never witnessed such a thing before, the mix of Utugani and lavaen." Another pause. "We do not know what kind of curse Alessan might have cast from inside a beast of fire. The power combination is too unpredictable, the magic too complicated. The answers you seek for Argus's curse do not lie with us. It is beyond our knowledge."

CHAPTER 57
NATE

The words seemed to echo inside the tent.

Nate's heart dropped into his stomach, and he let out a disappointed breath. What would they do now? He hadn't realized until just this moment how much he'd been hoping the memories would give them the answers they needed.

"Can we find the knowledge elsewhere? Is there anyone else who might have the answers?" asked Jena, her voice filled with despair. Bree's life was hanging in the balance, as well as Argus's.

The bear-memories paused and then opened its mouth again, the strange growling voice making all the hairs along Nate's arms rise. "Those who have spent centuries studying the evil curses, poisons and pestilence of this world might have an answer. There is one such place. Find the Society of the Myrtle. They hide in plain sight, but they may have the cure you seek."

Nate frowned. He'd never heard of such a society. "Where do they hide?" he asked. "How do we find them?" At least it gave them someone else to look for.

"They are very secretive, but we know they live in the shadow of Flame City. That is as much as I can tell you. They are your best hope for finding a cure for a lavaen-witch's curse." The bear-memories twitched its nose, and it was exactly like a real bear.

"Thank you," whispered Jena, from her position right next to the bear's face. She looked up at Nate, worry lines standing out on her face. She cleared her throat. "We have another question. We seek to confront Prince Lothar, the usurper on the Flame Throne. Nate is the rightful King. Do you have any information that might help us defeat Lothar?"

There was another pause as the question filtered through to the memories. "The Great Mage created the Flame Throne more than a century past." The bear-memory's voice echoed around the tent. "Before that, chaos reigned. The Flames hold us together, make our kingdom great."

"So we need the Flame Throne?" asked Nate. The memories were confirming what he had thought.

"Yes. They are integral to our society. The Great Mage was a Firecaller, a man destined to control the flames, and the beasts ruled by the flames. A man able to walk between the Edges and our world, to talk to the demons and those who remain after death, and to affect the ripple of time."

The ripple of time? "What..?" Nate's eyes widened. "That's—"

"Shhhh," said Jena.

He stopped, but couldn't help the thoughts that were raging inside his head. He missed some of what the bear-memories were saying because he couldn't figure out how he was supposed to affect the ripple of time. What did that even mean?

He shook his head and focused again.

"…. the Royal Flames must not go out. If they do, it will bring about the destruction of Ignisia," the bear growled eerily. "That was the law laid down by the Great Mage, and it stands today."

A chill went down Nate's body. "We know that Prince Lothar is planning to put out the flames. How do we stop him?" he said.

"The Firecaller must stop him. That is the only way."

"But how? *How* do I stop him? He's more powerful than I am. More experienced. I can't even control my flames. I'll end up killing everyone—if Lothar doesn't kill me first." Nate felt bile rising into his throat.

"You will find a way. A Firecaller is chosen for a reason. It is not accidental."

Nate just stared at the bear's face. "Everyone is so sure I'll figure it out, but no one knows exactly what I need to do to make that happen. No one seems to understand. *I have no idea what I'm doing.* This isn't something that's intuitive, or that will come naturally to me. I have less than three weeks to figure this out, and so far, I'm failing."

Just like he'd failed everything else in his life.

He didn't say the words out loud, but they echoed in his head, a reminder of the lessons he'd learned as a child.

"You will have help from unexpected quarters," growled the bear-memories. "The fates always send Firecallers those they most need to help them. If you fail, it will not be because the fates were stacked against you. It will be because you did not believe in yourself and those sent by the fates to help you."

Nate swallowed hard, wishing he could find a way to believe in himself like that. He glanced at Jena. The fates had sent her to him.

"But beware," the bear-memories continued, "there is always one, a person close to the Firecaller, who will betray them. Do not trust blindly, for there are those who would rather see Ignisia burned to the ground, than have you on the Flame Throne."

Nate blinked, his eyes going wide. "Who is going to betray me?" he whispered, horrified. "I don't have any enemies."

He glanced at Jena. Would she betray him? He didn't think so.

Then who would it be?

"We do not divine the future. We simply tell you what has gone before."

Nate nodded and tried to push that information away. It didn't help. "What else can you tell me?"

"Prince Lothar is but one man. You must find your allies. The Great Mage had many people willing to die for him. You must do the same. It is the only way you will succeed against Lothar."

First, someone would betray him, and he should trust no one, and then he had to find more people to work with? Nate shook his head. It was contradictory advice. Trust no one, but trust everyone? He glanced at Jena. He didn't know anyone who would die for him. Not even Jena, who had vowed to stay by his side.

"Anything else?" he said in a low, defeated voice. He felt worse, not better.

"The Great Mage put several safety provisions into the Flame Throne room, and around the castle where he lived. Rooms to hide where no one can find you, places to keep yourself safe until the time is right. Just look for the symbol of the Great Mage and the rooms will be close at hand."

Nate blinked, wondering how some hidden rooms

would help him fight Lothar. It didn't seem enough. "Anything else?" he asked again, desperation clawing inside his stomach.

"The Great Mage would often visit our leader, the second-ever Utugan. Our Utugani tribe was founded around the same time, and they were friends on their journey." The bear-memories paused, as if talking to someone inside its memories. "The Great Mage always said that belief in yourself was the only way to make your magic stronger. The power comes from inside you, not outside. There is nothing more you need to overcome Lothar and take back our kingdom than belief in yourself."

"But—"

"We are done. There is nothing more."

And the magic inside the tent disappeared with a whoosh of air. The bear-face immediately started to move and deflate, shrinking back down into Catarina's face.

Nate felt deflated. "That didn't tell us anything new," he said. He couldn't help the disappointment that colored his voice.

"Sure it did," said Jena. "We now have more knowledge of the castle to add to our strategy. And we know where to go for Argus's cure, so we can free Bree. This is more than we had before."

Nate nodded, trying to see the positive side. "You're right. It's just that I was hoping..."

"For the exact recipe for how you're going to defeat Lothar?" said Catarina. Her eyes were still closed, and she lay on the bed as if she was asleep. She looked weary, the shadows under her eyes dark with exhaustion.

"I guess," said Nate reluctantly. He felt embarrassed to admit it.

"No such thing exists, son. You just have to take everything as it comes, and hope the Flames are on your side."

"That's not exactly comforting," said Nate.

Catarina opened her eyes. They were still all-dark, like the bear's. "It wasn't supposed to be."

CHAPTER 58

JENA

"I cannot spare as many men as I had planned," said the Utugan.

Jena and Nate were standing with him outside his tent, watching as several Utugani men and women efficiently broke it down, led by Eldrin. They weren't wasting any time—everyone was eager to leave. It seemed like years had passed since their pre-dawn breakfast of porridge by the central hearth, but it was only mid-afternoon.

"We understand," said Jena. "You need everyone to help with the move to the Hidden Hearth."

The Utugan nodded. "Thanks to Rothell, we're more prepared than we would have been, but it's still a long trek and my people are suffering after the attack. So many deaths, it's difficult to take it all in." He took a steadying breath and hesitated as his dark eyes watched the tent being rolled into a fraction of its original size. "I can send someone with you who knows the city like the back of his hand. He also volunteered."

The Utugan glanced at Eldrin as he strode toward them,

a bag over his shoulder. The tent was being carried in the other direction on the shoulders of four men.

"You're coming with us?" Jena blinked in surprise.

"Argus is my brother. I want to make sure he's okay. And you'll need some extra help when you get Bree back." Eldrin flicked her a cheeky grin, although it was smaller than it used to be and it disappeared almost immediately.

Jena felt her heart leap at the reminder. They still hadn't discussed how they were going to rescue Bree without Argus signing himself over to Remus again. She could only hope something would occur to them after they got Argus free from the lavaen's curse. "Thank you. If you're sure?" She glanced between the Utugan and Eldrin.

Eldrin stared around at the broken hearth, his expression hardening into a seasoned warrior's. "I plan to make sure the monster responsible for this carnage is punished properly. My people deserve that much."

Jena nodded. She understood vengeance. That's what started her on this journey.

"Promise to take care of Eldrin for me. I need him back," said the Utugan. He stood straight and tall, dressed in traveling clothes, and didn't hint at the turmoil she was sure he was feeling. He was sending his second son to rescue the first. What if he lost them both?

"We'll keep him safe," she promised. *As safe as he could be, anyway.*

"I'll push him to the back of every battle," said Nate with a small smile.

Jena shook her head as Eldrin grinned again. If Eldrin was anything like Argus, he'd be at the front before they could say a word.

"And you've packed?" asked the Utugan, looking between the three of them.

"Yes, all done," said Nate. "Rothell is ready."

"I have my bag," said Eldrin. "Let's go before anyone else realizes and makes a big thing of it." He gave his father a fierce bear hug. "Take care of yourself, Father. I'll see you again soon."

"Yes. I'll see you soon," agreed the Utugan. His expression was sterner than usual, the lines on his face more pronounced.

Jena wondered why he'd agreed to let Eldrin go on a mission that he clearly didn't want him to go on. Was the desire for vengeance really that strong?

"Thank you for everything you've done for us," she said.

"The fate of the kingdom rests on your shoulders. It is my duty and pleasure to help you." The Utugan bowed, then turned abruptly and strode off.

Jena, Nate and Eldrin looked at each other, then Edrin shrugged. "He doesn't like goodbyes." Then he walked toward Rothell, his stride matching his father's.

"Family trait?" said Jena.

"Probably," agreed Nate. He was still staring down at Jena.

"What?" she said, shifting uncomfortably under his intense gaze.

"Earlier... when I thought we wouldn't make it out... I kept thinking, not yet. Just... not yet. Because I haven't told you—" He stopped. Looked away, his cheeks going red.

Jena frowned. He seemed... flustered? Was he upset with her? She couldn't read his expression. "Told me what?" Her raven moved on her stomach, feathers shuffling. She held her breath but didn't know why.

Nate cleared his throat. Looked her in the eyes. His gaze burned. "Told you that I—"

"Come on you, two!" yelled Eldrin from up ahead. "We don't have all day."

Jena waited a beat. She felt edgy and hot. What was Nate trying to say?

Nate closed his mouth abruptly. His expression became shuttered. "Don't worry. It's not important," he said. "We can talk about it later."

Jena glanced quickly to where Eldrin was gesturing at them to hurry, then back at Nate. "Are you sure?" she said, trying to decipher his strange mood.

Nate nodded. "Come on, we need to get going." He turned and strode toward Eldrin, his back straight and stiff.

Jena let the air out of her lungs in a long breath. What just happened?

Confused, she trailed behind him, glancing back at the disappearing hearth. Soon, the only trace that they'd been here would be the bloodstains on the ground and the ashes of the dead creatures that had attacked. The Utugani were experienced at packing up and moving on. It didn't matter that they were mourning.

Getting to safety was paramount.

Who would drive Elsa's wagon, now that she was gone? The thought made her heart ache. Their last conversation had been awful, but she hadn't wanted Elsa to die. She touched the raven amulet Elsa had given her only that morning. If nothing else, she was thankful she had her father's amulet back. She touched the silver raven amulet where it rested at her throat on a silver chain.

She'd moved the small pouch of Thornal's ashes to a special belt that Catarina had given her, with secret pockets for precious objects. She'd stored the lavaen stone there as well, keeping it well hidden from Nate.

But instead of storing the amulet with her other important objects, she'd worn it. The faint buzz of her father's magic made her feel connected to her family, including Bree.

Tears rose unexpectedly, and she blinked them away. She didn't have time to feel sad, or wallow in pain. They had a quest to complete, and no time to lose. Re-settling the bag on her back, she ran to catch up to the others.

"You're ready to depart?" asked Rothell, tipping her large glowing head in their direction.

"We are. We need to find the Society of the Myrtle."

"I know where they live," said Rothell, surprising them all. *"But they are not good people."*

"They don't have to be good. They just have to tell us how to break Argus's curse," said Nate, his expression grim.

Jena nodded in agreement. Their focus had to be on Argus and Bree. They needed to do whatever it took to get them both back.

Silently, they climbed onto Rothell's back. Jena was in front, Nate behind her, and Eldrin at the back.

"Everyone ready?" asked Rothell. *"Eldrin, remember to hold tight."* She took off without waiting for a reply. Jena's heart leaped in time with Rothell's sharp ascent into the sky. No matter how many times she experienced it, she would never get used to flying. Her fingers clung to the back ridge in front of her, and she squeezed her thighs tight, trying to hold on with her legs.

The air whooshed past them, and Jena scrunched her eyes closed, leaning forward to balance out the angle Rothell had leaped up at. She might never get used to traveling on the back of a shimagni—it was too terrifying for that—but there was also a rush to the entire experience.

Flying was like nothing else. The raven moved its tattooed wings in agreement, and she saw pictures in her mind as if she were the one flying. The raven was allowing her to experience flying from its perspective, and it was just as thrilling as being on the back of the shimagni.

When it felt like everything had evened out, Jena opened her eyes again.

She squinted so the wind wouldn't hurt her eyes and looked down. Below them, the patchwork of the landscape was spread out. Fields, forests, and rivers were all part of a greater whole. Even the mountains in the distance. Houses looked like insects, and the people weren't even visible. The only sounds this high up were the beating of Rothell's wings and the pounding of her own heart.

Jena let out a sigh. They were on their way. They had a destination, and people who might help with the curse.

They were one step closer to getting Bree back.

CHAPTER 59
NATE

"What's happening down there?" yelled Nate.

"What?" yelled Jena, her words whipping past him in the wind.

"She cannot hear you," said Rothell in his head. *"But I see what you mean. They are in trouble, are they not?"*

"I think they might be," yelled Nate, even though he knew the only person who could hear him was Rothell. Hopefully, she'd pass the words to the others.

Far below them, a group of travelers had stopped on the road. There seemed to be fire, confusion, and lots of running around.

In the distance, they could see the stone turrets of the highest buildings and the enormous red stone wall that circled Flame City. They'd been flying for several hours and had covered a distance that would have taken weeks on foot. Nate's whole body was stiff and sore from holding onto Rothell in a death-grip, but he could appreciate the benefit of traveling on her back.

They'd seen more travelers than usual on the roads

below, especially as they flew closer to the capital city. The coronation was in two and a half weeks. People were obviously excited to be part of the celebrations and to see a new king on the throne. It was always a spectacle.

"Maybe we should stop and make sure they're okay?" he yelled.

He wouldn't mind the break from flying, if he were honest.

"We are close to our destination," said Rothell. *"Are you sure you want to delay?"*

In front of him, Jena peered over the edge of Rothell's side. "They're being attacked," she yelled, looking back over her shoulder. "We could help without too much delay."

"As you wish," said Rothell, and she dipped her right wing, circling down toward the ground.

As they got closer, Nate could see that several carts and wagons had been placed in a circle on the road, as if they were protecting themselves from an attacker. There were people in the middle of the circle, and some on the outside, swinging weapons that varied from brooms to swords covered in... blankets? Nate squinted at the scene below but couldn't see anything. Small bursts of flame seemed to come out of nowhere and burn sections of the wagons.

"What's attacking them?" asked Nate.

Rothell landed on the road just ahead of the carts. Jena, Nate, and Eldrin climbed down, leaving their bags beside Rothell.

"I will stay here so I don't scare them," said Rothell.

Nate nodded back at Rothell. They walked cautiously toward the strange scene. Rothell shimmered behind them, staying mostly invisible.

It was only once they were about ten steps away from

the configuration of wagons that Nate finally realized what was happening. They were being attacked by insects.

Thousands and thousands of fire ants were swarming toward the group of travelers and their wagons. The fire ants at the front of the swarm were being brushed back by men wearing guard uniforms of green and black, but they were close to being overwhelmed. The expressions on the faces of the guards said they knew it, too.

"By the flames, why are they attacking in such numbers?" said Eldrin as they walked cautiously closer. "Fire ant colonies rarely grow to that size. They always break off and form new colonies."

Nate shared a glance with Jena.

"Lothar," they both said in unison.

"A better question might be, why are they attacking these particular travelers?" said Jena, searching the faces of the men and women hiding behind the wagons.

"They won't be saved by hiding in the wagons," said Eldrin, his expression concerned. "Fire ants will just climb through and around. And brushing them back will only work for a short time. They're aggressive and determined little creatures."

"They're too small to fight individually."

"Like the flies on the Riders," said Jena. "We have to fight them as a group."

Nate peered closely at the massing fire ants. "Honey won't work on them. They're not attracted to it like flies are."

"And there are so many of them, they'd just storm over top of the ones who died in the honey and keep going," agreed Jena.

A pained scream reminded Nate of the urgency of the situation. The ants were winning in their fight against the travelers. There were just so many. As soon as they swept one lot away, another thousand swept in behind them.

"Help us!" yelled one guard, who was attempting to brush away the ants with his sword, covered with a blanket. They'd finally noticed their potential rescuers. "They just started attacking. We've lost two people already. They just consumed them while they were still alive." The fear in his voice made it rise almost to a squeak on his last words.

Nate noticed two person-sized lumps of ants near the first wagon. He swallowed hard.

"We're here to help," called Jena. "We're just trying to figure out the best way to do it."

"How do we help them?" asked Nate in an undertone. "*Without* getting eaten alive by fire ants?"

Jena got that distracted look on her face that meant she was looking up fire ants in the Book of Spells. "I can't see much in the Book of Spells about them," she said. "They live in fire; that's how they make their eggs, in the heat of the flames. They have bodies that can withstand high heat. They're often found in lava, so they're immune to it."

"My fire won't help," said Nate. Not that he wanted to use it. He was secretly relieved he didn't have to.

"Fire ants hate snow," said Eldrin unexpectedly. "We used to throw snow at them if they came too close to the guard forts in the mountains."

"Not that helpful right now," said Nate, looking around at the dry landscape surrounding them. "And we don't have time to fly to the mountains and back. The ants would have consumed them by then."

Eldrin gave him a look. "They also don't like the cold. Any kind of cold. That's why they're usually found in and around volcanoes. Keeps them warm." Eldrin frowned, looking around them. "When I think about it, this is a strange place for them to have accumulated."

"It has to be Lothar controlling them," said Nate. "He loves to force creatures outside of their normal behavior. These people must be a threat to him somehow."

"You know what they say. The enemy of my enemy is my friend," said Eldrin.

"We need to find something cold to throw at them," said Jena.

"There's a stream nearby," said Nate. "I saw it as we came in on Rothell. We could get water from there. Maybe pour it over them?"

Jena hesitated, then said, "There's a spell to make water into ice. Would that be cold enough?"

"Definitely," said Eldrin with a grin.

Nate knew how hard it was for Jena to admit she could do spells. He raised his eyebrows at her, and she gave him a small half-smile back. She was okay.

"Let's get this rescue going," said Jena.

Nate turned to Rothell. "We need help with getting enough water over here to freeze the ants, and hopefully kill them," he called out to her.

Rothell bowed her head. *"I will fly to the stream, gather water in my mouth."*

"I'll go with her and fill our water bottles," said Eldrin. "Maybe find more ways to carry water back."

"We'll stay here, help the travelers however we can," said Nate.

Eldrin nodded, then ran back to Rothell and climbed up her flank and onto her back. He looked like he'd been doing it for years. Rothell took off in a flash of wings.

"We need to find out if they have any barrels of water.

Wealthy merchants often travel with that kind of thing," said Nate.

They cautiously moved closer, keeping a wary eye on the fire ants. They were moving in a wide clump around the wagons, little bursts of flame coming from their bodies. So far, they didn't seem interested in Jena or Nate, but there was no guarantee that would continue.

"I wonder who it is that's so dangerous to Lothar," said Nate softly. He peered at the people inside the circle of wagons and carts. They didn't look like a special group.

"The ants are certainly determined to get to them," whispered Jena, not taking her eyes off the scene in front of them. "We need their water. You're a mage. They'll trust you more. You need to be the one to talk to them."

Nate made a face at her but didn't disagree. People tended to be in awe of mages. He cleared his throat. "What supplies do you have? Do you have water barrels?" he yelled across to the men defending the group.

"We're not dead yet," shouted the same guard who'd yelled for help. "You can't have our supplies."

"We're not trying to steal anything. Fire ants don't like the cold. We need the water so we... um, I... can turn it to ice and use it on the fire ants," yelled Nate. Jena would be the one doing the spells, but they didn't need to know that. Everyone would see the tattoo on his face and assume it was him.

The guard called back to someone behind him, and moments later two big barrels were being rolled out from the middle.

"Now what?" asked the guard.

"Open the barrel and pour the water toward the ants. Cover as many of them as possible," said Nate.

They watched as the guard and one of the other men

pried open the first barrel. The ants started swarming nearby as soon as the men stopped brushing them away. One man yelled in pain and swatted away a group of fire ants that had crawled up his leg.

"Hurry," said Nate. He glanced at Jena. "Is there nothing else you could do? Maybe an air spell?"

Jena moved behind Nate and closed her eyes. Suddenly, the ants near the two men were being pushed back by a mysterious wind. "Put your hands up as if it's you doing it," whispered Jena from behind him. "They expect the theatrics."

Nate put his hands up, swaying them around as if he were doing something more than acting.

"I feel like an idiot," he whispered to Jena.

"As long as we save them, it doesn't matter."

The wind pushed back the ants, but they kept trying to move, and as soon as the wind stopped, they stormed forward again. But in the time they'd been flying, the men had opened the first water barrel and started pouring out the water.

At first, the fire ants didn't seem to care about the water, charging through it on their tiny legs. Then he heard Jena chanting the spell behind him, and the water started to look frosty and freeze over. He waved his hands around again to pretend it was him making the spell and watched as the ants slid over the newly formed ice. Their movements grew jerky and hesitant.

"More!" shouted Nate. "Pour out more of your water."

Behind him, he could feel the energy coursing out of Jena as she continued casting the ice spell. She was murmuring the words under her breath. He waved his arms about as they poured more of the water out of the barrels, pushing back the front edge of the ant invasion.

"Incoming from above," said Rothell into their heads, and then water was tumbling out of the sky.

It immediately turned into ice and snow, so it landed on the middle section of ants and sent them scurrying away. An unpleasant cracking noise filled the air.

"What's that noise?" asked Jena, her voice worried.

"The ants. I think it's their outer shell. It's cracking from the cold," said Nate, peering closer.

"No wonder they don't like ice."

"All that matters is that their survival instincts are finally overriding whatever spells Lothar put over them," said Nate.

The ants at the front were retreating, many with their outer shells cracking. But all the ants at the back were still stomping forward. Some of them were going around the edges of the water, moving out wider like they'd figured out the ice didn't go on forever.

"More water," yelled Nate up to Rothell and Eldrin.

"As you wish," said Rothell.

She flew back toward the stream, and they felt the downstream of air as she turned overhead.

"Maybe we can get Rothell to beat her wings and blow them backward?" said Nate. "The travelers can move on while she's doing that."

"That's a good idea to save the people here. But will they just attack the next group of travelers who come by?" asked Jena, her face scrunched up with worry. "We don't know for sure that this is a personal attack. Maybe he's just trying to disrupt travelers coming to the coronation?"

Nate looked back at the remaining ants that were trying to climb over the icy barriers. "You're right. We need to make sure the ants are completely disrupted."

"Now what?" asked the guard in front of the wagons.

They were pouring out the second barrel of water over any ants that remained, and the water turned to ice almost as soon as it touched the ground.

"You need to get moving, away from here, as fast as you can," shouted Nate.

A weak cheer went up from all the travelers.

"I can't keep the water icy for long," Nate warned, trying to get them to hurry.

But he needn't have worried. The group was just as eager to get out of there as Nate was to have them leave. They climbed into their wagons, the first two leaving quickly.

As the third and largest vehicle rolled by, it stopped by Nate, and a large middle-aged man with a ruddy complexion and twinkling eyes leaned out the window.

"Many thanks to you, young mage. If you ever have need of me, my name is Gerge the merchant. I owe you a debt for your work this day. Not everyone would help strangers on the road." He nodded to both Nate and Jena.

Nate bowed his head. "Thank you. We're happy to help. Now please hurry away before the fire ants figure out a way around."

Gerge nodded and banged the roof of the carriage. It sped off down the road, blowing dust into the air.

CHAPTER 60

JENA

They watched as the various conveyances rumbled off down the road, almost forgetting about the ants. Only when Rothell returned and poured more water down over the middle and back of the group did they turn back to their current problem. Jena concentrated on the water and whispered the words that would send her magic out. It crystallized and then froze the water, trapping many of the ants inside.

"We can't just leave the rest of the fire ants here to attack the next group of travelers who come by," said Nate.

Jena nodded in agreement. "Why would he just leave them to attack anyone who comes this way?" she asked. "Doesn't he want people at the coronation?"

Nate shrugged. "Maybe he doesn't care?"

A sudden roaring scream from the air made Jena jump. Her heart leaped into her throat, and as she looked up, Rothell tilted sideways and fell a few feet. There was a group of tiny creatures flying around her wings. A burst of flames hit Rothell's wing and burned the delicate membranes. She screamed again.

"Fire ants in the air," she yelled into their heads, panicked.

"Since when do fire ants fly?" said Nate, staring up in horror at Rothell.

"Go to the stream!" yelled Jena. "We'll meet you there." Jena took off running across the grassy field, with Nate only a breath behind her.

She ran as fast as she could, and still when they got to the stream, Rothell was writhing in pain in the water, part of her left wing burning from the flames, winged fire ants landing on her and sending bursts of flame onto her skin and biting her. Jena cast the cold spell again, turning the water in the stream into slushy ice, and several of the ants fell away into the stream.

"They're still flying around her," said Nate urgently. "We need to throw the water at them, then turn it to ice."

Eldrin had jumped from Rothell's back and was flinging his sword around at the flying creatures that were still zipping around them, but he wasn't fast enough.

"They're biting her as well," he shouted. One of Rothell's wings had some of the transparent skin burned away from their initial attack, and the fire ants were zooming in to bite the torn shimagni flesh.

They ran to the water and waded into the section that wasn't frozen over. Jena cupped her hands under the running water and flung it toward the closest flying fire ant. She chanted the spell under her breath, and just as the water hit the insect, it turned to ice. The flying fire ant dropped like a stone into the water, a loud cracking sound filling the air.

"And again," yelled Nate. "There are more of them. They're still attacking her." He was throwing water at the flying fire ants as well, but even if the water hit them directly, it just made them fall a little in the air, then rise again moments later. Only Jena's ice was stopping them.

Jena flung more water at another fire ant, then another, muttering the spell over and over, as she hit them with ice and water. Rothell's screams of pain became moans, but it was still the most awful sound Jena had ever heard. Without thinking, she gathered magic from her very core and flung it out toward Rothell, this time using it to soothe the shimagni's wounds. Spells for healing were difficult, and required energy and concentration, two things she had in short supply right now. The best she could do would be to stop Rothell from hurting.

She worked quickly on the healing spell, but even so, when she turned back to the fire ants she saw they'd been able to gain some ground. Two had landed on Rothell's side and were biting her, while another was aiming its flames. With a sound that seemed more like a wounded animal, Jena grabbed a handful of water and threw it at the three ants. She growled out the words of the freezing spell, and the ants fell to one side, their shells cracking.

It was the most beautiful sound she'd ever heard.

The remaining ants kept diving at the shimagni as she lay in the water, and Jena kept throwing the water, casting the spell, tears falling down her cheeks. They couldn't lose Rothell.

"She's stopped making noises," said Jena. "Is she okay?"

Nate ran to Rothell's head. "She's passed out," he yelled. "She's still breathing." He put one hand on the top of her head, as if he was trying to soothe her.

"From the pain," said Eldrin. "Fire ant bites hurt like you're being burned on a stake."

Jena cupped her now-frozen hands into the water again. Could fire ants kill a shimagni? It shouldn't be possible, but there were so many of them, and they kept burning and tearing at Rothell's skin. She flung the water at the closest fire ant, muttering the spell again. It plummeted into the stream with a satisfying thunk as it hit the slushy ice near Rothell.

There were only about five fire ants remaining, but they still buzzed angrily around Rothell, diving in whenever they had the chance. Jena doubled her efforts. She threw water on more than one at a time, cast the ice spell, and made them fall with a crack to the ground. Her arms felt like they were on fire, and ever since she'd cast the healing spell her brain had been fuzzy. She was exhausted, but she wouldn't stop, not until every single one of the flying fire ants was gone. She could see the sides of Rothell's body moving up and down. That's all that mattered.

"Almost done," shouted Eldrin. He was still trying to hit them with the side of his sword, but even when he slammed it into them, they would just move away for a moment, then dive back in.

Jena just kept casting spells, hitting the ants with ice, and trying not to think about what they had done to Rothell.

Someone touched her arm, and she flinched, jumping back.

"It's okay, Jena. They're all dead. You did it." Nate stood close by. "You killed them. It's okay."

Jena let out a breath and dropped her hands. She staggered to one side in the stream, only staying upright because Nate leaped forward and grabbed her arm.

"That took more out of me than I realized," she said. She stepped away from him and stood on her own two feet in the stream, shivering.

"Come on, Jena. You need to get out of the stream. It's

freezing." Nate held out one hand, his expression questioning. Without thinking too much about it, she took his hand and let him lead her back to dry land. She almost stumbled again, her trousers and boots soaked and heavy, but Nate kept her upright.

With gentle hands, Nate helped her sit on the ground. She sat with her legs bent and her arms resting on her knees. Breath rasping, she kept her head down and stared at the grass. Her magic felt like it was stretched tight, like a thin layer of glass coating her body that might break at any moment. Who knew that fighting such a small creature could be so exhausting?

And terrifying.

A low moan from Rothell brought her back to her senses. She pulled herself to standing and went over to the shimagni, who was still lying across the stream, her head laid on the earth next to the water. One of Rothell's wings was smoking from the fire ant flames, and patches of skin were burned away.

Jena put her hand on Rothell's head and closed her eyes. She tried to push energy into the shimagni, but there wasn't much left to give at this point.

"It is fine," said Rothell, her voice faint. *"Don't waste your magic. I have magic of my own."*

Tears fell down Jena's face as she looked at the devastation of Rothell's wing. "You won't be able to fly," she said.

How would they get Rothell to safety?

And how would they save Bree now?

CHAPTER 61

NATE

"I don't need to fly. I have this." Rothell closed her eyes and a blue crystal—just like the ones in her cave—appeared on a necklace around her enormous neck.

"What will that do?" asked Jena, peering at the gemstone.

"It will get me home," replied Rothell with satisfaction. *"It's tuned to my cave and set to appear if I ever get wounded. Once I'm back home, my wing will need some serious healing from my crystals. I am sorry, but I must leave you for now."*

Nate let out a relieved breath. He'd been worried that Rothell was permanently wounded. "You can get home? And you'll recover from those wounds?"

"Yes, the crystals in my cave will heal my body, but it will take time." Rothell stretched and winced in pain. "You must excuse me."

Jena stepped closer, placing her hand on Rothell's neck. "Before you go, Rothell, can you tell us where the Society of the Myrtle is?"

Rothell dipped her head. *"The Society of the Myrtle is due west through the forest. You will find it easily from here. Look for a crest with angel wings and a scythe. I will meet you outside the western gate of Flame City in three days. I will carry you back to Remus to rescue Bree."*

Nate listened to Rothell's words with growing apprehension. What would happen if the Society of the Myrtle didn't know how to break Argus's curse? Would they be able to free Argus in just three days?

In three days, they might be no further ahead than they were today.

"We'll be there," said Jena, her voice ringing with conviction. She glanced at Nate. "We have to be."

Rothell nodded. *"I will see you soon. But now, I must heal."* She closed her eyes, and the blue crystal glowed brighter and brighter until Nate couldn't look at it anymore. The glow seemed to spread until it was covering Rothell's entire body.

And then she was gone. Just disappeared from the stream.

Nate blinked, then looked at the other two.

Eldrin grinned. "That's one way to leave the room."

Jena shook her head, astonished. "I've seen many magical things in my time, but never anything like that."

"Come on, we have to keep moving," said Nate. "We only have three days."

Jena gave a tired sigh, but followed Nate as he turned back to the road and headed in the direction Rothell had indicated. Eldrin followed behind Jena, his usually cheerful expression grim. They grabbed their bags from the roadside and walked toward the dark forest.

Two hours later, Nate was tired, hungry, and sore. The forest was dark and thick with trees and underbrush, but compared to traveling in the Forest of Ghosts, it had almost seemed easy at first. Now exhaustion was making it difficult to walk in a straight line, and his eyes were so blurred he wasn't sure he could tell what was a tree and what wasn't.

He climbed over a fallen log and stumbled to a halt behind Jena, who'd stopped abruptly in front of him. She was staring up at an overgrown, crumbling stone building that loomed over them. Patchy late afternoon sunlight hit the arched stone entrance, and vines crawled over the side of the building that looked like it had caved in many years before.

It almost looked like a church where people might go to worship the Royal Flames and say the protection psalms.

Except Nate felt unnerved and edgy, not calm and peaceful like in a church. He immediately sensed why. Someone had placed a spell over the crumbling ruins to keep people out. There was a dark menace that hung over the area and sent a shiver along his skin.

He put his hand in his pocket and felt the fire ruby in its little pouch. It was hot to touch, a tiny reminder of why they had to do this. He pulled it out and held it in his palm. His heart hitched when he realized that the ruby had dimmed even more.

Argus was dying. Bit by painful bit.

The angry buzz of magic felt like a warning they should heed. All his instincts were shouting at him to turn around and leave. But he refused. He would do everything he could to save Argus, even if it meant facing this dark and twisted magic. He put the fire ruby back in his pocket for safe-keeping.

Ahead of him, Jena cleared her throat and pointed. Nate followed her gesture with his gaze.

A strange symbol was etched into the stone just under the apex of the roof. Three interlaced crescent moons inside three downward-facing triangles, with a scythe at the base, and two angel wings at the other two corners.

"That's it, the symbol of the Society," said Jena. "Exactly how Rothell described it."

"What does it mean?" asked Eldrin uncertainly.

"I'm not sure we want to know," said Jena. "They're a magical society that deals with curses, pestilence and dark magic. It's probably not something nice."

Nate agreed. He didn't think anything good was going to come from this place. But they didn't have a choice. They had to rescue Argus. He glanced at Jena. And then they'd go get Bree.

The door was unlocked and slightly off the hinges. It squeaked noisily when Nate pushed it aside and ducked his head to enter. Jena and Eldrin followed behind him, both silent as they stared around the inside of the ancient building.

"Is this really the right place?" asked Eldrin. "It seems abandoned."

"It's a protection," said Jena, her nose wrinkling. "Keeps people away, makes them think no one is here. But I can feel the magic pulsing around us. There's a powerful presence here."

Nate paused a moment and opened his senses wider. The pulse of power he'd felt earlier was stronger now. It wasn't clear and clean magic like Jena's. It was oily and murky, prickly and poisonous.

This was the dark magic of curses.

"They're dangerous and evil. The king should have ordered them destroyed years ago," said Thornal, appearing unexpectedly, his mage robes flapping in a non-existent breeze.

Nate ignored him, trying to take in all the details in case they were helpful later. It looked like a church on the inside too, with rows of benches for people to sit on and a pulpit up front. Except the wooden benches were old and rotting, the pulpit had been tipped on its side, and vines grew up out of it.

"Do we really have to do this?" asked Eldrin. He looked around at the broken furniture and the decaying rug on the floor.

"Yes," said Nate. "We need help with the curse. These people know about curses."

"They're going to want to trade something," whispered Jena. "I don't think money is going to be enough for these people."

"You better not trade me," said Eldrin. He didn't smile as he said it.

"We're not going to trade anyone, even you, Eldrin. We'll just have to take it as it comes," said Nate, wishing he felt as calm as he sounded. "We won't do anything crazy."

"They'll try to trick you at every moment that you're inside this place," said Thornal, his expression concerned. *"You'll need to have your wits about you."*

A door squeaked at the front of the room, and all of them jerked their gaze toward the sound. A tall, thin man wearing a long robe emerged from a set of stairs going down into the ground. He had long, thin arms, with thick blue veins that stood out. His eyes were small, and his nose was too large for his sharp face. He paused at the top of the stairs and stared at them.

"This place is abandoned, as you can see. I must ask you to leave." His voice was scratchy and raw, like he didn't use it much. Nate couldn't tell how old he was; his pale face seemed almost green in the forest light coming in through the half-open roof.

"He's one of the leaders. I met him many years ago. You're in the right place," said Thornal.

"We're in the right place," said Nate. "We're here to speak to an expert in curses from the Society of the Myrtle. We have a curse we need help with."

"Society of the Myrtle? I'm sorry; you have been misinformed. No such society exists here." His words were slow and measured, as if he were not a native speaker.

"We know we're in the right place," said Jena grimly. "We need your help. My sister and our friend are both in trouble. We need help with an unusual curse."

"I'm sorry, I don't know what you're talking about."

"We know you're lying," snapped Jena, clearly losing patience. "All we're asking for is a bit of time with someone who can answer our questions."

"It's okay, Jena. We'll find someone else," said Nate, glancing at Jena with a fake casual expression. "They clearly don't want to admit they don't know enough about curses."

The man's eyes flashed. "Of course we know—" He halted. Scowled at Nate.

Nate lifted his eyebrows, waiting.

The cadaverous man looked between them, his movements jerky. "Tell me about this supposed curse," he snapped.

"It was cast upon our friend by a lavaen," said Jena.

"Ridiculous. Lavaens don't cast curses. You waste my time." He started to turn and leave.

Nate took a step forward, his arm out as if he could pull the man back toward them. "They do if they're an Utugani witch who's been turned into a lavaen," he blurted.

The strange man's eyes lit up, and he turned fully back toward them. "An Utugani curse? But through a lavaen's body? Now that *is* interesting. Which one of you holds the curse?"

"He's in here," said Nate, holding up the fire ruby in his hand.

"He's inside a fire ruby?" His eyebrows rose. "Even more interesting."

He didn't ask how Argus got inside the fire ruby, and Nate didn't tell him. He didn't want this man to know any more than was necessary.

"Will you help us?" said Jena impatiently.

The man hesitated. He gazed at them for several awkward moments, his beady eyes flicking between them as if assessing their worthiness. "Yes. We will help you. Follow me." The man turned and disappeared back down the stone steps at the far end of the room, his long legs moving awkwardly underneath his long robe. He looked like a giant insect with overly long limbs.

Jena glanced back at Nate and Eldrin.

"I don't know if this is a wise decision, son," said Thornal.

"We have no choice," said Nate. "This is what we came here for." He walked forward, moving past Jena and taking the lead. He glanced back over his shoulder at the other two. "We stick together. We don't fall for anything they might say. And we leave as soon as we can," he said quietly, then took the first step down into the bowels of the building.

Jena and Eldrin nodded quickly, just as unnerved by this place as he was.

Thornal disappeared as soon as they walked through into the murky tunnels.

CHAPTER 62

JENA

"First you must accept our hospitality," said the man. He said it as if they were seriously imposing on his time. "I will take you to the food hall where you may partake of our evening meal. Then I will take you to your rooms. In the morning, we will look at your curse." They were walking along a dark, damp stone hallway, lit only by fire in sconces along the wall. Their host had to duck his tall body to fit into the low narrow space.

Jena shook her head, shuddering at the thought of any food provided by these people. "No thanks. We're fine. We just want your help with the curse."

The man stopped and turned with a swish of his robes. His eyes were bright in the light of the nearest flame. "If you do not accept our hospitality, we cannot help you. Partaking of our food and sleeping in our rooms are the price you pay for our help. It is our tradition."

Jena glanced at Nate, who shrugged. "Fine. Food and sleep, then curse." She was tired and hungry, and the food would be good. She just wasn't sure she wanted anything from this creepy place. "But if we're going to follow you around, we should get your name."

"You may call me Joro," he said with a smile that showed off rows of sharpened teeth.

Jena had a hard time controlling her shudder. "Thank you Joro," she said, a tiny quiver in her voice the only reaction she allowed herself. Before she could give him her name in reply, he turned and strode off. "Clearly not bothered about getting to know us, then," said Jena in an undertone, before moving off after him.

They followed Joro through a rabbit warren of hallways. Water dripped down the stone walls, which were covered in moss, and dampness. The smell of rot filled the air. In one particularly putrid spot, Jena put her hand over her mouth and nose to keep out the smell. Eventually, they came to a large carved wooden door. Joro hesitated outside the door and glanced back at them.

"I must go inside by myself. Prepare my fellow society members for the arrival of... guests. We do not usually entertain." Joro slipped in through the door and shut it firmly behind him.

"Are we sure this is a good idea?" whispered Eldrin. "Did you see his teeth?"

"They know about curses," said Jena. "And whatever they throw at us, we can take care of ourselves. We're not without our own protection." She hesitated, watching the door. "But we all need to be wary. I don't think this will be straightforward." The raven shuffled its feathers on her stomach, and she had the sense that it was uneasy too.

"Nothing about this place is straightforward," muttered Nate.

Joro slipped back out through the door, his eyes glittering with what could only be called malice. He was up to something. Jena narrowed her gaze and watched him even more closely.

"Follow me inside. There is food and drink for you."

He opened the door wider and gestured for them to walk through. After a moment's hesitation, Nate led the way inside, followed by Jena and then Eldrin. The first thing to hit Jena was the smell. It was a mixture of the moldy, damp smell that had permeated the underground hallway, combined with the smell of old socks, rotten eggs, and boiled cabbage all mixed together.

Jena put her hand over her mouth as she looked around the room. Long trestle tables filled up most of the space. There were five other men in the room, all of them in the same robes as Joro, and sitting together in a clump in one corner of the room. They were all watching with glittering eyes and smug smiles.

"There are three options for stew. You must take only from one pot. No mixing, that is extremely important. Pick your bread last." Joro gestured toward a long table at the front of the room that held three steaming pots of food.

"Is that where the smell is coming from?" asked Eldrin under his breath. "If so, I don't want to eat any of it." He was standing next to Jena, his whole body tensed.

"I get the impression it's not negotiable. I think this is the cost of being here," whispered Jena.

"My people know about hospitality. This is not hospitality."

Nate had moved ahead, walking closer to the large pots of stew at the front of the room. Jena hurried forward, worried he would touch the wrong thing.

The more she thought about it, the more certain she became that this was some kind of test. She grabbed Nate's arm and pulled him back a little, then peered down at the stews. She immediately recognized the mushrooms in the first pot. Silverworm mushrooms were highly poisonous. Even touching them could be dangerous.

"Don't touch anything," she said sharply to Nate.

"It smells the best," he said, peering into the first stew pot.

"It's poisoned," she said. The malicious way Joro was watching them made her even more certain this was to amuse members of the society, rather than their sustenance.

"So it's not a taste and see situation?" he said.

"No. I choose what we eat," she whispered to Nate and Eldrin. "Don't eat anything unless I tell you it's okay."

"What is this place?" said Eldrin, looking around at the society members with wide eyes. "Why are they trying to kill us?"

"For the fun of it, if their smirks are anything to go by," said Jena. "Rothell warned us that they weren't good people."

"That's an understatement."

"Here, take this," said Nate, handing them each an old earthenware bowl. "Let's get this over with."

Jena walked slowly between the three large pots of stew. The first one held the Silverworm mushrooms, the second looked like a beef stew, and the third seemed to have a whole chicken inside it, including the head.

"I'm not eating that one," said Eldrin. "I can see the chicken's eyes."

Jena leaned over the beef stew in the middle, trying to catch a whiff of the smells coming out of it. There was something in it, an undercurrent of a scent that caught her attention.

What was it?

She closed her eyes and pictured Thornal's spell room. Where had she smelled that particular note before? In her head, she walked the shelves of his room, sniffing the various powdered and dried herbs.

"He's watching us," said Nate. "He looks annoyed."

"The beef stew seems the second-best bet," said Eldrin. "It smells alright. The chicken stew smells bad."

Jena opened her eyes and help up a hand. "Just let me do my thing. There's something in the beef stew that I can't place." She closed her eyes again and thought hard.

It was prickle root.

A tiny plant with almost no smell that was used to poison people.

"We're not eating the beef stew. It's poisoned as well." Jena sniffed. "I'm not even sure that's beef."

Nate and Eldrin stepped back from the beef stew in unison.

Jena looked over at Joro. "Is there any way that we could do this without eating your food?" she said.

"No. This is the price," he said, amusement in his eyes. "You eat our food, sleep in our room, and then we talk. If you refuse, you will leave with nothing." He smiled again, showing off his sharpened teeth. "Choose wisely."

CHAPTER 63

JENA

S hivering, Jena went to the whole chicken stew.

It looked and smelled the worst. There were feathers from the chicken in the broth with the rest of it. She sniffed, trying to figure out the ingredients from the scent alone. It had worked for her so far.

She smelled garlic, onion, salt, thyme and other herbs. There didn't seem to be anything poisonous. A hint of cilantro, but that wasn't a poison either. But the chicken pieces were certainly not edible. Some of the bones had snapped and were like sharp little needles inside the pot. She glanced over at the other Society of the Myrtle members eating their dinners. They just seemed to have a clear broth to go with their bread. Was there a fourth option?

She stared intently at the long table. They couldn't eat the first two options. The third one... she wasn't excited about eating sharp chicken bones or accidentally getting a chicken foot in her bowl. There must be another option. She walked around the table looking for other ideas. That's

427

when she noticed something poking out from behind the third pot. A sieve hidden from sight.

Why would a sieve be hidden behind the third pot?

She glanced back at the other men, who were all studiously eating their dinner and trying not to look like they were watching them like vultures around a dead animal.

"I think we eat the third pot but make it into a broth by using this sieve to leave out all the chicken parts," said Jena. "It's a two-person job."

Nate held the sieve while Jena held her bowl under it and used the soup spoon to pour out some of the chicken mixture. Pieces of bone, one clawed foot and an eyeball ended up in the sieve. The broth below was thankfully clear.

She handed her bowl to Eldrin, and he passed her his. She filled all three bowls using the same technique.

"Now for the bread," she said.

"Are you sure we should eat this?" said Eldrin. "They're still looking pretty smug."

"This is the best option from those three pots. Maybe there's a problem with the bread as well? He definitely said we had to eat the bread." She walked down to the bread-basket and peered at the two different options. One seemed to be a sourdough loaf, and the other was some kind of dark rye bread. She glanced back at the men already eating, but they'd learned since last time she looked. All their bread was gone. She couldn't remember which of the two sorts of bread they'd been eating—or even if they'd all been eating one type.

"Does anything about either of these breads seem wrong to either of you?" she said.

The two men came closer and sniffed near the bread.

"Not really," said Nate.

"That doesn't mean they're not still tricking us," said Eldrin. "We can't trust them."

Jena leaned forward over the bread, looking over it without touching. There must be something that would tell them which bread to pick. She peered at each loaf of bread, trying to pick out the various smells and grains that were visible. All her years of learning about the herbs and spices and other ingredients in Thornal's workroom were proving useful in this situation.

The sourdough seemed... innocuous. The rye bread seemed to have too many other possible ingredients, several that she couldn't exactly identify. She was leaning toward the sourdough as the best option simply because it was the one that seemed less likely to be a problem.

Except... Jena hesitated. The rye bread had strange little seeds throughout it that seemed familiar. Not ones that were normally used in bread. Jena peered closer. Where had she seen them before?

She searched her memory, trying to place the seeds. They looked like a cross between sesame seeds and poppy seeds.

"They're chuga seeds," she said, pulling back. "Chuga seeds are used as an antidote for the leaves of the chuga plant, which is a completely undetectable poison that smells a little like cilantro and causes convulsions, and then foam at the mouth, then death."

"So we eat the sourdough?" said Eldrin, hopefully.

"No," said Jena grimly. She glanced back down at the broth in her bowl. "The chicken broth has the leaves of the chuga plant in it. I think we eat the broth and the rye bread together. The chicken broth is poisoned, and the rye bread is the antidote." She looked over at Joro and he seemed slightly less smug than he had a few moments before.

"We can't eat poison," said Nate. "That's ridiculous."

"He said that eating and drinking their food, plus sleeping in their rooms, was the price of their help. I don't think we have a choice." Jena hesitated over the food. "We just have to eat it carefully."

Jena grabbed two pieces of the rye bread and walked over to Joro. "This is definitely the only way to get your help?"

"You must accept our form of hospitality." Joro gestured with his long thin arm for them to take a seat and eat their dinner.

Jena took a deep breath and then went to sit at the closest trestle table. Nate sat next to her, and Eldrin sat across from them.

"You sure about this?" asked Nate, looking dubiously down into his bowl.

"No," said Jena. "I'm not exactly excited about doing this either. But according to the Book of Spells, the ratio of poison to antidote is one to one. So I think we have one spoonful of the broth, then have a bite of our bread. We eat it like that. No having more soup than the bread. Eat slowly and don't eat more than necessary." She'd only given them a small serving of the broth.

"I'll go first," said Eldrin. "If I die, you have to kill Lothar for me."

"You're not going to die," said Jena, feeling more certain. Joro looked like he'd just sucked a lemon. "I'm right about this. The other pots are wrong. We have to do it like this."

"This is the most messed up dinner party I've ever been to," said Eldrin.

Nate gave an amused snort but said nothing. He was watching Jena to see what they should do.

She put a spoonful of the broth to her lips. It tasted a little like old socks with garlic and cilantro. She swallowed and quickly took a bite of the rye bread, chewing it and swallowing it almost whole. She didn't want to give the chuga leaves a chance to poison anything before she put the antidote into her stomach.

Nate and Eldrin copied her method of eating exactly.

A tiny spoonful of broth, a bite of bread. Over and over. Jena felt hot and feverish, sweat breaking out on her forehead. She took an extra bite of the rye bread, worried that she was being poisoned by the broth. She looked at the other two. They both seemed pale but were determinedly eating alongside her.

"Take an extra bite of the bread," she said. "Just in case."

They both followed her instructions precisely. Eldrin's hand was shaking as he took another bite of the bread. Nate seemed more comfortable, possibly because he'd grown up in an environment where he was an outsider. In fact, if you believed Nate's stories, they hated him. He was used to uncomfortable situations.

Finally, the broth in Jena's bowl was gone. She ate the last of her rye bread in three small bites and then leaned back. The other two were already done.

"Everyone okay?" asked Jena.

"I think so. Would we know if the poison was affecting us already?" asked Nate.

Before Jena could answer, Joro walked over and answered for her. "Yes. If you hadn't chosen the rye bread, you'd be convulsing on the floor in front of me." He sounded sad that they weren't. "Come. Follow me. I will take you to your room."

Jena's stomach was churning as she stood up, and she hoped it was because of the fear and discomfort of their situation, and not a delayed reaction to the poison she'd just intentionally ingested.

They silently followed Joro out of the food hall, and back out into the dark stone hallway.

CHAPTER 64

NATE

"Here are your chambers. I apologize that it is a shared room. But everything else is taken," said Joro, clearly lying.

Nate peered into the room, his flames burning inside his chest, like they were just waiting for the moment he'd let them out again. He squashed them down, pushing away the panic and fear he'd felt in the dining hall as they'd deliberately eaten poison and antidote together in one meal.

He never wanted to do anything like that again.

The room had three beds that were basically raised wooded pallets with a single dirty blanket on it. There was a bucket in the corner and a bowl of water next to it. There was no window, and the only light was from a small candle sitting on a nightstand in one corner.

They'd clearly tried to make it uncomfortable, but it wasn't even the worst place Nate had stayed. And the fact that it was shared? Not a problem. Nate wasn't about to let Jena or Eldrin out of his sight in this place. They needed to stick together if they were going to survive.

They'd made it through dinner and all they had to do was survive a night in this little room before they could find out how to save Argus and Bree. Surely they could manage that?

Joro shut the door with a clang, the gust of air from the action blowing out the candle. The room was suddenly pitch black, a darkness that felt heavy and cloying, and more than simply a lack of light. They all heard a key being turned in the lock on the other side.

"Did he just lock us in?" said Eldrin, his voice shaky.

A silver glow lit up the room as Jena brought forth her unusual flame. She stomped over to the door and tried to turn the handle. "Yes, he did. Asshole."

"I officially hate this place," said Eldrin. In the glow of her silver flame, he looked pale and agitated. It was the opposite of his usual effortless charm.

Nate understood exactly how he was feeling. This place was like living in a nightmare.

He looked around the room. Took a calming breath. "We just survive a night in here, then we get answers. Surely we can do that?"

Jena picked up the candle and lit it with her flame. As the flame jumped from her hand to the wick, it turned back into an orange and yellow flame. He didn't know how she did it, but he'd never seen anyone else who could change the color of their flames like that. It made the flames inside him leap in response.

She put the candle back on the side table by the door. The two flames—one silver and one orange, lit the room with an eerie competing glow.

"We take turns on watch. We can't all be sleeping at the same time in here," said Eldrin briskly, like he was just a normal lieutenant arranging shifts. "He's going to try something."

"I don't think I can sleep in here," said Jena with a shudder.

"I'll take first watch," said Eldrin, as if she hadn't spoken.

"You can wake me next," said Nate.

"I doubt I'll be asleep," said Jena again, this time with a visible shudder. "But I can go third."

"We all need to sleep," said Eldrin sternly. "We've had a long day."

"We'll need all our wits about us tomorrow," agreed Nate. "These people clearly enjoy toying with people's lives. Let's not make it easier on them."

He sat tentatively on the edge of the nearest bed. It was hard, and the blanket smelled of horses. It was no doubt supposed to make them feel like they'd just grabbed some horse blankets to put on the bed, but it was actually comforting. It reminded him of the traveling he'd done to get here, the nights when it had just been him and Argus, sitting by the campfire, wrapped in their blankets, eating some delicious stew that Argus had made, seemingly out of nothing.

The other two followed suit, sitting down on their pallets, testing out their beds. Jena lay down, pulling the blanket over her. Eldrin stayed seated.

"How will you know when to wake me?" Nate asked, looking around the window-less room. "We don't have any way to see the moon or stars."

"I've been doing guard duty for so long now, I can tell the passage of time," he said with a weary shrug. "I'll do the first two hours. You do the next two. Jena can do whatever is left."

Nate nodded, and lay down, thinking how unlikely it was that he'd get any sleep. He felt wired and wide awake. This place was too scary, too unknown. The blanket was scratchy, and the wood had splinters. He turned onto his side and closed his eyes.

Next thing he knew, he was inside his flames. They were burning all around him, wild and uncontrolled. He tried to push them down, to control them like he'd been practicing. But they ignored him. Then he remembered he was supposed to be treating them more gently, offering love and compassion to them. Treating them like a piece of his own body. He reached out to the flames and tried to show that he meant them no harm. But that didn't change anything; they still burned wildly around him, flames reaching higher and higher.

Through the flames, in the distance, he saw people. Jena and Eldrin. The Utugan and Catarina. Other faceless people he couldn't quite place. He tried to reach out, to tell them where he was, but the flames kept him hidden from view.

And then Lothar stepped into the flames next to him. They licked at his body, but he didn't seem to notice. They didn't burn him like they should have. His only power, and it didn't affect Lothar at all.

"You're going to die," said Lothar with a small, sad smile. "I am too powerful. You and your pitiful group of ragtag travelers are all going to die."

Nate screamed, tried to push Lothar away, but he couldn't move.

Couldn't do anything except stare into the smug face of his enemy.

"Nate," said a familiar voice from outside the flames.

Lothar leaned closer to him. "It will all be your fault when they die."

Nate shook his head desperately. "No. No!"

"Nate, wake up." Someone shook his shoulder.

"No! Leave me alone." He pushed at Lothar, trying to force him to leave the circle of flames.

"Nate, you're dreaming. Wake *up*."

He felt a sting on his cheek as someone slapped his face.

The flames disappeared. He felt the rough bed under him, and the scratchy horse blanket over his legs. He opened his eyes. He was back in the dark cell, Eldrin leaning over him.

"You were calling out in your sleep," whispered Eldrin. "I figured you weren't having a pleasant dream. It's your turn to take watch, anyway."

Nate blinked, still trying to adjust to being back in the room. He shook his head to rid himself of the last vestiges of his nightmare. "Thanks," he croaked out.

Eldrin moved back to his bed, giving Nate privacy to pull himself together. He looked over at Jena's pallet, but thankfully she hadn't woken. She shuffled about in her sleep, but her eyes stayed shut.

He sat up, rubbing his tired eyes, wishing he was back at the beginning of this journey, sleeping by the fire under the blanket that smelled of his horse, no other worries than how he was going to escape Argus the next moment he could.

Now he had the worries of the entire kingdom on his shoulders, like an overwhelming burden that only got heavier the more steps he took.

Was this what it would feel like to be king?

This feeling that if he didn't do everything exactly right, people were going to die?

He'd always thought kings had a life that ordinary folk should envy. All the riches they wanted. All the glittering parties and glorious clothes. They could do whatever they wanted, go wherever they wished. A few decisions here, sign a document there.

No pressure or worries.

But if it felt like this awful weight all the time?

A job he'd never wanted would become a duty he didn't think he could cope with.

CHAPTER 65

NATE

He put his feet onto the floor and tried to wake up properly.

He pushed his hands through his hair and wished he could see outside. This tiny cell with no windows and very little space was making him feel even more edgy. His flames started flickering in the back of his mind. He was sure they sensed he was close to the edge, that maybe his control over them might crack and weaken.

They'd be there to take over, he was sure.

He hardened his resolve and stared around the room. He counted the number of stones on the far wall and peered at the moss growing next to the corner. He watched the flame from the candle—which was burning seriously low and might not last the night—and tried to memorize everything he could about the room. The only noise was the slight snore from Eldrin, Jena's snuffles in her sleep, and the flickering of the candle.

Except.

There was another noise now that he was listening. A patter of feet. A scrape. Another scrape.

439

What the hell was that? He stood up on the floor, ignoring the cold this time. Moving cautiously, he crept closer to the door where the sound was coming from.

The sound of tiny feet on stone was so soft, he didn't know how he could hear it, except perhaps through his flames. He peered at the bottom of the door, and then nearly fell over as he recoiled in horror. Coming under the door were several hairy, long-legged spiders. Not just any spiders—they were midnight black with three blood-red splotches on their bulbous bodies.

Poisonous blood-back spiders.

One bite and you'd be dead in minutes—after experiencing the worst pain known to the world. No one ever survived a bite from a blood-back spider.

He sprinted to Jena's bed and jumped up on it beside her. She spluttered awake, her arms out in readiness for a fight. "Wha... wh?" she said.

"Blood-back spiders. About ten of them just crawled into the room under the door," he whispered. He jumped from Jena's bed to Eldrin's and woke him in the same dramatic style.

Eldrin sprang to life as soon as he heard what was happening. "By the ashes. These people are diabolical."

Jena stood on her bed. "The book says blood-back spiders are timid, and more likely to run if you see one."

Nate looked at the row of spiders marching out from the door toward them. "I don't think they're normal blood-back spiders," he said. "Does it say how to kill them?"

"Not really. I don't think they usually march about single file like they're on a mission." Jena looked over at the other two, her eyes wide. "These aren't normal spiders."

"I hate spiders," said Eldrin with some feeling. He was

standing on his bed, his arms out as if he could defend himself from a spider bite with his fists.

One spider leaped onto Nate's bed, and without thinking, Nate threw fire from his fingertips toward the spider, burning it to ashes before it could take another step. It also burned a hole through the wooden pallet and charred the stone beneath.

He blinked and looked at Jena, his heart pounding. For a moment he was terrified that his flames were about to take control of his body, and he tensed to push them down.

But they were still securely inside him, although burning more agitatedly than usual.

"You controlled it," Jena whispered.

Nate nodded.

"Are you okay?"

He nodded again. Jena had been there when he'd lost control of the flames last time. She was clearly worried about it happening again.

"Can you do it again? Burn the rest of them?" asked Eldrin.

Nate looked around the room. The other spiders had scattered as soon as he'd blasted the one on his bed. He'd done it on instinct, not overthinking what he was doing. The flames had worked with him on instinct as well. Perhaps that might be another step toward harmony with the magic inside him?

Maybe he needed to let go of the terrified hold, and be a little more relaxed?

Operate a little more on instinct?

He took a breath, shook out his hands and then looked for the closest spider. One was crawling up the door to the hallway. He held out his hand and thought about a flame being thrown out of his hands, the same way he'd just done it.

Nothing happened.

A flare of light came from Jena's side of the room, silver and brighter than the day. A spider sizzled on the bed next to her. Two more were crawling on the wall behind her.

"Don't move," said Nate, flinging up his hand. Flames burst from his fingers, and he burned the two spiders on the wall, leaving a scorch mark and an indentation in the stone.

Jena stood stock-still on the bed, eyes wide, staring at him.

"They would have bitten you," he said defensively.

She blinked, then nodded.

"There's another one," yelled Eldrin, pointing at the wall above Nate's bed.

Nate held out his hand, and the flames shot out, burning the spider to ashes.

"How many is that?" asked Jena.

"I don't know, maybe five or six?" said Nate.

"You think there were about ten?"

Nate blinked wildly. "I don't know for sure. I saw them coming through and panicked. There could have been more."

"We need to burn every piece of furniture in this entire room," said Eldrin. "It's the only way to make sure there aren't any hiding under something."

"He's not wrong," said Jena.

"Okay. I'll do my bed first." He lifted his hand and again convinced his fire to come out in an even line of flame, hitting the bed in multiple places. They watched as it burned, smoke filling the room. When two spiders ran out from underneath, Jena threw tiny silver fireballs at them, and they both died before they could make it across the floor. Nate coughed, trying not to inhale too much of the smoke.

"You need to come over here," said Nate to Jena. "Your bed is next."

Jena jumped from her bed to Eldrin's, standing awkwardly at one end. Nate switched places with her and sent another burst of his flame to her bed. They stood watching silently as the bed burned in front of them. When another spider ran out from the flames up the wall, Jena threw a silver fireball at it.

Smoke from the fires filled the room, mostly in the top half. Nate accidentally breathed in the smoke and coughed.

"We need to let the smoke out somehow," said Jena, crouching down on the bed to avoid it. She covered her face with one arm.

Nate looked at the door. "It *is* wooden," he said.

He lifted his hand, aimed for the middle of the door, and sent a burst of his flames into the center.

The door erupted in fierce flames, crackling with the intense heat. Even the metal lock melted under Nate's magic, falling like ooze to the ground. The fire burned out quickly, with nowhere to go once the door was ashes. The smoke filtered out into the hallway, and Nate took a couple of deep breaths as musty air from the hallway filtered in.

"We have to burn this one as well," said Eldrin. "There could be more hiding under here."

"But we also can't just step down," said Jena. "They could be waiting for us to do that."

"We just have to jump as far as we can," said Nate. "If we all do it at the same time, I'll turn back and flame it straight away. Jena can use her fireballs on any of them that rush us."

"Okay. One... two... three!"

They jumped, Jena screamed, and Nate blasted Eldrin's bed with fire.

He turned to figure out why Jena had screamed and discovered another blood-back spider looming in the doorway to the hall.

Only problem?

This one was a hundred times bigger than all the others combined.

CHAPTER 66
NATE

"I fucking hate spiders," yelled Eldrin as they all cowered back away from the enormous spider that now filled the entranceway.

"Nate, burn it, burn it now!" screamed Jena.

Instead, Nate turned to the burning remains of Eldrin's bed and blanket, in case this was a distraction so that another spider could crawl out and bite them while they were focused on the one in the hall. He knew mages who'd be able to create an illusion like that without too much effort.

When no other spiders appeared behind them from the burning ruins of their beds, he turned back to the apparition in the doorway.

The gigantic spider in the doorway snapped its fangs and seemed to buzz with agitation as the flames burned down beside it.

"Is it the mother spider?" whispered Jena. "Is that why it's so upset?"

"Maybe," said Nate, observing it. "It could also be an illusion."

"It doesn't seem like an illusion," said Eldrin.

"I can hear it and smell it," said Jena. "Not many mages could do an illusion that vivid."

"She's right," said Thornal, appearing beside Nate.

Nate jumped back and knocked into Eldrin, who only just managed to steady himself and Nate before they both fell over.

"Don't do that," said Nate angrily to Thornal. "You could have killed us."

"I didn't know you were so jumpy," said Thornal with a shrug.

"Is that Thornal? Can he tell if it's a real spider?" said Jena, never taking her eyes off the enormous beast in the doorway. It seemed to be considering its options. She moved back a couple of steps until all three of them were grouped together in the center of the room, trying to avoid the worst of the flames from their burning beds and staring at the enormous spider. Smoke still curled around them, making it hard to breathe.

Nate covered his mouth with his sleeve and looked at Thornal.

"It's not an illusion, if that's what you're asking. It's also not a normal blood-back spider."

"No kidding," said Nate to Thornal. He turned to the others. "He says it's not an illusion."

"Then how do we kill it?" whispered Jena, her voice squeaking in the middle.

"I think you might be better off not killing it," said Thornal, wandering closer to the spider for a better look. His ghostly shape shimmered in the light from the flames devouring the last of Eldrin's bed. *"At least, not yet."*

"Why wouldn't we kill it?" said Nate. "It's about to eat us."

"Well maybe just injure it a little, to show it you mean business."

"He says we can't kill it, we have to just injure it," said Nate. The spider at the door moved backward, putting the bulk of its body behind the stone, as if it had heard Nate's comment.

"Did you see that?" said Nate. "It's like it understood what I was saying."

"If it's not an illusion, then how does a spider get that big?" asked Jena.

"When it's not a spider," said Thornal.

"Thornal says it's not a real spider," said Nate. He peered at the creature, trying to figure out what Thornal wasn't telling him.

"Sure looks like a spider," growled Eldrin.

"There's something about the eyes," said Jena. "It seems familiar."

Nate glared at Thornal. "Just tell us what you know. Enough of your guessing games."

"It's your host, Joro. This is his other form. If you wish to have his help, I wouldn't kill him."

"What?" Nate gaped at the giant spider, trying to see the connection to the gaunt man who'd shown them around the night before. "Thornal says it's Joro."

"I knew I recognized it," said Jena. She scowled at the spider. "But that just makes me want to kill him even more."

The spider clicked its fangs at her warningly.

"Don't think I couldn't take you on," growled Jena.

Nate took a step forward. "We know who you are, Joro."

"That's it boy, tell him who's boss!" cheered Thornal. Nate ignored him.

The spider snapped its fangs again, as if it were threatening them.

"We killed your spiders, and we'll do the same to you unless you change back into your other form and help us. We tried to be polite, but you've given us no other choice."

The spider stomped its legs about in agitation.

"Doesn't like being told what to do. Silly spider creature." Thornal was standing close to the spider, peering into its face.

Nate lifted his arm and sent a small flare of flames out from his hand. It hit the ground just before the spider, and right next to Thornal. It was satisfying to see Thornal jump backward at the same time as the spider scuttled back out of range. A blackened scorch mark was all that remained.

"Watch where you're aiming those flames, Nate. That almost got me."

"I'm not messing with you, Joro. Turn. Back. Now," said Nate, ignoring Thornal's indignant words. He felt the flames in his eyes, and he had to work hard to keep them from surging forward and taking over. But the spider didn't need to know that.

The spider scuttled away, and they looked at each other.

"Has it gone to get reinforcements?" asked Eldrin.

Jena shuddered. "I hope not."

"At least there's only one entrance to guard," said Nate. "I think we could take them, whoever they are."

"Maybe he won't come back," said Thornal. *"Seemed like a nervy creature."*

But a moment later, Joro reappeared in the doorway in his other form, wearing the same robes as the night before. His dark eyes glittered as he looked at the three of them standing in the ash-filled ruins of the room. "You had some trouble with your room, I see."

"Of course we had trouble. You sent your little spiders in to kill us!" said Jena angrily. "What did you think would happen if you did that?"

"Most people just die quietly," said Joro mournfully.

"Most people aren't us," said Nate. "And I can see there's a good reason people don't visit the Society of the Myrtle. But enough of the games. We did as you asked. We ate and slept. Now tell us about this curse."

Joro bowed. "Of course. You have survived the trials. Helping with your curse is the least I can do. Follow me."

None of them moved.

"Where are you taking us?" asked Nate.

"To the Curse Room. The place where we keep all our books and information about various curses. We have rooms for each of the malevolent magics that we study."

Nate glanced at Jena, who shrugged. "We did just demand that he help us," she said. "It would be silly not to follow."

With a sigh, Nate went first, following Joro along the dark stone hallway. He didn't know the time; it was impossible to tell in this stagnant underground environment, but it felt like it was still the middle of the night. It certainly felt like he hadn't had any sleep.

Joro led them further into the rabbit warren of hallways, and Nate started to worry that they'd never be able to find their way out if they needed to. Every hallway looked the same—stone walls, floor and ceiling, with moss growing everywhere, and little rivulets of water dripping down the walls—with no markings that showed the way.

Eventually, Joro stopped in front of a wooden door that looked like all the other wooden doors they'd passed. He used a key from a chain around his neck to unlock it, then led them into the room. It was a dimly lit with candles and covered lights, and a large wooden table sat in the middle, with papers and quills scattered over it. On three of the walls were shelves packed full of books of all shapes and sizes. The last wall had shelves full of strange objects—including glass jars filled with liquid and strange floating body parts—and even from near the door, Nate could feel the malevolent magic crawling off them.

A doorway on the far side of the room led into another chamber, and just at that moment, a boy walked through, stopping with a start when he saw he had visitors. He looked about fourteen, with scraggly brown hair and a robe the same as Joro's.

"This is my acolyte Seether," said Joro. "Seether, these are our visitors, the ones who have the cursed friend inside a fire ruby."

Seether looked from Joro to Nate, Jena and Eldrin. "I thought—"

Joro cleared his throat over whatever Seether might have been about to say. "They wish to look for cures for the lavaen curse, and I said we'd help them here."

Joro said the words carefully and was giving Seether a significant look.

The boy seemed to understand. He nodded and turned around, disappearing back into the room he'd just come from.

CHAPTER 67

NATE

"He's young, hasn't learned all our ways yet," said Joro with a frown. "But he will bring you any books he can find on curses and lavaens."

Nate walked further into the room, avoiding the wall with the creepy, seething objects. Even the books inside this place seemed angry. The air smelled heavy with a metallic tang of copper and the rotten smell of sulfur.

"Touch nothing," whispered Jena, at his elbow. "There's so much dark magic in here, it's hard to tell where one awful thing ends and another begins."

"We are the foremost experts on curses, pestilence and dark magic," said Joro. "We take great pride in our collections."

"What do you do with all your knowledge?" asked Nate, although he was pretty sure he already knew the answer.

"We simply gather it here for the greater good. So people like yourself can come here and find cures for their friends." Joro smiled insincerely, his sharpened teeth glinting in the candlelight.

Nate had never heard anyone lie so blatantly to his face before. It hit him like a slap to the cheek. His flames burst into life again, and he stepped away from Joro. "Don't bother saying anything at all if you're just going to lie to us," he snapped, unable to hold in his anger at everything that had happened to them since arriving in this place. His whole body felt dirty, and all he wanted was to bathe in a river and get the smell of this place off him.

"Nate," said Jena, reaching out to grasp his arm. "Take a breath. It's the effect of this room, the books. You need to control your reactions, or you're going to burn us all."

Joro's eyes widened at Jena's words. He glanced warily at Nate. "Come this way," he said, gesturing to the second door. "This room has a calmer feel. It won't affect your emotions quite as easily."

They followed Joro through the next door and found Seether placing several books on a second, smaller wooden table at the edge of the second chamber. This one didn't have the books or strange objects. Instead, it had several tables, and an area that was clearly for testing various spells or emulsions. There was a large glass tank of water, with several round, bulbous fish inside.

"Are they? Is that a...?" Jena didn't seem able to finish her sentence. Her expression was horrified.

"Yes, it's a Spiker Fish," said Joro with some satisfaction. "Carries a deadly spike that can kill you faster than a blood-back spider's venom."

"Why do you even have them here?"

Joro spread his arms. "I am not fully certain. Perhaps simply the joy of collecting? Or perhaps the intellectual pursuit of knowledge? Or maybe even the knowledge that I could kill a man, and no one would ever figure out how I'd done it. It's hard to know."

Nate felt a chill crawl along his spine. This man was dangerous. He'd known it all along, but now he felt it in his bones. They had to tread carefully.

Joro smiled with a flash of his sharpened teeth. "I believe Seether has found some mention of how to escape a curse set by a lavaen who was once a person. An old text, rather a unique situation I would have thought. But apparently it has happened before."

"What do we do?" asked Jena. She peered at the books that Seether had opened on the table.

Seether cleared his throat. "This one 'ere says that we need to do a simple binding spell, to bind yer friend to one of you instead of the curse. That oughta get him free."

"The price is that we would like to keep the fire ruby with the curse inside it." Joro swept his arm toward the shelf of creepy objects. "For my collection."

"Will that make him bound to one of us forever?" asked Nate. That didn't sound like a good alternative.

"It should be a simple matter to overturn the binding to you, and then your friend would be free," said Joro.

"Then let's do it," said Jena, clearly eager to leave this place.

"You think this is the best option?" asked Nate, feeling a little more cautious.

"It's the only one I found that offers a solution to your problem," said Seether with an unconcerned shrug.

"We don't have much time," said Jena. "We need to get this sorted quickly." She gave Nate a significant look, and he knew she was thinking about her sister.

Nate took a breath. She was right. Where else would they find a solution to this complicated curse? "Fine. We have no other choice. And you may keep the fire ruby as payment."

"I'll need time to collect everything we need for the spell," said Seether. He rushed into the main room and, moments later, they heard bottles clinking and things being shuffled around.

Jena and Eldrin moved closer to Nate, forming a circle.

"You think we can trust them?" asked Eldrin in a low voice.

"No," said Nate. "But they're our only option. We have to try."

"We need to keep a close eye on both of them," said Jena. "They're going to try something."

"Agreed."

They waited in silence for Seether to finish his preparations. He came back and settled three bottles and a small stone bowl on the wooden table. "It's a simple binding spell. You probably know it, Mage," he said to Nate with a nod of his head.

"I want to check the ingredients," said Nate. He glanced at Jena, and she stepped forward with him to check small vials. Nate unstoppered each of them, sniffed and held it close enough to Jena that she could sniff them too. She gave a subtle nod.

Seether added a spoonful of each of them to the stone bowl, then stirred them together. A tiny wisp of smoke drifted up from the bowl. This close, Nate noticed his eyes were a strange shade of dark green, like the deep patches of an alpine river. They made him look older than he had before.

"We add a couple of extra ingredients to help keep the curse inside the fire ruby and pull your friend out." Seether showed them two small, unmarked bottles that he pulled from his pocket.

Nate took the bottles and opened each one. Again, Jena took a sniff. She hesitated for a moment, but eventually nodded.

Jena frowned as Seether added a couple of drops from each of the unmarked bottles.

"Who's gonna be the person he's bound to?" asked Seether.

Nate stepped forward. "I'll do it." His hands felt were sweaty and his whole body was shaky, but he was the only logical choice.

"Are you sure?" asked Jena. "I could—"

"No, it has to be me. I'm used to that kind of thing. And I know Argus better than you do. If anything happens..."

"Nothing will happen," said Jena fiercely. She glared at Seether, who went pale.

Joro chuckled as if she'd made a particularly good joke. "Nothing will happen," he repeated.

Nate went to stand next to Seether.

"Hold out the fire ruby in your hand," said Seether. "I'll pour the liquid over the ruby and say the spell." He glanced over at Jena and Eldrin. "You should both touch his shoulders, to add power to the binding."

Nate felt Jena's light hand on his left shoulder and Eldrin's heavier hand on his right. He desperately hoped they were doing the right thing.

Seether poured the liquid over the fire ruby and started chanting under his breath.

As soon as the liquid hit his hand, Nate knew it was wrong. He tried to move his hand but couldn't.

He looked over at Joro and saw him smiling, this time a wide smile that showed every single one of his sharpened teeth.

He tried to yell, to move, to do anything, but he couldn't. He was frozen in place by whatever spell Seether had just placed over them.

CHAPTER 68

JENA

J ena tried to scream, yell, do *anything*, but her whole body was frozen in place. She couldn't even move her hand from Nate's shoulder. The raven was still and silent on her stomach and back.

"It's done, Master," said Seether. He gave them a sad glance, then bowed to Joro.

"Well done, Seether. For once, you've come through. Bring me the mirror."

Seether raced back into the other room and returned with a large circular mirror with an ornate frame, held in both hands. He stood with it in front of Joro, shaking slightly. Jena couldn't see the face in the mirror, even though she was straining to move. For a moment, nothing happened, and then a familiar voice spoke from inside the mirror.

"You have them?" asked Lothar. His voice sounded strange, like he was talking through water rather than the glass of the mirror, but Jena recognized it instantly.

A chill went over her skin, but she couldn't even shudder. Joro had been working for Lothar this whole time.

"Yes, my Prince. We have them." It was like Joro was a different person, the way he was fawning over Lothar.

"Show me."

Seether turned the mirror to face Nate, Jena and Eldrin. Jena saw Lothar's face for the first time without the flames. He didn't look evil—not like Joro and his spidery form—he simply looked like a distinguished older gentleman, someone who would never hurt anyone, let alone send assassins and every conceivable dark beast after them. Perhaps that was how he did it. He looked so innocuous that no one would believe that he was the mastermind behind so many devious plots.

And they'd walked right into his trap.

"My dear Nathaniel. How sorry I am to have to do this. But I must ask Joro to dispose of you. You understand how it is. We've talked of it before." He turned his face to Joro. "You may kill the other man as well. He is of no consequence. But the woman, you must keep her alive. She has something I want. I will come for her after the coronation."

"As you wish, Sire." Joro bowed regally, like he was at court addressing the king.

"I will ensure you receive your reward once everything is settled down."

"Thank you, Sire." Joro bowed again and then Lothar disappeared.

Joro looked at Jena thoughtfully.

He moved until he stood right in front of her. "He wants you alive. But he didn't say in what kind of condition." He leaned close to Jena's face, pinching her chin between two fingers, even though she couldn't move. No matter how hard she strained, she couldn't retreat as he came closer, putting his cheek to hers. His breath was sour, but his skin was strangely smooth and soft.

Jena was screaming on the inside, terrified of this man and what he might do to her. But on the outside, she could do nothing but look at him.

"If you give me any trouble, you'll wish I'd killed you with these two," he whispered into her ear, his hot breath brushing blowing strands of her hair into her face. "Perhaps I'll tell Lothar you died and keep you with my other collected objects?"

Jena couldn't even widen her eyes in reaction to his words.

She tried to move, to scream, to do anything, but she was all locked up. In front of her, she thought she could see Nate straining against the same spell, Eldrin doing the same next to her. They were all trapped, unable to move. At the mercy of a monster who had already proven that he didn't care if they lived or died. A sob worked its way up her throat but had nowhere to go. It sat at the base of her throat, making it feel tight and her chest numb.

This was it. Their quest to destroy Lothar was over. But it wasn't the failure of their quest that most upset her. It was what Joro was planning to do to Nate. He was brave and funny and caring, and didn't deserve to die like this. He didn't deserve to have his life cut short just because of who his parents were. Her heart felt like it was being wrenched from her chest. Every muscle strained as she tried to force her body to move through the spell.

It couldn't end like this.

She had to find a way out. She couldn't bear the thought of Nate dying. Where would that leave her? Without Nate to make her laugh, to tease her when she was too serious, to look after her when she was upset.

She would be alone again. Friendless.

An object in Joro's collection. Or worse, a toy for Lothar to destroy.

Joro leaned closer and put one of his hands on her neck. Jena tensed. What was he doing? He was very close. His thumb rubbed over the bumpy scars on the side of her face. "There's something about you, Jena, that I find compelling. These scars. Your magic." He sniffed her hair. "I think you would make a fine addition to my collection."

He tugged on the silver raven at her neck. "I can feel the power emanating from this necklace," he said. He reached forward and undid the clasp at the back of her neck. Jena tried to cry out.

He showed her the silver raven in his hand, then smiled, showing too many teeth. "This is mine now," he said.

Then Joro moved away, dismissing her. "Take them all to the cell," he said with a wave of his hand. "I'll deal with them later. I'm taking the fire ruby and my new amulet and putting them somewhere safe."

"Yes, Master," said Seether tonelessly.

Joro plucked the fire ruby out of Nate's outstretched hand, gave one last malicious smile in Nate's direction, then scuttled out through the main door and into the hallway.

Jena tried to moan, to make any kind of noise. Joro now had her raven necklace, her only connection to her parents, and Argus, still inside the fire ruby.

They'd failed.

What was going to happen to Bree when she realized no one was coming to rescue her?

Regret rose inside her chest, fierce and desolate. They'd made a terrible mistake. They'd been stupid to believe Joro and Seether would do anything other than betray them.

And even stupider to believe they could fight the evil that smothered this place in its foul odor.

Seether returned the mirror to the other room, then stood in front of them. He looked like he had something to say. Jena strained to move, to grab him, or even just flick her fingers at him. She wished she could punch him in the face.

She couldn't believe she hadn't noticed anything out of the ordinary. She'd been trained by the best. Seether was just a skinny kid with a few books.

She should have been able to *tell*.

"I'm sorry," said Seether. "I didn't want to do it. But that's what it's like here. They're not good people."

He lifted his hand and, as if they were on a string, the three of them started moving. Jena tried to resist, but the compulsion was too powerful. She walked after Seether as if she were a dog on a rope.

CHAPTER 69
JENA

They stumbled after Seether as he led them down the hallway.

She couldn't speak to the others or even give them a pointed look. They were completely locked up tight.

Seether opened a wooden door and led them inside. It was a dark, moldy room, completely made of stone, with no windows and no other light.

"You're to wait here. Until he's done with you, that is. You can move around—once I've gone—but your magic cannot be used."

Jena tried to yell out, to call to Seether, to beg for their lives if that's what it took. But she couldn't do anything except stand there and watch as he closed the door and left them in pitch darkness. Her stomach felt like she'd swallowed a stone.

As soon as the lock clicked, Jena felt her ability to move unlock.

"I can't see a thing," she said. It was an inky darkness. Not the kind their eyes would adjust to, but the magical kind. It lay across them like an extra blanket. In a panic, she stumbled forward and knocked into someone. "Is that you, Nate?"

"No, I think it's me, Eldrin," said Eldrin dryly. "Unless Nate has his hands on my chest."

Jena jerked back. She reached for her magic to light a flame in her hand, but it wasn't there. No, that wasn't true. It was there, but she couldn't access it.

"My magic. He's blocked it." Her voice cracked on the words as she realized what it meant for them. They couldn't even use their magic to escape.

"I can't access my flames either," said Nate. His voice was strained.

"How are we going to get out of here if we can't use our magic?" whispered Jena, her eyes wide. Even her raven wasn't moving. It was like it had died just like her magic. The thought made her panic surge.

"I'm more concerned about the fact that a scrawny young kid has control of all three of us. He could make us do anything he likes," said Nate, his voice grim. "Even worse, Joro has Argus."

Hanging in the air was the reminder that if they couldn't save Argus, then Bree was as good as dead as well.

"What are we going to do?" said Jena, almost choking on her words. She forced herself to take some deep breaths, trying to calm down. She hadn't felt so vulnerable in years, not since she started learning magic from Thornal.

"Luckily for both of you, I'm used to not having magic," said Eldrin. Suddenly, a light appeared in the darkness, as Eldrin lit a candle with a small portable spark and taper, made of a piece of flint and a highly flammable stone found in the depths of the volcanoes. It lit his face from the bottom up, giving him spooky shadows across his skin.

Nate lurked just outside the circle of light, his eyes dark.

"You carry those around with you?" said Jena, surprised, despite herself.

"Of course," said Eldrin. "You never know when you're going to need a light. It was a present from my father when we went off to join the flame guard. He gave one to Argus as well."

Jena couldn't help tipping her head to one side and peering at the spark. A small flame burned up from the volcano stone. She'd heard of them, but never seen one. "Is that common among the Utugani?"

"No, but my father believes in using every tool at his disposal." He put both the spark and the taper back in a small metal box that he tucked away in his belt.

Nate interrupted. "We're getting away from the main point. How do we get out of here?"

"We obviously can't use our magic. Can we overpower the boy when he comes back?"

"Who says he's going to come back?" said Nate. "You heard Lothar. He wants us dead." He glanced at Jena. "Me and Eldrin dead, at least."

Jena shuddered. "Joro strikes me as the kind of person who likes to push boundaries. I don't think he'll do anything until he's gathered every bit of useful magic out of us he can."

"So he's just going to leave us down here?" said Eldrin with a grimace.

"Maybe. But they'll have to feed us sometime. Surely we can overpower one boy," said Nate.

"That magic he was wielding was strong," said Jena. "I don't think we'd be able to attack Seether. If he sends some other lackey to attend to us, maybe we'd have a chance."

"We'd have to be really lucky," said Nate, his expression grim.

Jena nodded, trying not to scream. Everything about this place had been awful, but this was the worst of it. She wished they'd listened to Rothell when she'd said the Society of the Myrtle was bad. She peered into the darkness beyond the circle of light provided by the candle. "Eldrin, hold up the light for me while I search the walls," she said. Now that they'd been given a reprieve, she couldn't just sit here and wait to die. She had to do something.

She had to at least try.

"What do you think you'll find?" asked Eldrin, following her gaze. "This place seems pretty secure."

"Another way out? Something that might help us escape?" she said, her frustration rising. "I don't know. I just know I can't sit around and wait for them to come back and kill us."

"Fair enough." He held up the small taper, and they all walked to the nearest wall. "What are we looking for?" he asked.

"A hole in the wall? A breeze that might lead to a drain? I don't know, but surely we must be able to find something. This can't be the end of our journey." Jena started feeling her way along the wall, leaning down to the base where it met the floor, pushing her fingers into gaps. Nate followed them over and crouched down on the other side of Eldrin, doing the same thing.

Jena kept trying to think of a way to get out of here without using her magic.

All it did was make her aware of how much she relied on it.

They went slowly around the whole room. It was painstaking and tedious. And in the end, they had nothing.

"I need to sit down," said Nate. He slid down the wall

opposite the door, landing on his butt. He pulled his legs up to his chest and laid his head down on his knees.

"Me too," said Eldrin, following suit. He held the candle aloft in one hand.

Jena hesitated for a moment, looking at the two men sitting in front of her. They looked so defeated. Their situation seemed impossible. They'd lost Argus. If they died, Bree would die too. She couldn't let that happen. If not for herself, then for Bree. Her sister had never done anything to harm anyone. She'd been the model of a good, kind person. She didn't deserve to die like this. "Come on, you two. We can't give up. Argus and Bree are relying on us."

Nate didn't even look up. His shoulders were hunched and his hands clenched tight.

"We're just taking a break, not giving up," said Eldrin.

A scratching sound beside the door grabbed Jena's attention. In the dim light, she saw a dirty piece of paper being shoved under the door.

She strode over and picked it up, bringing it close to Eldrin's candle. Her eyes widened as she read.

"What does it say?" asked Eldrin.

"Be ready to run. I will come for you soon. Tell no one." Who wrote it? Could they trust a note like this to help them? She couldn't help the flutter of hope in her stomach.

"Who are we going to tell down here?" asked Eldrin. "Sounds like someone with a penchant for the dramatic."

"Or maybe just someone who wants to help," said Jena defensively. She knew she sounded naïve, but this piece of paper at least represented a possibility of getting out of here.

"It's probably just Joro playing with us," said Nate. "That's something he would do."

"I hope not." Jena sat down next to the other two, knees bent, and leaned her head on her arms.

They waited in silence, no one talking.

When the lock clicked a while later, Jena jerked her head up. They all stared at each other. This was it. Jena scrambled to her feet, and Eldrin blew his candle out, just as the door opened. In the doorway, a small figure was silhouetted.

"I promise to help you, but you have to take me with you," said Seether.

"I told you," growled Nate. "It's a trap."

CHAPTER 70
NATE

"It's not a trap," said Seether, his voice a desperate whisper. "I'm as much a prisoner in this place as you are."

"I don't believe you," said Nate, still sitting on the floor opposite the door. He glared past Seether, trying to see Joro's shadow just out of sight. He wouldn't put it past the spider to manipulate them into thinking they could get free of this place, then take it away again.

"I can get you out of here, but you have to take me with you."

Eldrin stood up. "How do you plan on getting us out of here without your buddy Joro finding out?"

"He's not my *buddy*," hissed Seether. "He's my captor. My parents sold me to him. They were about to lose the farm." Seether shrugged. "They thought I could earn my way to freedom. But Joro... he's a monster."

"Literally a monster," said Jena, taking a step closer to Seether. Could he possibly be telling the truth?

Seether's strange green eyes flashed. "No one ever survives being Joro's pet. He's going to kill me eventually, and I plan on getting out of here before that happens." He shuffled awkwardly in the doorway. "You gotta believe me."

"You could always force us to believe you," said Nate softly. He was the only one who remained on the floor, the only one not willing to give Seether the benefit of the doubt. He didn't trust Seether, even with this new information.

"It doesn't work like that," said Seether. He paused. "And I wouldn't do that even if it did."

"What proof do you have that you're telling the truth?"

Seether shook his head sadly. "I ain't got nothing. Only that you've met Joro. You've seen what he's like. You really think I'm lying?"

"I think he's telling the truth," said Eldrin. "And even if he's not, we need to get out of this cell. Come on Nate. Let's get out of here."

Jena reached out with one hand, and he took it, and allowed her to pull him up.

"We don't have to believe him, but if he gets us out of this room, that's one step closer to being free," she said in a low voice next to his ear.

He nodded. He didn't for one second believe that Seether meant what he said. But Jena was right. If it got them out of this room... "You need to take the binding spell off us. Right now."

"I can't take it off here. Joro will hear. We need to go back to the curse room."

"And you need to help us get the fire ruby back from Joro."

Seether shook his head frantically. "We can't. Joro has the fire ruby with him in his room. We can't get it back off him."

"We're not leaving here without it," said Jena fiercely,

her control held together by the merest sliver of string. "So you better work on a way to make it happen, if you really want to get out of here."

Seether paled, swallowed hard. Then nodded. "Okay. Sure. I'll figure out a way to get it back off Joro. But we must hurry. He's asleep, but he doesn't sleep long."

They followed Seether down the hallway, mimicking his silent footsteps along the edges of the walkway.

"Can we really—" started Eldrin.

"Shhh!" whispered Seether. "No noise at all until we get to the curse room."

Nate followed the others at the back of their little group. He kept glancing behind them, worried that Joro would leap out at any minute, laughing at them for thinking they could escape.

They made it back to the curse room without incident. Seether led them into the back room and closed the door.

"Okay, we can undo the binding in here," he said in his normal voice. "There's a muting spell around this room. No one will hear or feel it."

"How do we know that you're not going to just put a worse spell over us?" said Nate.

"Because I'm going to work with him on the spell," said Jena with a stern look at Seether. He cowered under her disapproval.

"Just hurry, whatever you do," said Eldrin, who was pacing nearby. "We need to get out of this place as fast as we can."

"He's right," said Seether, his strange green eyes flickering in the dim light. "My master is powerful. The only way to leave here is to do it while he's asleep."

"Come on then," said Jena. "I know the spell ingredients. Let's get them." She led Seether back into the other room, and they returned not long after with a few bottles that looked the same as the ones he'd used to cast the spell.

Seether placed the bottles on the wooden table. "You need to promise me you'll take me with you. And that you won't just kill me when I release the binding."

"What makes you think we'd keep a promise?" asked Nate.

"Because you're insisting on getting your friend back," said Seether simply.

Nate shared a glance with Jena and Eldrin. "Okay," he said, nodding once. "We'll take you with us, and we won't hurt you if you can get us out of here—but we're not leaving without the fire ruby."

Jena cleared her throat. "Was there ever a spell to cure Argus's curse?"

"Joro made me do the binding spell, but your friend's cure was never anything to do with a binding. It's a spell I created out of two other spells, one for an Utugani curse, and one for a lavaen bite. I'm pretty sure it would cure your friend. You'd have to get him out of the fire ruby, though. I don't have that power."

"You don't know for sure?" said Nate, glaring at Seether. Was it possible to just make a new spell like that?

Seether hesitated, then shook his head. "No. Not for sure. It's never been done before, the spell you want. Not as far as I could find, anyway."

"Is he right? Would a spell like that work?" Nate asked Jena. She was staring around at the books in the room, but she seemed to snap out of her thoughts and turned her gaze back to Nate and Seether.

"It's experimental," she said, staring at Seether thoughtfully. "And it's unusual for someone so young to be so good at creating new spells like that. But it could work."

"Let's do it then. Unbind us. Then we go get the fire ruby," said Eldrin urgently. He was clearly edgy about being inside the Society's walls. Nate didn't blame him. He felt the same way.

Seether looked at Jena, who shrugged. "Let's get started. Just don't try anything."

Nate snorted. If he wanted to, Seether could force them to do anything he wanted. The binding spell was still in place, and they were puppets in Seether's hands. He kept glancing at the door to the room, waiting for Joro to come through, smiling through his pointy teeth.

"I just want to get out of here.," said Seether. "You're my only hope."

"Don't worry, we'll take you with us. Now give us our magic back," said Jena.

Looking relieved, Seether opened the bottles. Jena stood right next to him as he measured out the ingredients and then started mixing the ingredients together. "Hold out your hand, like before," said Seether to Nate. "You two need to put your hands on his shoulders again, too. The unbinding spell affects all of you."

Nate reluctantly held out his hand. Seether seemed genuine, but he couldn't help the feeling that something was wrong. All his instincts were screaming at him. If Seether was telling the truth, maybe Joro had set him up too? Whatever was happening, Nate knew he wouldn't feel safe until they were out of this place.

Jena and Eldrin settled their hands on his shoulders, as they had last time. Seether poured the liquid over his hand, the same as before, muttering an incantation.

The flames inside Nate burst into life again so suddenly that he almost lost control of them. They rushed up and out of him like a tree of flames, growing faster than any living tree had ever grown.

"Hold on to them, boy," said Thornal, appearing by his side. *"You'll kill them all if you don't."*

As if Nate didn't already know that.

The flames wanted to burn whoever had kept them trapped. They wanted to make someone pay. He struggled for a moment, eyes closed as he fought to keep them inside. They would kill not only Seether, but Jena and Eldrin too. Maybe even everyone else inside the subterranean rabbit warren of the Society of the Myrtle. He didn't want all their deaths on his hands.

Except maybe Joro. He'd be happy to kill Joro.

He focused all his attention on the flames. It took everything he had to keep them from escaping. He could feel Jena's hand on his shoulder, and he knew she was trying to help. For a moment, everything seemed to be tipped on a knife's edge... and then unexpectedly, he was the one who held the reins. He took a gasping breath, then another.

"Are you okay?"

He heard Jena's voice but couldn't answer at first. The flames were still fighting for control. Eventually he opened his eyes and saw the flames reflected on Jena's worried face.

"I'm okay," he said, his voice strained.

"Don't lose your focus, Nate. They're still eager to get out." Thornal was pacing behind the others, his ghostly form barely visible. Behind him, there were three ghosts that Nate had never seen before. They all seemed to fear Thornal and were cowering in one corner. Nate caught Thornal's eye and nodded to let him know he'd heard the warning.

"I've never seen anything like that before," said Seether, his eyes wide. "What *are* you?" He looked worried. Maybe he was only just realizing that he didn't know very much about them.

"Someone you shouldn't mess with," answered Nate. He still felt salty toward Seether, but at least now they had their magic. "You okay?" he asked Jena. She seemed fine, but he couldn't help asking.

"Yes. Everything is back to normal," she said with a small smile up at him.

"Me too," said Eldrin dryly. "In case you were wondering."

Nate flushed slightly but ignored Eldrin's remark. "So how do we get the fire ruby?" he asked Seether. "We need to get it and get out of here."

"Are you sure you need it?" asked Seether in a wheedling voice.

"Yes," said Nate, Jena and Eldrin all at once.

Seether shook his head as if he thought they were crazy. "Joro has it in his personal chambers. He likes to spend time with the objects he collects."

Jena shuddered visibly.

"Then take us there," said Nate firmly. He refused to leave Argus here for Joro to hoard.

"Do you have a plan?" asked Seether.

"Threaten Joro with my flames unless he gives us the fire ruby," growled Nate. He was losing patience with this place.

"I don't know... Joro is cunning. I don't think he'll fall for that a second time."

"The young mage is correct. Joro is not an adversary to be taken lightly," said Thornal.

"It's not an idle threat," said Nate. The flames in his eyes burned brighter for a moment, and Seether's eyes widened.

"Just take us there, Seether. Let us do the rest," said Jena. She gave Nate a look, which he tried to return. He didn't know what she was thinking. He just knew that he wanted to burn Joro to ashes at his feet. And he'd do it if the spider gave him any opportunity.

"Just be prepared for anything, that's all I'm saying," said Seether. "He sleeps with one eye open. Maybe more."

Seether led them out of the curse rooms and down another dark, damp, stone hallway. No matter how much he tried, Nate couldn't figure out where they were or remember how they got from one place to another. "Is there some kind of spell on these tunnels?" he asked.

Seether nodded. "Yeah. Joro likes to keep everyone disoriented. He only gives the antidote to a few select people."

"So we can't get out of here without you?" said Nate. Thornal was striding next to him, his expression grim.

"You might guess your way out. It's not completely impossible."

"Just really, really difficult," said Jena.

"Yeah."

Nate gave up on trying to remember the twists and turns and just followed Seether. Eventually, they ended up in front of an enormous carved wooden door. Nate knew it was Joro's door, because the carving was an enormous web, with baby spiders running over it.

"This is it. Joro's room," said Seether unnecessarily. "I've never been inside, and I don't know what spells he might have placed in there. I think there might be webs." His eyes were wide, and he clearly didn't want to go any further.

Nate tried not to let the mention of spiderwebs make his skin crawl. What size web would it have to be to fit Joro?

He was an enormous spider. Webs that could capture each of them with ease, he was sure. "Eldrin and Seether, you wait out here. Make sure no one else comes in. Jena and I will handle Joro and his bedroom of webs." If nothing else, both he and Jena could use flames on the webs.

Jena swallowed hard and then nodded. "What's the plan? Are we sneaking in, or going in blazing?"

Nate glanced at Thornal before he answered, but the ghost mage was standing next to Seether, staring at the door like he might find answers in the carvings, ignoring the rest of them.

"Sneak to start, switch to blazing if it goes wrong," he said grimly. Nate turned the handle on the door slowly and pushed it open. A wall of heat slammed into them. The room was hotter than the lavaen's cave. There was only a dim light coming from a glowing stone on a shelf near the door.

Jena grabbed hold of Nate's hand before he could go too far. He looked back at her, but she wasn't telling him to stop. She was just using touch to gather courage.

He swallowed.

He was glad to have her hand in his. He needed the courage too. The room was giving off seriously creepy vibes, and they hadn't even stepped foot inside. Thornal stepped up beside him, clearly planning to follow them in.

He hoped they weren't making a serious mistake.

CHAPTER 71

JENA

The raven shuffled on her stomach, and Jena could only be glad that she had the feeling back in her body. She hadn't realized how much she relied on the raven keeping her company until it was gone.

The raven moved again, this time in a stroking motion, like it had heard what she'd been thinking, and was soothing her. She appreciated the sentiment.

Her hand was tight in Nate's as they tip-toed silently into the overheated room. She couldn't believe she was doing this, going right into the heart of Joro's sleeping room —she was pretty sure they wouldn't find a bed in here—to rescue Argus. But they had no choice. They couldn't leave him behind. Not for his sake, and not for Bree's sake.

The dim light from a strange glowing stone helped them move further into the room. It was on a shelf with other trophies—it was the only thing to call them—lined up next to it. Glass jars filled with liquid and eyeballs. Jugs, metal chalices, a crown. Horns from various creatures, even a unicorn. She'd never seen one, but the Book of Spells had a drawing that looked the same. There were a couple of animal heads on the wall next to the shelves, and next to that—Jena almost gagged. There was the head of a man, mounted as if he were a stag on the wall.

And Seether had been right. There were large webs everywhere, dripping from the ceiling, emerging from the corners, and lines running along the floor. They weren't going to be able to avoid them, not if they had to go right into the room.

Jena knelt and pulled up the leg of her trousers. She unhooked the buckle and pulled out her Hashishin knife. "Here," she whispered to Nate, who was leading them further into the lair. "Use this."

He took the knife without saying a word. When they got to a point where the webs were so thick there was no going around them, he used the knife to cut the webs. The fire ruby on the hilt glowed as he used the knife and led them further into the room. Nate glanced back at Jena, his eyes wider than normal. She shrugged. Nate had a connection to fire rubies. That was how he'd put Argus inside one and saved his life—hopefully. It was also how they planned to find the one that Joro had stolen from them.

They walked deeper into the lair, the cobwebs getting thicker. Jena felt one tickle her face, and she jerked away, certain that if she touched anything in here for too long, she'd regret it. Nate stopped abruptly, and she bumped into his back. Up ahead, in a thick web, was Joro in his spider form. He was enormous and hairy, the three red splotches on his bulbous back visible in the low red light from the Hashishin knife in Nate's hand. Jena felt sweat prickling down her back. She tried to stay quiet, but even her breathing sounded loud in the silence of the room.

Up ahead there was a matching red glow coming from

the web where Joro was perched, his long legs stretched out across the web and his body was low and unmoving. He appeared to be sleeping peacefully, just as Seether had said he'd be.

Jena felt a burst of optimism. Maybe they really could rescue Argus and the fire ruby and make it out of here alive. Seether had seemed so sure that Joro was too powerful, and it had affected her confidence. But perhaps it was time for something to go right for them? A little good luck to make up for all the bad...

Whatever happened, there was no way they were leaving without Argus.

They crept further into the room, both focused on Joro. Where was the fire ruby? Could Nate sense it yet? How were they going to retrieve it and escape in one piece?

Jena stopped abruptly and pulled Nate to a stop as well. What exactly *were* they going to do once they found it? Just dance over and grab the fire ruby and leave?

Unlikely.

Suddenly, she felt stupid for plowing into the room without a more thought-out plan. The only reason they weren't still rotting inside that cell was luck. If Seether hadn't been so desperate to leave, they would have been at Joro's mercy. He was a cunning adversary, with years of planning within his web.

And they were the idiots who kept getting caught.

Her hand was still on Nate's arm, and he was watching her with his brows raised. She cleared her throat, about to whisper her doubts—

"I'm glad you finally realized the insanity of your plan," said Joro, his voice distorted and sounding like it was coming from a long way away.

Jena's horrified gaze jerked back to the enormous spider

in the web. He had moved so that all of his eyes were focused on her and Nate.

He was awake.

Had maybe been awake the whole time. Jena felt sick.

Joro gave a wheezing laugh. "Seether is nothing if not predictable. That useless boy has been trying to escape ever since he arrived."

"You knew he'd let us escape?" asked Jena, her mind spinning.

"I assumed he would. He doesn't have the stomach for this kind of work. I knew he'd make the attempt, and I assumed you would come to steal my treasure. I'll have to eat him just to get my money's worth."

Jena felt dizzy. How many people had Joro already eaten?

"We don't want any trouble, and we don't want your treasures," said Nate quickly. "We just want our fire ruby back, and to go on our way."

Joro clicked his fangs sharply together. "But it doesn't belong to you anymore. It's my treasure now. And I don't take kindly to people attempting to steal my treasures."

Joro whipped out two legs and scuttled down toward the ground. He came to a stop in front of his web, his large black and red abdomen pointed in their direction. A length of milky white spider web strands flew out of his backside, and Jena and Nate only just managed to leap to one side in time to avoid the trap.

They fell heavily into the web on one side, and Jena immediately realized they were stuck there instead. Panic filled her chest as she lit her silver flame in her palm and burned herself free, while Nate used the Hashishin knife to cut at the sticky web.

Just as they climbed free, another blast of web hit them both on the back and spun them around, covering them both. They fell to the ground, trapped and straining inside Joro's sticky web. For a few seconds, the threads held tight, strangling Jena's body, making her feel trapped and help-less—then her silver flames burst out from her hands for a second time, burning the threads into nothing. She tried to be careful—she didn't want to burn their skin—but it was better to have a few more burns than to be stuck in Joro's web.

"Thanks," gasped Nate as he tumbled free. He was panting hard, and Jena could feel his flame magic rising to the surface.

"It seems I might have underestimated you, Jena. You've a few tricks hidden below the surface. No wonder Lothar wants you for himself." His long front leg tapped a pattern in the stone. "I don't think he deserves to have you, after all. I decided I'm going to suck out your magic and kill you myself."

"I'd like to see you try," sneered Jena, with far more bravado than she was actually feeling.

Joro continued as if she hadn't spoken. "Of course, no one will complain about how I killed you when I tell them you were doing mage spells." Joro's voice sounded painful in this form.

Even though she knew he was just baiting her, Jena froze. He was right; no one would care if he killed her. She was considered an abomination by most people in Ignisia.

Using her moment of fear to advantage, Joro sent another blast of web in their direction.

This time, Nate used one of his fireballs to destroy the web before it even reached them. He'd shoved the

Hashishin knife into his belt to give himself two hands. Joro made an annoyed ticking sound and scuttled to one side, hiding in the shadows.

"Destroy the big web," whispered Jena.

Nate sent out another blast of his flames. But this time, instead of incinerating the giant web, it got caught up in the strands, making the web glow brighter.

"Did you see that?" said Jena. "He's protected it somehow."

"Not just protected it, my stupid guests. My web absorbs power. Every time you blast a spell at me, it strengthens me even further," snarled Joro from somewhere in the darkness. "You think you're so powerful, but you're mere children compared to me." Joro stepped out of the shadows again, and Jena couldn't help her gasp. He was now even bigger than before, glowing red and pulsing from his abdomen.

"There's no way for you to beat me with your magic. I will simply use it back on you tenfold."

Flames burned in Nate's eyes. He sent another burst of his flames into the web, and this time they watched as the strands lit up, and then Joro grew bigger, glowed brighter.

"Stop it, Nate. It's just strengthening him," said Jena, her voice raw. Her heart was pounding so hard it would surely break in her chest. How could they fight a creature that could simply suck up their power and use it against them?

"We can't let him win," said Nate, his voice a low growl.

Jena tried to think of a good spell, other than sending flames at Joro, but her mind came up empty. It would all just amp up his power. "What do spiders hate? More than flames?" They needed something that didn't involve magic. Something that Joro wouldn't expect.

"I don't know. Being stomped on?"

Jena practically growled at him as she desperately tried to think.

What else might work?

"Vinegar," she whispered. "Elsa used a mix of vinegar and water to get rid of the spiders in her caravan. Those bottles, they're preserving the... eyeballs and...and... *things*. They probably have vinegar in them." Her eyes darted over to where the jars and bottles filled with disgusting body parts were sitting on the shelf. Before she could think too much about it, she raced over and pulled off the lid of the first one she came to. The smell of rotting flesh made her gag, and she almost dropped the jar. Then she bent back her arm and threw the jar and its contents at Joro.

"Nooo," yelled Joro. But he wasn't worried about the vinegar. It was the contents of the jar that he was screaming about. "Those took me years to collect." He moved, so the jar sailed over his head, slamming into the web, with some of the vinegar and eyeballs falling out over him. It didn't seem to hurt him even a little.

He stomped closer to Jena. "Now you've really made me mad. Instead of giving you a quick death, I'm going to let my babies have you. They'll tease out your death for days, maybe even weeks, as they feed on your flesh." He used one of his spindly spider hands to turn a lever on the wall.

Suddenly there were thousands of blood-back spiders behind Joro, rushing toward them.

"Nate!" screamed Jena. She threw fireballs at the spiders, but there were so many, she wouldn't be able to hold them all off. From behind her, she felt Nate's flames building up, and then his fire burned over her shoulder and into the crowd of spiders. Jena ducked down and crawled backward, out of reach of his flames and the oncoming spiders.

Joro screamed in the background.

Nate burned.

Jena threw her silver flames and tried not to think about the thousands of poisonous baby spiders heading straight for them.

CHAPTER 72
NATE

"Use the ghosts," yelled Thornal as he appeared next to Nate.

"What?" yelled Nate, as he threw more fire at the oncoming spiders. He'd thought ten in their cell earlier was terrifying. This was so much worse.

The flames were keeping them back a little, but it wouldn't give them much time. He was also scared of using his flames too much and giving them a chance to take over.

"*The ghosts. The spiders don't like them. Call all the ghosts, like you did at the farm. Hurry!*"

"There aren't any in the room," said Nate, frantically peering around.

"*Doesn't matter. They'll come if you call. Do it now, or you're both dead.*"

Nate didn't hesitate a moment longer. He stopped throwing fireballs and concentrated on calling all the ghosts in the surrounding area to him.

It turned out there were a lot of them.

And they were *furious*.

They'd probably been killed by members of the Society

of the Myrtle. There were already about twenty in the room, and more coming. They were all sorts of ages, some dressed in fine clothing, others in rags. There were some that were barely visible, ragged around the edges, and there were a couple that looked clear and new and kind of shocked to be there.

There was nothing that connected them as a group—other than that they'd somehow gotten tangled up with the Society of Myrtle.

"Nate, what are you doing? Don't stop throwing fire. They're getting closer." Jena's voice was pure desperation.

Nate shook his head, still trying to concentrate on all the ghosts in the corridors and shadows of the underground lair. "I'm doing... something else. Calling ghosts."

"Well, do it fast," she said. She was covered in dirt and spiderweb remnants and sending silver flames into the oncoming spiders. She'd never looked more beautiful.

He wasn't going to let her die.

Nate stepped closer to the ghosts. "We need you to help us kill the baby spiders," he said. "I think—" he glanced at Thornal to confirm—"I think the spiders won't like you going anywhere near them, especially as a group."

Several of the closest ghosts nodded their understanding. They strode forward, arms out, as if they could catch the baby spiders in their hands.

Nate watched, holding his breath. At first, it didn't seem to work. The baby spiders didn't even seem to see the ghosts. But then the first ghost reached the leading edge. His foot went right through the baby spiders, and trod the floor, but it was like something had stung them. They leaped backward, scuttling away from the ghosts. Several more ghosts strode into the swarm of spiders, and it had the same effect. The ghosts were repelling the tiny creatures.

They scrambled backward, away from Jena and Nate.

"What are you doing?" asked Joro, his voice rising to a screech. "How are you doing that?"

"More of them," said Thornal urgently. *"Send more of them in, as many as will go."*

Nate turned to the ghosts who still lingered at the edges. "Please help us," he whispered. "We're trapped here, like you were. If you help us, we'll make sure he never hurts anyone again."

"What are you saying? Who are you talking to?" Joro was still screeching in a high-pitched voice.

More of the ghosts waded into the sea of spiders. Several of the older, more ragged ghosts seemed to take great pleasure in stomping on the baby spiders. Maybe they'd been killed by them?

Whatever had happened to them, now they were determined to make Joro pay.

"What's happening?" said Jena next to him. Her face was pale, and she kept glancing over to where the spiders were scuttling back. She couldn't see the ghosts, so it must have looked like they were scuttling back from nothing.

"I called any ghosts who were nearby," said Nate in a low voice. "And there were lots of them. Joro and his buddies have been killing people, maybe for years. The spiders don't like the ghosts."

"Will it stop Joro?"

Nate shook his head. "We can't bet on it."

Joro had scurried back up onto his web. He watched as his spiders scurried backwards, away from the ghosts.

"What are you doing to them?" he screeched again. His voice was panicked, and his eyes were all looking in different directions, trying to assess a threat he couldn't see. He sent out a shot of his cobwebs, but they sailed right through the ghosts to land harmlessly on the floor.

The ghosts were piling into the room now, pressing in on top of each other. It was getting cold, and Nate could see puffs of air as he breathed out. They were crowding toward the spiders, stomping on them as if it would do something in their ghostly forms.

The strange thing was... it seemed to be affecting them. Some of them were collapsing onto the ground and trembling like they were cold before dying. Others were running around in circles like they were drunk. Even the ones who made it back behind Joro's web were running more slowly and stiffly than before.

"What's it doing to them?" said Nate to Thornal, who was standing right behind him.

"As a group, ghosts can affect the living. But they must be especially strong in their convictions, and there must be at least a certain number of ghosts. And they need someone to lead them."

"What do I do with them now they're all here?" he asked. "I feel like I should help them somehow."

"Just killing Joro will help many of them," said Thornal with a shrug. *"I'm betting most of them are hanging around because they feel they were unfairly murdered by Joro or one of his minions."*

Nate looked back over to Joro, who was standing on his web, squinting down to where the ghosts were milling around in front of him. Many of the blood-back spiders were gone or dead, but the ghosts were holding those that remained back. More ghosts kept arriving, and it was freezing in Joro's lair. Nate had goosebumps on his arms.

"We have to kill Joro," Nate whispered to Jena. "It's the only way to truly be free of this place."

Jena nodded grimly. "We can't use our magic. It just makes him stronger. Can the ghosts affect Joro?"

The ghosts were moving toward the web, crowding in beside the enormous spider. He crawled higher on the web, as if he could tell they were there. The web was pulsing with power, but it wasn't absorbing the energy of the ghosts.

"I'm not sure," said Nate.

"What else would kill a giant spider? The vinegar didn't work."

"What about a good old-fashioned knife?" asked Nate, pulling the Hashisin knife out of his belt where he'd stashed it earlier. It felt heavy in his hands. "How are you at knife throwing?" he asked. "I'm okay, but if you're better...?"

Jena shook her head. "It's not one of my strengths. You need to do it." She hesitated. "I just need the knife back. It's... it's the one that killed Thornal. I have plans for that knife."

Nate nodded. He could imagine what she had planned. It was partly why she was here with him on this journey. Nate turned back to Joro, who was still standing uncertainly on the web. "Where's a suitable spot to hurt a giant spider?" he asked.

"The eyes," said Jena.

Nate took a breath. "I think I need to get closer," he said in a low voice. "Stay here. Get the others and run if something happens to me."

"No, I'm coming too. I can help."

"Let me try throwing the knife. Maybe he won't expect it from a magic user. Then, if that doesn't work, we can regroup."

Jena nodded, her expression grim. He doubted she'd

retreat like he'd asked, but at least she was going to wait on the other side of the room.

He looked back at the ghosts. He knew what it was like to walk through a ghost. He'd even had some try to take over his body that way. But he had to do it. It was the only way to make sure he killed Joro. He stepped out into the crowd of ghosts. Instead of moving apart, like people in a normal crowd might do, all the surrounding ghosts crowded closer, like they could sense his power and wanted more of it.

"I need to get closer to Joro," he said, but they didn't seem to hear him.

"Come on, son. Hurry," said Thornal. *"Time is ticking."*

He hesitated, then just strode through the ghosts, feeling the cold sensation of their remaining spirit over his skin. It felt... strangely soothing. He'd almost been expecting it to hurt, but it was more like he was gathering courage from their presence.

He stopped once he was nearer the enormous web. Joro had retreated ever further up. His eyes were whirring frantically, as if he was trying to find an escape. He snapped his fangs at Nate when he saw him moving closer.

"What are you doing? What is happening?" he said to Nate, his pincers clacking in agitation. "Stop it. I will give you anything you want, just stop hurting my children."

"You know what I want," said Nate, holding out his hand. "Throw down the fire ruby and we can talk."

Joro hesitated. Nate saw the calculation in his eyes moments before he sent out a length of sticky web and caught Nate. The web circled Nate's upper arms, and then Joro pulled him up into his web. Nate dangled below Joro, trying not to panic. He could hear Jena screaming his name.

But this was better than he'd expected. He was closer to Joro, and his knife arm was only constricted from the elbow upward. He still had enough movement to stab the spider. He just had to do it before Joro killed him.

"Call it off. Whatever creature is down there hurting my babies, call it off. Or I will kill you here and now."

"It doesn't have to be like this," said Nate, wriggling himself into the perfect position. "There's still time to come to some kind of resolution."

The ghosts below him growled in unison at his words, but Nate knew Joro had no intention of working out a compromise. It was all or nothing with the spider. He expected to win and had no thoughts that there might be another way for this to end.

Nate just hoped that if Joro was right, and he managed to kill Nate, that Jena and the others would make it out of here before the enormous spider could regroup. Nate intended to hurt him badly if he couldn't kill him.

"Maybe," said Joro slowly, as if he was considering Nate's offer. "Maybe we could work out a compromise. Just call off your creature, and we can talk." His eyes flicked between Nate and the invisible ghosts that he could only sense.

The ghosts were pushing closer, making a solid wall of transparent bodies. More were arriving all the time, as if they'd heard there was a party and didn't want to miss out. Some were even climbing the web like they still thought they were alive; others were just floating upward. They were all making threatening noises as Nate faked his negotiation with Joro.

Nate shook his head. "I can't do that. They don't belong to me. They're yours."

"They?" Joro tipped his spider head to one side, confused. "There is more than one creature?" His eyes spun between Nate and the ground. "If they were mine, they wouldn't have attacked my babies. They wouldn't be making this room so cold." He shuddered. "I hate the cold."

Joro pulled Nate closer, peering into his face. "I don't understand what you are. Lothar said you were the Fire-caller, and that you were dangerous. But you seem very ordinary to me. This unnatural cold is the first time you have surprised me since you have been inside my home."

"I *am* ordinary," said Nate. "More ordinary than you could imagine." Without giving himself time to think, he jabbed the knife up into Joro's soft body, again and again, grunting with the effort.

Joro screamed and cut through the silken web that was holding Nate. Except instead of falling, Nate felt a gust of wind—where none should have been—and it pushed him back into the sticky web at his back. Nate didn't have time to look to Jena, but he knew where the sudden gust had come from.

He was still close enough to Joro that he could keep jabbing at his exposed body. He couldn't get high enough to reach Joro's eyes, so he just had to hope this was enough. Joro was scrambling and shrieking and clicking his fangs, but he didn't seem to know how to defend himself against Nate. He tried kicking out with his front legs, and Nate hacked at a leg that came close, cutting through the hard outer shell. The limb cracked and fell to the ground. Joro screeched and tried to back himself up the web. He kept missing the web, like his brain was a little scrambled by the knife wounds and the missing leg. Nate hoped so.

The ghosts were also crowding closer to them, and Joro

seemed to sense their presence, even if he couldn't see them. He turned his body away from them, trying to escape the cold invasion. Except it brought his most vulnerable body part close enough for Nate to reach.

Nate slammed the knife with all his might into one of Joro's eyes. His flames burned inside his chest as the blade slid to the hilt. The fire ruby in its design lit up like the sun.

Joro screamed and fell from the web, landing with an unpleasant squelch. The ghosts nearby crowded around the enormous spider, pushing themselves over and into its body. Joro was shuddering and moaning on the ground, the Hashishin knife still poking out from one of his eyes.

Nate tried to pull himself free from the spider web, but he couldn't move. He leaned back and just watched as the ghosts swirled around Joro. Someone would eventually remember to let him free.

He hoped.

The door to the hallway burst open, and Eldrin raced inside, sword held aloft. He took in the scene and ran toward Nate. Instead of helping Nate down, he skidded to a stop in front of Joro's twitching body and plunged the sword into his abdomen and face. Again and again, he slashed his sword into the enormous spider until it stopped twitching. And then Eldrin stabbed him again for good measure. He was clearly still angry about Joro trying to kill them.

Eldrin stood over the limp body, breathing heavily. "That felt good," he said, between ragged gasps.

Jena moved closer to look at Joro's body, as if she couldn't believe he was dead.

"I waited as long as I could. But that last scream sounded bad," said Eldrin. "Turns out it was the spider, and not one of you two." Eldrin stepped over the body and raised his sword to cut Nate free.

"I've never been so glad to see anyone in my whole life," said Nate as he tumbled free of the web, onto the ground.

Eldrin grinned. "I have that effect on people," he said as he held out his hand and pulled Nate to his feet.

CHAPTER 73
JENA

Jena didn't think her heart would ever stop beating at its current double-pace.

She'd thought Nate was going to be killed by Joro when the spider had captured him in his web. Even when the spider had screamed in response to being stabbed and had tried to drop Nate again, it hadn't seemed like Nate was going to succeed. She'd blasted him with wind to help him stay next to Joro, and tendrils of her magic had hit the web, causing it to glow, but by then, it was too late. Joro was too badly injured to be helped by such a minuscule amount of magic.

She could only be glad that Joro wasn't as invulnerable as he'd thought.

She crouched beside the body—careful to stay away from his mouth in case he was only pretending to be dead —and looked for Argus's fire ruby. It wasn't hard to find; the dim red glow gave it away. It was hidden in a silky cobweb pouch on one side of Joro's body, alongside her silver raven amulet. Making a face, she pulled them out, trying to touch as little of the enormous spider as she could.

The ruby had dimmed significantly since Nate had first put Argus into it. She curled it tightly in one hand, then placed it in her shirt pocket. She put the raven amulet back on around her neck. The weight of the silver raven steadied her, as did the faint buzz of her father's residual magic. She touched the fire ruby in her pocket, and was heartened by the faint warmth.

They would get Argus out in time. They had to.

Then she reached over and pulled the Hashishin knife out of Joro's eye.

He'd been killed with an ordinary knife. In the hands of a hashishin, maybe this knife was something special, but in the hands of someone like Nate, it was just a sharp edge. And it had done the job.

She stood and went over to where Eldrin was helping Nate pull free of the sticky spider web. "I think we need to really make sure he's dead," she said. A puff of cold air appeared as she spoke.

"Using my flames?" asked Nate. He had cobwebs in his hair and draped over his body.

Jena pulled some away from his shoulder, flicking them loose when they tried to stick to her hand. "Yeah. Otherwise, I'll have nightmares where he comes back to life."

Nate gave himself a shake and then walked to where Joro's lifeless body lay on the floor, a disgusting green fluid still oozing from his stab wounds. He gazed around, nodded at something Jena couldn't see, then let his flames come out of his hands in a small burst of light. It only took a moment for Joro's body to become nothing more than ashes on the floor in front of them.

Jena let out a breath. She saw Seether by the door, staring down at Joro's body like he couldn't believe it was real. Perhaps he'd never really expected them to kill his master.

There'd been quite a few moments when she'd doubted it herself.

"Come on, let's get out of this place," said Jena.

"One thing first," said Eldrin. He grabbed both Jena and Nate and enveloped them in a tight bear hug. Jena didn't have the strength to object to his manhandling of her. Her scars stretched and scratched uncomfortably, and yet somehow it was exactly what she needed right then. She clung onto both Eldrin and Nate. They'd almost died at the hands of a giant spider. Her brain hadn't quite caught up with the fact that they'd survived.

"Okay, now we can go," said Eldrin with a grin as he pulled back.

When they all trailed out of the room, Jena glanced around at some of the horrific keepsakes that Joro had inside his lair. "We can't just leave all this here," she said. "I think we have to destroy it."

Nate stopped and looked behind them. He nodded. "The ghosts agree. They say we should burn down this whole place, so that none of the other Society members or his acolytes can continue on with his work."

"I ain't gonna continue his work," said Seether firmly. "But they're right, there's them that would."

"We need an earthquake. Something to fall down on all this. Fire wouldn't do the same thing."

"What about an explosion?" said Seether with a glint in his eye.

Jena nodded, thinking quickly. "An explosion would do. If you have the right ingredients, I could make an explosion down here."

Seether grinned. "I can do better than that. I already have explosion spells made up."

Jena gave him a curious look. "Why didn't you just kill Joro yourself? You seem resourceful enough."

Seether's face darkened instantly. "First thing he did was put a spell on me so I couldn't hurt him. He seemed to know my thoughts before I had 'em."

"He'd probably had many apprentices before you," said Jena. "He was talking about eating you so he'd get his money's worth."

Seether shrugged. "He used to say that to my face."

Jena looked at him in horror.

"Hence, the explosion spells," said Eldrin grimly.

"Before we explode everything, we have to free Argus," said Nate, pulling the fire ruby out of his pocket.

"Where should we do it? In the curse room?" said Jena. She looked at Seether. He seemed much less of a henchman and more just a boy, now. Which made his mage skills even more extraordinary.

Seether shook his head. "We need to wait 'til we get outside. The others will have realized something has happened by now. They're all connected to Joro. They'll be after us. We need to leave here as fast as possible and explode everything in our wake."

"Should we warn them? Are there any innocent victims inside this place?"

Seether glanced to the side as if he were thinking. "All of the Society of the Myrtle are bad. Evil. They were all drawn here by the desire to do evil magic." He glanced down at the floor.

"I feel a 'but' coming on," said Jena.

"There might be people in the dungeon cells. They're below us. It's just... they're difficult to get to. And you're all

498

under the misdirection spell. I'm the only one who can lead you places."

"They're directly below us?" said Nate. He looked around the room, then raised his eyebrows and nodded at someone only he could see. "The ghosts say they'll lead me down there. I can free whoever is there. You can set up the explosion spells."

Jena immediately shook her head. "I don't think we should separate. What if something happens?" An irrational fear clawed at her insides.

"We've cut off the head of the snake. I don't think anything will happen, at least not until they rally their forces." Nate said the words calmly, as if they weren't still trapped down inside the Society of the Myrtle rabbit warren.

"We don't have time to have everyone doing everything all together," agreed Eldrin. "Nate's right. If we're going to get all this done and get out of here, we need to separate. I'll go with Nate and the ghosts; you go with Seether. Any trouble, burn them to the ground. No second-guessing, okay?"

Jena stared at Eldrin, then Nate, trying to decide if they were trying to keep her away from some fight they could see coming. But they just seemed like they wanted to save a few people and not accidentally burn them to death. "Okay fine. But the same goes for you two. If anyone even looks at you funny, burn them and get out of there."

Nate nodded solemnly, his usual lightness long gone. Killing Joro had taken more out of him than she'd realized at first. She couldn't help herself. She stormed over and grabbed him in a tight hug, burn scars be damned. He seemed surprised but put his arms around her and hugged her back.

"Take care of yourself," she whispered.

"I will," he said.

She pulled away and found Eldrin standing next to Nate, looking at her expectantly, his arms out. She sighed and hugged him as well. "Take care of yourself, too," she said. Part of her couldn't believe she was hugging him, but they'd been through so much together down here. It overrode her usual dislike of touching other people.

Then she turned to Seether. "Let's go. We need to work fast."

She didn't look back as she took off at a run behind Seether, heading back to the curse room where she'd first met him.

When they arrived, he pulled out a small bag and put several ingredients into the bag from the shelves. Then he opened a small cupboard and pulled out a basket of carved wooden boxes. Each box had a lid that was tightly held in place.

"Are they the explosion spells?" asked Jena.

"Yeah. I've been stockpiling them, just in case."

"And the other bottles were the ingredients for the spell to free Argus?"

"Yes."

"Is there anything else you want to take with us?" Jena stared around the room. There were so many ingredients in the room: bottles, boxes, baskets, and cups filled with an amazing array of herbs and spices, plus all the other ingredients that she didn't want to look too closely at. The books that lined one wall seemed intriguing, too.

Seether looked around as well, as if seeing it for the first time. "There's not much here that I want to take with me. It's all tainted with Joro. I'd like to start fresh." He grinned. "Besides, I've read all the books, and I've got a good memory."

"Is there anything about the prophecies in these books? Anything that mentions the next firecaller?"

Seether frowned, scanning the shelves as if cataloguing the books in his head. "There was one, I think, maybe?" He strode to the bookshelf, and pulled out a small, thin book with a leather cover and thin paper pages. He handed it to Jena. "Here, you have it, if that's what you're interested in. I want nothing more to do with Joro's magic."

Jena tucked the book under her shirt, making sure her belt held it in place. "Right. Shall we go plant some of these explosion spells, then?"

"There are certain places we can't go. Too likely to be caught. But I've been thinking about this for a long time. I've got it planned how we plant them for the most impact. We're gonna destroy this place," said Seether with satisfaction.

CHAPTER 74

NATE

As they ran after the three ghosts who had agreed to lead them, Nate just had to hope they were telling the truth. He didn't know where he was and was sure he'd never find his way out again if left on his own. The confusion spell was still in place, even after Joro's death.

They descended another set of stairs, going as fast as they could. It was even more damp at this level. He couldn't imagine what the cells down here were going to be like. He'd thought where they slept last night had been bad enough.

The ghost up ahead slowed to a walk. Then stopped. *"It's been a while since I was down here, but these are the dungeons."* He was an elderly man dressed in expensive clothes—a red velvet coat, and thick black breeches.

"How did you end up here?" asked Nate.

The ghost growled. *"I had a gambling debt, and Joro offered to let me pay it off by allowing him to test his magic spells on me."*

"That sounds... awful."

"What was worse was that I died too quickly, and he decided

I hadn't paid off my debt, so he brought my wife and son down here, and tested on them as well. I have been trying to get them free for a long time."

Nate struggled to swallow over his suddenly dry throat. Joro really was a monster.

"Are they still alive?" he asked carefully.

"My son lives," said the ghost with a tragic expression. *"He is weak, but if we can get him free, I will be forever grateful to you."*

"We'll get him out of here," promised Nate. It was the least he could do for the help the ghost had given him.

"Thank you. Once my son is out of this place, I will move on. There are many like me with similar stories. Your actions today have set many innocent souls free. You are a great man."

Nate shook his head quickly at the ghost, denying the claim. "Anyone could have done what I did. And I had help from my friends as well as all of you. We might not have survived if you hadn't helped us."

"There have been many people who have tried to kill Joro over the years. None succeeded until today."

"Come on," said Eldrin. "We need to hurry." He pushed Nate gently forward, and Nate remembered what they had to do.

"How do we break the locks?" he asked.

"I imagine you can use your flames, and I'll use the back end of my sword," said Eldrin.

"Makes sense," said Nate. He approached the first of the cell doors. It was a small square room, not tall enough to stand up in, with metal bars across the front. Inside, a man crouched, staring up at them. He was covered in dirt, his clothes were rags, and his eyes looked... like he was elsewhere.

"I'm going to open your door," said Nate. "I'm a mage, and I'm going to use flame to do it."

The man blinked but didn't acknowledge him in any other way. Nate swallowed. What had Joro done to him to make him like this?

Eldrin was talking to someone further down, and then there was the sound of metal striking metal. It reminded Nate that he had to hurry. They didn't have much time. He pushed a small amount of his flames out through his hand, careful to control it. His flames were getting stronger, but so was he. He'd learned how to push out only a small amount of flame since being here in the Society's walls. That was positive at least.

The flames melted the lock, and then Nate pulled open the door.

"You need to come with us. We know the way out. Joro is dead, and you're free."

Nate's words didn't seem to have any effect on the man. He glanced at the ghost standing next to him. "Can you watch him for me? I need to help Eldrin release the other prisoners."

He ran down the corridor, throwing his flames at the doors, telling the people inside that they were free. He had different reactions from all of them. Some cried. Some didn't believe him. Some just walked out of the cell, stoic. All of them immediately left their cell. When he found the cell that held the ghost's son, he knew him instantly. He had the same nose and eyes as his father.

"Come quickly. We need to get out of this place," he said to the boy, who looked to be in his late teens. He was so skinny that Nate couldn't understand how he was still alive. Strength of will, probably.

"What's happening?" the teen asked in a croaky voice. He sounded suspicious.

"We need to leave here quickly. Joro is dead, and we're going to destroy this place. You need to come with us if you want to live."

The boy pushed himself to his feet and tottered toward Nate on legs that didn't seem strong enough to hold him. The ghost of his father moaned behind Nate as he watched his son leave the cell. Nate grabbed the boy under his arms and helped him to the front of the cell block.

"You all need to follow us," said Nate once they'd all gathered back beside the entrance. "There's a confusion spell inside these walls. You won't make it out alive if you don't stay with the group." People murmured amongst themselves, but they all understood. The only person not moving or interacting with them was the man in the first cell. He still sat inside, eyes staring straight ahead.

"Does anyone know anything about this man?" he asked the group.

"He's been like that for a while now," said another man, his bare, muscled arms crisscrossed with scars. "Dunno what Joro did to him, but it musta' bin bad."

Nate peered inside the cell. "We have to go. You need to come with us now."

"I'll grab him," said Eldrin. He ducked his head, grabbed the man's arm, and pulled. Nate held his breath, worried that the man might put up a fight. But he simply stood and followed Eldrin out.

"I'll look after him," said the same muscled man who'd spoken earlier. He stepped forward and stood next to the blank man.

The ghost's son was being looked after by one of the other prisoners, an older woman who seemed in better shape than most. She had the boy's arm over her shoulder and a determined expression on her face.

With one last worried glance at the prisoners, Nate turned back to the entrance. "Follow me closely. We must hurry."

Eldrin and Nate led the group back out of the dungeons, led, in turn, by the three ghosts.

"I have a bad feeling about this," murmured Eldrin, as they neared the main floor again. He held his sword in front of him, at the ready.

"This whole place gives me a bad feeling," said Nate.

The ghosts up ahead came to a stop at a corner in the stone hallway. Nate frowned at the leader. "What's the matter?" he whispered.

"They're waiting for you around the corner. There's an ambush planned," said the red-velvet coat ghost. He kept glancing behind Nate's head to the group of prisoners, probably making sure his son was okay.

"How many? What's their arsenal?"

One ghost peered around the corner again. He was a much younger man, with tiny scars crisscrossed all over his body, like the muscled man in the group. What had Joro been doing to these people? Was it really just magical experiments? Or simply a desire to cause pain?

Nate felt queasy just thinking about it.

The ghost turned to Nate. "There are about seven of them, all dressed in the robes of the Society of the Myrtle. They appear to be magical; they have little in the way of actual weapons. They seem confident they'll be able to kill you."

"I'm getting impatient to get out of here," growled Nate, glancing at Eldrin. "Should I just go out and throw my flames at them?"

Eldrin shrugged. "Seems like a good plan to me. I don't have any magic to combat them."

"Wait," said Thornal. *"Let the ghosts take care of them first."* He turned to the other three ghosts that were standing at the corner. *"Come, we will frighten them, like they frightened all the people who have ever been stuck in this place."* His expression was grim, to match his voice.

The other three ghosts nodded in agreement and swished off around the corner.

"The ghosts are going to do something first," said Nate. He crept forward and peered around the edge of the stone corner.

Up ahead, something strange was happening to the mages who'd been lying in wait. They were either prone on the ground, cowering against the walls, or running away, their sandals slapping on the paved floor. One of them was wailing in terror as something he couldn't see attacked him.

Nate didn't recognize any of them—they'd barely been in the underground network a day, so perhaps that was unsurprising—but it was satisfying to see them so afraid.

"I think we can keep going," said Nate. "The ghosts have destroyed their desire to fight."

Eldrin and Nate led the group of prisoners toward the now-disrupted gathering of Society mages. He watched as the ghosts soared in and out of their bodies, sometimes staying inside for longer, until the eyes of whoever they were inside bugged out.

Thornal, in particular, was taking great pleasure in messing with the remaining mages.

"We need to keep going. They won't follow us now," said Nate.

"They deserve everything they're getting," said Thornal, his

voice tight with anger. *"And more. They pretend to be scholars, to be researching for the greater good. But they're monsters."*

"The others are setting up explosion spells. We need to leave before we get blown to pieces."

Thornal sighed. *"I guess you're right. But I enjoyed tampering with their minds."*

"Come. We are near one of the exits to the surface. I will lead you there," said the red-velvet ghost.

Their group set off again, led again by the three prisoner ghosts and Thornal, then Eldrin and Nate. Following behind them, the prisoners were starting to tire. They hadn't been outside their cells in who-knew-how-long, and their bodies were probably starved of food and water.

"I don't know how much longer they'll be able to keep going," said Eldrin in an undertone to Nate, with a glance behind them.

"It can't be much further. We just have to get them outside this place," said Nate. "Then we can treat them for their wounds."

Before he even finished speaking, there was a moaning cry, and then one of the prisoners fell to the ground. It was a woman, her gaunt frame folded on the ground. The prisoners around her were hovering, unsure what to do.

Nate strode back to her, gathered her thin body into his arms, and then strode back to the front of the group with her. "Let's get out of here."

The corridors all looked the same to Nate, with the stone walls dripping with moss and dampness. He had to concentrate on walking carefully so as not to slip on the stone surface of the floor. The woman in his arms weighed almost nothing, like perhaps she hadn't been fed in a long while. She was still unconscious, but he could feel a faint breath, and he hoped that she'd make it long enough for Jena to heal her.

He didn't want any of their prisoners to die.

He couldn't bear the thought of it, in fact.

They kept moving through the corridors, mostly silent now. No one else bothered them, and when the ghosts led them up a set of stairs that had a small landing with a carved wooden door, Nate didn't realize at first that this was it.

"We cannot open the door for you, and I believe it is locked," said Thornal. *"You will need to use force to get through it."*

Nate looked at Eldrin. "Can you break down the door?"

Eldrin strode up to the door and pushed his weight against it. The big man with the scars moved forward as well, and started pushing his shoulder against the wooden door, next to Eldrin.

The wood started to crack, and then the door broke under the combined weight of the two big men.

Sunlight burst into the darkened stone landing. Nate let out a breath. Behind him, a woman started crying.

Nate walked forward, stepping over the remains of the door, leading his group back out into the world.

CHAPTER 75
JENA

J ena raced behind Seether, hoping that Nate and Eldrin were safely out of the Society of Myrtle underground tunnels. They'd planted explosion spells everywhere around the tunnels, inside the curse room, and inside other rooms that Seether found. They set two up inside Joro's rooms, not because they needed to, but because it made Seether feel better.

Now they were running for their lives to the main entrance. Jena could barely keep up with Seether, he was so determined to get outside.

They turned a corner, and Jena barely managed to duck her head in time to avoid an old tree root that ran across the top of the corridor. "Seether, wait up," she called. He was almost too far ahead.

She got to the next junction of corridors, and turned in the direction she thought Seether had gone. Except she couldn't see him. "Seether," she called, annoyed that he'd thoughtlessly run ahead. She kept going along the corridor, hoping he wasn't too far away.

"Stop right there," snarled a rough voice. A bald man

with a scar running down one side of his face, dressed in the Society of the Myrtle robes, stepped out from a tiny alcove. He held a struggling Seether against his chest with a knife at his throat.

Jena took an instinctive step backward. She held up her hands. "We don't mean you any harm. Just let him go, and no one will get hurt."

"Who do you think is going to be hurt?" sneered the bald mage. "I'm not the one with a knife to my throat."

"Let him go. He's just a child." Jena surreptitiously looked around the corridor. There was nothing she could use to hit the mage with. The temptation to just burn him with a fireball was strong, but she didn't want to hurt Seether. What else could she do? They didn't have time to mess around; they needed to get out of here.

"Is that what you think? He's been Joro's pet for longer than any other unfortunate could manage. I'd say he's more spider than child these days."

Jena couldn't help it. She looked at Seether, surprise on her face. Seether gave a tiny shrug, his face impassive. "I'm a survivor," he said.

"So am I," said the bald mage. He dug the knife a little deeper into Seether's throat. "Now you're going to lead me out of here. Which way?"

Seether pointed down the corridor they'd already been going down. "This way."

Jena couldn't decide if he was leading them the wrong way or not. "You don't have to die down here. Just let the boy go, and we'll let you go."

"I think you're misunderstanding the situation. I'm the one with the knife. I decide who lives and who dies."

Jena had had enough. She held up her hand, the silver flame coming to life in her palm. The bald mage's eyes widened. She drew from the power of the Book of Spells, and a fireball formed in front of her hands. Her hands glowed silver in the reflection of the fireball.

"If you don't let him go immediately, you're going to be toast," she said calmly. "I've had a bad day, and I don't intend to let it get any worse."

"Who are you? How are you doing that?"

Jena stepped forward and held up her hand as if to throw the fireball at the bald mage. He lurched backward, still holding onto Seether. Instead of throwing the fireball, she muttered the words for a wind spell under her breath, and a howling blast sped down the corridor. It hit the bald mage face on, pushing him backward. The mage howled and, taking advantage of his distraction, Seether kicked his foot backward into the bald mage's groin.

The mage dropped the knife, Seether leaped away, and Jena threw the fireball.

The bald mage didn't even have time to scream. The fireball burned its way through his body, and he slumped to the ground, dead before he landed.

Seether stood to one side, staring down at the body. Then he looked up at Jena. "Joro really underestimated you, didn't he?"

Jena strode forward, grabbed Seether's hand, and ran in the direction they'd been going. "I hope this is the right way," she said.

"Sure is. Not far now."

Jena just gritted her teeth and ran. Her magic sizzled along her skin, making the hairs rise on her arms.

"You know, I can feel your magic," said Seether, as if they were having a nice Sunday walk. "You're pretty strong for a girl."

"I'm pretty strong for *anyone*," said Jena.

"I didn't think girls could do mage spells."

"They're not supposed to. I'm just different. I don't play by the rules."

Seether nodded. "I like that. I don't play by the rules either."

They ran on in silence for the next couple of minutes until Seether slowed down near a side corridor. He dragged Jena left down that hallway, and then stopped at a narrow set of stairs that led up. "Just be careful. These steps are old. Some of 'em don't hold a person's weight."

He started up the stairs, quick as a flash of lightning, and Jena could only follow and hope nothing would give out under her. Seether waited impatiently at the top.

As she climbed the last couple of steps, Seether pushed his way through an old wooden door. The sunlight blinded her for a moment as she stepped through the doorway, with one hand over her eyes. When she finally looked around, she realized they were back in the church ruins where they'd first met Joro, at a slightly different entrance.

It felt like it had been years, but it had only been a day and a half.

Seether kept running, like now that he was out, he didn't know how to stop.

At first, Jena sprinted after him, just as eager to leave the church and the society behind. But once they were safely in the forest, she slowed.

He was still a distance ahead of her when her foot slipped on a patch of moss. She skidded, then hit a tree root, her foot catching painfully. With a yell, she fell to the ground, landing with a heavy thump, her foot twisted painfully under her.

For a moment she sat there, stunned. Then she looked up and saw Seether still running in the distance.

"Seether. Stop. Come back," she yelled.

He didn't turn around.

"We need to wait for the others."

Seether still didn't stop running, but he glanced back over his shoulder. She could tell he was weighing up the benefits of just continuing on...and leaving her there.

She tried to think of something that would make him come back. "We still have to activate the explosion spell. You can't do that if you've run away."

She held her breath, waiting to see if the thought of blowing up Joro's lair would change his mind.

CHAPTER 76
JENA

At first, he kept running.

But then he slowed down and came to a stop, leaning his hands on his knees and gasping for air. He glanced at her over his shoulder again.

He turned around and trudged back to where she was sitting on the ground. She was fairly sure that blowing up the Society of the Myrtle chambers was the only reason he had changed his mind.

"What happened to you?" he asked.

"I fell," she said, holding out one hand. "Help me up. I think I've twisted my ankle."

Seether helped her to her feet, and she tried not to notice the stretch of her scars, or the pain that streaked up her leg from her twisted ankle. She leaned one hand on a tree, breathing heavily.

Seether stepped back, watching her warily.

"Do you know where the others would have gone? They wouldn't have come all this way back here, would they?" she said.

"Nah. I think they'd go to the south entrance. It's the closest to the dungeons." He pointed in the opposite direction from where they'd just been running.

Jena tightened her lips and glared in that direction. "Then let's go. We can't set off the explosions until we've confirmed they're all out. You'll have to help me." Her skin crawled at the thought of getting that close to another person, but it was the only way.

Seether gave her a mutinous glare, like maybe he thought they should just set off the spells right here and now.

Jena gave him a stern look back. "They're trying to save innocent people. We can't let them all die just because you're feeling impatient."

Seether let out a huff of air, but said nothing. He let Jena put one arm over his shoulders, and they slowly walked back toward the church, every step agony for Jena. It was slow and painful going, and Jena was trembling by the time they made it back to the church ruins.

They turned and continued moving slowly through the forest to the south entrance. By the time they arrived, Jena felt like her whole body was on fire. She collapsed onto a nearby log, her breath huffing.

"You sure you're going to get out of here on that leg?" asked Seether.

"I'll be fine," said Jena. She'd crawl out of here if she had to.

They were sitting silently on the log when Eldrin, Nate and all the prisoners burst through the door a moment later.

"We should have unlocked it for them," said Jena, feeling stupid. "I didn't even think about it." She stood and tried to limp over to Nate, who was carrying a woman who looked half dead. She didn't get far—it was too painful.

He laid the woman down. "What happened?"

"I tripped. If you could just help me over, I can check her out," she said, indicating the woman lying beside him.

Nate ran over and put an arm around her middle. Jena put her arm around his shoulders and, for a moment, just enjoyed the warmth of his body. He was strong and stable, and she almost cried right there and then.

"Can I blow it all up now?" asked Seether. He was standing next to her, staring at all the prisoners they'd rescued.

"Not yet. I need to help this woman, and then we'll move further away," cautioned Jena. She stared down at him until he gave a sullen nod of agreement.

With Nate's help, she hobbled over to the woman and knelt down beside her, putting one hand on her forehead. The woman moaned as if it hurt to be touched.

Nate stood right beside them. "Can you save her?"

"I'm going to try," she said. Jena placed her hands on the woman's temples and closed her eyes. She was only clinging to life by the merest tendril.

Jena pushed some of her magic into the woman, like Bree had done with Argus and Nate in the Forest of Ghosts. She wasn't as talented as her sister, but she was good enough. She just had to help the woman enough so that she could survive until they could get her to a proper healer.

Which reminded her...

"Argus," she said. "We need to free Argus from his curse."

Nate nodded. "But first, we need to get as far as possible from here. Is she okay to continue traveling? At least for a little while?"

Jena glanced around. People were milling about, some sitting and lying down. All of them were too thin and covered in dirt and grime. "She'll be okay if someone carries her. But we can't carry everyone."

"We just have to get them further into the woods. Then we destroy the lair and free Argus."

Jena nodded. "Let's go."

Nate cleared his throat and moved a little more into the center of the group. "Everyone, we need to keep moving. I want to be well away from the Society of the Myrtle when our explosion spells go off. We don't want anyone else to be hurt."

Many of the prisoners groaned, but they all stood up again. No one wanted to escape only to be killed in the aftermath.

Eldrin came over and picked up the woman on the ground. "I'll carry her. You can look after Jena," he said.

Jena let out a relieved breath. She hadn't wanted to ask, but something about Nate's powerful presence steadied her more than she could express in words. Every time he touched her it hurt a little less. Every time, she felt herself wanting to stay a little longer.

Nate carefully put one arm around her waist again, and she reached her arm around his shoulder. They took a couple of slow hobbling steps, and then with a curse, Nate leaned down and grabbed her under the knees and picked Jena up in his arms.

"I can walk," she objected, tensing up.

"It's faster this way," he said, not looking at her. He just kept striding through the trees.

Jena held herself tense for a moment longer then let out a breath. She lay her head on his shoulder and let him carry her, just for now. Once she'd had the chance to heal herself a little—after she'd helped as many of these people as she could, then she'd walk by herself.

Jena watched as a man hobbled past, limping on one side. His leg looked like someone had tried to cut off pieces of his skin. She shuddered. That's probably exactly what Joro had done to him.

From then on, she kept her gaze forward, rather than looking too closely at the terrible wounds of the people around her. She would break down if thought about Joro torturing them.

She'd already been glad they'd killed Joro, but seeing all these people, she was doubly glad.

It was slow going through the trees and undergrowth, but they eventually made it to a clearing that was far enough away. Nate put her down on the ground next to the unconscious woman.

"I'll leave you to help her?" he asked. "I want to talk to a few of the people we rescued, make sure they're okay."

Jena nodded. "I'll do everything I can."

While she used her limited healing magic to help the woman, Seether ran back to the entrance to cast the last part of the spell.

Jena worried about him the whole time he was gone, but she should have known better—he'd survived all on his own inside Joro's lair. Setting a few spells was easy.

But she still breathed a sigh of relief when he returned.

"What now?" she asked him as he settled down on a tree root near her. Her patient was sleeping, but it was a healing rest.

"We wait."

"You sure you did them properly?" asked Eldrin a few minutes later. He was sitting nearby on the ground, next to the other large man with crisscrossed scars over his body.

Seether scowled at Eldrin. "Of course I did. It just takes time."

The first of the explosions rocked the ground about five minutes later, and Seether's frown became a pleased smile. It sounded like a rumbling earthquake, and the ground moved slightly, even as far away as they were. Some in the group managed a weak cheer, but others cried out in fear.

"Don't worry, you're okay. We're far enough back that we won't be affected," said Nate soothingly to the group of survivors. Despite the streaks of dirt across his face and the rips in his clothes, he provided a reassuring presence.

When he came back and sat next to Jena, they were close enough that their shoulders touched. Jena gave a small half-smile, deciding she enjoyed feeling him next to her. "How are we going to get them all to safety?" she murmured only for his ears.

"They're stronger than they look," he replied.

"We need to take them somewhere so they can recover."

Nate nodded. "There's apparently a town close by with a healer mage. One of the survivors mentioned it."

Jena let out a breath. "That's a relief. I'm not as good at healing as Bree..." She trailed off. Her chest felt heavy. "When are we going to get Argus out of the fire ruby?"

"We'll do it right now," said Nate. He stood and held up his hands for quiet from the main group. "We'll rest here, then we'll walk to the nearest town," said Nate. "It shouldn't take long." There were groans and mutterings, but everyone was eager to get out of the forest, so no real objections were raised.

Nate looked at Jena and Seether. "And while they rest, we get Argus out of the fire ruby and cure his curse." He pulled the fire ruby out of his pocket and held it out, his hand shaking ever so slightly. The ruby's glow had dimmed even further.

Jena stared at the fire ruby, then at the young boy sitting nearby. This was it. The moment of truth. Could Seether really do it?

It was a terrifying responsibility to give to a child.

Seether meanwhile, seemed unconcerned as he rummaged around in the bag he'd brought with him. He pulled out three bottles filled with different colored liquids —green, black and red—and an empty glass vial. He poured three drops from each of the small glass bottles into the vial. The mixture immediately started to sizzle.

Jena watched him, wondering how he came to be so good at mage work. Was it all down to Joro? Or had Seether had some natural talents before he'd been sent here? What dark magic secrets did he have stored in his head?

"You ready to bring your friend out of the fire ruby?" said Seether.

"You won't have long once he's out. The curse was powerful and fast," warned Nate, his brow furrowed. He was just as worried about this as Jena was.

"It won't take long. This is fast acting too. Your friend will be back before you know it." Seether grinned with all the cockiness of a teenaged boy.

Nate took an audible breath, and even as they watched, seemed to go in on himself. His visible skin glowed in the dim light of the forest, and for a moment, Jena could almost see the echo of flames flickering around his whole body. The fire ruby glowed a brilliant red, almost too bright to even look at directly. But Jena refused to take her eyes off what was happening in case Nate or Seether needed help.

Smoke and flames erupted out of the ruby, spiraling and swirling around them like a storm, blowing everyone's clothes and hair in all directions. Jena held her breath and watched as the storm died down and the smoke and flames came to rest in the outline of a man's form right in front of Nate.

The form collapsed, and then Argus was lying on the ground in front of them, curled up into a ball, arms wrapped around his stomach as if he were in extreme agony. He moaned and clenched his eyes tightly closed. It was like he was trying to hide from whatever was causing the pain.

Eldrin went straight to his brother's side, putting one hand on his shoulder. "Argus. We're here. We're going to save you. It's going to be okay."

Jena leaned forward, but she could only watch as Seether took the liquids that he'd mixed, and poured them drop by drop over Argus, muttering a spell under his breath. Where each drop landed on Argus's body, it made a sizzling sound, and smoke rose into the air.

Argus stiffened each time, whimpering and moaning as the drops hit. Seether ignored his reaction and kept going until there was no more liquid in the vial. He closed his eyes and started chanting even louder over Argus's body. The smoke coming from the drops on Argus's body billowed and thickened, continuing to rise as Argus writhed in pain. He grasped Eldrin's hand tightly like it was a lifeline.

Maybe it was.

Seether kept chanting until Jena didn't think she could take it anymore. The smoke churned and writhed, almost as if something was fighting the magic. The surrounding energy thickened until it felt like the magic was pushing them away.

And then Seether stopped. The smoke cleared. Argus lay

in front of them, his body limp for the first time since he'd been pulled out of the fire ruby.

"It's done," said Seether breathlessly. "The curse is gone." He hesitated, then seemed to think better of his words. "Probably."

"You're sure?" said Nate. "Shouldn't there be more to it?"

"I can do it again, if that makes you feel better," said Seether accommodatingly. The look on his face showed them what he thought of anyone who took him up on his offer.

"No, thanks," said Nate and Jena at the same time.

Argus coughed, and it sounded like his chest was rattling.

Everyone's focus went back to the mercenary as he opened his eyes and looked around dazedly. Then he pushed himself to sitting, batting away Eldrin's attempts to help him. Argus looked like he'd been living at the bottom of a swamp for a month. His hair was hanging around his face and his stubble had grown into a beard. But he was back.

Tears welled in Jena's eyes. She wiped them away before Argus could see she was crying.

"I'm not an invalid. It was just a curse, and now it's broken," growled Argus at Eldrin, his voice rough from disuse.

"For once in your life, accept some help, you ash-filled idiot," said Eldrin. His expression was determined as he held out one hand to his brother.

Argus sighed and gave Eldrin a look, but he accepted the hand that his brother held out and allowed himself to be dragged to standing. Eldrin pulled Argus into a hug, despite his brother's protests.

"I'm glad you're safely out of that fire ruby," said Eldrin as he pulled away. "Father will be pleased."

"Why did you involve Father in all this? He'll only worry." Argus glared at his brother.

His tone and words were so familiar, Jena almost started crying.

"Where's Bree?" asked Argus, looking around.

And then Jena really did start crying.

CHAPTER 77
NATE

Nate cleared his throat.

"Remus kidnapped her," he said quickly, before he lost his nerve. "He said he'd give her back in exchange for you. We had to save you to save her."

It felt like time skipped for a second, and everything hung in silence. Then Argus let out an enraged bellow. "What?" He glared at Nate and took an aggressive step forward, hands clenched as if he were going to throw a punch. "You should have saved her first."

Nate stepped back, putting his hands up, palms facing out. "We can still save her. She's going to be fine."

"We need to leave now. We have to get her away from that ash-begotten asshole," Argus barked, his voice hard, eyes wild. He looked as if he wanted to murder someone.

"We're meeting Rothell again tomorrow," said Nate hastily. "She'll take us straight to Remus. Faster than we could walk or ride, even if we left right now."

"Who—or what?—is Rothell?"

Nate gave a sad half-smile. He'd been carrying around the fire ruby the whole time, and he'd assumed Argus was experiencing everything they were. But he had no idea what had happened.

"We met her after I put you into the fire ruby. She's a shimagni who was living on Remus's mountain. She knew you."

Argus's dark eyes glittered in the setting sun. "There were stories of a shimagni on the mountain, but I never saw her," he said. He rubbed his hand through his hair as if he were trying to force his brain to think properly again.

"She was traveling with us when we were attacked by fire ants and she was wounded. She's gone back to her cave to recuperate. She'll be back tomorrow." Nate tried to keep his voice soothing and calm.

"Between then and now, we can plan what we're going to do," said Jena softly.

Argus turned suddenly to Jena, like he'd only just noticed she was there. "Don't you care that your sister is in the hands of that monster?" he snarled. "How can you be so calm about all this?"

Jena's eyes filled with angry tears. "Don't you dare say I don't care about my sister," she growled back at him, just as angry, just as close to the edge. "We've been through hell, while you lounged around in that damned fire ruby."

Argus looked like he was about to explode.

Nate stepped between them and held up his hands, one to each of them. "Calm down, both of you. Fighting won't help. Argus, of course Jena wants Bree back just as much as you do. But we can't do anything until Rothell comes back tomorrow. Jena, you know he was hurt."

Argus let out an angry growl. Then ran his hands through his already mussed-up hair for a second time. He closed his eyes and took a breath. Then opened them and nodded once at Jena.

"I'm sorry," he said. "Ignore me. But there must be something else we can do. I refuse to just sit here and wait."

"Like Jena said, we can share information and plan what we're going to do."

Jena leaned closer. "For a start, Remus was strangely desperate to have you returned to him," she said quietly. "Why would that be?"

"I don't *know*. None of this makes sense." Argus stormed off in one direction, then paced back to them. Energy rolled off him, and he didn't seem to know what to do with himself.

"I think you need to sit down," said Eldrin, placing one hand on his brother's shoulder. "Maybe have some food, get your strength up."

Argus allowed himself to be dragged to the nearby log, sitting down while Eldrin got some jerky out of his pack.

Nate glanced at Jena. He hadn't thought about it, but she was right. Why *did* Remus want Argus back so desperately?

Argus chewed on the jerky in agitated bites, while the others shared pointed glances.

"Who's this Remus guy?" asked Seether.

"He's a nasty little mage who used to have Argus trapped in a spell," said Jena. "Bree freed Argus when they fell in love. But when Argus was hurt, Remus kidnapped her. He wants to trade Argus for Bree."

"If giving myself up to him is the only way to get her back, that's what we'll do," said Argus in a voice that brooked no argument. "I would be his slave forever, if it meant Bree was free."

"*The shrinking mage will double cross you. Probably try to keep them both somehow,*" said a voice in Nate's ear. He jumped, then turned to where Thornal stood next to him and glared.

"We'd rather not just hand you back over to him, if we can help it," said Jena.

"Smart girl," said Thornal.

Nate nodded in agreement. "Remus can't be trusted. But we need some kind of plan for how we deal with him. Figure out his weaknesses and use them against him."

"He's also called the shrinking mage," said Jena to Seether. "He had a spell cast on him many years ago, and he's been slowing getting smaller ever since."

Seether tapped one finger on the side of his head. "Stands to reason, the only thing that would make him this desperate is fixing that spell, right?"

"I suppose so," said Jena. "It's all he talked about while we were there."

"For as long as I've known him, that's been his obsession." Argus had stopped chewing the jerky. He looked a little less wild.

"So you must be able to help break the shrinking spell," said Seether.

Argus gave him a glare. "The spell was cast many years ago, and was nothing to do with me," he said.

Nate shared a look with Eldrin and Jena. "That's not entirely true. The lavaen that cursed you, also cursed Remus. And we think it was your Aunt Alessan, your father's sister."

"What?" He looked at Eldrin to confirm.

Eldrin nodded. "There has to be some kind of connection. It's too big a coincidence."

"Rothell said the lavaen is too far gone, she'd never take the spell back, even if Remus could turn her into a human again," said Nate.

They lapsed into silence. Nate tried to think of what kind of connection Argus was supposed to have with his aunt, other than the obvious family ties. He couldn't do curses or magic like she could.

"Maybe Remus just needs his blood?" said Seether into the silence.

"What good would that do? He still needs someone to undo the original spell," said Nate. "Argus doesn't have a magical bone in his body."

He glanced at Argus. "No offense Argus."

"None taken."

Seether narrowed his eyes and stared up at the trees for a moment. "There is dark magic, blood spells, that would allow Argus to take over the spell from his aunt."

Nate shivered. "You're saying Remus is planning to use dark magic?"

Jena gave a short laugh. "He'd use whatever it took."

"It makes sense," said Nate. "He's desperate."

"Then we have to figure out a way to get Bree back without that happening," said Argus. He looked past where Jena was sitting, and seemed to notice the prisoners milling around behind her for the first time. "Who are all these people?"

Seether spoke up. "They're the people we rescued from the Society of the Myrtle."

"And who are *you*?"

"I'm part of your group now," said Seether irrepressibly. "My name's Seether."

"What kind of a name is that?" said Argus, scowling at the young boy.

"Seether helped us escape from a monstrous spider creature called Joro, and he's now free to do what he wishes," said Jena with a sideways glance at Seether.

Seether crossed his arms. "And what I *wish*, is to join your crew."

"We don't have a *crew*," said Argus.

"You know nothing about us, or where we're going," Nate added sharply. "You don't want to join us." All he could see in their future was death and destruction. No place for a kid.

"I do too," said Seether indignantly. "Prince Lothar told Joro that you're going to Flame City to try to overthrow him. He was pretty happy when Joro said he'd caught you."

Nate raised his eyebrows in surprise, then glanced at Jena. Joro had taken Seether into his confidence, after all. Or maybe he didn't bother hiding anything because he'd been planning to have him as a snack.

"Did you learn anything else from Joro and Lothar?" asked Nate.

Seether's expression turned sly. "I'll tell you once you agree to let me join your crew."

"In what kingdom do we seem like a safe group of people to get yourself involved with?" asked Nate with some asperity. "It won't be a picnic, facing off against Lothar. We'll probably end up dead."

"At least it won't be boring," shrugged Seether.

"I see why your parents handed you over to Joro," muttered Nate.

"We can find someone who'll take care of you," interrupted Jena. "Someone who won't sell you."

"I don't want anyone else. I want to stay with you." Seether's face took on a mulish expression.

"Let's talk about it later," said Nate. He didn't want to get into an argument right now and agree to something he'd regret later.

"What's the plan, then?" said Argus, watching them all

with a guarded expression. He was probably calculating the ways he could leave on his own and give himself up to Remus for Bree.

"The best way to get to Remus is to travel with Rothell," said Nate, hoping Argus was listening properly. "If you try to get there on your own, you'll be days. Rothell will get us there in hours."

Argus glared at him but said nothing.

"We need to get everyone here to the safety of the next town over," said Jena. "Then we rest for the night, meet Rothell, go to Remus and save Bree. Simple."

"Things are never simple around you three," said Eldrin.

Argus snorted. "That's for sure."

It took them more than two hours to get everyone in the group up and walking toward the town, a little hamlet called Forest Cove.

Nate had offered to carry Jena again, but she'd healed her ankle just enough so she could walk on it. He could see that it still hurt, and wished she weren't so determined to fend for herself. She was up ahead, talking to some of the survivors, and surreptitiously healing their wounds as they walked.

He missed the feeling of holding her close, even while he admired her dedication.

"You look at her like she's a spell you're too scared to cast," said a voice beside him. He looked down to find Seether grinning smugly up at him.

"Don't be stupid," he said with a sharp edge to his voice. He tried to laugh it off, but it got stuck in his throat.

Seether shrugged. "You gotta take charge. Girls like it when you do that."

Nate almost choked. "Where did you get that piece of relationship advice? Joro?"

"Now, now. Don't be defensive. I'm just tryin' to help you get your lady."

"I don't need your help. Jena and I... have an understanding." He wasn't sure what their understanding was, but he sure as Flames wasn't going to discuss it with this precocious urchin.

"Your loss."

Seether ran up ahead, winking back at Nate as stopped to walk beside Jena.

Nate desperately hoped Seether wasn't having a similar conversation with her.

He watched them for a minute, trying to read by her facial expressions whether he was giving out more dodgy advice, and had just decided to catch up to them, when he noticed that the surrounding trees had thinned out. They were on the edge of the forest, and Forest Cove lay just in front of them.

As they stepped out of the forest and into the main square, some of the survivors—those who were from the small hamlet—were tearfully greeted by their friends and neighbors. The local healer, an older mage, greeted them and opened his healing dormitory to the rest of the group.

"I don't get the use out of it I once did," he said in a slow and measured voice.

"Can we trust him?" asked Jena in an undertone to Nate. "Surely someone living this close to Joro and the society must be in league with them?"

Thornal, who had been walking silently behind Nate the whole time, cleared his throat. *"I believe you can trust him. He was always a loyal and honest man when I knew him in life."*

"Thornal says yes," said Nate.

They gathered everyone up and helped them move into the beds provided for them. Those who were strong enough sat around a table that was filled with plates of fresh food provided by the villagers.

"I'm just so glad you could get my Jimmy back to me," said a weepy woman with powerful forearms and a ruddy complexion. She looked over at the large man with the crisscrossed scars.

Nate nodded. He was glad they'd asked Seether about prisoners before setting up the explosion spells.

The old mage went around and healed those he could, giving medicine and bandages to those he couldn't. Seether followed behind him, adding his own version of healing to each of the people. Sometimes it was gratefully received, and sometimes not.

Jena, Nate, Argus and Eldrin left the mage with his new charges and went to sit in a corner of the local tavern.

"So what happens when we get to Remus?" asked Eldrin.

They looked at each other, their faces grim.

"He's smart," said Argus. "We'll have to be smarter."

They sat over their ales and planned late into the night. When they finally left the building, Nate felt like they had a scenario that might work. When he awoke the next morning, he was sure of it.

"My name is Arthur, and I'm the town mayor," said a large man with an even larger belly as they stood in the town square, ready to leave. He was well-dressed and smiled like a politician. "Thank you for saving so many of our people from the clutches of the Society of the Myrtle. They have been the scourge of the forest my entire life."

"Happy to help," said Nate, shaking the man's sweaty hand.

"Anything you need, just ask," said Arthur, gesturing around at the people who'd gathered to see them leave.

Argus cleared his throat. "What about horses? And someone to bring them back to you today once we meet up with the rest of our group?"

The mayor blinked, and Nate tried to hide his smile. The offer of help had clearly been more of a ceremonial type of help.

"I'll loan them my Betsy for the day," said a loud voice from the back of the group.

"Aye, I'll let them have my red-chested mare," said another.

Soon they had four horses that would take them to their destination.

Nate's chest felt tight as he looked around at the people helping them. "Thank you so much," he said to the man who was settling the bridle on his horse, a medium-sized black mare.

"There's not many who could take on that spider and win," said the man. "We'd given up. Worse than that, we lived here knowing that our loved ones might disappear, and that we might disappear too. You've saved us from that. And we're grateful to you. More than grateful. We're in debt to you. Loaning you a few horses ain't gonna fix that."

"You owe me nothing. I'm glad to help," said Nate. He put one foot in the stirrup and swung himself onto the back of his horse. Beside him, Argus and Eldrin were astride larger stallions, and Jena and Seether shared a chestnut horse that must be the red-chested mare.

"Thank you all," said Nate with a wave.

He didn't look back as they all rode swiftly down the forest path toward their meeting place with Rothell.

CHAPTER 78
NATE

N ate squinted up into the sky.

They'd been waiting all afternoon at the meeting point, and so far, no sign of Rothell. The edge of the forest stood to their backs, green fields flowed around them, and a dirt track that joined to the main road into Flame City was nearby. In the distance, they could see travelers heading toward the entrance to the capital city, where enormous wooden doors were guarded by a heavily armed contingent of the palace guards.

"Are you sure this is the place?" said Argus for the hundredth time. He was pacing back and forth at the edge of the treeline.

"I made the arrangements, brother. This is the place," said Eldrin, who was seated on a nearby log, casually chewing on an apple from the supplies the townsfolk had given them.

"Then where is this creature? We waste time, while Bree is trapped."

Privately, Nate agreed with Argus. He was getting impatient. The walls of the Flame City towered over them in the distance, and it was making him edgy. The thought of being able to jump on Rothell's back and head in the opposite direction was... tantalizing.

Suddenly, Jena stood up.

"There," she said, pointing into the distance.

Nate squinted in the direction she was pointing. He could see a tiny dot, nothing more than a speck in the air. "You sure that's her?"

Jena scowled at him and lifted her shirt. The raven on her stomach burst free and flew off in the direction she'd pointed. "The raven will check. But it looks like her."

"I believe you. I'm sure it's her." *He hoped it was Rothell.*

They waited and watched as the speck grew larger until Nate was certain it was the shimagni. He let out a breath. Ten minutes later, Rothell landed next to them, her large wings blowing dust and debris into the air.

Argus had the grace to look awed by the sight of her. Eldrin looked resigned. Nate was just glad to see she was okay. She'd sustained so many injuries from the fire ants he'd been worried it would do her permanent damage.

"How are you all?" asked Rothell. *"I see you found a cure for your curse?"* Her gaze stopped at Seether. *"And that you have another among your number."*

Seether stared up at Rothell with wide eyes. For once, he didn't have anything to say.

Jena smiled at Rothell and stepped up to run one hand down the side of her neck. "I'm so glad to see you," she said. "Rothell, this is Argus, free of the fire ruby and his curse, and this is Seether, a young apprentice mage who helped us escape from the Society of the Myrtle."

"Escape? It was not the friendly visit you hoped it would be?"

"It was the least friendly visit you could imagine," said Jena with a slightly feral smile. "But we survived."

"Just," agreed Nate.

Argus stepped forward, his whole body tensed. "As much as I appreciate your desire to catch up, we need to get to Bree to save her from Remus—" His voice cracked.

"Of course. We will leave immediately." Rothell held out one foreleg to help them climb onto her back.

"What's that in the sky over there?" asked Seether as he waited for his turn to get on Rothell's back. He was squinting in a similar direction to where Rothell had come from. "Do you know any other flying creatures who'd be heading this way?"

Nate and Jena put their hands over their eyes and looked in the direction Seether had pointed.

Rothell was the one who recognized who it was. "Everyone into the forest. Hide! Hurry, she is almost here."

"Who is?" said Argus.

"The murghah," said Rothell grimly.

Nate's heart pounded in his chest as he ran after Jena and the others into the forest. He'd been told several times that he should be able to overcome the murghah with ease, but the creature still terrified him.

It was only Lothar's power that brought her out into the world to do his bidding. And all Lothar wanted right now was to kill Nate.

Rothell stood in front of the forest, her scales changing color until she was invisible. They all watched silently as the murghah came closer.

"Has she got something on her back?" asked Eldrin. "It's that, or she's got some kind of deformity."

"It would be really unusual for them to carry someone," said Jena. She had that look on her face that said she was checking what it said in the Book of Spells. "They resent people riding on their backs."

Nate watched from inside the forest, a swirl of confusing emotions making him feel sick. He was supposed to be able to control this creature, not cower in the trees. But what if he couldn't? What if they were wrong? He didn't want his journey to end here, just because he couldn't hold himself still for a little longer.

Rothell was watching the murghah with narrowed eyes. She growled. "It's a woman."

Nate's gaze immediately went to the murghah. He squinted. A familiar flash of white-blonde hair was visible.

"Is that...?" He didn't want to say the words aloud.

"It's *Bree*," said Jena. "How did the Murghah get *Bree*?"

"Remus must have traded her for something," said Argus, clenching his hands at his sides. "I knew we couldn't trust him." He stumbled out of the forest and stood staring up at the murghah in the distance. In a few minutes the creature would be over the wall, and Bree would be inside the Flame City. His whole body was tensed as if he was considering trying to run after them.

"What do we do?" asked Jena, her voice panicked.

Nate understood exactly what she was feeling. They'd thought it was over. They'd rescued Argus from the curse. They were going to get back to Remus well within the timeframe he'd set.

Bree was supposed to be safe.

Except... she was lost to them again, and this time it was much worse.

This time, Lothar had Bree.

Jena turned to Nate, her eyes bright with unshed tears. "Nate? Can you...?"

He shook his head, a lump forming in his throat. "I can't control the murghah from this distance." He wasn't sure he'd be able to control the murghah if she'd been standing in front of them.

"It's too far for us to fly and catch up with the murghah before she gets to the city," said Rothell. *"And I cannot fly you into the city myself. I would be too easy a target. If my magic fell into Lothar's hands, he would win."*

"We have to follow her into the city," said Argus, his expression a mask of despair. He clenched his hands at his sides. "Any way we can."

"It's our only option," agreed Jena.

She was right. The time had come for his confrontation with Lothar. "We'll get her back," said Nate. "Or die trying."

❧

THANK you so much for reading Oath of Embers!

HOW WILL THEY RESCUE BREE? Will they find a way to beat Prince Lothar at his own game? Or will the Throne of Flames burn them alive...

Find out in the third and final book in the Firecaller Chronicles, King of Flames, due out in 2026.

★ ★ ★ ★ ★ **"Started reading and couldn't put it down..."**

~ Amazon review for Fire Mage.

CHAPTER 79
THE PROPHECIES OF IGNISIA

Flamehaven Prophecy

The dead city of Flamehaven lives in our memories,
As a refuge for outcasts and souls on the Edges.
The seeds of the Guardian were planted here,
While the mighty fall,
Their blindness leading to a false path.

THE FLAMES of Flamehaven shall rise again,
When the Fiery Redeemer returns,
And leads the Way.
Until then,
Let those who remember,
Be the gatekeepers,
And those who have forgotten,
Fear what they don't know.

TWO OUTCASTS UNITE **Prophecy**

When the Rose crushes the Flames,
'Neath its curly thorns,
Ignisia will fall.
Demon beasts take wing,
While the rightful King,
Will see death.

WHEN THE WAY IS DESTROYED,
The Guardian's Mark must fly,
With a child of two powers.
Outcasts unite,
The Flames burn bright,
And the Way will continue.

A WITCH and a Mage Prophecy

The fall of Ignisia,
Begins when a witch and mage unite.
Darkness follows,
And a union of unholy power.

WHEN THE DARK ones come in the night,
The Guardian must protect
The Way above all else.
The Book will burn,
His mark will fly free,
And his seed will follow
A path no other can see.

CHILDREN OF FLAME and Shadow Prophecy

When seven sleeping giants stir beneath the earth,
And fire murmurs
Of endings and beginnings,
From the embers shall come
Children of Flame and Shadow.

THEY WILL TREAD a narrow path
    Where creation and ruin intertwine.
    The mountains bow
    Or break beneath their touch
    And the Throne of Flame will tremble.
    From the farthest dark,
    Monsters creep,
    Seeking the heart,
    Of the Flames and Shadows.

THE GUARDIAN'S shadow will lengthen,
    And the Way may may falter.
    The faces of ruin and deliverance
    Shall look alike to blinded eyes,
    And only choice,
    Fragile as smoke,
    Can steady the world's flame.

If you'd like to read more in the Firecaller world, join my Secret Society to get access to free prequel stories about Nate and Jena.

You'll also get the top secret, highly hush-hush weekly Trudi Jaye Secret Society bulletin with inside information on characters, ongoing stories, and early notification about sales and new releases.

www.trudijayewrites.com/shadow-archives

OTHER BOOKS BY TRUDI JAYE

Other Books by Trudi Jaye

Dragon Rising Series (Completed)

Lost Dragon (Prequel Novella available via the Trudi Jaye Secret Society)

Hidden Dragon

Searching Dragon

Fighting Dragon

Cursed Dragon

Warrior Dragon

Demon Hunter in Hiding Series (Completed)

Dreams & Demons (Prequel Novella available via the

Trudi Jaye Secret Society)

Secrets & Demons

Agents & Demons

Magic & Demons

Dragons & Demons

Spells & Demons

Elemental Witch Series (With Tania Hutley, Completed)

The Trouble with Magic

The Problem with Witches

The Danger with Demons

Firecaller Series

Salt (Prequel Novella available via the Trudi Jaye Secret Society)

Subtle Knife (Prequel Novella available via the Trudi Jaye Secret Society)

Fire Mage

Oath of Embers

King of Flames (due out in 2026)

Dark Carnival Series

The First Ever Wish (Prequel Novella available via the Trudi Jaye Secret Society)

If Magic Were Wishes

The Gift

Magic for Lost Souls (available via the Trudi Jaye Secret Society)

High Flyer

Hidden Magic

The Shadow Prophecy

ABOUT THE AUTHOR

Hi! I'm Trudi Jaye. I live in New Zealand on a beautiful rural property surrounded by horses and cows (not mine!) with my lovely husband and my cheeky teenaged daughter.

I've been writing since I was young, and for many years I worked as a magazine writer and editor, on topics ranging from hardware and electronics to holidays, recipes and university-level research projects.

Now I write novels full time.

I enjoy yoga, although I'm not very bendy, and karate, although I don't like the idea of hitting anyone.

f facebook.com/Trudijayeauthor

instagram.com/trudijayewriter

tiktok.com/@trudijayewrites

BB bookbub.com/authors/trudi-jaye

www.ingramcontent.com/pod-product-compliance
Lightning Source LLC
Chambersburg PA
CBHW032255020726
47495CB00001B/117